Praise for Paul Gitsham

'Once again Paul Gitsham has produced an utterly gripping thriller'

'Brilliant from start to finish. Love this series'

'Paul never lets you down'

'Beautifully written, well plotted and well researched'

'Up there with the best series'

PAUL GITSHAM started his career as a biologist working in the UK and Canada. After stints as the world's most over-qualified receptionist and a spell ensuring that international terrorists hadn't opened a Child's Savings Account at a major UK bank (a job even duller than working reception) he retrained as a Science teacher.

Also by Paul Gitsham

The DCI Warren Jones series

The Last Straw
No Smoke Without Fire
Blood is Thicker Than Water (Novella)
Silent as the Grave
A Case Gone Cold (Novella)
The Common Enemy
A Deadly Lesson (Novella)
Forgive Me Father
At First Glance (Novella)
A Price to Pay

Out of Sight

PAUL GITSHAM

ONE PLACE. MANY STORIES

HQ
An imprint of HarperCollins*Publishers* Ltd
1 London Bridge Street
London SE1 9GF

www.harpercollins.co.uk

HarperCollins*Publishers*
1st Floor, Watermarque Building, Ringsend Road
Dublin 4, Ireland

This paperback edition 2021

1
First published in Great Britain by
HQ, an imprint of HarperCollins*Publishers* Ltd 2021

ISBN: 9780008395308

MIX
Paper from
responsible sources
FSC™ C007454

Printed and bound in Great Britain by
CPI Group (UK) Ltd, Melksham, SN12 6TR

To Cheryl xx.
For putting up with me.

Thursday 24th November

Prologue

Five days before the new moon and the country lane was close to pitch black, thick cloud obscuring what little light was available. The car headlamps, dipped to minimise unwanted attention, illuminated the shallow brook beneath the bridge.

For the next few minutes, the stillness of the night was broken only by grunts of exertion, until, with a wet thump, the wrapped bundle splashed noisily into the lazy flowing stream.

A bare arm flopped loose of its binding.

Quiet descended once more until the sound of metal on bone and teeth startled the creatures in the underbrush; an unseen bird squawked loudly, its wings fluttering.

But three miles outside of Middlesbury, in the middle of a late-November night, nobody was there to hear it.

Sunday 27th November

Chapter 1

The house was cold. Not just because of the late-November weather, or the lack of heating, but because it was empty. Warren Jones turned slowly on the spot. The kitchen was old-fashioned; the new owners would need to rip it out and replace it. The bathroom was also past its prime.

He tried not to think about the changes that were coming. The kitchen had been the same for as long as he could remember, but now he barely recognised it. He'd never noticed how the wallpaper had faded until he'd taken down the photos and the clock. The linoleum floor was shiny with wear, four small indentations the only evidence of the wooden dining table that he'd sat at for so many years. With the leaves folded down, it had been just the right size for three people to eat dinner, or for him to do his homework. Fully unfolded, the table had doubled in size. With his eyes closed he could picture it laden with food. How many Christmases and birthdays had he celebrated here? He could almost smell his grandmother's cooking; they had never had double-glazing fitted, and he remembered the dripping condensation every time they had a roast dinner.

Reaching out, he scraped a trace of Blu Tack off the wall with his thumbnail. Christmas was less than a month away, but the

7

ancient decorations that his grandfather hauled out of the loft each year were now gone, sent to the council tip down the A45 along with everything else the charity shops had turned their noses up at. A handful of ancient baubles that he couldn't bear to part with were wrapped in bubble wrap in a box in the back of the hire van parked outside, along with some old books and childhood possessions that he'd never quite got around to moving to his own home.

This year it would be another family's decorations hanging throughout the house – somebody else's Christmas tree in the living room. A different collection of voices would be laughing and singing and loving each other.

He hoped they would be as happy there as he had been.

He felt his wife's arm snake around his waist, her head resting on his shoulder. 'Do you want me to take a photo? For old times' sake?' she asked him quietly.

Warren shook his head and swallowed the lump in his throat. 'No, I've plenty of pictures. Back from when … you know. I'd rather remember it that way.'

That's the first thing he'd do when he and Susan arrived back at Middlesbury that evening, he decided. His computer's hard drive was full of images that needed sorting and printing out, all of them treasured memories – newer, digital snaps of recent gatherings, older ones with Warren and his grandparents from Christmases before he even knew Susan, and scans of faded prints of Warren, his brother and his mother. There were far fewer than he'd like with his father also in shot. Even when his dad had been alive, he was usually the one behind the camera, selfies a technological impossibility with a point and click 35mm.

He pushed back his sleeve to look at his watch; it was almost eleven o'clock. Susan's parents would be back from church soon and Warren and Susan had promised that they'd all meet for lunch, before visiting the graveyard and then driving the van the two hours back to Middlesbury.

Suddenly, he wanted to go.

Ever since Granddad Jack had had his fall, the house had ceased to be a home. The old man had never spent another night under its roof. And what was a house without its owner?

Warren took his keys out of his pocket. The key to his grandparents' house was the oldest one on the bunch – he still remembered his grandfather handing it over to him the day he started secondary school. 'So you can let yourself in if you pop in on the way home and we're out.'

He'd felt so grown up.

Soon it too would be useless, the locks doubtless changed within days of the new owners taking possession. He twisted it off the keyring.

'Let's go. We can drop these through the estate agent's letterbox on the way to lunch,' he said, turning and walking briskly to the front door.

Following him, Susan said nothing as they emerged into the weak, autumnal sunlight.

A faint buzzing came from Warren's coat pocket. Stopping on the threshold, he took out his phone, looking at the caller ID.

'I need to take this,' he said.

Today was booked as a rest day. His colleagues knew that he was busy this weekend. It must be important. Answering the call, he listened intently, asking only a few questions. Eventually he hung up. 'We need to get back to Middlesbury. Can you drive? I need to make some calls on the way. I'll text everyone and let them know we won't be meeting them for lunch. We can post the keys when we get back.'

'Why, what's happened?' asked Susan, although she could already guess.

'They've found a body.'

Chapter 2

The body had been discovered a little after ten o'clock that morning. By the time Detective Chief Inspector Warren Jones, the Senior Investigating Officer at Middlesbury CID, arrived at the scene shortly after lunch, the narrow country lane had already been closed at both ends with fluorescent-clad, uniformed officers diverting the traffic.

Charlie Pitt, the farmhand who'd made the grim discovery, sat on the tailgate of the ambulance, his hands clasped around a steaming mug of coffee, his feet covered in plastic forensic booties and his shoulders wrapped in a thick blanket.

'He spotted a strange-looking bundle underneath the bridge when he was out fixing some fencing, and clambered down for a look-see,' said Detective Constable Moray Ruskin. 'The CSIs have taken his work boots and his coat for trace analysis. The lad that was with him stayed in the van and didn't get out. He didn't see anything.'

'Is he up to speaking?' asked Warren, grabbing the boot lid of Ruskin's car for support as he climbed into a protective white suit. Ruskin was already clad in one of the super-sized paper overalls that he was forced to bring to crime scenes himself; the Scenes of Crime van didn't routinely carry suits big enough for his six-foot-five-inch bulk.

'Yeah, I think he just wants to get it over with so he can get back into the warmth.'

'I can't blame him for that,' said Warren, already shivering despite the thick coat he'd kept on underneath his protective clothing. He didn't know what time of year was worse to deal with a body outside – summer, when the smell and the flies had set in, or winter when you lost the feeling in your fingers and toes.

Pitt was a wiry man in his late thirties, with short-cropped, brown hair. 'I wouldn't normally come down here at this time of year, we won't be planting anything until the spring, but some of the fencing needs replacing after the storms last month.' He gestured to a flat-bed truck. 'I brought young Kyle with me to give me a hand. Luckily, he didn't get out and see the body,' Pitt shuddered. 'The lad's too young to see that sort of thing.'

From what Warren had been told on the drive back from Coventry, nobody should be seeing that sort of thing, but it was his job to do so and he couldn't put it off any longer.

Leaving Pitt to continue giving his statement to one of his uniformed colleagues, Warren picked his way carefully along the bank. The CSIs had laid down raised metal plates to prevent any footprints being disturbed, but they were already slick with wet mud. He didn't fancy slipping over and landing in the icy stream.

The body had been dumped beneath a low, concrete bridge that crossed the water, allowing access to the field beyond. The space beneath the bridge was about five feet high; whoever had dumped the body would have been bent double as they did so.

A white tent had been erected around the site in an attempt to prevent further degradation by the elements. Inside, three white-clad technicians were busy searching for evidence, one of them wearing waders and kneeling in the stream.

'Aah, DCI Jones, good to see you, Sir.' The jovial Yorkshire accent and portly figure identified the speaker as Crime Scene Manager Andy Harrison; his greying ponytail was hidden from view by his hood. The face mask he wore prevented Warren from seeing the progress of the elaborate moustache he'd been cultivating during Movember.

'Lovely day for it, Andy.'

'Yeah, trust Meera to be on a rest day today.'

'What have we got?'

'One body – looks like a male adult, probably South Asian. The pathologist is due any minute, I'll leave it to him to confirm.' His mask twitched. 'I'd say he's been here a couple of days. But it's going to take a while to identify him.'

Warren nodded, as he followed him under the bridge. The details he'd already been told suggested as much.

The naked body lay in a few inches of water, partially wrapped in a white cotton sheet. The head was barely visible, but what Warren did see looked mangled. Both of the man's hands were free of the cloth. Again, Warren could see that they had been mutilated.

'They removed his fingertips?'

'Looks like it. All ten digits.'

Warren bent towards the head. The lower part of the face had been battered beyond recognition, the jaw a gaping mess.

'Not much blood. Post-mortem?'

'I'd say so.'

Warren straightened, careful not to hit his head on the concrete above him.

'Well, whoever he was, the killer didn't want us identifying him too soon.'

*

The expectant buzz in the briefing room quietened immediately when Warren walked in. It was now mid-afternoon, and all those assembled had heard about that morning's discovery at Carrington Farm. Detective Superintendent John Grayson had just arrived back at the station; judging by his casual jumper and lack of tie, he'd been out for Sunday lunch when he was notified. Much of what Warren had to share with the assembled officers would be new to him as well.

Warren started by bringing everyone up to speed with what little they had so far. There were looks of disgust around the room as he detailed the post-mortem violation of the victim's body.

'As always, the most pressing priority will be identifying our victim. He's naked with no mobile phone or wallet; fingerprints are out of the question, obviously. I'll speak to the pathologist about using dental records but judging by the state of the mouth that's not looking promising. That leaves DNA; maybe he's on the system already.

'Andy Harrison thinks that the victim was dumped within the last few days – certainly not long enough for significant decomposition to set in, despite his exposure to the elements. Moray, I'd like you to liaise with Missing Persons. See if anyone matching his description has been reported in the past week. If you don't find anything, continue working backwards; our victim might have gone missing some time before he was killed.'

Ruskin started making notes on his pad.

'That body had to find its way to the dumping ground somehow. Mags, I want you to secure CCTV and number plate recognition from the surrounding area.'

'I'll see what I can find, Sir,' said DS Richardson, the team's resident CCTV expert, 'but I'll warn you now, that far out of town, there's not going to be much. The closest speed cameras are a couple of miles away, and there's almost no ANPR out there.'

'Could the killer have known that?' asked DS David Hutchinson. 'Are they familiar with the area? Did they know where they were going to dump the victim, or were they driving around with a dead body in the boot, looking for a convenient ditch? It looks as though the body was well-hidden.'

'It was,' confirmed Warren. 'It was spotted by a farmhand from

13

the field side of the ditch. Bushes block the view from the road, even at this time of year.'

'They may well know the road, Hutch,' said Richardson, 'but I wouldn't infer too much. It's a busy cut-through linking the A506 with the Cambridge road. My satnav has directed me down there when the traffic is bad on the A506. Anyone living that side of town probably knows the road.'

'But do they know about the ditch?' mused Warren.

'What state are the verges in?' asked Hutchinson.

'A bit chewed up, since it's the widest point that'll let two vehicles pass, and the weather hasn't been ideal,' said Warren, glancing at the scene report, 'but there are some recent-looking tyre prints that Andy's looking at. There are also some shoeprints on the riverbank that may be usable.'

'There are houses either end of that road,' said Ruskin. 'If the body was dumped late at night, maybe somebody remembers a vehicle?'

Warren nodded his agreement. 'Hutch, can you organise some door-knockers?'

With nothing else pressing, Warren looked at his watch. 'OK, folks, this is far from ideal. We don't know who the victim is, nor do we know when the body was dumped. But we can probably assume that our golden twenty-four hours are long past, and our killer has a significant head start. The forecast is for more rain, so any evidence that we haven't secured yet is at risk. We're against both the clock and the weather. Let's get going.'

Monday 28th November

Chapter 3

The body lay on a metal trolley. Beside Warren stood Moray Ruskin. As usual, the young detective constable appeared to be more fascinated than repulsed by the sight in front of them. Warren wished he felt the same way; he really hated autopsies.

'The victim was an early-middle-aged male of what appears to be South Asian heritage, 174 centimetres in height. He was a little overweight, weighing eighty-nine kilogrammes, with moderate muscle mass.'

The speaker was Professor Ryan Jordan, the American-born Home Office Pathologist who covered the part of eastern England where Middlesbury was located. With rain threatening to flood the shallow brook and compromise the scene still further, the body had been transported to Jordan's morgue late the previous night, ready for the post-mortem first thing that morning, and Warren had driven Ruskin to the Lister Hospital in Stevenage to witness the procedure.

'Lividity from blood-pooling is fixed and indicates that he spent some hours lying more or less flat on his back before being moved to his current position.'

'So he wasn't killed where we found him?' asked Ruskin.

Jordan rocked a hand from side-to-side. 'All I can say at the moment is that the positioning of his body was changed after death. He was mutilated post-mortem; that might account for the change in posture.'

He carefully lifted the right hand. 'All of the fingerprints have been sliced off with a very sharp blade. I'll take nail clippings as best I can, but I'm not promising.'

'Any indication what they might have used?' asked Ruskin, his mask rustling against his beard as he spoke.

'Hard to tell. It could have been a scalpel or a box-cutter; you know, one of those Stanley knives that crafts people or wood-workers use. The lack of blood indicates that they were sliced off after death.'

'Organised crime?' asked Ruskin.

'Possibly,' said Warren, fervently hoping not – it was fair to say that his working relationship with the Serious Organised Crime department had had its ups and downs over the years.

Warren moved to the head of the trolley. 'I take it dental records won't be much use?'

'I'm afraid not. You need teeth and an intact jaw for that. Whoever did this put a lot of effort into making sure that wasn't an option.'

'Any idea what was used?'

'From the shape of the impact marks, I'd say a blunt instrument with a round head, approximately three centimetres in diameter. Could be a hammer, or similar.'

Warren had seen a lot of deaths over the years, but it was rare to see this degree of mutilation. 'Post-mortem again?'

'Yes. The killer was probably covered in blood clots and bits of flesh, but it won't have been spraying everywhere.'

'So, what did kill him?' asked Ruskin.

'I don't know yet, there's no other obvious serious trauma. I've sent off for blood toxicology. I did find this though,' Jordan picked up a tablet computer. He flicked to a high-resolution photograph of the back of the man's head. The victim had been bald on top, with jet-black hair covering the sides and the top of the neck. An ugly-looking gash was visible just above the hairline. The flesh around it was raised and swollen.

'From the bruising, this was definitely pre-mortem. That was a hell of a smack to the head. I'd be willing to accept that it would have knocked him senseless, but my gut feeling is it wouldn't have been enough to kill him. I'll know more when I've examined the brain. A brain haemorrhage might have finished him off, but I haven't seen any other indications of that yet.'

'What about these scars?' asked Ruskin, leaning forward. The man's upper arms and thighs were criss-crossed with lines and scratches, some of them purple against the bloodless beige of the man's skin.

'They're several years old, possibly even dating back to child-hood or adolescence,' said Jordan. 'Probably self-inflicted. From the depth and angle of the cuts, I'd suggest self-harm, rather than serious attempts at suicide. They don't extend beyond the middle of the forearm, and wouldn't be visible if our victim chose not to wear short-sleeved shirts or shorts.'

'Private trauma, rather than public display,' said Warren quietly. The way that the man had been dumped and then mutilated, like a problem that needed to be solved rather than a living human being, had felt callous and uncaring. Had the man's death been the tragic culmination of a life full of sadness and pain, or had he at least found some peace and contentment? Had he loved and been loved? Warren pushed away those thoughts, returning his attention to Jordan.

'Well, we can't use fingerprints, and I doubt a photograph will be much help in identifying him, so it looks like it's DNA,' he said. 'We might get lucky and find he's been arrested previously.'

'Even if he isn't listed, it might not matter,' said Jordan. 'Our victim was fitted with a pacemaker. If it was done on the NHS, then the serial number should lead us right back to him.'

*

Warren slumped behind his desk, a sudden feeling of weariness banishing the excitement and adrenaline that had driven him for the past twenty hours. It had been well after midnight the previous evening when he'd finally caught a taxi home, Susan having driven him straight to CID in the hire van. She was in bed when he returned and he'd slept in the guest room so as not to disturb her, his hope that he could use the weekend in Coventry as a catalyst to discuss their own future plans scuppered. He resolved to get on the web and order a brochure first thing – one of them needed to take action to break the unspoken deadlock between them.

As always, the first few hours of the investigation had been a whirlwind of activity. Andy Harrison's team had worked the scene through the night, but even with powerful lamps to assist them, there was little the officers combing the nearby fields for evidence could do after sundown. They'd resumed at first light.

Meanwhile, the rest of the CID unit had swung into action. In the vast majority of cases, the killer was known to the victim; the clues to why the person was killed and who was responsible were there to be found within the victim's day-to-day existence. Not knowing the victim's identity put the team at a disadvantage from the start.

Despite Jordan's hopes that the victim's pacemaker might provide a clue to his identity, Warren knew that would take time. Every hour that passed was another hour that the killer had to cover their tracks. Fast-track DNA matching would potentially yield results within the next twenty-four hours, but only if their victim was on the database.

Ruskin had been working with the Missing Persons Unit since the previous afternoon and had compiled a list of men matching their victim's rough description. But it was lengthy, and aside from the scars – which may well have remained hidden from view – the deceased had no distinguishing marks. Patient records weren't routinely recorded on the database, meaning that they couldn't even use the man's heart condition to whittle down the candidates. And again, that assumed he was even on the system;

depending on how recently he vanished and the closeness of his personal relationships, it might be that no one had yet noticed his absence. And if his closest acquaintances had a role in his death …

Warren fought down a feeling of impatience. Every member of his rapidly expanding team was busy doing their job, but until they started feeding back to him, there was nothing much he could do.

Well, not quite nothing.

He eyed his in-tray. The end of year was fast approaching, and the mounting paperwork for appraisals was causing the wire mesh tray to lean at a precarious angle. The sensible thing to do would be to make a start on it – to make the most of the temporary lull before the investigation took over everything. And before the tray toppled onto the floor.

The door pushed open.

'It didn't look as though you've had much time for coffee, Boss.' DI Tony Sutton placed a steaming mug on his desk.

'In on your day off and bringing me coffee. Somebody's just scored full marks on his appraisal,' joked Warren.

'Thought never crossed my mind,' said Sutton, sitting down. 'How did it go yesterday?'

Warren shrugged. 'Pretty much how I thought it would. My cousin donated most of the remaining furniture to the British Heart Foundation. Just a few last boxes of photos and keepsakes left – less than I thought to be honest; we probably could have saved ourselves some money and loaded the car instead of hiring a van. But then Susan loves minibuses, so any excuse. She reckons it's nice to drive one without a dozen puking and screaming kids in the back.'

Sutton snorted. 'Yeah, I remember those days from when I used to take Josh and his teammates on football tours.' He took a swig of his own drink. He'd known Warren long enough to recognise when he wanted to steer clear of something. 'How do you think this one is going to play out?' he asked, changing the subject. 'I've been looking at the photos of the body. Somebody really didn't want us to identify him. Organised Crime?'

Warren let out a sigh. 'Christ, I hope not. Hopefully, whoever disposed of the body has just watched a lot of gangster movies or true crime documentaries.'

'Well, hopefully not too many, it makes our job a lot more difficult when the buggers know what they're doing.'

'Fingers crossed.'

*

The first real breakthrough came shortly after lunch.

DS Rachel Pymm phoned Warren in his office to tell him, 'Just got a shout from the search teams at Carrington Farm.' He hastened over to her desk, Sutton following.

As 'officer in the case', it was Pymm's job to manage the team of analysts that kept the sprawling HOLMES2 case management system up-to-date. Situated in the corner of the office, her workstation boasted three large monitors arranged in a horseshoe. To the side of her, the table housing her colour laser printer was already accumulating stacks of paper.

Pymm had joined Middlesbury's CID team two years ago when the tragic events of the previous summer had left them in need of a new case manager. An experienced detective sergeant, Pymm had been forced to retrain and take on a more deskbound job after a diagnosis of multiple sclerosis had started to impact her mobility. These days, Warren found it hard to remember a time when she hadn't been a part of his team and he had come to rely on her instincts.

'What have they found?' he asked.

Pymm spun her ergonomic chair to face him, pushing her red plastic glasses back on her nose. 'A hammer and a Stanley knife, wrapped in a towel and hidden under a tree stump, two-hundred metres from where the body was found. It looks as though they're covered in blood.'

'Bingo,' said Sutton. 'Now we're cooking.'

Chapter 4

Mid-afternoon on the second day and so far they weren't even certain how long the victim had been dead or who he was.

Warren was reminded of a course he had attended back in his early days as a detective constable. The distinguished pathologist giving the lecture had been disdainful of TV coroners who were able to insert a thermometer into a dead body, then pronounce that the deceased had died between 11.35 p.m. and 12.10 a.m. 'Total bollocks,' the man had proclaimed. 'If you ask me how long a person has been dead, I can tell you with great confidence that they died sometime between now and when they were last seen alive.'

Of course, he was exaggerating. But with the cold weather slowing decomposition, all Prof. Jordan could say with certainty was that the man had been moved after death, and that he had died enough hours prior to the discovery for his body to reach ambient temperature. Given the weather conditions, and assuming the body hadn't been kept in cold storage, he could have been killed anywhere from the night before he was found, to as much as a week earlier. In the meantime, all the team had to go on was the scene analysis.

'We found his fingertips,' said Andy Harrison over the

conference phone. Warren had invited him to address the afternoon briefing directly and he'd been happy to join the discussion from his base at the force's headquarters in Welwyn Garden City.

'Dare I ask …' said Warren.

'Not good,' said Harrison. 'They'd been discarded a bit further downstream from the body. Looks as though they made a tasty lunch for some of the local critters. No chance in hell of printing him.'

Warren looked around the table; the various expressions of his team told him he wasn't the only person unwilling to linger on that image. He moved the conversation on.

'What else have you got from the scene?'

'Well, the good news is that we've found some pretty clear tyre tracks that I'm fairly confident come from the vehicle used to dump the body. If you could show everyone the first slide, Sir.'

Warren turned to the wall screen that displayed the presentation that Harrison had emailed over before the briefing started. The first image was a top-down sketch of the dumping site.

'The stream is on the right-hand side of a narrow road if you travel in a westerly direction away from the A506. There is a verge on that side of the road that is used for passing vehicles. We've isolated clear tyre tracks from there that we believe are likely to be those from the vehicle of interest.'

'How can you be sure that they aren't from an unrelated vehicle using it to pass another car?' asked Hutchinson.

'Next slide, please,' instructed Harrison. The image changed to that of a tyre track on the muddy verge. 'If you look at the pattern of the indentations surrounding those small stones and the way that the grass is flattened, it's clear that the vehicle that made them was also travelling in a westerly direction, which means that it would have been on the left-hand side of the road. Passing cars that use the right-hand verge would be travelling in an easterly direction.

'In addition, as you can see on the following slide, the tyres

24

took some mud with them as they exited the verge, which then tracks back to the left-hand side of the road. Unless the driver had a complete brain-fart and forgot which side of the road we drive on in this country, I'm pretty sure it's the car we're looking for.'

'How good are the impressions?' asked Sutton.

'The ones on the verge are OK. But there are better ones 200 metres up the road, where the same vehicle used the entrance to a field to do a three-point-turn.' This time the image was a lot clearer. 'The bad news is that they are fifteen-inch Goodyears; they fit loads of small to medium-sized vehicles. The good news is that the tyres have plenty of wear on them; find me a suspect vehicle and I'll match them for you.'

'What else have you got?'

'Staying with impressions, we've isolated two different pairs of men's footwear on the embankment. The water level in the stream is just a few centimetres, and we have several clear imprints from each shoe on the mud underneath the bridge, plus lots of partials surrounding the body. The prints were clear enough to run through the database. Nobody we know unfortunately, but again I have make and size, so find me a suspect and I'll tell you if their shoes match.'

'That's brilliant, Andy,' said Warren, before the CSI hung up.

'Well, that gives us something to work with if we get a suspect,' said Sutton.

'I'd be happy just to know who the victim is at the moment,' said Warren. 'How is the search going for his clothes and belongings, Hutch? I'm willing to settle for house and car keys, wallet with photo driving licence and an unlocked smart phone.'

'Sorry to disappoint,' said Hutchinson. 'The search team are making the most of the last of the daylight. They did a fingertip search – no pun intended – along the verge this morning, that's how they found the hammer and knife. Tomorrow, teams with waders will do the rest of the stream and we've got a load more warm bodies coming up from Welwyn, plus dogs, to start on the fields. At least this time of year, there aren't loads of crops, but if the killer decided to bury them … well it's a big, rural area.'

Warren took his point. He'd already spoken to DSI Grayson regarding the logistics for such a large search. They'd agreed to throw everything available at the search for forty-eight hours, before reviewing that decision. The days of blank cheques authorising hundreds of hours of overtime on an SIO's say-so were long gone.

'It's early days,' he said, 'but let's start thinking about motives. We're already considering an organised crime angle, due to the mutilation.'

'No wallet or phone,' said Hutchinson, 'so normally I'd think robbery, but the teeth and fingertips seem extreme, and where does the bed sheet come in?'

'It feels pre-meditated,' said Warren. 'Or at least the disposal of the body does.'

'Stripped naked could indicate a sexual motive,' said Ruskin, 'but Prof. Jordan hasn't found any indications of rape or torture.'

'The man's of South Asian heritage,' said Sutton, 'so we should consider that it could have been racially motivated.'

'Or even a so-called honour killing,' said Richardson.

'We definitely need to look into that angle,' said Warren, 'but at the moment we're speculating.'

With little else to report, the meeting broke up. Warren fought the urge to look at his watch again. It's a marathon, not a sprint, he reminded himself.

Watching the purposeful strides of his team, he smiled humourlessly. He wasn't the only person who found that hard to accept.

*

'First reports are back on the tools found near the body yesterday,' said Pymm as Warren crossed the office to her desk. One of her monitors displayed a high-resolution image of the hammer. 'They're going to use cyanoacrylate to try and lift any residual fingerprints from it, but it's been wiped down very carefully.'

The tool in question was a typical claw hammer, made of stainless steel with a black, rubber grip. The circular head was stained a dark red, with further small spots on the shaft.

Warren squinted at the image. 'It doesn't look new, there are lots of scratches.'

'Is that a logo on the handle?' asked DC Karen Hardwick, leaning closer to the screen.

'Yes, but I don't recognise it,' said Pymm.

'Me neither,' said Warren. 'Karen, can you take a closer look and see if it matches anything in the tool database? Then see if we can narrow it down; you never know, it might be an unusual make.'

'There's a sticker on the base,' said Pymm, magnifying the image. 'It's pretty faded, but there appear to be some numbers printed on it. A batch number perhaps?'

'Excellent. Karen, run that by the manufacturer when you've identified them, see if they can tell us where it was sold. What about the knife?'

Pymm switched images. The tool was a Stanley knife, with a push blade. The handle was made of grey metal, covered in blood and flecks of what looked like paint.

'Again, no obvious prints,' said Pymm. 'It looks as though they used a new blade, but this handle has seen some use over the years. Forensics are going to dismantle it and check for trace evidence. Unfortunately, there don't appear to be any obvious serial numbers, and I'll bet Stanley have sold millions of these over the years.'

'Well, let's not assume anything. Check the database, Karen. Again, we might get lucky.'

Jobs assigned, Warren headed back to his office. Despite himself, he looked at his watch. They had made good progress, but it was reaching the end of the second day of the investigation

27

and so far they still had no clue who the victim was, when he was killed and why he was dumped in that ditch.

*

Warren and Sutton brought DSI Grayson up to speed with the progress of the case in the Superintendent's office.

'The CSIs are confident that blood spatter at the dumping ground was from a body that was already dead,' said Warren. 'Couple that with the inconsistency in the lividity patterns that Professor Jordan analysed, and I think we can state with confidence that the victim was killed elsewhere then moved prior to the body being dumped.'

Grayson nodded his understanding. The confirmation wasn't a huge revelation, but it did help focus the investigation.

'Hutch has been organising door-knockers for the houses either end of the road,' said Sutton. 'Nobody remembers any suspicious vehicles over the past week. They get a fair bit of traffic down there from people dodging congestion, so they are used to seeing unfamiliar cars.'

'I don't suppose there's any CCTV out there?' asked Grayson.

'I'm afraid not, Sir,' replied Sutton. 'A couple of the farms have their own system, but the road is well outside their camera range.'

'What about ANPR?'

'Mags is securing it for analysis, but if they obeyed the speed limit on the 506 and didn't drive into Middlesbury, they probably weren't captured. It doesn't help that we can't be more specific about the time frame; the list of cars that could have those tyres fitted is ridiculous. It'd almost be easier to ask what cars the tyres wouldn't fit.'

'Then we need to know who he is,' stated Grayson.

Warren agreed. If they knew who they were dealing with, then they could track his movements, speak to associates and construct a timeline of his last movements. Somewhere, buried within that information, the clues to his murderer would hopefully be hidden.

'Speaking of which, when will we hear back about the pacemaker?' asked Grayson.

'It's been removed and cleaned. If it was fitted on the NHS, it should be fairly easy to identify who it was given to using its serial number,' replied Warren.

'What if the pacemaker was fitted overseas?' asked Grayson.

'It should still be possible to track it down through the manufacturer, but it may take a bit longer,' said Warren.

'Well, here's hoping,' said Grayson.

It was past six when Karen Hardwick knocked on Warren's office door. 'I have some news about the tools.'

'Do tell,' said Warren, grateful for the interruption; he was drowning in a sea of appraisal paperwork. Hardwick's return to Middlesbury CID after her maternity leave had been far from certain, but the last few months had reminded Warren just how efficient she was. There was still some awkwardness between them, but he was glad to have her back on the team.

'I traced the logo using the database and identified the hammer. Would you like the good news or the bad news?'

'Go on, give me the bad news first. It's always nice to end on a high.'

'I contacted the manufacturer. They're a mid-range, mid-price product made in China and sold across several big DIY retailers. Last year alone, they imported five thousand units to the UK. I got the batch number off that sticker on the base of the handle, but they couldn't tell me where they would have been sold.'

'Damn. What's the good news?'

'I wouldn't get too excited. They were able to tell me that hammers with that batch number aren't sold as a single item, they come as part of a tool set, in a medium-sized plastic toolbox, with screwdrivers, spanners, hex keys, pliers and spirit level etc., all of them branded with the same logo. I found a picture of the set online.'

'That could be useful,' mused Warren. 'If we find a suspect then we can check their toolbox for a missing hammer.'

'The set also has a box-cutter, but according to the online reviews, it's a bit crap. A couple of buyers suggested ditching it and replacing it with a metal Stanley knife, which fits in the same space in the toolbox.'

'Which is the same brand that we found wrapped up with the hammer,' said Warren. 'Good work. I imagine that tracing sales of the knife is a non-starter?'

'The woman on the phone actually laughed when I told her the model; she couldn't give me the exact sales figures, but it's probably the most popular craft knife sold in the UK over the past ten years.'

'Then let's hope that forensics have a bit more luck,' said Warren.

Warren pushed down his sense of mounting frustration. Two days in and they still hadn't identified the victim.

Sleep would be elusive tonight.

Tuesday 29th November

Chapter 5

'We know who the victim is.' Rachel Pymm was jubilant.

The third day of the investigation started with some good news – at least for the investigative team.

'NHS England identified him from the serial number on his pacemaker.' She looked at the screen in front of her. 'Anish Patel, thirty-nine years old. The pacemaker was fitted eighteen months ago at Addenbrooke's to help manage a congenital defect leading to an irregular heartbeat.' She scrolled down. 'He was also on medication.'

'Is he on the PNC?' asked Warren.

'Nope, no arrests and no criminal convictions, so his DNA isn't on the system.' She clicked her mouse. 'He also isn't listed as a missing person; Moray will be delighted he spent all those hours trawling the database.'

'Who do the hospital list as his next-of-kin?' asked Sutton.

'His father, Gotam Patel. He lives in Cambridge; same home address as Anish.'

Warren sighed. 'If he's not listed as missing, then either his family know what happened to him and are suspects, they know that he is missing but aren't worried enough to contact the police, or they haven't even realised he's gone.'

'Which means the poor bastards are about to get some devastating news,' said Sutton quietly.

*

'Somebody's doing all right for themselves,' said Tony Sutton.

Warren pulled into the drive of the large, converted farmhouse on the outskirts of Cambridge. The two detectives were accompanied by PC Kevin Lederer, a Family Liaison Officer. Warren had been going to ask David Hutchinson to come with him on the visit, but Sutton had been desperate to get out of the office. For most of the past year, since returning after his mini-stroke, he had been on light duties. However, he'd persuaded Warren that breaking the tragic news to the Patels, whilst emotionally draining, would not be physically demanding.

Warren had regretted agreeing to Sutton's plea the moment he turned the engine on and backed out of his parking spot at the station.

'Duran Duran!' Sutton had cackled, as the radio burst into life. Warren had sighed; he'd put up with this for over five years. It never seemed to get old for his friend.

Turning in his seat to face Lederer, Sutton was gleeful. 'The DCI's taste in music died and was buried sometime around the late 1980s.'

'However,' Warren had interrupted, 'despite his advancing years, DI Sutton still listens to Radio One. He thinks it keeps him more in touch as a father.'

Lederer had laughed. 'No need to be ashamed, Sir. I saw them live on the Isle of Wight last year. In fact, me and the missus have seen loads of '80s bands over the years. Have you seen any recently?'

If Lederer thought that he could curry favour with the DCI by sparing his blushes, he'd miscalculated. Badly.

This time, Sutton's laughter was more of a guffaw. 'Go on, Chief, tell him.'

'I think that's enough.'

Sutton had ignored him. 'DCI Warren Jones is probably one of the few people in the world who has never been to a concert or a gig.'

'That's not true,' Warren had protested.

'An ABBA tribute band playing a student hall of residence doesn't count.'

'I can't see the point,' Warren had muttered. 'It costs a fortune, the songs never sound as good as they do on the stereo, and the queues for the toilets are massive.'

'Wow,' Lederer had said eventually. 'I'm not quite sure what to say.'

'Try "no comment", lad,' Sutton had advised. 'It's appraisal time.'

'I did a bit of research,' said Sutton now, as Warren pulled up next to a white Range Rover with personalised licence plates bearing the victim's father's initials. Parked next to it was a bright red, two-door Mercedes, also with personalised plates. 'It turns out that our victim comes from an extremely wealthy background. His parents, or rather his father now, owns a string of businesses across this area. Everything from dry cleaning to newsagents and one-stop shops under the brand name Everyday Essentials; they even have a small catering business. Net worth is in the millions.'

'That explains the cars and the house then,' said Lederer.

Even with Warren taking up a space, there was still enough room for several more vehicles, plus a detached, two-car garage. To the right of the main house, what looked like an old barn had been converted into a smaller, separate dwelling.

'According to a recent profile in the *Cambridge Evening News* business section,' continued Sutton, 'our victim is the third of four children; two older brothers and a younger sister. Judging by the initials on the Merc, I'd say the sister is home. The two older brothers and the sister work for their old man; no mention of what Anish did for a living. Their mother died a few years ago.'

Warren filed the tit-bit away for later consideration. If the family was as wealthy as Sutton claimed, it suggested a raft of potential motives for Anish Patel's murder. The fact that he might be the only child that didn't work for his father hinted at even more.

The three officers climbed out of the car, but before they even reached the doorstep, the door opened. A tall, thin, Asian man who looked to be in his sixties, greeted them.

Warren and Sutton had done many of these visits over the years, and the FLO was an expert, so if there was one thing that Warren knew, it was that the next few minutes could be critical. The reaction of family to the news of their loved one's murder often provided essential leads. Did they seem surprised, or were they expecting the news? Everyone reacted differently, but an experienced officer could often distinguish true grief from that put on for show. The details of the victim's death would be released slowly and carefully – not only as a kindness to help the family process them properly, but also to see if the family knew more than would be expected about the circumstances.

To this end, the FLO was a crucial part of the investigation. Part of the role was as a conduit between the investigating team and the family, keeping them apprised of major developments, and advising them on practical matters, such as when the body would be released. Equally important, the information exchange was two-way. Vital details that a shocked family might forget to tell Warren during interview, or they might have deemed unimportant, were noted, along with the FLO's observations and impressions.

But that was all in the future. First, they had to break the news.

'Mr Patel? My name is Detective Chief Inspector Warren Jones. May I come in and speak to you?'

*

Gotam Patel was yet to touch the brandy that his daughter, Reva Vasava, had poured him. Despite his size, he was almost engulfed by the four-person leather sofa that he'd collapsed into when

Warren broke the news. His hands shook as he took a long swig. Vasava lived with her husband in the converted barn that they had seen on the way up the drive. She had arrived at the front door moments after Warren had been invited inside.

'Was it his heart?' Patel finally asked, his voice shaking.

'Mum died of a heart attack nearly two years ago,' said Vasava. Her voice was barely a whisper, as she perched on the edge of a large armchair, her hands wrapped around a tumbler she had yet to take a sip from.

Warren spoke as gently as he could. 'No. I'm very sorry to tell you, but it appears that Anish was murdered. His body was discovered Sunday morning. We came as soon as we identified him.'

Vasava gave a low moan and raised her hand to her mouth. The tears that she had somehow held back as she poured the drinks and guided her stricken father to his chair, now flowed freely.

'But who …' She couldn't finish the sentence.

'We don't know yet,' said Warren. 'We have a large team working on that as we speak.'

'How was he killed?' she managed.

'We haven't yet determined the cause of death,' said Warren; this was not the time to go into details.

'So how do you know he was murdered?' asked Patel, his voice trembling.

Warren glanced over at Sutton. 'The circumstances that he was found in mean it is unlikely that he died of natural causes.'

'What circumstances? Where was he found?' demanded Patel.

Warren chose his words carefully. 'His body was found near a field just outside Middlesbury.'

'What was he doing there?' asked Vasava.

'We don't know yet, we're trying to establish his last movements. I'm sorry to have to ask at such a time, but when did you last speak to Anish?'

Vasava gave a sniff. 'Last week. Tuesday, I think. He phoned me.'

37

Out of the corner of his eye, Warren could see that Patel had turned his head to look out of the window.

'Was there anything unusual about the call? Did he mention any worries?'

Vasava looked over at her father, before looking away. 'No. Nothing.'

Warren turned to the father. 'What about you, Mr Patel? When did you last have contact with Anish?'

'I haven't spoken to him in a long time,' he said quietly.

'Anish listed this as his home address on his medical records. I take it he no longer lives here?'

'No, he moved out last year. I don't think he's got around to changing his GP or dentist.'

'Do you have his current address?'

Patel gave a tiny shake of his head and looked away. After a moment's pause, Vasava recited the address of a flat in Middlesbury. It wasn't in the nicer part of town.

Patel stirred. 'I knew this would happen.' His voice grew stronger. 'I said that, did I not?'

'Dad, not now.'

'What do you mean, Mr Patel?' asked Warren quickly, not wanting him to stop talking.

'His lifestyle, the people he hung around with.' He turned to his daughter. 'I told you not to speak to him. That until he changed his behaviour, he brought shame upon us.'

'Dad, please,' she said, the tears starting to flow again.

Outside the window, Warren heard a loudly revving engine, followed by the sound of tyres sliding on gravel. A black Range Rover, identical in model to the one bearing Gotam Patel's personalised license plates, ground to a halt.

Patel stood up.

'My son is here. I would be grateful if you could leave us alone now to grieve, Chief Inspector.'

*

38

Warren held an impromptu meeting on the drive home from the Patels.

'Thoughts?'

'I'm not happy with the family,' said Sutton. 'There's something funny going on there.'

'I agree,' said Warren. 'It's clear that Anish has had some sort of falling out with his father and his brothers.'

Anish's eldest brother, Manoj, had appeared shocked at the news, but unlike his younger sister, had also seemed angry. The middle brother, Jaidev, had yet to arrive by the time the officers left. Like their father, Manoj had mentioned Anish's lifestyle, and claimed not to have spoken to him in recent months. Under the scowling countenance of their father, neither Manoj nor his sister had been willing to elaborate on what was so concerning about the way he'd lived his life.

It had taken some persuasion for the family to take Lederer's business card, but they had eventually agreed to the FLO stopping by the following day. Warren was interested in the officer's impressions.

'Grief's a funny thing,' said Lederer. 'It's not uncommon for the relatives to initially blame the victim. But I agree that there is a lot going on in that family.'

'What about the dad's comments about Anish's lifestyle and the people he hung around with?' asked Warren.

'Maybe he had criminal connections?' said Sutton. 'The article in the newspaper suggested that Anish wasn't part of the family business, and his father claimed not to have spoken to him since he moved out. My immediate thought is, what did he live on?'

'If the family business is as lucrative as we think, then perhaps that made him a target?' suggested Lederer. 'Perhaps he was kidnapped and killed for money?'

'We should see if the Patel business empire is known to us,' said Sutton. 'From the article, most of the businesses are cash-based; plenty of scope for money-laundering.'

Warren grimaced. 'I'll get onto Organised Crime and see if they have any intelligence they'd like to share.'

'It was also a bit strange that his father seemed not to know where he lived,' said Lederer. 'And there were no photographs of Anish in the living room. Reva had to fetch one for us to borrow.'

'Reva said that she spoke to him last Tuesday,' said Warren. 'And of the three of them, she seemed the most upset at the news.' He glanced at Lederer in the rear-view mirror. 'I think Reva is likely to be the most cooperative. Can you try and build a relationship with her?'

'I'll do that tomorrow when I swing by to arrange for them to be interviewed,' promised the constable.

'In the meantime,' said Warren, 'we at least have a recent photograph of him, and Reva gave us his address. Tony, arrange a locksmith and a forensics team, and go and look at where he lives. Maybe that will shed some light on what has upset his family so much.'

Chapter 6

'The forensics are back on the hammer and knife,' said Rachel Pymm. Warren stood behind her as she shared the findings; a strange herbal smell that reminded him of throat lozenges drifted from the steaming mug next to her elbow. He didn't dare ask what this week's infusion of choice was; it was likely to result in another conversation about his caffeine intake. He was already being nagged by Tony Sutton, who claimed that his enforced switch to decaf coffee was the best thing he'd ever done, although he too declined to sample Pymm's collection of weird and wonderful teas.

Pymm pointed to an image of the hammer on her left-most screen. 'The stains have been confirmed as human blood belonging to our victim.' She gestured at the picture on the middle screen. 'The same goes for the stains on the knife.'

'What about trace evidence?'

'Nothing on the hammer. No identifiable prints, and the pattern of blood-smear on the grip indicates that the person wielding it wore gloves. If the killer did leave any DNA behind, it's too well mixed in with the victim's blood to be isolated.'

'No surprise. What about the knife?'

'That's a bit more hopeful. The handle is die-cast metal, with a rough texture to improve grip; there appear to be skin cells caught in it. They've been sent off for DNA typing, although it may take a little time to isolate any profile from the victim's own.'

'What about fingerprints?'

'Nothing on the outside, but they've found a partial print on the unused blades inside the handle.' She switched images. 'It has a retractable blade that is replaced when it becomes too blunt. They come in strips of three, which are loaded into the handle. When the blade is no longer usable, it's snapped off and the next one in the strip pushed forward. The print, a partial thumb, probably comes from whoever loaded it. The tool looks well-used, so hopefully the print was from the owner replacing the strip. I'd have thought that the factory assembles them by machine.'

'How good is it?'

Pymm made a so-so gesture with her hand. 'Probably not good enough to search the databases, but enough to match by eye if we have a suspect in the frame.'

'I'll take that. Anything else?'

'The dried paint flecks on the handle are being analysed to identify the colour and manufacturer.'

Warren pinched his lip thoughtfully. At the moment, the tools weren't pointing them towards the person that mutilated the victim's body. However, the trace evidence might be enough to confirm a suspect.

Thanking her, he headed back to his office, where he could hear his desk phone ringing.

*

'I'm in Anish Patel's flat.'

Tony Sutton stood in the living room of the tiny apartment, his voice slightly muffled by his face mask. His legs still trembled slightly from three flights of stairs, however his pulse, which he'd surreptitiously checked after the climb, remained fast but steady. Months had passed since the cardioversion that had corrected his arrhythmia and allowed him to finally return to work, but he still half-expected it to revert at any moment.

'Any sign of a struggle?' asked Warren, on the other end of the line.

'Nothing obvious. The place is a bit untidy, but I can't see anything noticeably out of place. The CSIs are going to take up the rugs and check for trace, but if he was killed here, his attacker was sophisticated enough not to clean the place up too much. I can't smell any bleach or cleaning chemicals.'

'OK, what's your first impression?'

'Living beyond his means. The flat is tiny, and I'd say the rent's probably about as low as you can get in Middlesbury without moving to the Chequers Estate. But there is a wheeled clothes rack with a load of tailored suits, and he has several very expensive watches. I'd say he's playing the role of a wealthy man but struggling to make ends meet.'

Sutton turned on the spot. 'It looks as though he's a big action movie fan; the only art on the wall is framed movie posters: James Bond, Jason Bourne, plus all the *Ocean's Eleven* films – the original and the remakes.' He took a few steps toward a pair of tall bookcases. 'Lots of paperback thrillers in the bookcase and similar DVDs, plus some compendiums of poetry.'

Sutton carefully leafed through a pile of envelopes on the small, fold-up table next to the kitchen counter.

'There's a load of what looks like bills here, all unopened, some with "final demand" on them.'

'Any electronic devices?'

'No laptop or desktop, but we've secured a tablet. There's an empty box for a Samsung mobile phone.'

'Any sign of a toolbox that the hammer could have come from?'

'Nothing – doesn't look as though he was much into DIY.'

'What about photos?'

Sutton moved around the flat, his booties rustling as he carefully trod on the metal stepping plates.

'There are a few on a shelf above the TV …' He looked closer. 'Three from his sister's wedding, including one with the two of them, and another that looks like it might be his oldest brother's wedding. Judging from his hairline, that one's a few years old. There's another one of him on holiday with an older woman, could be his mum. Big smiles, again a few years old, but aside from an awkward-looking one at his sister's wedding, I'm not seeing any other happy family gatherings. It seems like he really was the black sheep of the family.'

'That fits with what we've heard so far,' said Warren. 'Any indication of when he was last in the flat?'

'The neighbour across the hall says that he's pretty certain that he saw him Wednesday evening,' said Sutton. After a few more seconds, Warren heard the sound of a door opening and a compressor pump starting up.

'The fridge has some reasonably fresh-looking salad in the vegetable tray, and an opened two-pinter of skimmed milk with another three days left on its use-by date. I'd say his neighbour was probably right.'

'Well, that narrows things down a bit. Now we just need to know where he's been between last Wednesday and his body turning up in that ditch.'

Chapter 7

Three days in and already the late nights were starting. Warren knew from experience that things were unlikely to get any better in the short term, and at this stage of the investigation, speed was essential.

One advantage that the team still enjoyed was that it appeared as though the body had been found sooner than the killer might have hoped. It was all but impossible to see the site from the road; it had only been the unexpected presence of Charlie Pitt and his young helper Kyle in the adjacent field that had led to the body's discovery. With winter fast approaching, unless some unfortunate dog-walker stumbled across the decomposing remains, it was possible that Anish Patel may have remained alone and unfound for months.

Which raised the question as to whether the person, or persons, dumping the body knew this or just got lucky? Were they familiar with the ditch or did they stumble across it as they drove around with a body in the boot of their car, looking for somewhere to deposit it?

That made Charlie Pitt and young Kyle immediate suspects, along with anyone else that worked on Carrington Farm. As a matter of routine, everyone associated with the farm had been run through the PNC, but aside from a couple of motoring offences, nobody was listed. Unfortunately, with no time of death established, checking alibis was proving difficult.

Regardless, it was entirely possible that the killer had not yet realised the victim had been found, and so might be caught unprepared. A statement had been made to the press first thing that morning, but with few details, had barely made its mark on a news day still dominated by the recent US elections, ongoing legal spats over the future of the UK's relationship with Europe, and the latest minor celebrity to leave *Strictly Come Dancing*.

At this stage, Warren would take any advantage that he could.

Looking at his watch, Warren debated whether or not to make the call. It was well after 9 p.m. and he knew that out of necessity, bedtime was a highly regimented affair. He should have called the previous evening, but it had been impossible to get away for more than a few moments before it really was too late to phone.

To hell with it, he decided. If he didn't phone now, when would he?

He closed the office door as he waited for the phone to connect. It rang so long that he was mentally composing a voicemail message, when it was finally answered.

Another pause, followed by a raspy 'Hello?'

Warren smiled; the old man still hadn't got used to checking caller ID on the phone's screen. Warren had eventually found a handset designed with input from charities that helped the elderly, and whilst texting was still a work in progress, the staff in the care home had helped Granddad Jack learn to use the new technology.

'It's Warren, Granddad,' he said loudly. The phone was designed to work with hearing aids, but that assumed the stubborn nonagenarian hadn't removed them or turned them off; something he did regularly when he wanted some peace and quiet.

Immediately the man's tone shifted. 'How are you, son?'

'I'm fine,' Warren swallowed. 'Look I'm really sorry that I didn't get to pop by on Sunday, after … you know …'

'Of course, I know you're busy,' the old man injected a note of false cheer into his voice. 'I imagine you've been called into deal with that body they've found?'

'How do you know about that?' asked Warren. As far as he was aware, the case had yet to hit the national newspapers and the care home was in Coventry; they'd receive TV news from the West Midlands, not the East of England where Hertfordshire was located.

Jack's voice was full of pride. 'I figured it must be something like that, so I went to the day room and looked it up on the internet. It wasn't on the BBC internet page, but I used Google and put in "Middlesbury" and "murder".' He gave a throaty laugh. 'Goodness son, I'd forgotten how busy you'd been since you'd moved down there. That little town must be the murder capital of England.'

Warren gave a chuckle, although it wasn't really a laughing matter. Jack was right: Middlesbury had seen far more than its fair share of killings in the five years since he'd moved there from the West Midlands Police.

Pushing aside the dark topic, he reflected on his relief at how well Jack seemed to be coping. At ninety-two years old, the mobile revolution had pretty much passed Jack by and he certainly hadn't had access to the internet at home. Finding out that he'd started using the communal computers in the day room had astounded Warren. He'd even had a couple of brief emails from him.

It was a far cry from where they had been just nine months ago. The eventual realisation in February that Jack would not be able to care for himself in his own home, even with assistance, had left Warren with the heart-breaking task of telling the old man that he would need to move into a care home. And not only that, he would have to sell his beloved house to pay for it; the house that Granddad Jack had pledged would go to Warren and his brother, should Warren ever locate his long-missing sibling.

At first Jack had been in denial, insisting that the progress he'd made in the respite home since his accident showed he just needed a bit more time. But the doctors had been clear that there was only so much more a body that age could fix itself.

Warren had assumed that it was the loss of independence that bothered Jack the most; that after years of looking after himself, and before then his wife, he mourned the man he once had been. Eventually though, he'd confessed that he didn't mind living with other people; he'd been feeling lonely for the past few years. He didn't even mind being cared for; he was a practical man and welcomed the extra assistance. What upset him the most, after the loss of his house, was that he felt that he was breaking a promise. The night that Nana Betty had passed away, Warren and Jack had stayed with her until the end. Jack had lain beside her in the bed they'd shared for over sixty years: the bed that he'd told her he would die in one day also.

With that in mind, Warren had tried to find a care home that would let them move the old timber-framed bed into one of their rooms, but it had been no use. Even assuming they were able to dismantle and reassemble it, it simply wasn't suited to the needs of a modern care facility, especially if Jack needed increasing personal and medical attention in the years to come.

But by this point, Jack had come to accept the inevitability of his future. Most importantly for Warren, he'd stopped talking about how he'd 'had a good innings' and that he'd 'had it better than most'. For the first time, he'd started to engage with the whole process, expressing firm preferences for how he wanted to spend this next – and probably final – chapter of his life. The Fir Tree Lane Care Home had ticked all of the boxes. Less than three miles from where Jack and Betty had lived for so many years, it was close enough to Jack's old haunts that friends could still visit. Now that he could walk short distances with his walking frame, and with a steadying hand could climb in and out of a car, a steady rota of friends had stepped up, ensuring that Jack made it to church each week and had a pint at his local. Warren had made a list of these friends and was planning on sending them all a heartfelt Christmas card and letter thanking them for taking care of him.

'Well anyway,' said Warren, 'I'm really sorry we couldn't come by on Sunday for a bite to eat with you before we left.'

'Not to worry, son. I'm sure you'll get up here before Christmas.'

'Count on it,' said Warren, vowing that he would make time in his schedule, even if it meant he had to drive up and back in the same evening.

'Anyway, I had company,' said Jack.

'Oh? Did Bernice and Dennis pop over?' Susan's parents were one of the few reasons that Warren hadn't moved back to the West Midlands to be closer to Jack. Both retired now, they had been seeing even more of him than before. The domineering Bernice and her hen-pecked husband might be hard work at times, but Warren would never forget the way that they had taken Granddad Jack to their hearts. Warren and Susan had been due to meet them at Jack's home, which had a relaxed policy about guests visiting with food and would arrange tables and chairs for families to spend time together.

'Yes, Dennis has been busy in the kitchen again, it seemed a shame to waste it. And they had a surprise.'

'Oh?' Warren had no idea.

'Felicity and the kids were over for a flying visit, so they all came too.'

Warren's heart sank, even as he heard the happy note in Jack's voice. Susan hadn't seen her sister and her brood for months; Bernice and Dennis had obviously hoped for this to be a surprise. Susan would be gutted when he told her of yet another family get-together missed due to distance and the demands of his job.

'It's just as well you two didn't come, there wouldn't have been enough food. My God that boy can eat!'

'Sorry, Granddad, I missed that,' said Warren, dragging himself back to the conversation.

'Jimmy – I can't believe he's only eight. He looks at least eleven; I'm not surprised, the amount he eats. Burns it off though, apparently he's doing a different sport every day; Felicity showed me the calendar on her iPad thingy,' Jack chuckled. 'Not like when you were a kid. Your mum and dad would give you a football, kick you out the back door and tell you not to come back until your dad whistled.'

Warren smiled at the memory. A memory from a time when they had all been happy. Before his dad had died, and everything changed … he forced the gathering clouds away. He'd largely dealt with those demons, but sometimes they reappeared when he least expected them.

'How are the rest of them?' he asked.

'Growing like weeds. The boys must have put on six inches in the past few months, and the girls, well Annie has changed so much since she started school and Tiffany is such a little chatterbox, I can't believe she only turned two in the summer.' Jack gave a wistful sigh. 'They grow so fast at that age, but it's lovely to see them. Ranjit in the room opposite me has so many great-grandkids they have to take it in turns to visit him. I forget sometimes what it's like—' He stopped abruptly.

Warren closed his eyes and took a steadying breath, not quite trusting himself to speak. A little over a year ago, he and Susan had broken the news that Jack was going to become a great-grandfather for the first time. Over the years, he'd loved playing honorary great-grandfather to Susan's nieces and nephews, and finding out that he was going to finally have his own had lifted his spirits immeasurably.

The blow from finding out that it wasn't going to be, followed shortly after by the news that he was never going to return home, had pushed Jack into a dark place that he hadn't occupied since Nana Betty's death. Thankfully that had passed.

'Have you and Susan talked about, you know …' Jack said finally, the words awkward, coming from a man whose generation

50

rarely discussed such things. 'I know I promised I'd help you out with the money, and I'm sorry I can't now …'

'It's not about the money,' said Warren quietly, not wanting to discuss it any further.

The silence hung on the line like a blanket, neither man sure how to proceed. They were rescued by a knocking in the background.

'That's Alina,' said Jack, sounding relieved. His voice became muffled as he turned to the care worker. 'I'm just on the phone to Warren; a cup of cocoa would be lovely.'

'Look, I've got to go,' said Warren. 'I'll let you get ready for bed.'

After ending the call with his usual promise to call more regularly, Warren was again left feeling deflated. It was less than a month to Christmas; he was determined that he would spend at least some of it with his grandfather. But how many more would they celebrate together?

Wednesday 30th November

Chapter 8

'I have Anish Patel's phone records,' said Pymm at the morning briefing. 'Unfortunately, the handset went dark at 17:38 on Thursday evening, about halfway up the high street. It turned on briefly again Friday morning, when a text was sent, and then again, same number, Saturday morning.'

'Well that would have been too easy,' said Warren, 'but the timing might indicate when he was killed. Can we track the handset? If the phone was stolen by the killer they might switch SIM cards and use it themselves. The box that we found in his flat was this year's top-of-the-range model, that's got to be worth a few quid.'

'The network operator is working out the phone's IMEI code, they'll put a flag on it if it connects again.'

'What about call logs?' asked Sutton.

'I'm working out who he's called over the past few months. He spoke to his sister each week, usually for about half an hour. He also rang both his brothers and his father several times in the weeks after he moved out. Normally the call was unanswered or lasted only a couple of seconds before they hung up. He also texted them repeatedly, with no reply. Eventually he gave up.'

'Which would make sense if they were refusing to speak to him,' said Warren.

'True, but his middle brother, Jaidev, did answer properly once, on July 10th. The connection only lasted for about three minutes.'

'Before we were turfed out yesterday, his older brother Manoj claimed that neither of them had contacted him,' said Warren. 'I'd like to hear that denial directly from Jaidev's lips when he finally comes in for an interview. Who else did Anish call?'

'Lots of others that I am identifying. But there are a load of unregistered pay-as-you-go phones; some that he called several times, usually only over a short period of time, some he only called once.'

Warren tapped his teeth thoughtfully. 'Thoughts?'

'It could be anything from online dating to a drug dealer that changes their burner phone every couple of weeks. I'm cross-referencing the times of those with his known movements to see if there's a pattern. I'll let you know as soon as I've finished.'

'I'll tell you something, our job would be a lot easier if they banned unregistered handsets,' said Sutton.

Pymm shrugged. 'I agree. But then how would I conduct my extra-marital affairs?'

*

'You have a visitor, Sir.'

Janice, the support worker that acted as Warren's unofficial PA, poked her head around his office door. Warren looked up from the computer in surprise.

'I didn't think I had any appointments today, except for the budget meeting?' He glanced at the clock on the wall. 'Which I shall be enduring in about fifteen minutes.'

'It's a walk-in. Reva Vasava.'

'I'll be right there.' He paused, trying not to look too pleased. 'Send my apologies to DSI Grayson, he'll have to represent both of us.'

*

Reva Vasava was dressed in an expensive-looking cashmere coat and calf-length leather boots; her large, but tasteful gold earrings glinted in the fluorescent light. Her eyes were red and puffy. In her hand, she clutched a brown, A4 envelope. She looked around her, as if nervous at being seen.

After greeting Anish Patel's youngest sibling, Warren walked them both down to the 'smart meeting room'. Furnished with soft, comfy chairs and painted soothing pastel colours, it was purposely designed for meetings with grieving relatives, or conversations unsuited to a formal interview suite. Its machine also served the second-best coffee in the building after John Grayson's personal stash.

'As I said yesterday, I am very sorry for your loss, Mrs Vasava. How can I help you today?'

PC Lederer had been around to see the family that morning. He'd reported that they were still not opening up to him, and were reluctant to come to the station and give statements; much longer and they would have to insist. Lederer's attempts to forge a relationship with Vasava had been politely rebuffed, however his instinct was that she was willing to talk, away from her family.

Vasava laid the envelope on the table between them, then removed a tissue from her pocket. Warren waved away her apology as she wiped away the freshly formed tears. Eventually, she regained control. When she spoke, her voice was low, fearful.

'I'm sorry, DCI Jones. I should have come in sooner, but things at home are … difficult.'

Warren nodded his sympathy.

'The thing is …' She paused, and Warren could see that she was fighting back more tears. 'The thing is, I think my father might have been involved in Anish's death.'

*

'Why don't you start at the beginning,' said Warren, when the tears had finally subsided.

57

Vasava nodded. Warren noticed that her eyes took on a faraway cast. 'I'm the youngest child, with seven years between me and Anish. I guess that's why we are … were … so close. I love my other brothers of course, but there was always something special between me and Anish.' She sniffed. 'Even when I was a little girl, I knew that there was something different about him. Jaidev and Manoj – they were like little versions of Dad. They were into sports: cricket, martial arts, you name it. They still are.' She smiled tightly. 'It's no coincidence they all drive the same model of car. But Anish … well, he wasn't. Whilst the boys were out with Dad, Anish was home with me and Mum. He loved to cook. He was really good; he could have been a chef if he'd gone to culinary school. He also loved to read and write. I used to adore bedtime stories and when Mum finished hers, he would sneak in and read me another. I was trying to persuade him to do a degree in English Literature through the Open University; he'd have been great at it.'

She wiped her eyes, but her voice remained steady. 'Mum must have known, even then, she wasn't daft. But she never said anything. And I know that she never told Dad.'

Warren said nothing. He could see where this was going.

'As we grew up, the boys – sorry we always called Jai and Mannie the boys, but never Anish – were really popular with the girls. They're both handsome, and even back then were fit. Anish wasn't.' She sighed. 'Eventually it became so obvious that even Dad noticed; not that he wanted to believe it. It was one of the few things he and Mum ever argued about. Dad is really traditional – conservative with a small "c", you could say. He felt that Anish being the way he was brought shame on the family. And the boys agreed.'

She wiped her eyes again, and her voice cracked. 'I never realised just how much Mum protected him until she died. It was so sudden. None of us saw it coming. At the autopsy, they identified a congenital heart defect. Dad insisted that all four of us got tested. Me and the boys were clear, but Anish had inherited it.'

'Hence the pacemaker,' prompted Warren after a moment.

She nodded. 'It was a big shock, but they said that now they knew, it could be managed. They fitted the pacemaker, prescribed him some medication, and said that they'd just keep an eye on it.

'You know, you'd think that would have brought us all closer. And at first it did. But once the grief wore off, Dad started being really weird. He was obsessed about the family business continuing after he died. He said it was his and Mum's legacy, and that he didn't want anything to tarnish that reputation. The boys agreed. We've all worked with Dad since we left school. Anish didn't, he and Dad ... Besides, Anish wanted to be a writer.

'Although he would never say it out loud – as if admitting it would make it more real – we all knew what Dad meant by "tarnishing the reputation".'

'Anish was gay,' said Warren.

She gave a shuddering sigh and nodded, before continuing. 'The boys are married with their own families. I've been living in the barn, with my husband. Eventually, when Mum ... passed, it was just Dad and Anish living in the house.

'I could hear them arguing sometimes. Finally, last autumn, Anish moved out. Dad didn't even ask where he was going and he told the rest of us that "until Anish stopped shaming us all with his behaviour", he was no longer part of the family, and that we had to stop talking to him. The boys agreed.'

'But you kept in touch with him?'

'Yes. My husband comes from a big family, and he supported me. He even tried talking to Dad, but he was told to mind his own. Anish and I would speak on the phone each week and we'd meet up for lunch about once a month. I'm really sorry, I completely forgot, but I tried to phone Anish Friday night. I'd seen that an exhibition of James Bond memorabilia was coming to the local arts centre in the spring. I wanted to let him know about it.'

'What did he say?'

'He didn't. The phone went straight through to voicemail. He texted me Saturday morning and said that he had come down with the flu and was sleeping it off. I tried to ring that evening, but it went to voicemail.' Her voice caught. 'I was going to ring him again Sunday, to see if I could bring some food around, but I was busy ...' The tears started again, and Warren waited for them to abate.

Finally, she gave another sniff. Reaching into her pocket, she removed a set of keys. 'Anish gave me these in case he ever needed me to go round to his flat. You may as well have them.'

Warren had dozens of questions that he wanted to ask Vasava, but there was one big query he had to address first. He chose his words carefully. 'You said that you think your father may be involved in Anish's death? Why do you think that, Reva?'

Vasava took a deep breath and reached for the envelope. 'After Dad and Anish had their ... falling out, Dad changed his will.'

She opened the envelope, sliding out a bundle of papers held together with a paperclip. The text was slightly off-centre, indicating that they had been photocopied. The document was written in dense legalese, with the name of the law firm that had drafted it printed in the header at the top of each sheet. Two scrawled signatures were at the bottom of each numbered page.

'Look at the third page; I've highlighted it,' she said.

Warren was no legal expert, but the wording was not dissimilar to his and Susan's own wills, with one significant difference.

'Gotam Patel's estate will be divided equally between all of his children, but only if they are married with their own children,' he summarised.

She nodded. 'Jai and Mannie are both married with children.'

'But Anish isn't married, and he doesn't have children,' he said. It wasn't a question.

'No, and if you read further, it states that marriage is defined as between one man and one woman, and that children are defined by blood. And if one of us dies, then our share will be passed directly to our children.'

The implication was clear. If Anish Patel wished to inherit his share of his father's estate, he would need to marry a woman and have a child with her. It was a crude, but effective way of either cutting him out of his inheritance or forcing him to deny his homosexuality and 'stop tarnishing the family's reputation'.

'I see.'

'It was especially mean for Anish,' said Vasava. 'Dad knows that Anish has inherited Mum's faulty heart genes. Forcing him to have a child that might have the same condition is just wrong.'

Warren pushed back a sigh. Over the course of his career he had seen many spiteful and shocking things. But it never ceased to amaze him how the cruellest behaviour often came from the ones who were supposed to love you the most. He thought back to the scars on Anish's arms and legs – he wondered how much of the pain that he had clearly suffered came from his unhappy family life. But it still didn't point the finger at Gotam Patel as the culprit. He said as much.

'Anish found a way around it. He found someone to marry.'

Warren blinked in surprise. 'Have you met this woman?'

'No, I never had the chance. But Anish was happy. Apparently, she's in a similar situation; she needs a husband to keep her family off her back. The plan was to get married and live together, but have separate lives,' she smiled. 'Anish was happy. Apparently, they were a good match, similar hobbies and plans. They'd been out on a few – I suppose you could call them dates – and he said that they got on well. He said that plenty of successful arranged marriages have been built on less.'

'Where did he meet this woman?'

Vasava shrugged. 'I don't know.'

'What about the children?'

'Anish was looking into IVF and pre-implantation genetic testing. There's a company in the US that said they might be able to help.'

'Do you have a name for this woman?' They would need to contact her, if only to break the news of Anish's death.

'Just her first name, Latika.' Warren made a note of it. The name was hardly unique, but she and Anish may have been in contact electronically, and if they had met in person, he might have saved her phone number.

'Had Anish told anyone else?'

She shook her head. 'I don't know. He'd have had to tell people eventually, I suppose. I know my family would expect a big wedding. I guess hers would too.'

*

'We need to take a hard look at that family,' said Warren after filling in the team on his conversation with Reva Vasava. 'We should consider them all potential suspects, especially the father. He might have been upset at Anish trying to circumvent the stipulations in his will.' He thought for a moment. 'I'll see if there is any way of getting a confirmed copy. We'll look like fools if it turns out Reva wrote that document herself to cast suspicion on her father.'

'His brothers stand to gain the most from this,' said Richardson. 'If Anish did fulfil the requirements of his father's will, then suddenly their inheritance is being split four ways not three.'

'For that matter, so does his sister,' said Hutchinson. 'Hell, she could be behind this whole thing and trying to make us look at her brothers to get them out of the running.'

'What about this woman he recently met?' asked Ruskin.

'Try and match his phone records and social media contacts against the name "Latika",' said Warren. 'I'll speak to Pete Robertson and see if I can persuade IT to make analysing his internet history a priority. Karen, when the data arrives, I want you to try and identify her,' instructed Warren. 'If she is in a similar situation with her family, they could also be suspects.'

'As could she,' said Sutton. 'For all we know, she could have been stringing him along. An apparently wealthy but unhappy man looking for a partner?'

'Surely it would have been in her interests to marry him first, then kill him?' said Ruskin.

'Perhaps, but Tony's right. Let's not rule anything out,' said Warren.

'There's also the question of where they were planning on getting the money for IVF,' said Hutchinson. 'If they were looking at travelling to the US, that would cost a fortune with no NHS.'

'Good point. This is getting very complicated. For now, we need to keep an open mind. Get the family in and try and lock down their alibis; don't take no for an answer.' He turned to Lederer. 'For appearances' sake, if nothing else, bring Reva in again when you bring in the others. I don't want her family knowing that she's already spoken to us.'

'Should we show them the tools?' asked Hutchinson. 'See their reaction?'

Warren thought for a moment. 'No, let's hold that back until we have full forensics.' He turned to Pymm. 'Aside from Reva, they claim not to have had any contact with Anish recently, so look for lines of communication between everyone and see if we can catch any of them out in a lie. We already know that Jaidev spoke to him this summer.

'Let's also cast the net a bit further. Try and track down some of Anish's acquaintances, I'm a bit concerned that everything we have so far comes from those who stand to gain from his death. Find out where he works. I also think we need to dig a little deeper into his personal life; it sounds as though he kept that side of himself private. Reva has suggested that he found a woman who might have been willing to marry him, but what about the other side of his life? Was he active sexually? Did he have a regular partner? Did he use online dating, or go out clubbing? A bit of outside perspective would be helpful; see what the neighbours say.'

Rachel Pymm spoke up, her voice quiet. 'Of course, if Reva is right, and one or both of her brothers did kill Anish to increase their share of the inheritance, then there's something else we need to consider.'

Sutton beat her to the punch. 'Reva doesn't have any children of her own yet, and an inheritance split between two heirs is even bigger than one split between three.'

Chapter 9

By lunchtime, Constable Lederer's gentle persuasion had finally worked its magic, and the remainder of Anish Patel's family agreed to attend the station to give statements.

These initial interviews had been divided amongst the rapidly growing investigative team, but Warren had opted to do at least a couple himself. It was somewhat unusual for an officer of his rank to speak directly to potential suspects, but then the set-up at Middlesbury CID wasn't like most departments. It was one of the things that Warren loved about working there. Having briefly met Manoj Patel the day before, Warren decided to try and build on that relationship.

Anish's eldest brother was a well-built man with a trimmed black beard. Despite the cold weather, he was dressed in a thin jumper without a coat, and faded black jeans. He removed the jumper within moments of entering the interview suite, revealing a tight, black T-shirt tailored to show off his toned, upper body. Warren had little interest in high-end fashion, but it was clear even to him that the clothes weren't off-the-peg from Marks & Spencer. It looked as though he also shared his late brother's taste in expensive watches.

'As I said yesterday, Mr Patel, I'm very sorry for your loss,' Warren started.

Patel said nothing. For a man that had found out that his brother had been murdered barely a day ago, he seemed more irritated than grief-stricken. Family dynamics were complicated and unpredictable at times like this, and they clearly had much that they'd rather not discuss with outsiders, but Warren thought it unusual that the family had initially resisted requests to give formal interviews.

'I realise that the last twenty-four hours have been very upsetting, but we really need your help in tracking down your brother's killer.'

Again, Patel said nothing.

Warren decided to push on quickly. 'I wondered if you have had any thoughts about who might have targeted your brother? Are you aware of anyone that he may have had a falling-out with recently?'

Patel gave a snort. 'You mean aside from the rest of his family?'

At least Warren didn't need to work out how to broach the subject.

'I saw that there was some tension when I visited yesterday,' said Warren. 'Would you be able to tell me a bit about that?' Warren had no intention of revealing that his sister had already spoken to them. He wanted to see if their accounts agreed.

'Nothing to tell; Anish brought shame on us. None of us had any contact with him.' His lip curled. 'He was no longer my brother.'

Warren managed to keep his tone neutral. Over the years, he'd encountered many different ways that grief could manifest itself. He'd also witnessed many people faking grief. He'd seen families that were already broken before tragedy struck, and families broken by the tragedy.

But he couldn't recall ever seeing such a callous attitude towards a dead brother.

'How did he bring shame on your family, Manoj?' asked Warren.

'You know how,' Patel's eyes flashed angrily.

'I really don't,' said Warren, keen to hear Patel's version of the story. 'I know that there has been a serious falling-out, but nobody has told me what it was about yet.'

'Because it's private.' Patel sat back in his chair, his arms folded.

Warren could see that he wasn't going to get any more out of the man on that subject. He decided to change tack.

'When was the last time that you spoke to your brother?'

'Have you not been listening? I haven't spoken to him in months. I have – had – nothing to say to him. I don't know who he saw, who his friends were, or who he might have pissed off enough to kill him.'

Warren decided it was time to stop tiptoeing around the subject. So far – the text message to his sister on the Saturday morning aside – the last confirmed sighting of Anish was Wednesday evening, by his neighbour. The body had been found Sunday morning.

Warren asked him to account for his whereabouts during that time.

A look of surprise crossed Patel's face. 'Wait, you don't think I had something to do with this do you?'

'The thought had crossed my mind,' said Warren, struggling to keep his tone even. The man had just sat there, radiating his hatred for his brother, and yet was surprised that Warren might suspect his involvement somehow.

'Oh, for fuck's sake.' Patel glared at him. 'If it was a weeknight, I was probably at home with my family; during the day I would have been at work. Saturday morning, I took the boys to football training, then spent the rest of the weekend pottering about at home. I popped into work for a few hours Saturday afternoon. You can speak to my wife and work colleagues or the two-dozen other parents freezing their bollocks off on the sideline Saturday morning.'

'Thank you, I will,' said Warren.

'Can I go now? I've got a busy day ahead of me.'

'Of course, Manoj, thank you for your time,' Warren handed him his card. 'If you think of anything else that I need to know about, please don't hesitate to call me.'

*

'What an arsehole,' said Moray Ruskin.

'Amen to that,' muttered Warren. For the first time since he'd been promoted to DCI, he wondered if it was time for him to stop interviewing suspects. He'd assiduously kept up his interview skills, but it was hard to imagine an occasion recently when things had gone so poorly. He'd known that there were tensions in the family, but he hadn't expected them to be quite so overt. He'd only asked half the questions in the interview plan and he had almost lost his temper, something that should never happen in an interview.

Grayson saw the look on his face. 'Don't be too hard on yourself, I don't think any of us were expecting that degree of hostility. If his alibi doesn't stack up, he's just placed himself top of my suspect list.'

Warren thanked him.

'I think it's interesting that he stated that none of them had any contact with Anish,' said Ruskin. 'His call logs show that he ignored his brother's call and texts, or only answered them long enough to tell him to piss off, so fair enough. But does that mean he didn't know that Reva was speaking to her brother each week, or was he lying?'

'And don't forget, we know Jaidev spoke to Anish for a few minutes back in July,' said Hutchinson. 'I'll be interested to hear if Jaidev also denies having any contact with him.'

Warren contemplated what his team had said. He'd not met Jaidev yet; the middle brother had yet to arrive when he, Sutton and Lederer had been asked to leave the Patel family home. However, given how badly his interview with Manoj had gone, it was clear that a different approach would be needed. He just

68

hoped that the premature ending to the interview hadn't given the two brothers too much time to get their stories straight. Regardless, he needed to alter the interview strategy, and there was one obvious change they could make.

'Hutch, I suspect I have a little bit too much history with the family. Are you OK to take over for Jaidev?'

Hutchinson smiled grimly. 'Delighted to.'

'Mags, can you tackle the father, Gotam?'

'My pleasure.'

*

'Well, that couldn't have been more different,' said David Hutchinson after concluding his interview with Jaidev Patel. The interviews with the middle son and his father had been conducted simultaneously to minimise the chance that Manoj Patel could pre-warn them about what to expect. Because of that Warren had been unable to follow them closely on the briefing room screen.

'Unlike Manoj, he actually seemed upset about Anish's death and he was a lot more forthcoming about the family's problems.'

'He acknowledged that Anish was gay?' asked Sutton.

'Yes, and shed light on why it was such a big issue for his father. Apparently, old man Patel is extremely conservative in his views, and moves in very like-minded circles. I didn't get the impression it's particularly motivated by religion, more that he is old-fashioned.

'The biggest thing he craves is respect, which goes back to his own parents' experiences when they first came here from India. For political reasons that Jaidev was either unable or unwilling to elaborate on, they were shunned not only by the British but also by a lot of the local Indian community. He vowed to do better than his parents, and apparently was doing very well, until Anish started behaving "differently" – Jaidev's words, not mine.'

'That chimes with my impressions of him,' said Richardson, whose own interview had finished rather more abruptly.

'Apparently, Gotam's late wife, Suniti, ticked a lot of the right boxes socially,' continued Hutchinson, 'although Jaidev was keen to stress that his parents adored each other. Suniti acted as a buffer between Anish and his father, but when she died, their relationship really soured.'

'If the friction with Anish was causing so many problems, why didn't he move out sooner?' asked Ruskin.

'Hah! Well, that's where Jaidev says his father dropped the ball,' said Hutchinson. 'Gotam refused to give Anish any role in the business. If he had, then he could have paid him a good enough wage for him to build up a deposit for a flat so he could have moved out years ago. Unfortunately, he couldn't just kick him out, as making his youngest son homeless would have raised awkward questions, so they were stuck with each other.'

'I can picture the resentment building up enough for one of them to murder the other,' said Warren, 'but Anish finally moved out over a year ago. If he did kill him, there must be more to it than that. We'll come back to it. What did he say about his brother's recent activities?'

'Very little,' said Hutchinson. 'I gave him two opportunities to admit that he'd had contact with him after he left the family home, but he claimed they hadn't spoken in ages. He said he knows nothing about what he was up to, or even where he lived and worked, other than that it was in Middlesbury.'

'Well, we know that's not true, there was a three-minute phone call on July 10th,' said Pymm.

Warren tapped his teeth thoughtfully. 'Three minutes is a difficult length of call to pin him down on. You can say a lot in three minutes, or you can just argue about nothing and then dismiss the call out of hand and claim that you forgot about it when asked. I think we'll keep knowledge of his call history to ourselves for the time being. I don't want to give him time to make up excuses if and when we challenge him on it.'

'If the call was more meaningful, could Anish have told him

about his plans to get married?' asked Richardson. 'Reva said that she didn't know if Anish had told anyone else about meeting this woman, Latika. If Jaidev knew, and even told his brother, Manoj, then there's a potential motive staring us in the face. I know the call was a few months ago, but it could have been the catalyst that triggered everything.'

'What about an alibi?' asked Warren.

'Similar to his brother's. Work during the day, home with kids in the evening and football training with their boys on the Saturday morning. However, he plays badminton every Thursday evening at the Church End Gym in Cambridge; mixed doubles and they stay for drinks afterwards. Reckons he left by bus about 9 p.m. and got home about half-past.'

'Does he have any theories about who might have killed Anish? Did he point his finger towards anyone?' asked Hardwick.

'No, he just repeated that he hadn't had any contact with him recently.'

'What about the future of the family business?' asked Warren. 'Any indication that he knows about the changes to his father's will or Anish's attempts to circumvent it?'

'Nothing. He dodged the question when it came up; said it was insensitive to be talking about the death of his father the day after he found out about the murder of his brother. I backed off, as I didn't want him to shut down like Manoj.'

'Good call,' said Warren. 'Mags, tell us all about Mr Patel senior.'

Richardson snorted. 'Well, those of you who watched it on the screen can see who Manoj inherited his delightful personality from. He made no admission that Anish was gay and refused to elaborate on yesterday's suggestion that Anish's death was due to "his lifestyle" or why Anish left the family home last year.

'He dismissed my questions about why Anish was the only sibling who wasn't part of the family company as a "business decision" and flat-out refused to discuss what will happen to Anish's share of the estate when he dies.'

'Assuming we take Reva at face value,' said Hutchinson, 'I find it hard to believe that only she knows about this change to the inheritance. The will she showed us was dated some months ago, so it's not like Gotam hasn't had time to broach the subject.'

'That's true,' said Ruskin, 'but the amendments insisting on an heir would only affect Reva and Anish, both Manoj and Jaidev are married with kids. Perhaps Gotam felt that the changes weren't really any of their business?' He sounded sceptical of his own suggestion.

'Well, the two brothers would have an incentive to deny any knowledge of the changes if they did kill him to increase their share of the inheritance,' said Hardwick. 'If they discovered that Anish was planning on getting married and having children, not only would their share of the pie become smaller, but it might mean that Anish suddenly has a say in how the company is run, if he owns a chunk of it.'

'So, where does Gotam come into this?' asked Pymm. 'Reva said that she thought her dad might have been involved in Anish's death.'

'She did say that he was obsessed with his legacy; maybe he orchestrated the whole thing?' suggested Hardwick.

'Or perhaps the whole thing was dreamed up by the two brothers, and they kept his father completely out of it,' said Sutton. 'Reva could be wrong.'

'The problem I have is that they all seem to be each other's alibi,' said Richardson. 'We can check out the brothers' whereabouts Saturday morning easily enough and verify Jaidev's Thursday night badminton session, but during the week, only their wives saw them at night, and their work colleagues during the day. Gotam claims to have spoken to his daughter Friday evening, when he saw her bringing the groceries in about 7 p.m., but supposedly spent the rest of the evening alone; he can't account for his whereabouts for most of the rest of that period. Reva claims she did her grocery shop and then spent the evening with her husband and worked from home during the week. I'm not seeing any independent witnesses here.'

'I think we need to take any alibis with a pinch of salt,' said Warren. 'Their colleagues might be a bit reluctant to drop their boss in it.'

He turned to Hutchinson. 'Hutch, I want you to liaise with Cambridgeshire Constabulary to organise teams of door-knockers; we need to see if Manoj and Jaidev were home when they say they were. Check with their neighbours that their cars were in the drive etc. Mags, Jaidev says he caught the bus home after playing badminton; secure CCTV from the bus company for his likely route and check what he said is true, and try and pin down exactly what time he got home. Whilst you're at it, run all of the family's cars through the ANPR system, let's see if any of their vehicles pop up where they shouldn't.

'Moray and Karen, I want you to visit the football club that the brothers' kids train at. See if they were both there when they said and do a little probing about the wider family, I want an outside perspective. Whilst you're over that way, pop into Jaidev's badminton club. See if they remember him being there that Thursday and get the contact details of the people he was playing with.'

He turned to Pymm. 'I think we have enough to justify a warrant to look into the rest of the family's mobile phones, at least the ones that are registered to them. Download the call logs and cross-reference them against each other. If there was collusion, we may see unusual patterns of activity, particularly in the period before we told them his body had been found. I think we can also get a warrant to look at location data. I want to know where those phones were during the period we believe he was killed. Also, none of them, except for Reva, admit to having had any contact with Anish recently. We know that Jaidev has lied about that. Look and see what the others were doing around the time of that phone call. Did Jaidev contact Manoj or his father after speaking to Anish?'

Warren sighed in frustration. 'This would be a lot easier if we could narrow down exactly when he was killed.'

Chapter 10

'We've got Anish Patel's financial records, it looks as though he was spending significantly more than he earned,' said Rachel Pymm.

She fanned a series of highlighted sheets of paper in front of her.

'I looked at his bank statement and he received a monthly salary from Clancy's.'

'The department store in town?' asked Sutton. 'Aren't they an independent? I've never seen a branch anywhere else.'

'Founded over a hundred years ago as Clancy and Sons, according to the sign on the wall outside the main entrance,' Pymm confirmed. 'It's still owned by the same family; I'm amazed it's still going with the state of the high street these days.'

'I'll pop down and chat to their HR department,' said Sutton. 'Maybe his co-workers can give us some insight into his lifestyle.'

'Either way, his outgoings greatly exceed his income from Clancy's,' continued Pymm. 'I've looked over the past few years, and he has been consistently overdrawn on his main current account. Things only got worse when he moved out and started paying rent; his salary barely covers that and his bills. He also has five different credit cards that he has been shuffling the balances around on. He's paying off the minimum each month, just to stay solvent. I'm no financial expert, but he was heading for serious trouble, sooner rather than later.'

'What was he spending his money on?' asked Warren.

'It looks like he's a sharp dresser, I recognise the names of some of these boutique clothing stores. They aren't the sort of place you'd even walk into if you were on his salary. He pays almost as much each month to Mercedes as he does to his landlord, although it looks as though he was going to lose his car if he didn't pay the last two months' instalments. He also likes to eat out, and I'm not talking chicken and chips at Nando's. The food and drink bills are regularly over a hundred pounds, sometimes a lot more.'

'Bloody hell,' said Sutton, leaning over her shoulder and pointing at the statement. 'I took Marie there for our wedding anniversary. The starters alone cost more than we normally pay for a main course. He went twice last month.'

'That ties in with what I've seen on social media,' said Hardwick. 'His Instagram and Facebook are full of pictures of him dressed in sharp suits in luxury restaurants, although never with anyone else tagged. I've counted at least four different watches, which unless he's wearing counterfeits, have got to have set him back hundreds or even more. You said he appeared to be a fan of spy thrillers.' She looked down at her notepad. 'Lots of profile pictures of him posing like James Bond, and he's "liked" and followed lots of related pages.'

She curled her nose up. 'He was also one of those annoying people that tell the world exactly where they are and where they are going every time they leave the bloody house. I'm amazed he wasn't burgled.'

'Could that be a motive?' asked Ruskin. 'He's telling the world that he's wealthy. Maybe he attracted the wrong sort of attention?'

'Robbery gone wrong?' asked Hardwick.

'It's got to be worth considering,' said Warren. 'When was the last activity on his account?'

Pymm flicked through the sheets in front of her. 'That's another weird thing; aside from his direct debits and standing orders, the last time he used his cash card was over a month ago. He hardly ever draws money out.'

'That's not that weird,' said Ruskin. 'I hardly ever use cash these days. It's much easier to use contactless in pubs or for small purchases.'

'Yes, but he hardly ever uses it for that either. In fact, he hasn't even used his cards in the supermarket for months.'

'Which means he must be using cash for most of his day-to-day outgoings,' said Warren. 'But if he isn't using cashpoints, then where is he getting it?'

'Could he have another bank account, or card that we aren't aware of?' asked Ruskin.

Pymm shook her head. 'I doubt it. You need all sorts of ID to open a bank account or take out a credit card because of the anti-money-laundering regulations. That would have shown up when I requested his financial records.'

'So where was he getting cash from, then?' repeated Warren.

'Drugs?' said Ruskin. 'A bit of dealing on the side to make ends meet?'

'Which would have brought him into contact with some pretty undesirable individuals,' said Hutchinson.

'Well, it's another angle to investigate,' said Warren. 'I'll see if the drugs division have any intelligence. Maybe he's on their radar.'

'I found some useful information,' said Pymm. 'Even though he's not been using cash machines, there has been activity on his account.'

'Don't tell me somebody's used his cards this week?' said Warren.

'Nothing so obvious. But he uses an online banking app. According to Santander, he usually accesses it via his tablet. Probably not as much as he should, given the state of his finances, but the last time he logged in was just after 8 p.m. on Thursday the 24th of November, via his mobile phone. All he did was look at his balance. No transactions were made. He must have been using Wi-Fi; his phone was still disconnected from the mobile network at that time.'

'So he was still alive Thursday,' said Warren. 'That narrows it down slightly. See what more the bank can give us.' He turned to Sutton. 'Tony, speak to Clancy's as a priority; ask when he last turned up for work. His sister says that he texted her Saturday after he didn't return her call Friday night.'

'He also sent texts to a number Friday morning at 7.18 a.m., and at the same time Saturday morning,' said Pymm. 'Both times, he received a reply. I've identified the recipient as a Mrs Maureen Bentley; I've no idea who she is.'

'OK, see what you can find out about this Mrs Bentley before we pull her in for questioning.'

Warren looked at his watch. 'Right everyone, it's 7 p.m. There's nothing that can't be picked up by the evening shift or started in the morning. Take the opportunity to get yourselves home at a decent hour, I suspect there'll be plenty of opportunities to earn some pre-Christmas overtime in the next few weeks. Besides, it's the last day of November, and if I don't get the Christmas tree out of the loft tonight, Susan will have me out of bed early tomorrow to fetch it.'

Thursday 1st December

Chapter 11

Almost five days had passed since Anish Patel's body had been found, naked and wrapped in a sheet, and it was time to ask the public for help. Anish's sister, Reva Vasava, had supplied a recent photograph, but otherwise the family had declined to take part in the press conference.

The press office had released a statement earlier that week, confirming the discovery of the body and asking for information, but now they needed more assistance. The team still hadn't determined when or where he had been killed, and so the appeal focused on requests for information about his movements between the last confirmed sighting of him by his neighbour on the Wednesday, and the discovery of the body Sunday morning.

They had also released images of his vehicle. The dark-blue Mercedes sports car was nowhere to be found and as yet had not been captured on ANPR systems. Violent car-jackings were rare in the UK, but at this stage Warren and the team were in no position to rule anything out.

As usual, Warren had appeared beside a smartly coiffured DSI Grayson at the force's headquarters in Welwyn Garden City but said little; his boss enjoyed the limelight far more than he did. After a few questions from the assembled reporters that they were largely unable or unwilling to answer yet, the two men had headed back up the A1 to Middlesbury. Warren had successfully contrived to drive himself to and from the press conference; bad for the environment, but good for his nerves – Grayson had a notoriously heavy right foot.

His excuse was a planned meeting with Andy Harrison, who was lounging in Warren's visitor's chair when he returned, sipping from an insulated coffee mug with a picture of Darth Vader on the side. It matched his T-shirt.

'The victim was wrapped in a cotton double bed sheet,' said Harrison. 'Since the victim was mutilated post-mortem, there isn't a huge amount of his blood on the sheet. We're still trying to isolate any other fluids on there, but it was sitting in a stream.'

Harrison had yet to shave off his effort for Movember; he'd opted for a handle-bar moustache for this year's charity fundraiser. Warren wondered if anyone would have the heart to tell him that with his ponytail and generous build, he looked like an ageing porn star.

'Here's hoping,' said Warren.

'The good news is that the sheet is almost certainly from a hotel, and probably a budget one. The cotton is thicker and more hard-wearing than the material used in typical domestic bedding, since it needs to be boil-washed after every guest – or at least it should be, I have my doubts sometimes …'

'Well, that gives us something to go on,' said Warren. He made a note on his pad to organise a team to contact all of the hotels in the area and seize their CCTV footage. He'd have to decide on what radius to cover, but regardless, it would be a big job. An hour's drive would cover hundreds of hotels in the local vicinity.

Harrison gave a small smile and pushed his tablet across the table. 'I might be able to help you narrow it down. This is a picture of the bottom corner of the sheet.' He zoomed in. 'You can see here a small, square piece of blue fabric has been glued on.'

'I've seen those before. What is it?'

'It's a laundry tag. Most budget hotels send their laundry away

82

to be washed. If they aren't part of a chain, then they use a local company. Coloured tags help the launderette keep track of who the sheets belong to.'

'Brilliant,' said Warren, 'You've just saved us hundreds of hours of work. DSI Grayson will be delighted.'

'A pleasure to help,' said Harrison. 'Just keep it to yourself, Sir. Christmas is coming and I've just scuppered a load of overtime pay.'

*

'I had an interesting chat with Anish's workmates,' said Sutton, addressing the team briefing. 'He's worked at Clancy's for the past eight years and was promoted to department head a year or so ago. Which makes me wonder how his family didn't know that, given he would have been working there whilst still living with his father and sister.'

It was a good question; had his family really cared so little about him, or were they deliberately downplaying their relationship with him?

'Anyway, his employment record is unblemished, and he was very popular with both colleagues and customers, nobody had a bad word to say about him. It's a real family business in all senses and he fitted right in; regulars would ask for him by name and he would help some of their older customers load their shopping into their car etc. News of his death has absolutely rocked everyone I spoke to.

'We've secured CCTV footage from the past few weeks to see if anyone of interest interacted with him in the store, or he had any customer altercations, but none of his colleagues are aware of anything untoward happening. It turns out that the Maureen Bentley he texted Friday and Saturday morning is the manager in charge of staff absence. He was due to work nine-to-five both days. Sunday was his day off.'

'So does that mean he was still alive Saturday?' asked Hutchinson.

'Impossible to say,' said Pymm. 'His phone was powered off either side of those texts being sent, but if he really was ill with the flu, then he might just have been in bed.'

'Where was the phone when the texts were sent?' asked Sutton.

'The phone connected to the cell tower closest to his flat, both for those texts and the ones he sent to his sister,' said Pymm.

'Did you find out much about his private life?' asked Warren.

'A few snippets. Apparently, it was well known that he was gay, but he never spoke about his love life. He certainly didn't mention anything about his plans to marry. He was described as really kind and generous with his time, running the work social committee and he was organising the Secret Santa. He was obsessed with James Bond and spy thrillers; he even raised money for charity by dressing in a tuxedo at work for a week when the last Bond film came out.'

'Anything about his relationship with his family?' asked Hutchinson.

'Nothing much. I spoke to the two women that he works most closely with, and they knew that he wasn't on speaking terms with them. Outside of work they felt he was quite lonely; he never mentioned any friends other than work colleagues and aside from the cinema, didn't seem to have any hobbies, which they thought was a shame as he was so nice. Sometimes he'd even pop into work on his days off and meet co-workers for lunch. I showed his list of Facebook friends to Maureen Bentley and she reckons almost all of them were either current or former Clancy's employees.'

'What about the lavish existence he portrayed on social media?' asked Ruskin.

'They always assumed that he had some sort of inheritance or trust fund. He dressed very well, drove an expensive car and enjoyed dining out. His salary was pretty good, but not enough for the lifestyle he seemed to live.'

'Where are we with the interviews with the rest of the family and the siblings' co-workers?' asked Warren.

Sutton looked at his notes. 'DSI Grayson arranged for Welwyn to lend us a few warm bodies yesterday. Both Manoj and Jaidev Patel's wives backed up their husbands' version of events: no contact with Anish for months, both of them home playing dad each evening – except for Jaidev who had badminton on the Thursday night. He was back at his usual time. Both brothers manage corner shops, and their co-workers claim that they were present all day, Monday to Friday, with a couple of hours put in over the weekend.'

'And do we believe them?' asked Warren.

'Impossible to decide,' said Sutton. 'I've run back through the interview tapes and the wives are pretty cagey, but then it doesn't take a genius to figure out that their husbands are likely to be prime suspects, so you'd expect them to be on guard.'

'I spoke to the man who runs the kids' Saturday football club,' Hardwick took over. 'He remembers both men being there Saturday morning. He collected subs money off them both, so he's confident they were present. Interestingly, he knew about Reva, but had no idea they had another brother.'

'What about her?' asked Warren.

'Same story,' said Sutton. 'Her husband claims that aside from the grocery run, she was in each evening. He also says that Gotam Patel's car was in the driveway all that time, although he admits that he spends most of the day working in the back office so Gotam could have slipped out or left on foot without him knowing.'

'What about their relationship with Anish?' asked Warren.

'Pretty much what Reva told us,' said Sutton. 'He knew that his wife still spoke to Anish. In fact, he encouraged it. It doesn't sound as though he cares much for his in-laws; he was quite scathing about their decision not to speak to Anish because he was gay.

'He hadn't seen Anish since he moved out, but he always liked him. He even suggested Anish come and stay with them, since they have a spare room, but Anish said that he didn't want to cause any more trouble between Reva and their father. Besides which, they hope to make it a nursery someday.'

Warren considered the feedback. On the surface, the testimonies backed up what Anish's father and siblings had told them. But he was still aware that they had precious little truly independent verification. Given the potential financial benefits to the rest of the family from Anish's death, they needed some outside perspective.

'Hutch, anything back from his neighbours?' asked Warren.

'Well, it appears Gotam Patel doesn't reserve his sunny disposition for the police,' said Hutchinson. 'A few of Cambridgeshire's finest agreed to help us do some door-knocking around the cul-de-sac where the Patels' home is situated.'

He swapped a coffee – on it, a picture of a motorcycle helmet emblazoned, 'loving my mid-life crisis' – for his notepad. 'I'll warn you now, that some of their neighbours' impressions might be coloured a little by how well they perceive the Patels fit into their little world.'

'An Asian family with lots of money that they've earned through hard work, living in a corner of Little Britain normally occupied by good decent white folk who inherited their wealth by honest means?' asked Sutton.

'Pretty much,' said Hutchinson. 'Apparently more than one conversation started with "I'm not racist, but …"'

'Well, let's at least hear what they had to say,' said Warren.

'The Patels moved in about twenty-five years ago, which makes sense; the business started to make its money in the Nineties. The three boys would have been teenagers and Mrs Patel – Suniti – was still alive back then.

'Several neighbours said that Gotam can be abrupt to the point of rudeness; a trait that he's passed on to Manoj apparently. You'll be lucky to get more than a grunt out of either of them if you see them in the local corner shop. Not that Gotam goes there unless he has to; the family have their own stores. Interestingly, when the owner of that shop retired, he approached Gotam about buying it. He thought it was a win-win proposition; somebody local takes over, giving them an incentive to keep it focused on the neighbourhood's needs, whilst the Patel family gains a profitable business. He said that Gotam practically sneered. He didn't say as much, but implied that living essentially opposite his corner shop was only one step above living over it.'

'Sounds like he was eager to distance himself from the stereotype of the Asian corner shop owner,' mused Sutton. 'Which fits in with what Jaidev Patel told us about his drive to do better than his parents.'

'OK,' said Warren, 'so he isn't a pleasant man. I think we already knew that.'

'Well it goes deeper, if what his neighbours have to say is true,' said Hutchinson. 'Apparently he is rude and belittling to his kids also. The woman who lives next door says that she overhears them arguing a lot when she's out in the garden. That's got worse since the mother passed away.'

'That's not unusual after sudden deaths,' pointed out Ruskin.

'True,' allowed Hutchinson, 'but she reckons that he was extremely controlling. He rarely asks for anything, he demands it. She described him as "cruel".'

'Anything specific?' asked Warren.

'Reva lives in the converted barn on the property. The neighbour overheard him one morning, after his eldest son had just left with his boys, asking why she hadn't given him any grandchildren yet. She said that Reva burst into tears and walked away. Apparently, his parting shot was "if you're like that with your husband, it's no wonder he hasn't been able to get you pregnant".'

There were winces around the table.

'What about his relationship with Anish?' asked Warren. 'If Patel Sr was that unkind to his daughter, how did he act towards his estranged youngest son?'

'That's where the neighbour is a bit more speculative. She says that the relationship was cold, and on summer days with the windows open, she heard the two arguing, but she couldn't really understand what they were saying. Outside, where they could easily be overheard, the two rarely spoke. She got the impression that they were reluctant to "air their dirty laundry in public".

'Any suggestion what that dirty laundry might be?' asked Sutton, although they could all guess.

'That Anish was probably gay, and that his father was not supportive.'

'If the home life was so bad, why did they stay with him?' asked Ruskin.

'Well, she says that Suniti probably held the family together. Gotam adored his wife – that was obvious to anyone who saw them together. But the two older sons did leave, as soon as they got married. Only Reva and Anish were left. Apparently they pumped significant amounts of money into converting the barn into a house, which Reva moved into as soon as she got married. She had a look around when it was completed and said it is absolutely stunning.'

'I'd be interested to know if Reva and her husband are living there rent-free,' interjected Pymm. 'That might explain why she stays – how else could she afford somewhere that nice, in that area?'

'We know her mum was still alive when she got married,' said Sutton. 'Things might not have been so bad when she moved into the barn.'

'The neighbour did say that Reva was very close to her mother, as was Anish.'

'Which explains why Reva stayed, but what about Anish?' said Ruskin. 'He lived in the house with his father for months after his mum died.'

'We know Anish was a spendthrift; it may have taken him that long to raise money for a deposit on his own place,' said Hutchinson.

'All of which would have given his father ample motive to kill him back when they lived together,' said Warren. 'But he moved out over a year ago; that's a long time to hold a grudge. If Reva Vasava is right, and her father was responsible for his death, then whatever precipitated that event must have been more recent.'

'His engagement,' said Sutton.

88

Chapter 12

It was late evening when Warren's office phone rang; it was Sutton, calling on his mobile. 'They're just finishing up the forensics at Anish Patel's flat. Andy Harrison is here with me.'

Warren motioned for the rest of the team to join him in the briefing room, where he initiated a conference call with the crime scene manager and Sutton.

'First off, there are some unknown partial fingerprints on the handles to the front door and the bedroom,' said Harrison.

'Separate from Anish's?' asked Warren.

'We think so; I reckon we have examples of all ten of his prints. His bathroom only had a single electric toothbrush, so we lifted fingerprints from that on the assumption that they are his. Those match fingerprints on the TV remote control, his tablet and some of the clean crockery in the kitchen cupboard.'

'The neighbour down the hall doesn't recall him ever getting visitors,' interjected Sutton. 'At least nobody at the weekends or the evenings. There could have been people during the day when he was at work, but he's pretty confident that he didn't have a boyfriend or girlfriend staying regularly.'

'I could accept the postman or a delivery driver, or even somebody taking a meter reading, touching the front door,' continued

Harrison. 'But why would they touch the bedroom door handle? Unfortunately, they are too smudged to run them through the system as a blind hit. It'll throw up hundreds of potential matches.'

'What if we had a suspect to compare against?' asked Warren.

He could hear Harrison sucking his teeth on the end of the line. 'I doubt it would stand up in court, but we might be able to eyeball a partial match for exclusionary purposes.'

'What about this woman that he was supposed to have met online?' said Ruskin. 'Maybe she came by, or maybe his sister helped him move in?'

'Or the killer could have been there to remove any evidence,' said Sutton. 'We still haven't found his keys, wallet or phone yet.'

'We'll run them against any suspects that we find, and his family and friends if they'll let us print them,' decided Warren. 'What else have you found?'

'His sister says that he was ill over the weekend,' said Sutton.

'Yes, the flu. He also texted work on the Friday and again on the Saturday to say he wouldn't be in,' recalled Warren.

'Well it doesn't look as though he went out Friday night,' said Sutton. 'There was an unused ticket pinned to his notice board for a James Bond-themed evening at the community cinema. Thirty-five quid for two classic Bond movies, with a cocktail bar and canapés, and special guests. He has a black tuxedo with a bow-tie hanging on the back of the bedroom door. He even had a plastic gun.'

'I saw that on his Facebook feed,' said Ruskin. 'He was really excited about it. He must have been properly ill not to have gone.'

'And he'll have been gutted to miss it,' said Pymm. 'I read about it in the *Reporter*. The mystery guests included two former Bond girls, who signed memorabilia and mingled with the guests afterwards.'

Warren looked at his team. 'Are you all thinking what I'm thinking?' he asked.

'We know he went to work Thursday,' said Sutton.

'Nobody actually spoke to him when he texted work to say he was ill Friday,' continued Pymm, 'and he didn't answer when his sister called. And now we know he missed an evening out that he'd been looking forward to for weeks.'

'So he could have been killed Thursday evening or Friday,' concluded Warren. 'Which would mean the texts sent from his phone on the Saturday were sent by his killer.'

Friday 2nd December

Chapter 13

Friday morning started off bitterly cold, and Warren had taken extra care driving into work. He'd arrived well before dawn, pulling into the car park at the same time as Moray Ruskin who, as usual, hadn't let a little bit of ice get in the way of his triathlon training. The steam was rising off his colleague as he locked his bicycle up. Warren felt cold just looking at him.

David Hutchinson opened the briefing. 'We've traced the hotel. Cambridgeshire Commercial Laundry Services have identified the tag on the bed sheet as coming from the Easy Break Hotel out on the A506.'

Warren knew the establishment. Situated roughly halfway between Middlesbury and Cambridge, it was a small, independent hotel with conference facilities and cheap rooms for travellers on a low budget.

'Are we confident that the sheet came from the hotel, not the laundry firm?' asked Sutton.

'I asked them to check their inventory logs and they claim that they count each item in and out. No discrepancies.'

'Is that location consistent with the data from his phone?' asked Warren.

'No,' said Pymm. 'The handset was turned off Thursday

evening, so we don't have anything from then. The next time it was turned on was briefly Friday morning near his flat, when he texted work.'

'Karen, go to the hotel and show staff a copy of the photograph the Patels gave us,' instructed Warren. 'If he did stay there, seal the room he stayed in and secure any CCTV footage. Let's try and work out when he was there and if he was with anyone. It can't be a coincidence that his body was wrapped in a sheet from the hotel. Either he was killed there or his killer has a link to the hotel.

'We also need to try and pin down a timeline for when he was last physically seen, text messages aren't good enough. Also see if his car is there, we still haven't tracked that down. Anything else from the location data, Rachel?'

'Still analysing in detail, but so far, the brothers' movements match what they told us,' she replied, 'as do their dad and sister's. Working during the week and home in the evening. Reva and her father popped out on the Thursday and Friday respectively to the supermarket.'

Warren considered what she'd told him. As an alibi, mobile phone movements were hardly watertight, but at least they hadn't caught any of them out in an obvious lie.

'I've also been doing some more digging into Gotam Patel's finances,' said Pymm. 'First of all, the family businesses have a very impressive turnover.'

Warren looked at the spreadsheet displayed on the main screen.

He let out a low whistle. 'You're not kidding – it's like he's printing money. And presumably, his kids stand to inherit the lot when he dies?'

'Yes, and that's just his liquid assets. Almost all of these businesses are turning a significant profit. I'm no expert, but if the kids don't fancy continuing his empire after he passes, they could sell them as going concerns for a very tidy sum. He really knows how to make money: launderettes in areas where the residents are unlikely to own a washing machine,

96

the only newsagent-cum-grocery store in a neighbourhood, dry cleaning firms close to train and bus stations to capture business commuters. He has a real eye for choosing the most attractive locations. They also make Indian snacks that they sell through their shops and other local businesses; samosas, bhajis, pakoras, that sort of thing, under the brand name "Suniti's Sundries". It looks as though Reva worked with her mum and then continued after she died.'

'Well, that certainly makes his inheritance worth fighting for,' said Sutton. 'I've seen people killed for far less than that.'

'There's more,' said Pymm. 'We know that he pumped some serious money into that barn he converted for Reva to live in with her husband, including a professional kitchen. It turns out he also pays the mortgage on both his son's houses. And the lease on all three kids' cars.'

'Sounds like daddy loves his children very much,' said Sutton, his voice heavy with sarcasm. 'Who cares if he's a nasty piece of work if he's throwing money at you?'

'What about Anish?' asked Warren.

'Nothing that I can find,' said Pymm.

'Well, you'd think that they'd be a bit more generous about sharing their inheritance,' said Hutchinson. 'But then I suppose greed is like that.'

'His brothers and sister may well figure that given how hard they've worked to help build the family business, Anish doesn't deserve any part of it,' Warren said. 'Which to my mind gives them all a pretty strong motive for not wanting him to get married and have kids.'

*

Warren headed back to his office and dialled an extension at Welwyn from memory.

'How are you doing with Anish Patel's tablet, Pete?'

Warren didn't like badgering his colleagues in the forensic IT department, but he knew from experience that the explosion of digital evidence in recent years meant that even priority cases like murder investigations could find themselves sliding down the job list.

He could hear Robertson sigh at the end of the phone.

'We're on it. We've managed to bypass the lock code, and we're making a copy of its storage as we speak. I'll get it to you later today.'

That was quicker than Warren had hoped for, and he thanked Robertson.

'Are you able to access his email and app usage?'

'Yes, he uses push notifications, so there's no need to enter his passwords again.'

'Has he installed any extra apps?'

'How did I know you were going to ask that?' said Robertson. 'Hang on, let me have a look.'

There was the sound of plastic on wood as Robertson placed the handset down on his table, followed by the sound of rustling. Warren could picture Robertson moving around his tiny office. It never ceased to amaze him how someone so tall and ungainly could work in such cramped conditions.

'OK, let's see what we have here,' said Robertson, his voice suddenly very loud. Warren could hear his breathing down the line, as he balanced the handset between his ear and his shoulder.

'It's a Samsung tablet; most of the apps are the pre-installed ones. Let's see what he's added. Hmm, Netflix, Amazon and BBC iPlayer,' Robertson made a humming noise. 'This sounds interesting. Rainbow Hookups – that's a new one on me; looks like some sort of dating app for the LGBTQ community. And another one, this one's called Bespoke Pairings. According to the description, it's some sort of matching service for people looking for non-romantic, long-term partners.'

In the background, Warren could hear the rapid clicking of computer keys.

'Well I never, you learn a new thing every day,' said Robertson.

'Go on,' said Warren, trying not to sound impatient.

'According to the site, it specialises in setting up couples who need a partner for appearance's sake. There are a number of options on the search page, such as heterosexual or same-sex partners. You can even specify if you are looking for marriage, open relationships or companionship, with a tick box for whether you wish to enter a sexual relationship. Looking at the app on his tablet, he's a subscriber to the Pro edition, which allows users to get matches and make contact.'

'Bingo,' said Warren. It looked as though they had found a way of identifying Anish's lady friend.

Chapter 14

Bella, the receptionist at the Easy Break Hotel, squinted at the photograph of Anish Patel for several seconds, before nodding her confirmation.

'I didn't recognise him at first,' she said. 'He usually has his hood up.'

'Usually? Is he a regular?' asked Hardwick.

'Yeah, he stays about once a month.' She frowned for a second. 'He checks in under the name of Mr Smith.'

'Mr Smith?' Anish was of Indian heritage, 'Smith' seemed an unlikely alias.

'Yes. He just turns up and pays cash.' She lowered her voice slightly. 'He's a bit of an oddball, to be honest. Pleasant enough, but he doesn't stick around for the free breakfast or come down to the bar. He just takes his keycard and goes straight to his room.'

'Would you be able to confirm when he last stayed here?'

'Of course.' She turned to her computer. 'I'm sure I saw him recently.'

She tapped away for a few seconds. 'Yeah, we've had two bookings under Smith this month, but one was a couple who pre-booked through Expedia. The other one paid cash on Thursday the 24th of November. That's your man, I reckon.'

'Was he alone?' asked Hardwick.

'That's what he said. We offer free breakfast for all guests, so we ask how many occupants are in each room,' she paused. 'And for fire safety of course.'

'Of course,' said Hardwick. 'But he didn't have breakfast?'

'No, so he could have had a whole circus troop in there and we'd never have known,' she laughed for a few seconds, before falling silent.

'How long did he stay?'

'Just the one night.' She moved the mouse. 'No bar tab or room service because he didn't use a credit card.'

'Isn't that unusual, not insisting on a credit card?'

The receptionist paused and glanced over her shoulder. 'To be honest, we can't afford to turn customers away. We took a bit of a kicking on TripAdvisor after a food hygiene incident last year; we're still struggling to recover. Bloody online review sites. The owners completely gutted the kitchen afterwards, but mud sticks.'

Hardwick said nothing. She remembered reading about the 'incident' in the local paper. Two dozen extremely sick wedding guests – three requiring hospital treatment – after a badly prepared buffet. An inspection had revealed a raft of failings and poor practice in the kitchen and it had very nearly been shut down. Perhaps that was why Anish decided to forgo the complimentary breakfast.

'Do you remember seeing him when he checked out?'

'No, I wouldn't have been on shift then.' She pointed to a letter box on a table opposite the desk, a brightly coloured poster next to it exhorting guests to follow the hotel on Facebook and leave a comment on TripAdvisor. 'Besides, he won't have had any outstanding payments, so he could just drop the card in there and leave.'

'Do you have a record of the room he stayed in?'

'Yes, 201.' She looked at her computer. 'That's another weird thing about him. He always insists on staying in the same room.'

'Any reason why?'

'Not a bloody clue. We only have two types of room, family and twin slash double, and they're all the same. I'm sure I remember Juanita, the other receptionist, saying that he was quite agitated a few months ago when 201 was already booked out. He ended up staying in 202 across the corridor. Like I said, he was a weird one. Donnie, the manager, reckons he's a spy; always pays cash, insists on the same room, never comes out. I reckon he's just a nutter.'

A search of Anish's flat had revealed it to be full of spy memorabilia, and his sister had mentioned that he was a keen James Bond fan. Hardwick thought it more likely that Anish had enjoyed a bit of harmless role-playing.

'Has the room been let out since?' Hardwick held her breath; it had been eight days since Anish had checked in.

She manipulated the mouse again.

'Yes, sorry. There was a booking the night after he stayed, and there's an American couple in there now. They've been booked in for three nights, with one more left. I think they're visiting Cambridge.'

Hardwick sighed. 'I'm afraid I'm going to have to ask that they are moved out, and the room sealed until my colleagues arrive.'

'You are joking?'

'I'm afraid not.'

'Shit, Donnie is going to do his nut. The last thing we need is more crappy reviews on TripAdvisor.'

Hardwick gave an apologetic shrug. 'And I'm going to have to ask for any CCTV footage that you have from his stay.'

'It just gets better,' she muttered as she went off to find her manager.

*

'I've sealed the hotel room that Anish Patel stayed in, and I'm having a quick look at the CCTV before it's taken away for Mags'

102

team in Welwyn to look at properly,' said Hardwick. Her eyes felt gritty from another sleepless night with Ollie and the grainy footage had hardly helped matters. She stifled a yawn. The office behind the reception desk was over-heated and cramped; she was glad that Moray Ruskin hadn't come with her – he'd probably have had to wait outside.

Behind her, Donnie, the hotel manager, was looking on, irritation radiating off him. She'd only heard his side of the conversation, but it didn't sound as though the two guests in room 201 were very impressed about being phoned during their guided tour of King's College and told they needed to return to the hotel to remove their belongings from the room. Unfortunately, the Easy Break Hotel wasn't the sort of establishment that could soften the blow by upgrading them to a luxury suite, and breakfast was already free.

'Any sign of his car?' asked Warren, his voice tinny over the desk phone's loudspeaker. Mobile phone reception varied enormously throughout the hotel, and Hardwick had eventually tired of going into the kitchen to get a signal.

'They have free parking, but they don't record guests' licence-plates. There is a wide-angle CCTV camera covering the building's entrance, but the one that appears to cover the rest of the car park is a fake, placed there as a deterrent. We have no footage of cars entering or leaving the car park.'

'Naturally,' grumbled Warren.

'However, I have found him checking in and checking out on the reception camera.' She looked closer at the screen. 'Timestamp says he arrived at 18:28 on Thursday 24th.'

She manipulated the controls on the security system. 'He's on his own, carrying a grey backpack. It looks big enough for a spare change of clothes and wash kit, with a bit of space left over.'

'Get a screenshot and description, we'll add it to the list of items we need to find,' ordered Warren.

'It looks like there's a logo on the back of his hoodie,' said

Hardwick. 'I'll ask the Video Analysis Unit to examine it in more detail.'

'What about checkout?' asked Warren.

'He just left his keycard in the box. I have him leaving at quarter to seven Friday morning wearing the same hoodie. His keycard was one of only two dropped off before the morning receptionist swiped it to mark the room ready for housekeeping.'

'Good work. The CSIs will be there in about ten minutes to start processing the room and secure the footage, Hutch is organising a team to question the staff. I'll get Mags to pull up the traffic cams to see if we can find his car.'

Hardwick acknowledged him and hung up.

Behind her, Donnie shifted. 'Could you please tell me what the hell is going on?'

Chapter 15

'IT have accessed the logs of Rainbow Hookups, the dating app on Anish Patel's tablet,' said Pymm. She called up a fresh window on one of her screens.

'I've not heard of that one,' said Hardwick, before expertly pitching her finished can of Diet Coke into a nearby waste bin, the caffeinated beverage finally starting to combat her fatigue.

'It looks as though it's a fairly new, free service. It's pretty basic, just a profile picture and a few details such as location and preferences. No subscription, so no credit card details, name or address required. All you need is an email account.'

'Damn,' muttered Sutton.

'Anish has been using it for a little over twelve months.' She clicked a link. 'This is his profile. As you can see, he portrays himself on this site much the same way he does on social media.'

The pictures showed Patel in a variety of poses. In all of them he was dressed in well-cut suits, his sleeves rolled back just enough to reveal the expensive watches that they had found in his flat. In two of them he lounged confidently against the front wing of his convertible Mercedes.

'He's been honest about his age, but he describes himself as a businessman and entrepreneur,' said Pymm, 'and lists his interests as working out, fast cars and fine dining.'

'Sounds like quite the catch,' said Hutchinson.

'Or a good target,' said Warren.

'I've made a list of the contacts he's made since he joined. The site rather cutely refers to anyone who expresses an interest as a "nibble", and if that interest is reciprocated, a "bite". There are an awful lot of fishing puns on there.'

'How many are we looking at?' asked Warren.

'Twenty-six nibbles, and nine bites,' said Pymm.

'Is that normal?' asked Sutton.

'I have no idea,' said Pymm. There was an awkward silence.

'Well, don't look at me,' said Ruskin. 'Alex and I met the old-fashioned way after a few too many in the Students' Union. Neither of us have ever used one of these apps.'

'Sorry,' muttered Sutton. 'I shouldn't have assumed you'd know.'

'Have any of the bites turned into anything more substantial?' asked Warren.

'Five of them progressed beyond a bit of flirting within the app, and they exchanged mobile numbers. You can probably guess what that's referred to.'

'And do any of these "catches" appear on his phone log?' asked Warren.

'All five, but they usually only communicate for a few days; generally a brief flurry of text messages and maybe a phone call. Then a single exchange of texts and nothing more.'

'Thanks for a lovely date, best wishes for the future?' suggested Ruskin.

'I imagine so, although judging by the profiles that I've been reading, "date" might be a bit generous. There's no way to know without access to their phones,' said Pymm.

'Who hooked who?' asked Sutton.

'The first catch was initiated by Anish to a Johnny74 on October the 28th last year. A lover of all things car-related according to his profile, he was also the first to offer his mobile number – an unregistered pay-as-you-go, naturally. It looks as though Anish mulled it over for a bit, before finally texting him. I guess if this was Anish's first foray into internet dating, he might have been a bit nervous.'

'What happened then?' asked Warren.

'They exchanged two more texts each that evening, over the space of about an hour. The next text was from Anish at 7 p.m. the following evening, followed by a reply less than sixty seconds later. Then nothing until 8.30 the next morning, when Johnny74 texted. Anish replied within a minute and then nothing since.'

Pymm pushed her glasses back onto her nose. 'It's impossible to work out exactly what's going on without access to their phones so we can read the texts, but I think we can probably divide these relationships into two groups: those that are just a quick hook-up for sex, and those that are perhaps looking for something a bit more long-term.'

'And what do you think Johnny74 is?' asked Sutton.

Pymm looked thoughtful. 'I think the former. Looking at the pattern of the texts, I don't think there's much flirting going on. To be honest, if they were just hooking up for sex then all they'd need is to decide on a time and a place. The text the following day could have been "I'm at the bar, where are you?" and the next morning, "thanks for a lovely night. Don't call me."'

'You're a brutal woman,' said Sutton.

'You have no idea,' replied Pymm sweetly.

'Of course they could have moved their conversation away from text messages,' said Ruskin. 'There's not a lot of space for deep and meaningful conversation in a text.'

'Good point,' acknowledged Warren. 'See if Anish started any email conversations with new recipients at that time, Rachel …' He paused, looking at Ruskin. 'What?'

'Well, I don't want to be rude, Sir, but email is a bit … formal.'

'He means "old-fashioned",' interjected Sutton helpfully.

'So how else would they have kept in touch? WhatsApp?' asked Warren, ignoring Sutton.

'Perhaps,' said Ruskin.

'Can we access his WhatsApp account on his tablet?' asked Warren.

Pymm shook her head. 'It's not on the list of installed apps that Pete Robertson sent over. Besides which, WhatsApp is associated with a phone number. Most people don't sync it to multiple devices.'

'So, they could have continued their relationship via WhatsApp, and we'd never know it without his phone?' said Warren.

'Afraid so, Sir,' said Pymm.

'I'm not sure,' said Sutton. 'They met up months ago. But there's no phone calls either. I can completely understand using WhatsApp instead of texts, but it seems unlikely that they never phoned each other for a chat.'

There was a moment's silence, before Pymm spoke. 'Do you want to tell him, Sir?'

Warren smirked. 'You can make voice calls using WhatsApp. Perhaps you should ask one of our younger colleagues for a tutorial?'

'I did not know that,' muttered Sutton as the rest of the team laughed.

'Well let's at least see if we can track down this Johnny74,' said Warren. 'We know what time the texts were sent, so see if you can cross-reference the location data. Presumably they will have met up and gone somewhere if they had sex. Maybe we'll get lucky and find out that Anish went back to Johnny74's residence, or at least get a decent headshot of him on CCTV; I'm not sure if I trust these profile pictures.'

'Speaking of which,' said Pymm, 'Anish contacted a gentleman calling himself "Brown Bear" on the 8th December. Mr Bear claims to be thirty-two, but judging by his profile picture, either he needs to sack his photographer, or he's knocked twenty years off his age.'

Pymm's rather waspish assessment was correct. There was no way that the man calling himself Brown Bear was less than fifty.

'How did this relationship pan out?' asked Warren.

'Based on the evidence that we have here, they spent a bit more time getting to know each other. They flirted for almost a week within the app before Anish took the initiative and sent his mobile phone number.'

'How did that go?' asked Sutton.

'Pretty well by the looks of it. They sent a half-dozen texts each, and had a long phone call on the evening of Sunday the 13th. Again, there was a brief text exchange the following evening just before 8 p.m. Then a single text the following morning from Anish. No reply.'

'Ouch,' said Ruskin.

'Could it be that they had a date on Monday night which didn't go entirely as planned?' asked Sutton, 'and Mr Bear wasn't happy about the brush-off?'

'Perhaps,' said Warren. 'Or the date went very well and they decided to move to some other means of communication. Either way, I think that working out who this Mr Bear is should be a priority.'

'Regardless of whether the date went well or not, it didn't stop Anish from continuing to use the app,' said Pymm. 'He continued to pursue more nibbles.' She called up a new screen. 'Meet Blondie92.'

The screen showed an image of a young man in his twenties, with short, spiky blonde hair. The headshot was accompanied by three more photos, all taken at the beach, revealing a slim, lightly muscled torso.

'Can you zoom in on that tattoo on his left shoulder?' asked Warren.

Pymm clicked her mouse, and the man's shoulder expanded to fill the screen.

'Looks like he's a Chelsea supporter,' said Hutchinson.

'I'll take your word for it,' said Warren staring at the pixelated blur.

'Chelsea is a football team, Sir,' said Pymm with a straight face.

'Thank you, Sergeant,' replied Warren. 'And there was me thinking we had a netball fan. Tell me what we have for Blondie92.'

'Well first of all, he contacted Anish, who responded less than twelve hours later. That was on the 1st of January this year.'

'New year, new start,' said Warren. 'What happened next?'

'A bit of forward and backwards – I'll spare your blushes – suffice to say that it was Blondie92 who gave Anish his number.'

'Unregistered, I assume?' said Sutton.

'Naturally. Anyway, Anish was clearly interested. He texted within twelve minutes. I count eight messages between them over the next hour.'

'It looks as though Blondie92 hooked his fish,' said Warren.

'Possibly. There were two more texts from each of them the following morning, and a fourteen-minute phone call – initiated by Blondie92 – the following evening. The next day there are two more texts in the morning, and then one at lunchtime. The last text exchange that day was at half past five.'

'Setting up for an early evening date?' asked Ruskin.

'Well don't get too excited,' cautioned Pymm. 'That was the last time the two of them made contact. There wasn't even a follow-up text the following day.'

'Ouch,' said Sutton. 'That's harsh.'

'I don't want to be uncharitable, but I think Anish might have been punching a bit above his weight there,' said Pymm. 'We know that his profile pictures were flattering to say the least. Blondie92 may have been a little disappointed.'

'What about the other two bites?'

'Car_lover12 – I think we can spot a theme here. He claims to be thirty-five and offered his number on the 16th of June. There was a bit of back and forth over text and one phone call, initiated by Anish and a follow-up text exchange a few days later, first thing in the morning, again started by Anish.'

The photo this time was of a tall, well-built black man whose age seemed to match the one listed on his profile, photographed in front of a variety of sporty-looking cars.

'Do what you can,' instructed Warren. 'That was only five months ago. That's not that long to bear a grudge, if you're the sort of nutter who dumps a body in a ditch then removes the fingerprints and smashes the teeth in. Anyone else?'

'Most recently, HotnReady. They connected on September 28th. A few, frankly eye-watering exchanges, then HotnReady passed on his number. Two text messages apiece the following day, and then nothing. No idea if they met up or not,' Pymm clicked over to the man's profile pictures.

'Bloody hell,' said Sutton, 'I think we'll have to crop that one if we're going to show it to a jury.'

After the laughter had died down, Hutchinson spoke up. 'If Anish was continuing to see other men, even if he was in a relationship, that could have been a source of jealousy. Presumably his profile must still have been live if he continued to receive nibbles, so any boyfriend would know that he was still looking.'

'As far as I can tell, his profile has remained active from the moment he joined the site,' said Pymm. Her voice softened. 'It's still active now. Somebody nibbled yesterday.'

The room went quiet, nobody really sure what to say. The site had no subscription fees. Presumably, Anish's profile would remain active until somebody told the site to take it down, or the company archived it due to inactivity. In the meantime, how many users would click on the picture of the smiling man leaning against the bonnet of his Mercedes car, and feel a twinge of disappointment when he never responded?

*

'I've been looking at the Bespoke Pairings app installed on Anish Patel's tablet,' said Hardwick, addressing the late afternoon briefing. 'It appears that after a few false starts, he found a match. A young woman called Latika.' She gestured to the headshot of a pretty, Asian woman that she had projected onto the wall of the main briefing room.

'According to her profile, she's twenty-eight years old, a teacher, enjoys yoga and is looking for marriage and children without a sexual relationship.'

'Well the name matches what Reva told us,' said Sutton. 'Do we have contact details for her?'

'Yes. After a dozen exchanges through the site, Anish sent her his Gmail address, where they continued their relationship. They agreed to meet up at a café for coffee in March and Anish sent her his mobile number. Unfortunately, she didn't send hers back.'

'Damn. Without the address book stored in his phone handset, how can we contact her?' asked Ruskin. 'If she has any common sense at all, she isn't going to respond to an email out of the blue claiming to be from Hertfordshire Police asking her to get in touch.'

'Oh, ye of little faith,' said Hardwick.

She switched slides to a list of phone numbers, and gestured with a laser pointer. 'This is his call log. He received a text message from this number the day after he offered his mobile number to her. Since then he has made and received dozens of calls, pretty much up until the present.'

'Have you traced the owner of the phone?' asked Warren, although he had a suspicion he knew what her answer would be.

'Unfortunately, no. The number is one of the numerous unregistered pay-as-you-go numbers he has contacted.'

'That would make sense if she was conducting her relationship in secret,' said Ruskin.

Warren tapped his teeth thoughtfully. 'We won't get a warrant to tap her phone or track it; she's not suspected of any crime. So, unless anyone else has a bright idea, the only thing to do is call the number and see if she picks up.'

His request was met with an apologetic silence. Warren gave a sigh; it wasn't the way he'd hoped to end his day, but there was no way around it.

'Mags, what have you got for us?' he continued.

'Welwyn had a rush job done on the CCTV Karen found of Anish leaving the Easy Break Hotel on the Friday morning. He left alone, with nobody obviously following him.'

'Did he appear on any other cameras?' asked Hutchinson.

'No. There isn't much in the way of working CCTV around the hotel, but we don't see him in reception again and he didn't go to the bar or the dining room.'

Warren turned to Pymm. 'How does all this fit in with his phone's location data?'

'It doesn't. He turned his mobile off at 17:38 just outside Clancy's where he worked. It then doesn't power up again until he sent the text to work, later on Friday morning,' said Pymm.

'Sounds dodgy to me,' said Sutton.

'Not necessarily,' said Hardwick. 'The mobile phone signal in the hotel is atrocious, even the manager says as much; there's only a handful of spots you can get any reception at all, guests need to stand right in the middle of the car park to make a call. It's why they offer complimentary WiFi. If Anish was a regular there, he'd have known.'

'But why turn it off before he even arrived at the hotel?' asked Ruskin.

'Rachel, check his phone's logs against his confirmed stays when you get them,' said Warren. 'See if that's normal behaviour for him.'

'Well the obvious reason for his visits to the hotel is for sex with people he's met online,' said Sutton. 'Maybe he turns everything off before he gets there, so he can't be tracked?'

'But why?' asked Richardson. 'He's a single bloke, who doesn't live with anyone. If he was a married man, hiding it from his wife, I'd get that. But who's going to be checking his phone for evidence of an affair? Surely this Latika woman won't care?'

113

Warren turned to Hutchinson again. 'How has the questioning of the hotel staff been going?'

'Most that we've spoken to so far didn't recognise Anish's picture, but then the majority of them have little interaction with the guests.'

'What about the other photos?' asked Sutton.

'None of them recognised the profile pictures from Rainbow Hookups.'

'Mags?' Warren turned to Richardson.

'I've given the pictures to the Video Analysis Unit. They're collecting images of everyone who walked past the reception camera on the days he stayed to see if they can spot anyone of interest. Then they'll do all the other cameras. We've also got a list of the guests that stayed there over that time period, for all the good that'll do us – if Anish was able to check in under a false name, who knows how many other guests also did so?'

'There is another mystery we have to solve,' said Richardson. 'I've got the ANPR records from the fixed cameras on the A506 near the Easy Break Motel, but there's no sign of Anish's Mercedes on the day that he checked in, or the following morning.'

'Wait, we still haven't tracked down his car?' asked Sutton.

Richardson shook her head. 'It was last picked up twice on an ANPR camera the weekend before. Looking at the location of the camera, and the time between triggers, he was probably doing his grocery shop at Tesco.'

'The one we think he pays cash for,' interjected Pymm. 'It might be worth getting CCTV footage from Tesco at that time to see if he's alone when he does the shop, or if he is using a card we somehow don't know about.'

'Good thinking,' said Warren. 'Now, back to the cameras near the hotel.'

Richardson grabbed a pen and a piece of paper. 'The cameras are at a set of traffic lights about three-hundred metres south of the turn-off for the hotel. If he was travelling to the hotel from the direction of town, he'd have gone through these traffic lights, then turned left into the side road that the hotel car park entrance is on. The next morning, he would have come out of the hotel, turned right onto the A506, then passed through the traffic lights on the way back towards town.'

She sketched the junction. 'That would make sense, since his flat is in town, and if he came direct from work, he would have also travelled that way.'

'So, what would happen if he came from the other direction?' asked Warren.

'Well, that's where it gets weird,' said Richardson. 'There isn't a lot out that way. It's pretty much a straight road to Cambridge.'

'But there is a turning onto the country lane where his body was found,' pointed out Sutton.

'There is. And he could have continued down there to get to the main road that runs parallel to the A506, which would have led back into town. But that's a bloody strange route to take, it would add the better part of ten miles onto his journey. I looked at the ANPR cameras on that road and again I can't find his Merc.'

Warren closed his eyes, picturing the layout of the roads. 'Then was he coming to or from the direction of Cambridge? The family home is in that direction.'

If Anish had driven that way, perhaps he had visited his family or friends? In which case, why had nobody said? Aside from his sister, his family claimed not to have had any contact with him recently, and she hadn't mentioned meeting him that day.

'I spoke to Cambridgeshire, and they have no record of his car being spotted that Thursday either. Nor for that matter were any of the cars belonging to his close family, although we already know that according to their mobile phone location data, they were at home that night.'

Warren pinched his lip thoughtfully. 'So, all we know so far, is that he was still alive Friday morning when he checked out of the hotel. But it still leaves two questions. First, how did he get to the hotel if he didn't drive? And second, where the hell is his car?'

'There is a bus that stops near the hotel. The X262 runs between Middlesbury and Cambridge,' said Richardson, 'but it's an hourly service. Unless it was running very late, there's a forty-minute gap between him getting off and entering the hotel. It's less than a five-minute walk between the stop and the hotel. Plus, the weather was pretty crap that night, I can't imagine why he would have stayed outside any longer than necessary, especially given that he was just wearing a hoodie.'

'Well, we can't dismiss it out of hand,' said Warren. 'Get onto the company and secure their CCTV footage from the vehicle and, if possible, the bus stop. Also, ask them if the journey was delayed. We know what time he finished work, could he have jumped straight on the bus after finishing?'

'I'll also ring around local cab firms and see if they dropped him off,' said Richardson.

'We should also do the same for Friday morning, when he left,' said Sutton. 'Even if he was feeling ill and went straight home to bed, he still had to get there somehow.'

'Which still leaves the question, where is his car?' said Warren. 'Regardless of whether he drove to the hotel or used public transport, his vehicle is still unaccounted for.'

'Could it have been stolen?' asked Ruskin. 'Maybe he was carjacked as he was leaving that morning? And if he didn't give up his keys immediately, maybe that's why he was killed? He left pretty early and it would have been dark at that time.'

'If it was stolen from the hotel, then we'd have picked it up on the ANPR cameras if it was driven back to Middlesbury,' said Richardson.

'Not if they took his body directly to where it was dumped,' replied Ruskin. 'They'd have turned left out of the hotel, away from Middlesbury and missed the ANPR camera at that junction.'

'But it still wasn't picked up on any of the other ANPR cameras out towards Cambridge,' said Sutton. 'Surely they'd have passed at least one camera after dumping his body?'

'They could have switched the licence plates,' countered Ruskin. 'In fact, if they were professionals, they almost certainly would have.'

'But we didn't pick up his car on Thursday night either,' said Sutton. 'They can't have switched the plates before he checked into the hotel.'

Ruskin reluctantly conceded the point. 'So, either he used public transport, or someone dropped him off.'

'Could his killer have dropped him off and picked him up?' asked Hardwick. 'If they didn't come in, that would explain why they don't appear on the reception CCTV.'

'Damn, we could really use some CCTV footage of that car park,' said Warren.

The last confirmed sighting of Anish Patel was the morning he checked out of his hotel. Since then, aside from some text messages, they had no idea of his movements between then and his body turning up naked in a ditch two days later.

Patel's trip to the hotel might have been a coincidence, unrelated to the murder. But his body had been wrapped in a sheet from there. Whoever Anish Patel's killer was, they had to have some link with the hotel, either as a guest, a visitor or a worker.

But why had they killed Anish?

Saturday 3rd December

Chapter 16

Warren met Latika Luthra in a small coffee shop on the outskirts of St Albans. Despite her over-sized dark glasses, he recognised her from her profile picture on Bespoke Pairings as soon as she entered. She had clearly chosen their meeting place deliberately; this early on a Saturday morning it was almost empty, and Warren had snagged a table in the back corner where they could speak without being overheard.

Standing up as she entered, Warren waved her over. She declined his offer of a coffee, looking around nervously, as if expecting to be seen by someone. She didn't remove her coat, or her glasses.

'I knew what it was, the moment you called,' she said, after Warren had expressed his condolences. 'I saw it on the news, and I suppose I was expecting to hear from you eventually.'

Warren didn't ask why she hadn't contacted the police in response to their appeal; it was clear that it was a delicate situation.

'How did you get my number?' she asked.

Behind the dark glass, he could see that her eyes were wary. He knew that unless he mentioned how she and Anish originally hooked up, she was unlikely to be forthcoming about something so personal.

'I appreciate that this is a sensitive subject, but we identified you through the Bespoke Pairings app. We then used Anish's email account and telephone record to get your number.'

Her breath caught in her throat, and for a brief moment, Warren thought she was going to get up and leave. He quickly continued. 'You've heard what happened to Anish. We're trying to contact all his friends and acquaintances to find out more about him, and perhaps discover a motive for his death. I will do everything I can to ensure that anything you say will be kept discreet.'

She nodded, her shoulders relaxing slightly.

'Why don't you start by telling me a little about Anish?' said Warren gently.

She sighed, and for the first time since they met, her nervousness was replaced by a look of sadness.

'He was such a nice man. We met for coffee and dinner a few times, and he was funny and kind. I studied English Literature at university; Anish never went to uni, but he could talk endlessly about books and poetry. He'd even read some of the textbooks that I used during my course.' She looked down at the table. 'I suppose if you found me through the app, you can guess at the situation we were both in?'

Warren nodded, but said nothing, letting her do the speaking.

'I come from a very traditional background. Anish did too. There are expectations, especially for a young woman. I managed to delay things by going to university, but recently my mother has become more and more insistent. She says that she can't understand why a pretty girl like me can't find a suitable husband and settle down. Last year, she started trying to match me. Ever since my dad died, she and her sister have made it their mission to get me married.'

She stopped speaking for a moment and composed herself.

'I've always known that I was a bit different. When I was younger, I just thought it was a phase I was going through. That eventually, I'd get over it and then everything would be normal.' Her voice took on a bitter edge. 'But when I went to uni, I realised

122

that wouldn't happen. I know that I'm not some freak, that there are many others just like me. I felt so free when I was away at university, but then as soon as I graduated I returned home and I had to start hiding who I was again. I love my family very much, and I know they only want me to be happy. My mum and her sister are simply trying to help, but they don't understand. I cringe whenever anything comes on the TV about lesbians or gays, because my mum just sits there shaking her head. She's convinced that they are mentally ill or looking for attention. I don't think she's figured out why I haven't found a husband yet.

'I came across the Bespoke Pairings app by accident, and suddenly I realised that I'm not alone. I read some of the testimonies on the website and figured that if I could find someone who my mother approves of, she'd back off. I could move away and then I'd be free again. As long as I had a man at home, and perhaps a couple of kids, then it'd never occur to her that any woman I spend lots of time with is anything more than a close friend.' She wiped her eyes behind her glasses. 'We were even talking about getting a puppy; Anish always wanted one. I suppose he was perfect in a way.'

Her lip curled. 'There are some real weirdos on that site. Men who claim to be gay, but aren't really; they just want to see if they can "convert" you or "cure" you.' She gave a sniff. 'I was thinking about cancelling my membership when I finally met Anish.'

She gave a bitter laugh. 'You have no idea how hard it is. It's like looking for a roommate, but one that you are going to live with for the rest of your life. I'm not after a romantic or sexual partner, but if I am going to live with this man, marry him and have children with him, I still have to love him. For the first time since I joined that site, I thought I might have found that person.'

Behind her glasses, Warren could see her eyes shining.

Warren felt a wave of sympathy for her. He couldn't imagine how difficult her situation was. If there was one thing he'd learned over the years, it was that love took many different forms. Latika

Luthra and Anish Patel might not have been boyfriend and girl-friend in the traditional sense, but it was obvious that the two had formed a bond, and that she was grieving.

'I think I'll have that coffee, now,' she said, suddenly getting up. 'Would you like another?' She gestured at Warren's empty mug.

'Just a glass of tap water, if you don't mind,' he said. Despite the early hour, he'd already had two coffees, but he wanted to make sure she returned.

As she queued, Warren mentally reviewed their conversation. She'd started off understandably wary, but he'd noticed a softening of her attitude. He realised that this might be one of the few times she'd been able to openly discuss her situation. Did she keep in contact with any of her friends from university? Did she have anyone special? Warren decided that it didn't really matter and was none of his business. He was here to gain information on the life of Anish Patel. But if talking to a stranger comforted her ... well, Warren didn't mind.

'What can you tell me about Anish's situation?' he asked when she returned.

She gave a sigh. 'Very similar to myself. He was gay and had known it since he was very young, but his family had the same expectations as mine.'

She took a sip of her coffee, wincing at the heat.

'His father was in denial, and his brothers were ... ashamed, I suppose you could say. I think they thought that they could bully it out of him. Or at the very least, force him to hide it, so that it didn't "tarnish the reputation" of the family.' She mimed quotation marks with her fingers. Warren noted her use of the same phrase that Reva Vasava had used.

'And what about his sister?'

'She was different. So was his mother, when she was alive.' A slight smile softened Luthra's lips. 'I wish I could have met her; Anish spoke so highly of her. She taught him how to cook; I was really looking forward to that, I'm hopeless in the kitchen.

I was going to finally meet Reva when we formally announced our engagement. We were planning on doing it at Christmas and Anish wanted us to choose a ring next week.' Her voice caught and she masked it with another sip of coffee.

Warren waited until she returned her cup to its saucer.

'Do you know if he had told any other members of his family about your plans?'

Luthra shook her head. 'I don't think so; if he had, he didn't say.'

Warren thought about the unexplained phone call that his brother, Jaidev, had denied. Could Anish have brought it up then? Perhaps as part of an argument? If the response hadn't been what he wanted, then maybe he hadn't told Luthra about it.

'You said that they tried to bully it out of him,' said Warren. 'How?'

'When they were growing up his brothers were generally unpleasant to him: teasing him, calling him names, cutting pictures out of pornographic magazines and sticking them in his school exercise books to get him into trouble. His father was mostly cold. I'm sure that you are aware that Anish is the only one of his family who doesn't have a role in the business? When his mother was alive, she used to shield him, but after she died … well, that ended.'

Warren thought back to the scars that Anish had inflicted upon himself; he could only imagine how he must have felt, growing up in a family that struggled to accept him for what he was.

The next question Warren needed to ask was likely to be the most delicate. He chose his words carefully.

'You and Anish were not going to have a romantic partnership. Can I ask if you were planning on an "open" relationship?'

Luthra flushed pink. She cleared her throat, took a mouthful of coffee, then cleared her throat again.

'Yes. I suppose you could say that. We were planning on having separate rooms, and continuing relationships outside of our marriage.'

'Do you know if Anish was seeing anyone before he died?'

She paused again. 'I believe that he was … active. He used to go clubbing sometimes and I think he used an app for hooking up with other men.' She looked down at the table, her face still slightly pink. 'I regarded that part of our lives as private, and I never asked him about it. I trusted that he wouldn't bring it into our marriage. That neither of us would.'

'And he didn't mention anyone in particular?'

'No, he never spoke about it. And I didn't ask.'

Warren decided to move the interview onto less awkward territory.

'What about other friends?'

'He never really spoke about anyone, except for a couple of workmates. I think he was a bit lonely and shy.'

'What about any worries?'

'Aside from his family situation, I can't think of anything.'

'Nobody that he had had an argument with?'

'Not that he said. I always found him to be very laid back and polite, I find it hard to imagine him getting into an argument with anyone.'

Warren took that statement with a pinch of salt. Luthra and Anish had only been dating for a short time; he imagined that both of them were still showing each other their best faces. Nevertheless, it was worthy of note.

She bit her lip. 'I suppose you need to know this. Anish told me about it a couple of dates in. He was always very honest with me.'

Warren waited.

'After his mum died, Anish's father became obsessed with passing on his legacy. He rewrote his will to insist that his children could only inherit, if – at the time of his death – they were married, with children.' She shook her head, a flash of anger crossing her face. 'It was so cruel. He was basically saying that either Anish had to "give up being gay" or he was no longer his son.'

Warren contemplated her carefully, as he took a long sip of

126

his water. Luthra had just confirmed that she knew that if she married Anish and bore his child, she would be marrying into wealth. That might call into question her motives for marrying him, but it would have made it less, not more, likely for her to have killed him – at least before they were married.

Aware that he was about to risk revealing sensitive information that it wasn't his business to disclose, he decided it was time to shift the focus of the interview slightly.

'Were you familiar with the circumstances of Anish's mother's death?' asked Warren.

Luthra took another sip of her coffee before answering. 'If you mean, am I aware that Anish had inherited the same gene that killed his mother, yes I am.'

Warren waited.

'I'd be lying if I said it didn't worry me, but he assured me he was receiving medical treatment, and that there was no reason he couldn't live a long and healthy life.'

'And what about your future plans?' asked Warren carefully, unsure how much Anish had disclosed.

Luthra cleared her throat; the colour that had tinted her cheeks a few moments before returning. 'We weren't planning on having a baby the traditional way anyway. There is a company in the US that offers genetic tests for Anish's disorder. I was going to take one. If I don't carry the faulty gene myself, we were going to proceed with IVF on the NHS.'

'And if you do carry the gene?' asked Warren.

'Then we would discuss our options. The company will do pre-implantation genetic screening to ensure that none of the embryos that they implant will develop the disease.'

She looked down at the table again. Warren wasn't sure what to make of the woman in front of him. She was choosing to go through all of that to have a child with Anish. Warren had no reason to doubt that she wanted a baby for all of the right reasons, yet if all she wanted was a child and a man to pose as her loving husband, surely she could have waited for a better offer? Even as he thought it, Warren felt slightly ashamed at being so judgemental, but he pushed that aside. He needed to look at the situation dispassionately. Luthra was young enough to wait a few more years – longer even, given that she was planning on using IVF – so what was so special about Anish Patel?

Was she really that desperate for his inheritance? Warren's gut told him otherwise. From what she'd told him, and the look of genuine sadness and upset in her eyes, he felt that the relationship was not just transactional. He thought back to what she'd said. Latika and Anish may not have desired a sexual relationship, but it looked as though Luthra at least was looking for a loving partnership.

'I don't want to be indelicate, but those sorts of services don't come cheap,' said Warren.

Luthra sighed. 'I was going to pay. When my father died, he left my mother some money. It'll be passed on to my sister and me eventually anyway, because Mum won't spend it. The plan was that when we got married, I'd tell Mum that I was having problems having a baby and ask her for the money. Then, when Gotam passed away, we'd pay her back through Anish's inheritance.'

Put like that, it suddenly seemed a little more business-like. And raised another question.

'Is your sister aware of your ... situation?'

'Yes. Shyama is two years younger than me – married at nineteen to a very suitable man of course.' Her mouth twisted slightly. 'To be fair to her, she's always been accepting of me. She told me that she'd had her suspicions from when we were young, but she knew for certain when she visited me at university.'

'And what did she think about Anish?'

Luthra picked up her coffee cup again, although Warren noted that it had been drained some time ago.

Eventually, Luthra spoke. 'She was ... unconvinced.'

'How do you mean?'

'Shyama has always been a bit more forthright. I guess that's the privilege of being the younger sibling. She thinks I should just tell Mum that I'm gay and be done with it; there'll be tears and shouting, but eventually, Mum'll see sense,' Luthra snorted. 'Easy to say when you don't live in the same house.'

'And what about the baby?' asked Warren.

Luthra's face darkened. 'She knows about Anish's health problems, and she thinks I'm mad. She reckons that if I'm going to insist on having a child with somebody, then I shouldn't "limit myself to paddling at the shallow end of the gene pool", especially if I have to "pay for the privilege". My sister has never been one to let a person's feelings get in the way of a witty turn of phrase.'

Warren gave her a moment to compose herself, before continuing the questioning.

'Are you familiar with the Easy Break Hotel on the A506?'

Luthra frowned slightly. 'I don't think so.'

'It's about halfway between Middlesbury and Cambridge.'

'No, Anish and I steered clear of Cambridge.'

'So, you've never met Anish in a hotel?'

She looked surprised. 'No, of course not. After everything I've told you, do you really think Anish and I would be meeting up for … sex? That we were having some sort of affair?' She sounded incredulous now. 'Surely, I've made it clear, that we were not looking for that sort of relationship.'

Warren raised his hands. 'I'm really sorry, it's my job to ask.'

He paused, knowing that the next question could well end the discussion. He hoped not, thus far his gut was telling him that Luthra was as innocent as she claimed. But if she didn't cooperate with him now, the only alternative was a formal statement at the station.

'Can I ask where you were between the evening of Thursday the 24th of November and the following Sunday morning?'

'Wait, am I a suspect?' she asked, her voice rising slightly. Her shoulders tensed, and he could sense that she was contemplating getting up and leaving.

'I'm just being thorough.'

Even behind the glasses, he could feel the heat of her glare. He held his breath.

Eventually, she slumped back down. 'Yes, I do have an "alibi".' Her tone of voice made air quotes unnecessary. 'I was at home on the Thursday night with Mum, marking books, and then I was teaching all day Friday. I spent the weekend with friends.' For a brief moment, Warren saw another glimpse of her vulnerable side. 'But I would appreciate it if you don't go stomping around my family and friends demanding to know my whereabouts. The questions they ask could be … problematic.'

'I will do my very best to be discreet,' Warren assured her.

Luthra wrote down the name of the school she worked at and her home and friends' addresses. Warren pocketed the piece of paper. He would get someone to check it out. Unfortunately, no matter how discreet his officers were, he suspected that she would face a barrage of questions from her mother.

'Is that all that you need from me?' she asked. Her tone was still frosty.

'Yes, thank you for your time. I apologise for the intrusion and I'm sorry for your loss.'

Warren had deliberately delayed the team briefing that morning so that he could feed back his meeting with Latika Luthra.

'It doesn't sound as though it would be in Latika's interests to kill Anish before they were married,' said Richardson. 'If she wanted to get her hands on any of his inheritance, she'd need to be married to Anish and at the very least pregnant before Gotam Patel died.'

'Then maybe it wasn't Latika who was responsible,' said Sutton. 'What about her family?'

'I assume that you're thinking of her sister?' said Warren. He'd had plenty of time to consider his conversation with Luthra on the drive home.

'Exactly. Did Latika say how much money her mother was left after her father died?' continued Sutton.

'No, but we can probably find out,' said Warren.

'Well, assuming it wasn't a fortune, it's possible that a trip to the United States for expensive fertility treatment could wipe out the whole lot, including the half that her sister is expecting to inherit one day.'

'Which would certainly be enough motive,' said Richardson.

'Let's do a little digging then,' said Warren. 'Hutch, organise a team of colleagues from Welwyn to look into Latika Luthra and her family. But remind them to tread carefully where possible; there's no need to make things more difficult for her than we need to. At the moment, there's no reason to assume she's anything more than an innocent party.'

Moving on, Warren recapped where the investigation was at that moment.

'There's still no sign of Anish's clothing or backpack, his car or his mobile phone.'

'Then either the killer has done a really good job of disposing of them, and we'll never find them,' said Sutton, 'or the silly sod has kept them close by and we'll be able to hang them with them.'

'Well, here's hoping,' said Warren. 'In the meantime, what else have we got?'

'The good news is that we have identified the gym that Anish used, from the logo on his hoodie,' said Ruskin. 'Middlesbury Sports and Leisure. Apparently, the gym ordered a job-lot from the same supplier in a single batch and their records show that Anish bought one. They are sending us one over for comparison purposes, should we find his.'

'Good, what else did they have to say?' asked Warren.

'They confirmed that he was a regular, but not a member; he paid for individual sessions with cash.'

'That explains why I didn't pick it up on his bank statements,' said Pymm. 'I can't say I'm surprised; the last thing he needed was another monthly direct debit coming out of his account.'

'But where is he getting cash, if he isn't drawing any out?' asked Sutton. 'He must be doing something on the side.'

Warren turned back to Ruskin. 'Did he have a routine?'

'The receptionist reckoned he used the fitness suite on a Monday and went swimming on Thursdays; 6.30 to 8.30 early bird sessions both days, and always left in a suit and tie. He can't remember the exact times, but definitely saw him Thursday morning.'

'Well, he can't have been that ill if he was swimming Thursday morning,' said Sutton.

'Do we know if he was especially friendly with anyone?' asked Warren.

'Staff recognised him,' replied Ruskin, 'and one of the lifeguards reckoned he was on nodding terms with some of the other regular swimmers, but he pretty much got in and did his own thing. Probably forty-five minutes; maybe fifty lengths. The good news is that the fitness suite has CCTV. I've arranged for someone to pick it up for Mags' team to look at.'

'Good,' said Warren. 'See if they can build up a pattern of normal behaviour. Does he arrive and leave at the same time? Does he always get changed for work? If he deviated from that routine it might be significant. Did he catch the bus or drive? Does he speak to anyone in the fitness suite? Cross-check any faces of interest with the guests at the Easy Break Hotel, his family and those profile pics from Rainbow Hookups.

'We all know the stats, people; most victims are killed by someone that they know. We need to identify everyone in Anish Patel's life, no matter how inconsequential and determine if they were responsible for his murder.'

Chapter 17

It was the first time that Warren had visited the Easy Break Hotel. Standing in the car park, he could hear the constant rush of traffic on the A506, hidden from view by a row of hedges.

'There's no sign of Anish's Mercedes, but we know that he entered and exited the hotel via the front entrance,' said Ruskin, who'd cycled over earlier to avoid the roadworks. 'Forensics have done a fingertip search but haven't found anything of note. They're currently processing all the areas that he is likely to have been but locking down the whole hotel isn't really an option. The manager is pissed enough as it is.'

He turned on the spot, facing the hotel's front again, and gestured towards the security camera above the entrance.

'Fake.' He turned to his left. 'Same as the camera over the entrance to the car park. Apparently, they will be replaced when the hotel undergoes a revamp in the spring.'

'Fat lot of use it'll be to us by then,' Warren grumbled.

'Yeah,' agreed Ruskin. 'From what I've been hearing, the hotel took a real kicking after that food poisoning incident. And with competition from the new Travelodge, they're really struggling.'

He glanced upwards. 'Looks like it's going to rain, we'd better hurry up.' He set off towards the right. Warren was just over six feet tall, but he had to push himself to match the young constable's stride.

'There is a working camera here,' said Ruskin, as they reached the edge of the building. A painted sign informed them that it was staff only beyond that point. 'Although it's not much use to us; it mostly covers this service entrance. Anish doesn't enter or leave the hotel by this door during his stay.'

They rounded the corner of the building.

'As you can see, there is an access road along this side of the building. The other side of that hedge is a pavement that leads to the main road. There's a bus stop just along from the entrance to the car park that picks up passengers heading towards Cambridge from Middlesbury on this side of the road and another for the return on the opposite side. It's the only stop for about a mile or so each way.' He pointed to a gap in the hedge. 'Staff cut through there to get to and from the bus stops.'

The two men continued walking down the access road.

Ruskin motioned to the building edge. 'This is the wall of the breakfast bar.' They walked a few more paces. 'And this door is a fire exit.' The floor around the door was littered with cigarette butts.

He pointed upwards. 'That's a real camera, but it's broken.'

'How convenient,' said Warren. 'How long for?'

'Months at least.'

They continued walking to the end of the service road, emerging behind the hotel. A half-dozen cars were parked in a line, and three bicycles were locked to a curved metal rail. A yellow hatched box was painted on the tarmac in front of a rolling door.

'Staff parking and deliveries, including the laundry company. There's just enough room for a small lorry, although the driver has to be pretty good at reversing to get back out.'

Warren pointed at the corner of the building. 'Don't tell me, that's either broken or fake?'

'No, as it happens, but there's no movement on it the night of the murder. Apparently, it's a complete mystery why the camera over the fire exit keeps on conking out. It's been like it for ages, but they're waiting for the spring refit to get a new system.'

'Hmm,' said Warren. It was certainly convenient that there was no footage on this side of the building.

The spots of rain were becoming more frequent, and the cold wind was starting to bite. They made their way back to the main entrance and Ruskin pointed out the camera above the reception desk.

'We've managed to retrieve the keycard that Anish used that night. It's covered in loads of different fingerprints, as you'd expect, but hopefully forensics will find something interesting. We've taken exclusionary prints from the cleaning staff, and the couple who were booked into room 201 when we sealed it.'

'How did that go?' asked Warren. The couple had been rather vocal about being forced to return to the hotel and move their luggage mid-stay.

'They were pretty annoyed, until we said it was a murder investigation; the wife was taking selfies in front of the police tape the last I heard.'

To the left of the reception area was a lift. 'Let me guess, the CCTV is broken,' sighed Warren as they stepped into the car.

'Nope, fake.'

'Great. They don't like to make our job easy, do they?' said Warren as Ruskin punched in the floor number. A slight patina of fingerprint dust remained on the number two and Ruskin grimaced as he wiped his finger on his trousers.

The lift deposited the two men on the second floor with a loud 'ding'.

'This is another weird thing about our victim. Apparently, he insisted on always staying in 201,' said Ruskin, 'but as you can see, it's the furthest room from the lift. Guests usually prefer to be closer, so they don't have to drag their suitcases as far.'

Warren saw that he was right. The signs on the wall indicated that room 201 was at the far end of the corridor.

'Maybe he didn't want to be disturbed by the lift coming up and down all night?' suggested Warren, although he couldn't say it was something he'd ever considered himself when booking into a hotel.

'Hutch thought that maybe he had a thing about being near the fire exit,' said Ruskin, as they walked down the corridor. 'We know that he doesn't have a problem with lifts, because he used it after checking in.'

Warren could see that room 201, easily identified by the blue and white police tape and the bored-looking constable hiding his mobile phone, was next to the fire door at the end of the corridor. Directly opposite was 202, where Patel had grudgingly stayed some months before, when 201 was already in use. It too was being processed.

The scene was currently being examined by forensics, so the two men signed the log and slipped on latex gloves, a paper suit and plastic overshoes before ducking under the tape.

The room was a small twin, the two single beds currently rolled together to form a double, the mattress already seized for analysis. To the left of the entrance, an open door led to a tiny bathroom with a sink, toilet and a miniscule shower cubicle that Ruskin would have struggled to fit into.

The walls were painted a neutral beige, with a brightly coloured abstract print above the bed; the window overlooked the car park. In the corner, there was an open-frame wardrobe, with two shelves taking up the bottom third and a clothes rail above. A small shelf at the top had an iron and miniature ironing board. It reminded Warren of his room during his first year at university, although his digs hadn't had a flatscreen television mounted on the wall opposite the bed. Beneath the TV, with barely enough space for a large adult to squeeze between it and the bed, was a wooden desk with a selection of laminated menus and the hotel's WiFi password. A numbered, yellow scene marker had been placed on the corner of the table. The plywood was chipped.

'The desk has been wiped down, but the CSIs found traces of blood and a human hair caught in the split in the wood. They've sent the blood off for DNA matching,' said Ruskin.

'We have CCTV of him leaving the hotel the following morning, so if that's where he hit his head, it can't have been immediately fatal. Any reports of a disturbance?'

'None, but it was quiet that night; all the adjacent rooms were unoccupied.'

'What other trace evidence have they recovered?'

'Hundreds of fingerprints, and they haven't finished yet. The room has been cleaned since Anish stayed here, but it's still pretty grubby; it'll take days to process them all. They've also dismantled the sink trap and the shower's drain, but they didn't find anything interesting. It's unlikely that we'll be able to isolate any foreign DNA, even if we have a suspect.'

Warren had expected as much. Hotel rooms, by definition, were filled with strangers' DNA and hair. The best they could hope for was a fingerprint that matched a suspect – but if their suspect worked in the hotel, then proving that there wasn't a legitimate reason for the print to be at the crime scene could be extremely difficult.

'What about drugs? We know Anish was getting cash from somewhere.' If he had been dealing out of the room, then perhaps there would be traces.

'They've done some putative drug swabs, but there's nothing beyond the usual background levels of cocaine you'd expect for a hotel that caters for a lot of stag and hen parties. If they were testing merchandise in here, either they were careful not to make a mess, or it's been cleaned up since then.'

Warren looked over at the bed. 'What about bedding and towels?' The body had been wrapped in a sheet from the hotel, and the hammer and knife used to mutilate his body had been wrapped in a hotel towel.

'According to the housekeeping log, there was nothing missing from the room. But there is a cupboard full of cleaning materials and spare linen down the corridor. Unfortunately, they don't keep an inventory, but it is locked to stop guests pinching stuff. There's no sign that the lock has been forced.'

'Which means that if the killer did help themselves, then they must have had access to those keys. Could this be an inside job?'

*

After one last look around the room, the two officers left, removing their gloves and booties.

'Let's see where these stairs lead,' said Warren pushing through the fire door. It opened onto a vestibule, with bare metal steps heading up to the next floor and down to the ground level. The two men's shoes rang out as they descended.

At the bottom of the stairwell, there were three doors. The first, directly opposite the stairs had a narrow window with safety glass showing a glimpse of the reception area beyond. At the other end of the short corridor, a metal door with a steel crash bar was marked with a fire exit sign. To its left, a door without a window was staff only.

Warren shrugged and pushed his way in. Immediately, his nose was met by the smell of cooked breakfast, as the two officers entered the kitchen. A man in chef's whites and an apron looked up from the sink where he was washing a large metal pan.

'Hey, staff only. Can't you read?'

Warren flashed his warrant card. 'Do you mind if we ask you a few questions, Mr …?'

The man carefully placed the steel pan down on the draining board. He looked at Warren and Ruskin, licked his lips then shrugged.

'Sure. Nicholas Kimpton.'

Warren glanced around the kitchen. Two more steel pans, one

crusted with the remains of scrambled eggs, the other with what looked like scraps of bacon, were piled to the left of him.

'Is it just you working here today?' asked Warren.

'Yeah. I have a lad who helps out during the setup, but he's finished for the morning. Muggins here has to clean up. He'll be back in to help with the evening shift.'

Warren showed him the screen of his phone. 'Do you recognise this man?'

Kimpton glanced at it. 'I've already been asked this. No, I don't. I stay in the kitchen. The girls set the food out and bring in the dirty pans.'

Warren gestured towards the door that they'd just entered. 'Do the serving staff use that to come and go?'

Kimpton shook his head. 'No, that just leads to the emergency stairs and the fire exit,' he pointed to the other side of the kitchen at a pair of double-doors with eye-level windows. 'Those are the serving doors, they lead into the back of the dining area.'

'So, you can't get in and out of the building through that door?'

'Well, you can in an emergency obviously, but the fire door's alarmed. There's another door around the back of the fridges that leads onto the loading bay. Staff use that or reception when they finish their shift.'

'What time does the evening shift end?' asked Ruskin.

Kimpton sighed. 'We stop serving food at half-nine. If it's been a quiet night and we've managed to stack the dishwasher by then, I can be out of here a little after ten.'

'Then back first thing in the morning?' asked Ruskin.

'Yeah, the joy of split-shifts. Look, I'm sorry, but I really need to get on. I'm supposed to be taking my little girl out for the day, and my ex gets really pissy if I turn up late.'

'Of course, I won't keep you any longer,' said Warren. He and Ruskin turned and walked back through the door that they had entered.

'He claims that people don't use this door,' said Warren quietly, once it had closed behind them, 'but look at the floor, it's covered in shoe prints. You said that there was no movement on the loading bay camera?'

'Nothing. The last thing it picked up was a delivery van at four o'clock that afternoon.'

Warren pondered that for a moment.

'There's something that bothers me,' said Ruskin. 'If staff don't come in and out of the fire door because it has an alarm, how come there are so many cigarette ends on the floor outside it?' He bent over. 'And why is there a folded piece of cardboard in the shape of a doorstop lying here?'

'Exactly what I am wondering,' said Warren. 'I think it's time we brought in a few members of staff for a little chat, starting with our new friend, Nicholas Kimpton.'

Chapter 18

'Sir, we've just had a call come in on the tip line.' Rachel Pymm waved the printed message as Warren returned to the office. 'It's from Middlesbury Rental Vehicles, I have the details from the call-taker here.'

Warren looked at the note. 'It says here that Anish hired a car from them the day he checked into the hotel.' He frowned. 'There was nothing on his bank statements to indicate that he hired a car. Surely he can't have used cash?'

'That's what I thought, so I called his credit card company directly. Apparently, there was a ring-fenced sum of £500 placed on the card that day. It was removed two days later. That's why it wasn't on his statement. They suggest that he probably used cash for the rental, but used his card for the deposit. If he returned the car in good condition with a full tank, they won't have taken any of it.'

'Great work, Rachel.' He looked around the office, spying Hardwick who'd just arrived after dropping her son at his grand-parents'. 'Thanks for coming in on a rest day, Karen. Can you go and speak to a Mr Latham at Middlesbury Rental Vehicles?'

'Delighted to, it's far too stuffy in here.'

Warren turned back to Pymm. 'Moray and I just met somebody

interesting. Can you run a Nicholas Kimpton through the PNC?'

'Way ahead of you, boss. I received a list of all the employees from the Easy Break Hotel this morning and he's already come up. And he's not the only one.'

'Give me details,' said Warren, as he removed his coat. He could sympathise with Hardwick's desire for fresh air; the building's elderly thermostat thought it was a lot colder outside than it actually was.

'Kimpton is thirty-two years old and has multiple convictions for dealing drugs and aggravated assault. He's worked in the kitchen since last year, when they fired the old chef after the food-poisoning incident. He does a split-shift, working the breakfast buffet, then comes back in the evening and does bar food, six days a week.'

'Ouch, that's a long week,' said Ruskin.

'Welcome to the world of catering,' said Hutchinson. 'Why do you think I joined the police?'

'He's certainly worth a look,' said Warren. 'Who else?'

'Leon Grime. He's in charge of maintenance and also has a record, with two short sentences for drug dealing. We've nothing on the computer since 2000.'

'I'd be very interested to see if anything's missing from his toolkit,' said Warren, 'and that beige paint that covers every wall in the hotel looks a lot like the drips on the tools we found.'

'My thoughts exactly,' said Pymm.

Warren turned to David Hutchinson. 'Hutch, organise teams to bring in Nicholas Kimpton and Leon Grime for questioning.' He thought for a moment. 'Keep it low key, try not to spook them. Make out it's just routine questioning to help with our enquiries. Whilst you're at it, speak to the CSIs at the hotel. See if they've located Leon Grime's toolkit.'

*

142

Nicholas Kimpton was not impressed when he was invited into the station for an interview. His ex-partner, who had to cancel her own plans to look after their daughter, was apparently even less happy.

'Thank you for coming in, Mr Kimpton,' said Warren. Beside him, Moray Ruskin sat immobile, a notepad in front of him.

'You are not under arrest, but we will be recording this interview. You are free to leave at any time, or request legal representation.' He paused. 'I'm sure you know the drill.'

Kimpton scowled at the subtle dig. 'Yes, I know how this works.'

'Well let's start off by talking about Thursday the 24th of November. What times did you work that day?'

'I did a split-shift. I started breakfast at about five-past six for a six-thirty start. We prepare most of it the night before. Everything was cleared away and most of the prep for the evening done by about eleven, when I went home. I then came back in at half-five,' Kimpton scowled. 'I already told you this.'

'Sorry, Mr Kimpton, I'm just getting it on the record.'

'Fine,' muttered Kimpton, although his scowl didn't ease.

'So, was it just you?' asked Warren.

'Not all the time. Shane, the kitchen hand, started a bit after quarter past six, then left just after eight to catch the bus to college.'

'What about the evening shift?' asked Ruskin.

'I got the ball rolling about half-five, then Shane joined me about a quarter of an hour later when he finished college.'

'Tell me about Shane,' said Warren.

Kimpton shrugged. 'Not much to tell really. He's a good lad. He's doing catering at Middlesbury College and he works here mornings and evenings to earn a bit of cash and get some experience on his CV.' Kimpton scratched his chin. 'For the last few months he's done the Tuesday on his own since he doesn't have college then, so I finally get a day off. To be honest, I don't think he'll be here much longer.'

'Oh? Why do you say that?' asked Warren.

'He's got talent, he's wasted here. I reckon as soon as he passes his driving test he'll be applying to restaurants.' For the first time since his arrest, Kimpton's scowl was replaced with a smile. 'I'll be sorry to see him go, but I'll give him a bloody good reference.' The smile faded. 'Reminds me a bit of myself at that age ...'

Warren was in no mood to hear Kimpton lamenting how his poor choices had derailed his own career. 'Was there anything unusual about that Thursday evening?'

Kimpton stuck his bottom lip out and gave a half-shrug. 'Not that I recall, typical weekday night.' A brief flash of something crossed his face. Irritation? Bitterness? 'We ain't exactly a Michelin-starred kitchen with complex orders cooked to the customer's precise instructions. Burgers, chips, reheated lasagnes and curries; aside from the occasional allergy note, or request to swap the chips for a jacket potato, that's about as complicated as it gets. It's why I trust Shane on Tuesdays.'

'So, a bit different to what you're used to do then?' asked Ruskin.

Kimpton sat back in his chair and glared at the two men. 'Yes, very different. We all know why I'm here.'

'Why is that, Nicholas?' asked Warren.

'Because I did time. Because when I was a kid, I was a fucking idiot and decided to make a little extra money on the side dealing drugs out of the kitchen where I was working.'

'That wasn't the only reason,' said Warren mildly.

'Yeah, well that was bullshit. I got a bit greedy and took more merch than I could sell and pay for immediately. They sent in somebody to collect, and things got a bit heavy. What was I supposed to do? Let them cut a finger off over five hundred quid?'

'So, you got your retaliation in first?' said Ruskin.

'I didn't have any choice, did I?'

It was a somewhat sanitised and down-played version of what had been recorded on the computer, but they weren't there to rehash old offences.

Kimpton leaned forward, his tone bitter. 'Look, I was a stupid kid, and I paid the price, OK? I spent nearly two years in prison and went from working in the best hotels in the area, alongside some of the best chefs in the country, to working split-shifts serving pre-made scrambled eggs and frozen burgers in a bloody fleapit. I only have this job because they were desperate after the last dickhead they hired nearly killed a whole wedding party.' He rubbed his eyes, his tone suddenly weary, 'Look, this job is the first decent one I've had since leaving prison. I have my little girl to think of now; I'm hardly going to throw that away by killing some random bloke, am I?'

'A random bloke you claim never to have met.' said Warren.

'Why would I? I never meet the guests. I just come in, do my job then go home.'

Warren waited a beat. 'OK, fair enough. What time did you leave that night?'

'As I said before, I finished a bit after ten.'

'And how did you get home?' asked Ruskin.

'I cycle. I only live a few miles away, and the exercise does me good. Besides, the buses cost a fortune and they're never on time.'

Warren frowned and made a show of flicking through his notes. 'I don't see any record of a cyclist coming in and out of the reception area.'

'You wouldn't. I come in through the gap in the hedge by the service road.'

'Ah, where the camera is broken.'

Kimpton paused. 'I wouldn't know about that.'

'I assume that you lock your bike to the railings in the staff car park, and enter through the loading bay?'

'Yes, that's right.'

'So how do you leave? We have footage of you coming in through there that night, but nothing of you leaving.'

Kimpton licked his lips but said nothing.

'In fact, we've replayed all of the footage for the past week, and whilst we see you coming in through the loading bay at the start of your shifts, we haven't seen you exit once, by either the loading bay or the main reception. How are you leaving the building, Nicholas?'

Warren and Ruskin sat silently. Kimpton folded his hands in his lap, but not before Warren saw the slight tremble, and the faint sheen of sweat they left behind on the table's smooth surface.

Eventually, Kimpton cleared his throat. 'The alarm on the fire exit hasn't worked for months. I leave through there.'

'The fire exit under the broken CCTV camera?' asked Warren.

'If you say so.'

'And have you reported the broken alarm?'

He paused. 'Not really.'

Warren made a noise at the back of his throat. 'I see. Not really. Why not?'

Kimpton licked his lips. 'Just lazy, I guess. It's easier to leave through that door.'

'Is that all?' asked Warren.

'And you can go out there for a crafty fag.'

'Because the CCTV cameras are broken and no one can see you?'

'Yes,' Kimpton's voice was soft.

'How did you know?' asked Ruskin.

'How did I know what?'

'That the cameras are broken and the alarm doesn't work?'

Kimpton paused. Warren could see that his mind was spinning furiously. 'I overheard someone mention it.'

'Who?' pressed Ruskin.

'I can't remember.'

*

'He knows he's backed himself into a corner,' said Sutton, who along with the rest of the team had been watching the interview remotely.

146

'He has form for violence and drug dealing,' said Ruskin. 'If Anish was visiting that hotel on a regular basis to pick up drugs, maybe Kimpton is his supplier? Maybe they got into some sort of disagreement.' His voice grew more excited. 'That comment about losing a finger over five hundred quid was interesting, especially given what happened to Anish.'

Ruskin looked around the room, and his enthusiasm dimmed.

'Seems a bit of a strange setup to me,' said Sutton. 'If Anish was going to the hotel regularly to pick up drugs, why would he book a room for the night? That doesn't make sense. Surely he'd just turn up, buy the drugs and leave?'

'And if he was buying drugs, he wasn't buying very much,' said Richardson. 'I've been comparing the images of him arriving and leaving from the hotel, and that backpack he's carrying has barely changed in shape. There isn't much in there.'

'Well Kimpton is not an idiot, he knows how the system works,' said Sutton. 'I reckon that was our only shot at interviewing him without some bloody solicitor telling him to no comment when we ask him to confirm his name and date of birth.'

Warren agreed. Kimpton had been out the door like the proverbial rat up a drainpipe the moment Warren had finally given up trying to elicit the name of the person who told him about the broken fire exit.

'Well, we're not done with him, but in the meantime, I think it's time to have a word with the hotel handyman, Leon Grime. And whilst we're at it, let's bring in Kimpton's kitchen hand, Shane Moore, and see what he has to say for himself.'

*

Middlesbury Rental Vehicles was an independent firm specialising in short-term rentals for small vans and cars, and longer-term leases of mid-size vans and lorries. It was based on the East Lane Industrial Estate.

Richard Latham was a late-middle-aged man of average build with a comfortable-looking beer belly and a shock of grey hair. He closed the book of crosswords he was working on as soon as Hardwick introduced herself.

'You said that Anish Patel hired a car from you a couple of weeks ago.'

'Yeah, he's been renting cars from us about once a month since the start of the year. According to our records, he always returns them in perfect condition with a full-tank, or near as damn it.'

'So, what happened this time?'

Latham shrugged. 'Returned first thing the following day. We weren't open when he turned up, so he left it parked outside and posted the keys in our secure drop box. The tank was almost full and there was no damage.'

'Is that normal?'

Latham pinched his lip thoughtfully, before shaking his head. 'I'll be honest, I can't remember. Customers tend to book online or by phone, so I don't bust a gut to open the shop early unless somebody has arranged a morning pick-up; I work shifts down the homeless shelter in the evening so I like a bit of a lie-in if I can get it. Rental usually ends at midday, so I check all the vehicles are back by that time, give them a quick once-over, and ring around if somebody is late or hasn't filled the tank.'

'And did that ever happen with Mr Patel?'

'No, like I said, he's a good customer. To be honest, the late fine is a bit of a joke. As long as they don't bring it back half-empty or after we've closed for the evening, I usually waive it. With both Hertz and Europcar down the road, we try not to annoy customers too much.'

'Did he pay on a credit card?' asked Hardwick. She was almost certain that the answer was no, but if Anish did have another card that they were unaware of, it would answer a few questions.

'No, cash, but we ring-fence a deposit against the card we have on file.'

She handed over a copy of the photograph that they had borrowed from the Patels. 'Do you recognise this man?'

Latham looked at the picture carefully. 'Yeah, that's him.' His expression turned to one of embarrassment. 'I'm sorry I didn't call earlier. I'll be honest, I don't watch the news these days. It's all about bloody Brexit and the new Prime Minister. Too damned depressing. My youngest daughter saw his face in the *Middlesbury Reporter* and thought he looked familiar.'

'Were you the one that served him?'

'Yeah. He used our online booking page, then came by Thursday evening.'

'And how did he seem?'

Latham shrugged. 'Normal. He paid the cash, picked up the keys as usual and drove off.'

'Do you know what he needed the car for?' asked Hardwick.

'No idea. I know he doesn't go far in it, it rarely has more than a couple of dozen miles on the clock.'

'I don't suppose you have any CCTV footage of the drop box?' asked Hardwick, she'd noticed a couple of cameras on the outside of the building, and in the reception area where they were currently talking.

'No, I'm sorry. We tried to fit one, but there's nowhere to attach it that can't be easily vandalised.'

Hardwick repressed a sigh; that would have been too easy. 'Can you give me the details of the car that he hired?'

'Sure, I can print it out for you.' He turned to his computer, manipulating the mouse. He gestured towards a laser printer on the far end of the counter.

The car was a white Ford Focus; basic specification, about three years old.

'Where is the car now?'

Latham returned his attention to the computer. His face fell. 'Oh dear.'

*

'Scotland!' Grayson dropped into his chair.

'Sorry, Sir, the current renters of the car are on a driving holiday of the UK.' Warren winced. His own response had been much the same when Hardwick had returned from Middlesbury Rental Vehicles. 'They booked it for two weeks last Sunday. The good news is that Police Scotland have already tracked them down and impounded the vehicle, but who knows what's happened to any forensics over the past few days.'

Grayson groaned. 'How long will it take to bring it back here?'

'It's already on the back of a low-loader, but they're right out in the sticks. We're looking at tomorrow morning at the earliest,' Warren paused. 'We've also agreed that when our Scottish colleagues return, they will take a replacement car back to the couple – they're already going that way anyway ...'

Latham had been crestfallen that his car would be impounded, and doubly upset when the German couple currently renting it had threatened to write a scathing review on TripAdvisor if they didn't get a replacement vehicle the next day.

'Dare I ask how much that's going to cost?' asked Grayson.

'You'll probably be happier not knowing. On the plus side, we've solved the mystery of Anish Patel's missing Mercedes. He left it, along with the keys, with the owner of the car hire place. It's been sitting in their car park for the past ten days.'

Chapter 19

'He was a bit shifty, but I can't quite put my finger on why,' admitted Karen Hardwick after she and Moray Ruskin had finished interviewing Shane Moore, the seventeen-year-old catering student who assisted Nicholas Kimpton in the kitchen of the Easy Break Hotel.

'He confirms what Kimpton has already told us,' continued Ruskin. 'They do split shifts, finishing the evening shift around nine-thirty, out the door by about ten. They have serving staff to take the food out, so they spend all night in the kitchen with just the occasional loo or fag break. It's usually so quiet he plays on his mobile phone or they go through some of Kimpton's old cookery books.'

'There's a little bit of hero-worship going on there,' warned Hardwick, 'so bear that in mind. It sounds as though Moore looks up to him as a bit of a mentor.'

'Did he mention the fire exit?' asked Warren.

'Yes. Reluctantly,' said Ruskin. 'He admitted that everyone knew that the fire door had been tampered with. The hotel manager has tried to clamp down on cigarette breaks, so everyone turns a blind eye. Kimpton uses it himself.'

'Gut feeling?' said Warren.

'He was honest, up to a point,' said Ruskin.

'I agree, I think there may be more he's not telling us,' said Hardwick. 'He broke eye contact when we brought up the fire exit. I wouldn't be the least bit surprised to find out that there's a bit of drug-dealing taking place.'

Warren considered what they had told him. 'Well, given that we have yet to work out where Anish Patel got the cash that he preferred to use instead of his bank cards, you have to wonder if there is a connection. Kimpton has previous for drugs.

'Good work, both of you. It may be something or it may be nothing; we'll bring him back in again if we need to.'

At that moment, Warren's desk phone rang: Andy Harrison.

Waving his thanks to the two constables, he listened intently to what the crime scene manager had to say, before hanging up and accessing his email. Moments later he headed straight for Tony Sutton's cubicle.

'Any sign of Leon Grime, yet?'

'Should be here any minute, Boss,' replied Sutton.

'Good.' He held up the tablet computer on which he'd opened the photographs Harrison had emailed to him. 'Take a look at these before you speak to him, I think you'll be interested.'

*

Leon Grime was in his late forties, with several days' stubble. He'd arrived at the station looking more curious than nervous.

Grime's hands were gnarled and pitted, his nails dirty – the hands of a manual worker. Were they also the hands of a killer? Tony Sutton pushed that thought away, not wanting his suspicions to show on his face and scare Grime. The longer Sutton could keep him relaxed and cooperating, the better.

'Thanks very much for giving up your day off to help us, Mr Grime,' started Ruskin, smiling at him.

'Of course, anything I can do to help. Terrible thing that happened,' he continued. His voice was surprisingly soft, traces

152

of a North East accent lingering. Grime apologised profusely for taking so long to come into the station.

'You caught me on the way back from Newcastle. I try and pop up and see Mam about once a month; I had a bit of holiday needed using, so I went up Thursday and came back this morning. I took a bit of fresh veg up for the home; just some cabbages and sprouts. The residents love it.'

Sutton wondered if Grime was like David Hutchinson, who had also moved from the North when he was young? Pure east of England until he'd had a few pints or Newcastle United were playing, when he suddenly sounded like he'd just come wading out of the River Tyne.

'First of all, do you recognise this man?' asked Ruskin, pushing a tablet computer showing a headshot of Anish Patel across the table.

'Oh, aye, I've seen him on the telly. That's the poor sod from room 201.'

'And did you know him at all?' he asked.

'No, never met him. I hear he was a regular, like, but I rarely see the guests. Purely behind the scenes, me.'

'I believe you're in charge of maintenance,' said Sutton.

'Yeah, pretty much. Facilities Manager is my actual title, but basically I'm a handyman. Been there sixteen years. I keep the place running, fix anything that needs fixing. A bit of plumbing, a little bit of electrical. Painting, decorating, you name it really.'

'What were you doing Thursday the 24th and the Friday?' asked Sutton. 'Were you working those days?'

'Aye, just the usual. Couple of blocked toilets on the Thursday morning, then I spent the rest of the day and Friday doing a bit of refurb up on the fourth floor: new LED lighting to save a bit on the leccy bill, and some painting. Nothing too fancy.'

'What about 201? Have you done that recently?' asked Ruskin.

Grime frowned. 'It's been a couple of years since we spruced up the second floor. I don't remember any issues with the plumbing in there recently, so I would say it's been a few months since I've been in.'

'What time did you finish those days?' asked Sutton.

'Five o'clock. Just enough time to get home, have my tea, and then off to the Newlands to play a bit of pool. I had a league game on the Thursday. Friday I just sank a few with me mates.'

'And what time did you get there?'

Grime pursed his lips. 'On Thursday, the game started at six-thirty. Then I stuck around for a couple of pints. Friday, I probably got there about seven.' He gave a shrug. 'No work in the morning, so I probably stayed a bit later than I should have. At least that's what the missus said.'

If Grime realised they were establishing if he had an alibi, he didn't seem especially bothered. Did that make him innocent or arrogant?

'Tell me Mr Grime, would you also be in charge of maintaining the CCTV cameras?' asked Sutton.

'No, that's the job of the CCTV firm. Look, is this about that bloody camera over the fire exit? I've been on at them for ages to fix that thing, but they can't figure out what the problem is. They just keep on saying it's an old system that needs upgrading. And surprise, surprise, they can sell and install us one for a small fortune,' he snorted. 'That isn't going to happen, not under the current owners.'

'And what about the fire door?' asked Ruskin.

'What about it?' For the first time since he'd arrived, Grime broke eye contact.

'It has a broken lock and the alarm has been disconnected,' said Sutton.

'Really? I had no idea,' said Grime, but his voice had lost its confidence.

'Forensics have had a look at the alarm,' said Ruskin. 'Somebody just bypassed the wiring to make the door think it's closed when it's not. Also, the lock has been tampered with, so it doesn't actually lock when you clash the door. You can't open it from the outside, there's no handle. But since there's no alarm, you could just prop it open to make sure you don't get locked outside.'

'I had no idea,' said Grime. 'But that explains the fag ends outside. I'll bet the cheeky bastards have been using it for a crafty smoke.'

Sutton chuckled. 'Well, all credit to them for doing their best.' He shook his head. 'I tell you, if some people put half as much effort into doing their job as they do skiving off …'

Grime joined in with the laughter. 'Yeah. Well thanks for letting me know. They'll be pissed off when I fix it Monday.'

'Anyway, moving on,' said Sutton, reaching over and swiping the screen of the tablet. 'Do you recognise this?'

Grime squinted at the screen. 'Looks like my toolbox.'

'Are you sure?'

Grime looked a little closer. 'Yeah, I recognise the paint spots,' he pointed. 'It also has my initials on the handle.'

'Can you tell me what tools are normally in the box?' asked Ruskin.

'Wait, what is this about?' asked Grime, starting to look nervous.

'Just answer the question if you don't mind, Leon,' said Sutton.

Grime shrugged. 'Mostly the stuff it came with. Screwdrivers, hex keys, a tape measure, hammer.' He frowned in concentration. 'Christ, it's like the Generation Game,' he laughed nervously. Sutton and Ruskin said nothing.

Grime continued. 'Um, pliers, an adjustable spanner. I think that's mostly it.'

'Nothing else?'

'I swapped one of the screwdrivers for an electrical-testing one, and I added some wire strippers.'

'What about a knife?' asked Ruskin.

'Chucked it, it was crap. I bought a decent Stanley knife which fits in the same space.'

Sutton swiped to a picture of the toolbox opened up. There were empty spaces in the moulded plastic insert.

'Can you tell me where the hammer and the Stanley knife are? They don't appear to be in there.'

Grime frowned. 'I've no idea. I'm sure they were in there the last time I checked.'

'When was that?' asked Ruskin.

Grime glanced upwards, as if trying to remember. 'I've mostly been painting and decorating lately. I fitted some new energy-saving lights, but I used my electric screwdriver for that,' he shrugged. 'Sorry, could have been a couple of weeks.'

'And do you take your toolbox home with you?' asked Ruskin.

'No, I leave it in my office.' His eyes narrowed. 'Which is where you probably found it.'

Sutton swiped the screen again. 'Are these your tools?'

Grime blanched. The hammer and the Stanley knife were laid out on a table, next to a ruler. Under the bright light that the photo had been taken under, there was no mistaking the blood on both tools. The paint spots matched those on the toolbox.

'Shit.' He swallowed hard. 'Look, everyone knows the combination to my office, anyone could wander in there and help themselves to my tools.'

'Of course,' said Sutton. 'The CSIs saw that when they went in.' He gave him a reassuring smile.

'Going back to that dodgy CCTV camera,' said Ruskin. 'You said that the CCTV company can't work out what's wrong with it?'

'Yeah, that's right.'

'Well they aren't much good.' He swiped the tablet again. 'This is a photo of the junction box near the fire exit. The cable from the camera leads into it.'

Sutton watched Grime's face carefully.

Ruskin swiped the screen again. 'Now I'm no technical expert, but even I know that if you disconnect the aerial lead you lose the picture. Which is what appears to have happened here.'

Grime swallowed. 'Cheeky bastards. They were going to charge us a fortune to replace the system.'

Sutton shook his head in disgust. 'I'm thinking of getting a system at home, I'll have to steer clear of those buggers. Who did you say they were again?'

'North Hertfordshire Security Solutions,' said Grime.

'I know it,' said Ruskin. 'In fact, I called them earlier. And you'll never guess what they said?'

Grime said nothing, his Adam's apple bobbing up and down.

'They said that they haven't had any complaints at all from you,' continued Ruskin. 'In fact, they haven't had any contact with you since the service contract expired two years ago. Now why is that?'

Grime licked his lips.

'Whilst we're at it, could you also tell us why the inside of the junction box for the CCTV, including the cable connector, is covered in your fingerprints?' asked Sutton.

Grime said nothing.

'Not to mention the wiring to the alarm on the fire exit,' said Ruskin.

When Grime finally found his voice it cracked, his tongue thick in his mouth. 'I think I'd like to speak to a lawyer.'

'I think that's a very wise decision, Mr Grime,' said Sutton. He raised his voice, making sure that the microphones picked him up clearly.

'Leon Grime, you are under arrest on suspicion of the murder of Anish Patel …'

Chapter 20

The arrest of Leon Grime had given the investigation a much-needed adrenaline jolt, although nobody was under any illusions that the end was near.

'Search teams are looking over Leon Grime's house and car,' said Sutton. 'Nothing yet, but it's early days.'

'Have any links been identified between Anish and Grime yet?' asked Warren.

'We've had a data dump from his phone handset and from the phone companies,' said Pymm. 'The handset data is being analysed down in Welwyn, but you know what the backlog is like. However, I haven't found any calls or texts between Grime and Anish, or any members of his family, at least on the numbers that we have for them.'

'I've run the number plates of Anish's hire car through the ANPR system,' said Richardson. 'It's picked up at the junction before the hotel at 18:25, three minutes before Anish enters the hotel. The car is then logged again the following morning at 06:47. Again, just a couple of minutes after we see him leave through the hotel entrance.'

'Which doesn't leave him very long to get mugged or attacked outside the hotel,' said Ruskin.

'It's not impossible,' said Hardwick. 'If they were standing by the hotel entrance, or even hidden behind his car, and they were armed …'

The team were quiet for a few moments before Sutton broke the silence. 'If it wasn't for that damned bed sheet and the tools, I'd be tempted to dismiss the hotel connection entirely, but it's too much of a coincidence.' He turned to Richardson. 'Did any other cars follow him through that junction? Could somebody have followed him from the hotel, with the bed sheet and Leon Grime's tools?'

'We're looking into that,' confirmed Richardson. 'Traffic was still light that time of morning, so we're identifying every vehicle that passed through that junction.'

'Play it safe,' said Warren. 'If it was another guest at the hotel, they could have checked in a few days beforehand. Let's see if we can link guests to cars.'

'In that case, we should probably also record cars that leave some time after Anish,' said Hutchinson. 'If the killer did take him in the car park, then they might have needed to retrieve their own car after they killed him and disposed of his body.'

'Then we'll also need plate numbers of cars travelling back towards the hotel and CCTV from the bus company,' said Richardson. 'That's a lot of data.'

'Probably better to have it and not need it, than not to have it,' said Sutton.

'Was the hire car photographed again that day?' asked Warren. 'It would be useful to know what time it was returned to the rental place; that might help us narrow down the time of death. The vehicle was apparently parked outside, and the keys dropped off before Mr Latham opened up late morning.'

'No,' said Richardson. 'There aren't any cameras up near the hire place, and once you've passed the traffic camera outside the hotel, you can drive there easily without being photographed. We didn't capture him on the Thursday either when he picked the car up.'

Warren fought down a hiss of frustration. 'We can't pin down when or how he died, since we don't know when he returned his hire car; he wasn't shot, stabbed or strangled and Prof. Jordan isn't convinced that the bump on his head caused enough trauma to kill him. If we can't even prove the cause of death, we're going to struggle to prove he was murdered.

'We don't know where it happened – the blood lividity patterns show that he was moved after he died, and the blood spatter at the dumping site indicates the mutilation was post-mortem, but there's no evidence that he was murdered in his own flat. And if he did die there, why would they wrap him in a sheet from the hotel? Why not use one of his own?

'And we still don't have a motive. An attempt to stop him cashing in on his inheritance? An online tryst that went too far? A drug deal gone wrong? None of the above?

'Until we've answered at least one of those questions, we aren't going to be able to prove who killed him, or if they acted alone. Leon Grime might be our man, but everything so far is circumstantial; we aren't even close to charging him yet.'

'Which begs the question: what are we going to do about Nicholas Kimpton?'

Warren sighed; Sutton was right to ask. Kimpton had left after his interview had concluded; Warren doubted they'd see him again without a solicitor in tow.

'Do we have any links between Kimpton and Anish?' he asked.

'I've checked the mobile phone number Kimpton gave us against Anish's phone records and haven't found any connections,' said Pymm. 'The warrant came through a couple of hours ago for Kimpton's records and I've done a quick search for numbers of interest. So far, no calls or texts to Anish or any of his family members. None to any of the numbers we got from Rainbow Hookups, or Latika Luthra for that matter. There are a number of calls and texts to Leon Grime, however.'

'When?' asked Warren.

'None in the fortnight preceding the murder, or since,' said Pymm.

'They've worked at the same place for over a year, they could just be mates,' Hutchinson pointed out.

'I agree, but look into it,' Warren ordered. 'I don't think we have anything we can use to justify arresting him. My gut tells me he's dodgy, and I wouldn't be in the least bit surprised to find out that he's been moving drugs or stolen property through that fire exit, but that's not what we're investigating.'

'And the kitchen hand Shane Moore did claim that Kimpton was busy Friday morning,' said Hardwick.

'As did other witnesses,' added Hutchinson. 'Breakfast was served at the usual time; it's hard to see when he could have snuck out of the kitchen and killed Anish.'

'But you did say that you thought Shane Moore wasn't being entirely honest, Karen,' said Sutton.

'I got the impression that he knew more than he was letting on,' admitted Hardwick. 'But that could just have been because he didn't want to get anyone into trouble. We're investigating a murder; he might not have thought a bit of drug dealing through a broken fire exit was relevant.'

'Well, let's not dismiss Kimpton or Moore entirely,' said Warren. 'Even if their alibis hold up, we'll look at pulling them back in again in future and leaning on them. With Grime arrested, they might just remember something else.'

'Could Kimpton have killed Anish between his shifts on Friday?' asked Ruskin. 'Anish dropped the car back before the hire place opened. He should have popped back to pick up his own car later. Kimpton could have easily killed him in that window.'

'But why?' asked Sutton. 'We don't have a motive yet. And why kill him after he had left the hotel?'

'Didn't want it linking back to his place of work?' suggested Hutchinson. 'I doubt the killer expected us to connect the bed sheet to the hotel. Even if we found out that he'd stayed at the hotel that night, if he was killed after he left, why would we link the two events? And what about this flu business? Was it real, or was Anish skiving off work to do something else that day? Did his killer know?'

'In which case, did he send that text to work, or did his killer?' asked Ruskin.

'If Anish wasn't meeting his killer, how would Kimpton have known where Anish was at that time?' said Richardson. 'We have no evidence that they even knew each other, and if we believe that Kimpton didn't leave the hotel until after his shift had finished, Anish was long gone by that point. He should have been back in his sick bed.'

'Anish didn't use his credit card to check in,' pointed out Pymm. 'And he used a false name, so he couldn't have been tracked down that way.'

Warren gave a sigh. 'OK. Kimpton remains on the suspect board, but we can't justify his arrest yet. Keep Shane Moore up there as a person of interest, also.'

*

Warren inhaled the aroma of John Grayson's finest coffee gratefully. Beside him, Tony Sutton took a swig of the decaffeinated brew that the detective superintendent had recently started stocking just for him. It was a gesture that Sutton appreciated.

'All of the taste, none of the kick,' he said. 'You really should try it, Rachel.'

'I'm good, thanks,' said Pymm, her hands folded around the glass mug that Warren was convinced she used deliberately just to show off the brown, leafy mess that she favoured. His nose couldn't give him any suggestions as to what she was drinking today.

'There's no sign of any of these contacts from Rainbow Hookups on the CCTV?' asked Grayson.

'None,' said Warren. 'If they are coming in, then they're entering via the fire exit with the broken camera.'

'Tell me more about these mysterious visits that Anish Patel has been making to this hotel,' said Grayson.

Despite the presence of Leon Grime in custody, and the suspicions the team had about Anish's family, they were still pursuing other leads. With no definite motive, ruling out anything at this early stage would be premature.

Warren deferred to Pymm. It had taken her team much of the afternoon to work out the dates that Patel had stayed at the Easy Break Hotel. The lack of a credit card and his habit of using an assumed name had muddied the waters somewhat, but eventually they had a list of dates.

'The pattern we have established is that roughly once a month, always on a Thursday, he hires a car after work, then checks into the Easy Break Hotel under the name of Smith, paying cash. He asks for – and usually gets – room 201. It's at the furthest end of the corridor from the elevator, and the hotel typically allocates rooms sequentially, moving away from the lift.'

She took another sip of her drink. 'Once in the room he doesn't receive any visitors that the hotel is aware of, doesn't order room service – such as it is – and doesn't show his face in the bar. The next morning, he checks out by depositing his keycard and skips the complimentary breakfast. He then returns the car he's hired, either in person before the midday deadline, or by dropping the keys off before the hire place opens and retrieving his own vehicle after he finishes work.'

'Do we know what he does then?' asked Grayson.

'According to HR where he works, he is normally in on time the Friday following his Thursday night outing; there are no black marks against his name for lateness. In fact, the Friday he was killed is the first time he has rung in sick for months, and that previous occasion didn't coincide with one of his hotel visits.'

'What about the other guests?' asked Grayson.

'Nothing,' said Sutton. 'The good news is that Anish was the only person paying cash that night. Everyone else used a credit card, so Hutch's team have made contact. The rooms either side of him were unoccupied and nobody reported any disturbances. The duty log has nothing more exciting than somebody calling to report a dripping shower head. Nobody recognises him, so it doesn't sound as though he was wandering around the hotel late that night.'

Grayson leaned back in his chair, cleaning under his nails with a golf tee. 'What about his mobile phone?'

'What we have seen is that it is normal for him to turn off his phone before he arrives at the hotel, and it doesn't usually get switched back on until sometime the following morning, so we have no tracking data,' said Pymm. 'Why he does this isn't clear, but there is little or no phone signal in the hotel. They do provide free WiFi, so he may be using internet-based methods to communicate with other parties.'

'But not if his phone was off, surely?' questioned Grayson, indicating that he was paying more attention than it appeared.

'No, but it's possible that rather than turning the handset off completely, he might have switched to flight mode and then reactivated the wireless,' said Sutton.

'Seems a bit elaborate,' remarked Grayson.

'That's what's bothering us,' admitted Warren. 'We know that he has something of an obsession with spy novels and movies. Whatever his reasons are for being at that hotel, it looks as though he was using it as an opportunity to live out his fantasies as a spy.'

Grayson grunted. 'All fun and games until some bugger bumps you off and you've made it more difficult for the police to track down your killer.'

He drained his coffee and placed the mug on a coaster advertising a golfing supplier. 'Even if we don't know the details, the link to the hotel is indisputable,' he said. 'You've uncovered some

164

strong potential motives for why his family might want him dead, so what's their connection?'

'Unclear,' admitted Warren. 'None of their vehicles have been spotted nearby during the period we're interested in, and the tyres at the dumping site definitely don't match the type of vehicles they drive. None of them have appeared on the hotel CCTV. If they are involved, we've yet to place them there physically. They could have come in through that fire exit of course, but that means they would need to have known about it, so we're trying to establish if there is a relationship between them and Leon Grime or anyone else working there.'

Grayson said nothing. He didn't need to. 'Tell me more about this LGBTQ dating app,' he said eventually.

Sutton quickly filled in the DSI.

'And the text messages that Anish sent and received from these contacts don't entirely match the dates that he checked into the hotel?' said Grayson.

'A couple are two or three days beforehand, but it's tenuous,' said Pymm.

'I assume that the phones are unregistered?'

'Yeah,' said Warren, 'which is hardly surprising, I imagine that at least some of the people using that site are playing away from home.'

Grayson gave a long sigh. 'I can see why you're interested, but I know what the magistrate is going to say.'

'Not enough to authorise a real-time trace,' said Pymm.

'Realistically, it's the only way to track them down,' said Warren. 'We can't call the numbers that they gave to Anish and see who answers, we may as well stick up a wanted poster; if one of them is the killer, he'll vanish the second he thinks we're onto him. The headshots on Rainbow Hookups may be useful if we get a suspect but are next to useless otherwise. The staff at the hotel claim not to recognise them, but you only have to see Anish's profile picture to know that they are somewhat flattering.'

Grayson said nothing, just continued picking under his nails. Finally, he looked up.

'I can get you a warrant to look at their phone's call history, and I know a magistrate who will probably authorise historic location data, but I can't see her signing off on real-time tracking until you can bring me more. Sorry, best I can do.'

Sunday 4th December

Chapter 21

Warren was in early the following morning. He'd spent most of the previous night tossing and turning, regretting his late-night acceptance of John Grayson's coffee. Susan had already been sound asleep, so he'd headed to the spare room: another missed opportunity to speak about the subject they were both avoiding.

Compounding his low mood, he'd just received an email from one of the staff members at Granddad Jack's home. The attached video showed Jack, dressed in a baggy reindeer jumper, singing 'Jingle Bells' alongside other residents and their relatives at the home's Christmas family event the previous day. The video had brought a smile to his face and a lump to his throat. A glimpse of Bernice and Denis in the background had eased the pain somewhat, but it was times like this he cursed the hundred-mile distance between them. He absolutely had to get up there to take part in some of their pre-Christmas festivities.

Dropping some money into the old coffee pot that served as an honesty jar for the communal coffee fund, he heard it clink against the coins already in there. As usual most, if not all of them, were his. He noted that there was a pound coin in there that hadn't been there the day before. Perhaps one of his colleagues had actually paid for their coffee? Or more likely they'd just swapped it for a couple of fifty-pence to use in the rather temperamental vending machine.

Turning to leave, he almost slopped coffee down the front of Karen Hardwick.

'Sorry, Boss, didn't mean to sneak up on you like that,' she apologised.

'My fault, I was away with the fairies,' said Warren, pushing down the reflexive feeling of awkwardness he felt every time he spoke to her. It had been over two years since her fiancé Gary Hastings had been killed so violently. It had taken many sessions with the force's occupational health service before he had finally started to accept what everyone from the Assistant Chief Constable to his team and Karen herself had told him repeatedly: that Hastings' death was not his fault.

'Everything OK, Karen?' he asked, noting the dark circles under her eyes. Her hair, as usual, was tied back in a ponytail, but a few stray wisps had already worked their way loose. Her suit jacket looked slightly creased and he noticed that despite the early hour, the collar of her white blouse had a smudge on it.

She gave a weary sigh that turned into a yawn halfway through.

'Teething,' she stated. 'Not me, Ollie, but it may as well be me since if he's awake, I'm awake,' she gestured at her rumpled appearance. 'And then, to say thank you for staying up most of the night with him, he decided to bring up his breakfast on me as I gave him a last cuddle before leaving for work.'

Warren winced. 'Ouch, not what you need.'

Hardwick gave a short barking laugh. 'Yeah, of course the little sod never does it to his grandparents. Mum just texted me to say he's running around happy as anything and has just scoffed a whole banana.' She shook her head. 'I tell you what, Sir, I love him to bits obviously, but some days I do envy those of you who don't have kids.'

Warren smiled tightly. 'Well, try and get home at a decent hour and maybe Ollie will let you sleep tonight. In the meantime, there's always coffee.'

Hardwick nodded as he left, a sudden flash of embarrassment colouring her cheeks. Her tiredness notwithstanding, how could she have been so insensitive? Nobody had said anything obviously, but it didn't take a detective to realise that a couple that age, happily married for so long, might not be childless by choice. The tightness of his smile and the brief flash of sadness in his eyes had all but confirmed it.

And just as she felt that he had finally started to become more comfortable in her presence. She groaned. It wasn't even 8 a.m. Could the day get any worse?

*

Back at his desk, Warren winced at the bitter taste of the black coffee. Two spoonful's of granules when there was no milk left might have been unwise, but he had a feeling the caffeine hit would be necessary. Forcing away the unintentional sting from Hardwick's words, and biting into a custard cream, he opened his emails.

The previous night's search of Leon Grime's second-floor flat that he shared with his wife had thrown up some clothing with suspicious-looking red stains.

By all accounts, Grime's wife had been rather uncooperative, refusing to answer any questions. She'd been even less happy to be dispatched to stay with her sister overnight, wearing nothing but the clothes on her back.

Warren stifled a yawn. The duty solicitor had arrived late and unsurprisingly advised Grime to stop speaking and no comment. The lawyer had quite rightly pointed out that the evidence so far was circumstantial at best, and Warren was conscious of the fact that they were nowhere near the charging threshold. In fact, unless they pulled something out of the bag within the next few hours they might not even be able to extend his custody beyond twenty-four hours.

Warren's day didn't improve any.

'We've had teams showing photos around all the bars and nightclubs in the area, especially those popular with the gay community,' said Hutchinson at the lunchtime briefing. 'Nobody recognised Anish or any of the headshots from Rainbow Hookups, although given the quality of them, that's hardly surprising.

'We've also got multiple witnesses that say Leon Grime was at work all of Friday until his usual knocking off time around 5 p.m., and Mags' team have found snippets of CCTV footage around the hotel from throughout the day. It also looks as if he's right about not using his toolbox; every time they capture him on camera he's carrying ladders or decorating kit.'

Warren looked at his watch. 'Well we've got a few more hours to turn up something useful.' He turned to Sutton. 'How do you fancy giving his cage another rattle?'

*

'I think Leon Grime is trying to run down the custody clock,' said Sutton. 'I'll bet his solicitor has told him to keep quiet and see if we have enough to charge him or get an extension.'

Warren and Sutton were standing by the coffee urn.

'That's not decaf,' warned Warren, as Sutton picked up the metal tin of instant coffee.

'Seriously? You're storing regular coffee in a decaf tin, just to stop Rachel nagging you about how much caffeine you drink?'

Warren shrugged. 'What she doesn't know won't hurt her.

Sorry, I should have said.' He opened the cupboard above and removed a glass jar. 'Use this, it's labelled correctly.'

Sutton took the jar and helped himself to a custard cream. 'At least you're man enough not to give in on the biscuits.'

Coffees in hand, the two men headed back towards the office.

'Speaking of Rachel, I see you managed to get her to go home in time for Sunday lunch,' said Sutton. 'Did she put up much of a fight?'

'No more than usual,' said Warren.

Pymm's MS was the relapsing-remitting form of the disease, meaning that she enjoyed lengthy periods of relative good health, interrupted by bouts of debilitating illness. Stress, mild infections and fatigue were all known triggers. Pymm didn't like being told to take it easy, but Warren had made it clear that he had no choice in the matter, if for no other reason than he was her line manager and responsible for her well-being.

'I told her if she didn't go home and eat it fresh, I'd invite myself around and eat it for her.'

'I'd have joined you,' said Sutton; Martin Pymm's prowess in the kitchen was legendary. 'We don't usually bother with a roast if Josh isn't here. He's visiting his girlfriend's parents this weekend.'

'How long has he been seeing her now?' asked Warren.

'Over six months.'

'You'll be choosing a hat soon,' joked Warren.

'Hah, not for a while yet, but he could do a lot worse.'

'I think you're right about Grime running down the clock,' said Warren as they settled in his office. 'He's correct that anyone could have used that toolkit, and the keys to the laundry cupboard hang in plain sight in the office off reception. All we really have on him are his lies about the dodgy camera and door alarm. If we don't get anything soon, we're going to have to release him on bail, and I'm still coming up blank on a motive.'

'Well, he's clearly got something to hide,' said Sutton.

'The question is whether it's to do with the murder, or

something else,' said Warren. 'That CCTV camera has been broken for ages. Whatever reason he had for ensuring it wasn't fixed can't just have been to conceal the murderer's comings and goings that night.'

'Just a happy coincidence then,' said Sutton.

Warren's desk phone rang. He looked at the caller ID. 'Andy Harrison. Fingers crossed he has something.'

Warren picked up the handset and put it on speaker.

'We've finished processing Anish Patel's room at the Easy Break Hotel. Hundreds of partial fingerprints, including a few that are definitely Anish's. We've also got a few hundred more from other areas of the hotel. It won't be cheap processing this many prints, I'll need authorisation.'

Warren tapped his teeth. In theory, a murder investigation came with a blank cheque, but in practice Major Crime had not managed to escape the swingeing budget cuts that had decimated the rest of the police service. Andy Harrison had been right to seek authorisation before expending so much money and resources. Warren considered the suggestion for a moment, before deciding to kick the decision upstairs; that's what superintendents got paid for.

'We also found something that may or may not be interesting,' said Harrison. 'Just above the TV there is a small patch of fresh paint. It looks the same as the stuff already on the walls, but a little shinier. I'd say it's only a couple of weeks old at most. The paint is covering up Polyfilla – the walls are made of plasterboard and there was a drill hole a little over a centimetre in diameter that has since been filled in.'

Sutton and Warren looked at each other. 'Leon Grime claims he hasn't been in 201 for months,' said Warren.

*

Conscious of the dwindling time remaining before they had to apply for an extension, Warren and Sutton decided to challenge

Grime immediately over the strange patch of fresh paint in room 201. Unfortunately, the handyman had been advised by his solicitor to 'no comment'. It was sound advice; the case against him was weak, with no obvious motive, and Warren worried that he would soon be walking.

Another call came through less than half an hour before Warren needed to plead his case for a custody extension. Hanging up, he went straight to Grayson's office. Unusually for a Sunday, the superintendent was working.

Too cold for golf, had been Sutton's suggestion, who made no secret of the fact that he thought Grayson was only hanging on in the hope of a final promotion before retirement to secure a bigger pension pot. Warren thought that was somewhat uncharitable, but there was no denying that the man spent a lot of time socialising with senior leadership outside of work hours.

Grayson was on the phone, but waved Warren in.

'Just filling in the brass on where we are,' he said after finishing.

'Forensics rang,' said Warren.

'I'm not seeing a smiling face.'

*

Walking back into the office, Warren called for quiet.

'The tyres on the hire car don't match any of the prints at the dumping site.'

A chorus of groans rippled around the room.

'The vehicle team at Welwyn looked at the tyres as soon as they received the car, and they aren't even the same manufacturer. The blood spot in room 201 has been confirmed as belonging to Anish and an attempt was made to clean it up, but Prof. Jordan is still doubtful that the bump on the back of his head was enough to kill him. Given that the CCTV shows Anish leaving the Easy Break Hotel on the Friday morning, it looks as though he returned the car before he was killed.'

The team had been hoping that Patel's hire car had been used to transport his body to the ditch where he had been dumped. Logically that would mean that the killer – or killers – had to have driven the car to the dumping site and then back to where it had been originally hired from. Warren knew from long experience that vehicles were a potential forensic goldmine. He'd really been hoping for something useful from the car.

'And we're certain we've got the right car?' asked one of the seconded detectives from Welwyn.

'I can only go by what Mr Latham told us,' said Hardwick. 'But he printed off the car's rental history and it looks as though it checks out.'

'So where and when did he meet his killer? And when was he killed?' asked Ruskin. 'There has to be some link to the Easy Break Hotel, the bed sheet and Leon Grime's tools can't be a coincidence.'

'Well unfortunately, the red stains on Leon Grime's clothes have tested negative for blood,' said Warren. 'So there's no easy link there.'

The news was disappointing, but not surprising. It would have been an incredible stroke of luck if Grime had kept the clothes that he had worn the night of Anish Patel's murder in his wardrobe. It would have been even more remarkable if he hadn't bothered to run them through the washing machine.

'They're still testing his shoes, coat and car, but we won't get anything back before we have to release him. Furthermore, none of the shoes we have recovered match any of the impressions on the grass verge next to the ditch. We've no choice, I'm afraid; I'm about to go and bail him.'

As Warren trudged down to the custody desk, the atmosphere he left behind him was sombre. That morning, they'd had a suspect in custody and were awaiting several promising forensic leads. Now it felt as though they'd gone back to the beginning.

Monday 5th December

Chapter 22

Warren spread the doughnuts across the briefing room table. It was a small gesture, but after the disappointment of the day before, it would boost their blood sugar, if not their morale, as they planned their next steps.

'I'm not ready to dismiss Nicholas Kimpton or Leon Grime just yet,' said Warren. 'But clearly our priority has to shift. We still need to work out exactly when, where, why and how, before we get to who.'

'The alibi of Latika Luthra, Anish's … girlfriend? Well anyway, it checks out,' said Hutchinson. 'She's a full-time English teacher and was at work both Thursday and Friday. Her mother confirms that she was in all of Thursday night doing her marking. Friday evening, she went to the pub after work for drinks and spent the weekend with friends.'

'That's confirmed by the location data on her phone,' said Pymm. 'I've also cross-referenced it against all of our numbers of interest, and there are no links. If she was involved somehow, she had the common sense to either use a burner phone or use a messaging app.'

'Thank you,' said Warren, turning next to Richardson.

'But maybe she wasn't the one with the motive,' said Pymm.

Warren fought down a sigh, as everyone around the table chuckled at Pymm's dramatic flair.

'Go on,' he said, returning his attention to her.

'Latika's father died just over three years ago. I looked up the probate records and in addition to the house he owned, he had a bit of money stashed away. According to the will, it all went to his wife in the first instance, with everything being split between their daughters on her death.'

'How much?' asked Warren, hiding his impatience at hearing information he already knew.

'About twenty-five thousand.'

'Which means that given the cost of private fertility treatment in the US, Latika would probably have had to borrow her sister's share of the inheritance also,' said Warren. 'Which is risky as their long-term plan relied on Gotam dying after she got pregnant, but before her mother passes.'

He looked closely at Pymm. 'What else have you got up your sleeve, Rachel?'

'I got a friend in Business and Fraud to do some sniffing around. Latika's sister's husband runs a small graphic design business. In June their biggest client went bust. That's left a significant hole in their income. What they really need is a cash injection of about twenty-thousand to get them over the next twelve months whilst they pitch for new business.'

'And who better to ask than the Bank of Mum?' said Sutton.

'Nice work. Get a small team to keep on looking into that,' said Warren. 'Over to you, Mags, assuming Rachel hasn't any more surprises.'

'We've retrieved the CCTV from the leisure centre that Anish was a member of,' said Richardson. 'First off, the morning of the Thursday that he went to the hotel looks pretty much normal compared to previous weeks. He arrived a little before seven-thirty, in a tracksuit, and came out just after eight-thirty in his suit. He exchanged a few words with the lad on the till and paid cash, then changed on his own in a private cubicle. He said hello, or nodded to a couple of the regulars, but I don't see any meaningful conversation. CCTV outside the entrance shows that he drove there in his own car.'

'What about his Monday fitness suite sessions?' asked Warren.

'We have videos for the last few weeks, but again nothing stands out. It's the same crowd each time, but they pretty much follow their own routine and hardly speak; Anish has his headphones in the whole time. I don't think it was a social thing, he just turned up, did his thing and got on with his day.'

Warren could sympathise with that. He and Susan had tried exercising together, but they found it a distraction. Warren had started running again over the summer but hadn't enjoyed it, particularly after the clocks had gone back. Maybe he should look into swimming instead?

'How did he look on that Thursday morning, given that he called in sick the next day?' asked Warren.

'Normal,' said Richardson. 'He seems to have been in there for the usual length of time, and he wasn't obviously sneezing or blowing his nose as he left.'

'That doesn't necessarily mean anything,' said Ruskin. 'Sometimes, if I'm coming down with a cold, I find a good swim clears my head.'

'True, but he didn't mention feeling ill at work,' said Sutton.

'So why did he text in sick on the Friday morning?' asked Hardwick. 'Was he planning to rendezvous with his killer that day?'

'If he was pulling a sicky, then either it was a last-minute thing, or he's an amateur; he doesn't seem to have laid the groundwork very well,' said Hutchinson. 'Surely he'd have been sneezing or complaining about feeling ill the day before?' He stopped and looked around the table. 'What? My brother-in-law's an expert skiver. I'm amazed no one has thought to look for a correlation between the football fixtures and his "Monday morning migraines".'

'I'll remember to check if Newcastle are playing the next time you start complaining you're feeling a bit under the weather,' replied Warren drily.

'We still don't know if Anish was alive when he sent those texts,' said Ruskin, after the laughter had died down. 'We think his killer sent the text on Saturday morning. We see Anish leaving the hotel at quarter to seven Friday morning and the first of those texts was sent at 7.18 a.m. He could have left the hotel and returned the car, then met his killer straight afterwards. That's not much time for him to be killed before his phone was switched back on and the text sent.'

'The text was sent from the vicinity of his flat,' said Pymm.

'Anish could have been forced by his killer to send the text and murdered later,' said Ruskin.

'If we go down that route, then he could have been killed after the Saturday text,' said Sutton.

It was a sobering thought. Had Anish been kept against his will for a prolonged period of time?

'Which again raises the question of how well he knew his killer,' said Hardwick. 'How else would they have known where he lived?'

'He'd hired a car, so presumably he had his driving licence on him, with his address printed on it,' pointed out Sutton.

'On the subject of how well he knew his killer, do we still think he lived alone?'

'I reckon so,' said Sutton. 'He had pretty much one of everything in the bathroom; it doesn't look as though anyone was staying over on a regular basis.'

'Which matches his supermarket trips to Tesco,' said Pymm. 'He paid cash, but he also used a Clubcard for the points. We've got some images of him from his past few trips and he's on his own; his purchases for the past year are consistent with a single person living alone. He also buys petrol at Tesco and considering how much of a gas-guzzler that Merc is, he doesn't fill up very often. The dealer he leases the car from says he drives barely five thousand miles a year.'

'Which makes you wonder why he even owns such a fancy car,' said Ruskin.

'Appearances,' said Sutton. 'It's all part of the playboy image he cultivated on social media.'

'It's an image that might have got him killed,' said Warren.

It was a sobering thought to end the meeting on and the team were subdued as they left. Walking past Pymm, Warren saw that she was scrolling through her email as she waited for the room to clear out – her body language made him pause.

'This just came in from traffic. I think you are going to be interested.'

Rachel Pymm pushed her glasses back onto her nose and directed Warren's attention to her screen.

'Audi A5 caught twice on the A506 on Tuesday the 29th at 12.32 and 12.52,' he read out, before pausing to picture the area.

'The car was clocked doing eighty-five along the fifty stretch heading towards Middlesbury, then doing seventy-two back out of Middlesbury towards Cambridge, twenty minutes later. That's about twenty-five minutes after you did the death knock at the Patels.'

'OK, why is this important?'

'Have a look at who owns the car,' said Pymm.

Warren squinted at the name. 'Is that …'

'Yes.'

'I think we need them in for a chat.'

Chapter 23

Kamala Patel was relaxed as she was led into the interview suite. The wife of Jaidev Patel had been briefly interviewed previously about the death of her husband's younger brother, but it was time to probe a bit deeper.

'I'm very sorry for your loss, Mrs Patel,' started Warren. 'I've asked you here to help us clear up a few things about Anish.'

'Of course, anything I can do to help.'

The woman had a slight accent familiar to Warren, so he decided to start the interview by putting her at ease.

'That sounds suspiciously like a Coventry accent, Mrs Patel.'

'Close enough. Nuneaton originally, although I've lived down here for so long I doubt most people would recognise it. I'm guessing you're from Coventry?'

'Guilty as charged, although I've only been here a few years. I still call bread rolls batches.'

Patel smiled. 'I've not heard that for a while.'

'Why don't you tell me a bit about Anish.'

The smile faded and Patel gave a sigh. Unlike her husband and in-laws, it took little probing for her to admit the tensions raised by Anish's sexuality, confirming that Manoj, the eldest son shared his father's disapproval, whilst his sister was more supportive.

184

'What about Jaidev?' Warren pressed.

'Jai was a bit more accepting. He figured that you are born the way you are born. Anish was still his brother, but he was conflicted; he didn't want to upset his father.' She took a sip of the water that Warren had poured her. 'It was a lot easier when their mother was still alive. Gotam listened to Suniti and knew that it upset her when he spoke ill of Anish. When she was around, they were at least civil to one another.'

'But things changed after she died?'

'Yes. We had no idea that she had heart problems. Gotam insisted the family all got tested for the faulty gene that killed her.' Patel smiled, but it didn't reach her eyes. 'It was a tremendous relief when it turned out that although Jaidev, Manoj and Reva were carriers, Jaidev and Manoj hadn't passed it on to the kids.'

'Did Jaidev keep in contact with his brother? Against his father's wishes?'

'No. I tried to talk to him about it, but he kept on telling me to let it go. I didn't want to upset him, so I didn't push.'

'What about Manoj?'

'Not that I know of. I know Reva spoke to him sometimes, but I don't think the brothers have spoken to him since Anish left the family home.'

'Where did Anish move to?'

She frowned. 'I'll be honest, I'm not actually sure. I think it's here in Middlesbury somewhere.'

'So, you didn't help him move then? What about his brothers? Did they help?'

'No, I think he hired a van.'

'I see ...' Warren paused. 'Can I ask when you heard about Anish's death?'

Patel frowned slightly. 'It must have been a little after midday, that Tuesday. Jaidev phoned me at work to tell me what had happened. He was already in the car on the way over to the house. Reva had just called him.'

Warren glanced down at his notepad. 'That would have been about 12.20?'

'I guess.'

'And where do you work?'

'I manage the dry cleaner's near the train station.'

'In Cambridge?'

'Yes.'

'Did you go over to the family house that day?'

'Yes, in the evening. Jaidev picked me up after I finished work.'

'May I ask why you didn't go over until then? I don't mean to sound insensitive, but your husband's brother had just been found murdered. It doesn't sound as though you joined him until some hours after we broke the news.'

Patel's eyes narrowed. 'Unfortunately, the company that does our dry cleaning doesn't collect until 6 p.m. I was the only person in the shop, and so I couldn't leave until the pick-up happened. A lot of our regular customers rely on our twenty-four-hour service; if I missed the collection, they wouldn't have got their garments back the following day.'

'Do you drive an Audi A5?' asked Warren.

Patel blinked at the change in subject. 'Yes, I've owned it for a couple of years. I'd prefer something a little smaller, but it's good for the kids.'

'A nice car. Quite nippy.'

She shrugged. 'I suppose so. To be honest, I'm not much of a petrol head.'

Warren opened the folder by his envelope, removing a black and white photograph. 'This was taken at 12:32 on Tuesday the 29th of November.' He pushed it across the table and pointed at the licence plate. 'Is this your car, Kamala?'

Patel squinted. 'Yes.' She frowned. 'I don't understand.'

'It was photographed doing eighty-five miles per hour in a fifty limit.'

Warren pushed a second photograph across the table. 'This

was taken twenty minutes later, going in the opposite direction, this time at seventy-two miles per hour.'

'Shit.'

*

'We're waiting for Jaidev's lawyer,' Sutton greeted Warren, as he left the interview suite.

'Now why would a man with nothing to hide, who hasn't been arrested, want a lawyer?'

'A very good question. He knows something is up, because his wife had to arrange for someone to pick up their kids from afterschool club.'

'But she didn't tell her friend the reason she needed them to babysit?' asked Warren.

'No,' Sutton smiled grimly. 'Jaidev's going to have a lot of explaining to do. That's one pissed-off missus.'

'Good, keep them apart, I don't want them swapping stories,' said Warren. 'The less he knows about why he's here, the less he'll be able come up with a convincing lie. One or both of them was up to something that day, and I want to know the truth. In the meantime, it gives Moray and Karen more time to ring around and find out what we need.'

*

Jaidev Patel affected nonchalance as he accepted a cup of water. Warren was struck once again by how much he resembled his older brother, Manoj, and how little he looked like Anish.

'We've just got a few questions to help us clear up a few details,' started Warren.

'Where is my wife? I got a call from one of the other parents at school to say that she had been asked to pick up the kids. Is she OK?'

'Your wife is fine, she's also helping us with our enquiries.'

'I don't understand, what has Kamala got to do with anything?'

'All in good time, Jaidev. The sooner you help us with what we need to know, the better.'

The solicitor raised her pen but said nothing.

'We've been looking into your late brother's affairs. We know that he moved out of your father's house in October last year. Did you help him?'

'No. He hired a van, I think.'

'I don't suppose you know where he moved to do you?'

Patel shrugged. 'Not really. Towards Middlesbury, I believe.'

'Any idea why he would choose Middlesbury?'

'I guess it was convenient for work. Rent's probably cheaper than Cambridge as well.'

'Do you know where he worked?'

'Some department store.'

'So, you've never visited him at work or at his flat?'

'No.'

'What about your wife? Do you think she has ever visited him?'

'No, why would she?'

'Just clearing up a few loose ends. We need to work out who he has come into contact with in recent months.'

'I'm sorry, I really haven't had any contact with him since he moved away.'

'No contact at all?'

'No.'

Warren opened the folder to the right of his elbow. He pulled out a printed sheet. 'Do you recognise this mobile phone number?'

Patel looked at the sheet. He swallowed.

'That's …' His voice cracked. 'That's my number.'

'I see. Well, according to Anish's phone records, you texted him on November the 5th last year. He replied after about two minutes. What was that about? You claim not to have had any contact since he moved out of your father's house in October.'

188

Patel paused, swallowing repeatedly; eventually he spoke. 'Oh, yeah. I remember now, I decided to ask him out for a pint. Just to see how he was doing. He said no. I guess that's why I forgot about it.'

'And that was the last time you spoke to him? Over a year ago?' asked Warren.

'Yeah, that sounds about right.'

'So what happened on July the 10th? He phoned you and the call lasted for three minutes, before he terminated it.' Warren sat back and waited.

The silence stretched as Patel's eyes darted from side to side. Finally he spoke, his voice almost a whisper. 'No comment.'

Warren waited, letting the silence build uncomfortably.

'OK. Let's go back to last Tuesday, the day that we came around to your father's house to break the news about Anish's death. Can you tell me what time you heard about it?'

'I'm not sure. A bit after midday, I think.'

'We arrived at the house at five past twelve and your sister, Reva, phoned you about five minutes later. Does that sound right?'

'Yeah, I guess so.'

'And you came straight to your father's house? We left at about ten to one; Manoj had arrived in his Range Rover, but we never met you.'

'I think I arrived just after you left.'

'When did you call your wife, to tell her about Anish's death?'

He pursed his lips. 'Probably a few minutes after Reva called. It took me a moment to get my head straight.'

'Of course. And you were at work?'

'Yes, I manage the Everyday Essentials on Henson Street.'

'In Cambridge?'

'Yes.'

'How long would it take you to get to your father's house from there?'

Patel paused. Again, his eyes started darting around; it was

189

obvious that he had no control over them when he tried to fabricate a story – which would make Warren's job easier, he reflected. Finally, Patel clearly decided that there was no point trying to fudge an answer that could easily be contradicted by a few moments research on Google Maps.

'I guess ten or fifteen minutes, depending on traffic, but I had to close the shop. That's probably why I missed you at the house.'

'Ah, that makes sense,' said Warren. 'What about your wife, did you go and get her first?'

'No, she had to wait for the dry-cleaning pick-up. She couldn't join us until later that evening.' Patel relaxed slightly.

'Do you own an Audi A5?'

He paused, briefly. 'No, but my wife does.'

Warren opened his folder again and removed the two photographs taken on the A506.

'Can you explain why your wife's car was caught on cameras, travelling at high speed a few minutes after you called her to tell her about Anish's death?'

'Umm …'

'And was then caught again, travelling in the opposite direction, about twenty minutes later?'

'I don't know,' Patel's voice had gone croaky again.

'Did she not say anything to you? I thought she had to wait for the dry cleaning to be collected?'

'I really don't know. I thought she stayed at the shop until I picked her up later.'

'Whose car did you use to pick her up, Jaidev?'

Patel opened his mouth, before closing it again.

'You see, according to your wife, you were driving her car. She was using the bus because yours was in the garage.'

'She must be getting her dates wrong,' said Patel. A hint of desperation had crept into his voice.

'No, I don't think so. We phoned the garage that was repairing your car and they confirmed it. Furthermore, the firm that you

190

contract to do your dry cleaning say that the daily pick-up happened as normal that day. The driver even remembers passing on his condolences to your wife when she explained why she was in a rush.'

'No, you're wrong. I didn't drive over to Middlesbury that day.'

'I didn't say anything about Middlesbury,' said Warren quietly.

Patel looked over at his solicitor, who said nothing.

'I need a break,' he said finally.

*

'He's well and truly on the back-foot,' said Sutton with satisfaction.

Warren squeezed out the red bush teabag from Sutton's mug and handed over the steaming drink. At his friend's insistence, he'd tried the naturally caffeine-free tea substitute. It wasn't as foul as some of the concoctions that Rachel Pymm had tried to force down his neck, but he wasn't a convert yet. And today, he really needed the boost. He took a slurp of his coffee before answering.

'I'll be interested to see where Jaidev goes from here. At the moment, we don't have enough to arrest him, and even if he doesn't realise that, his lawyer certainly does. All we know is that he's lied about what he did the afternoon that he found out about Anish's death, and his contact with his brother. Heavy right foot aside, driving towards Middlesbury and then away is hardly a crime.'

'I can't imagine he'll be foolish enough to stick with his story that it was his wife driving the car,' said Sutton. 'He's going to be in enough trouble as it is when two speeding tickets in her name drop through the letter box.'

'So, if we assume that he was driving that way, the question is why? What was so important that moments after learning of his brother's death, he went racing over to Middlesbury before he even joined his family at their father's house? I know Anish was estranged, but Manoj appears to have driven over immediately. You'd think Jaidev'd be there to support his sister, if nothing else.'

'The obvious conclusion is that he went over to Anish's flat,' said Sutton. 'But why?'

'If he was involved in the murder, then perhaps he was looking for evidence that could have implicated him?'

'Which would imply that he had some way to access the flat,' said Warren. 'We still haven't found Anish's missing keys, wallet or phone.'

Sutton looked at his watch. 'Kamala Patel hasn't asked for a lawyer yet, which suggests to me that she's got a clear conscience. But at some point, she's going to figure out that unless we arrest her, she's free to go home at any time. Particularly if she's worried about her kids.'

'Well we can't stop her,' said Warren. 'But let's not put the idea in her head, eh?'

Chapter 24

The custody sergeant rang just as Warren was finishing the last of his coffee. Jaidev Patel had returned from his break and wanted to speak to him. No sooner had Warren replaced the handset, than the phone rang again.

After listening intently for a few moments, Warren thanked the caller and hung up.

'Who was that?' asked Sutton as he climbed to his feet.

'I'll fill you in on the way,' said Warren. 'Things just got interesting.'

*

'You are right, I did speak to my brother,' said Jaidev Patel.

'May I ask why you told us that you hadn't been in contact recently?' asked Warren, mildly.

'I didn't want to upset my father any more than he has been. He already knows that Reva speaks to Anish, despite him forbidding her to do so,' Patel looked down at the table. 'Despite everything, my father did love Anish, but he couldn't accept what he was. We pretended to go along with his wishes to keep him happy, but I think if he knew that we were going behind his back, it would break him.' He looked up again, and Warren could see what appeared to be genuine pain in his eyes. 'Please, if at all possible can you not let Dad know about this?'

'I'll do what I can, but I can't promise anything. Now tell me about those calls.'

Patel shrugged. 'I was just checking in, seeing how he was.'

'Did he mention any worries that he had? Anyone that he had fallen out with?'

'No, nothing like that. He seemed fine.'

'What about new acquaintances? Any friends that you knew of?'

'No, Anish didn't really speak about that. I think he was friendly with some of the people he worked with, but that was all I knew.'

'What about older friends, perhaps people he kept in touch with from school?'

Patel frowned in concentration, before shaking his head again. 'No, sorry. He wasn't the most popular kid you know.'

'Because he was gay?' Warren let an edge creep into his voice, picturing the scars that spoke of Anish's unhappy adolescence; a brief look of shame crossed Patel's face.

'Yeah. And we hardly made it easier for him.'

'What about other, more intimate relationships?'

'I think we would have been the last to know about such things.'

'OK, well that explains the phone call. But it still doesn't explain why your wife's car was seen racing towards Middlesbury shortly after you received the call about Anish's death.'

'That was my mistake. I got confused. I was driving my wife's car.' Patel met Warren's eyes squarely.

'So why did you go that way? It's the opposite direction to your family home.'

Patel continued to meet Warren's gaze, but he licked his lips. 'I needed petrol.'

'You needed petrol?' said Warren.

'Yes, I'd been driving around all week in Kamala's Audi and I was running on fumes. I realised that I would probably run out of fuel if I didn't fill up, and with everything that was happening, the last thing I needed was to find myself stranded on the side of the road.'

'Where was this garage?'

'Dunno, somewhere along the A506.'

'Let me get this straight. You drove all the way out of Cambridge to the A506, to get petrol, then drove back to your father's house, which is in Cambridge?'

'Yeah. I wasn't really thinking straight.'

'But there must be half a dozen filling stations between where you work and your father's house. Why didn't you stop at one of those?'

Warren looked over at Patel's solicitor; her face was a mask, but he could imagine what was going through her mind.

'Most of them are BP garages, they cost a fortune. I try and avoid them.'

Warren stared at him for a few more seconds, wondering if it was some sort of joke. Patel finally dropped his gaze and looked back down at the table.

'So why were you travelling so fast?'

'Well I wanted to get to my father's house as soon as possible.'

'Yet there is a gap of twenty minutes between you being caught on camera the first time, and the second time.'

'There was a queue at the petrol station.'

Warren took a deep breath. The man's story was so preposterous, he didn't know whether he should challenge him on it right now or come back to it later. In the end, he decided to move on. It would be easy enough to ask all of the garages along that route to check their forecourt cameras for Kamala Patel's Audi. They could then blow his story out of the water.

It was time, Warren decided, to bring up the search warrant for the couple's home. He braced himself. Patel didn't disappoint.

'What, you can't do that!' shouted Patel.

'We can, Jaidev, your wife has agreed. Now would be a very

good time for you to tell us everything. Have you ever visited your brother's flat?'

Patel scowled, before leaning back in his chair and folding his arms. 'None of your business.'

'Are you sure about that? I have to say, it's not looking great for you at the moment, Jaidev. You've lied repeatedly about how much contact you had with your brother, and despite claiming to have never visited his flat, the first thing you did after hearing of Anish's death was race towards it.'

'I told you, I was getting petrol.' He turned to his solicitor. 'This is bullshit. Can't you do something?'

'I would remind you that Mr Patel is here voluntarily,' said the solicitor. 'He is not under arrest and has not been charged with any crime. He also has alibis over the period you believe his brother was killed. I ask that you either arrest my client or let him go.'

'Jaidev,' said Warren, 'the more help you give us the better. If, as you say, you have nothing to do with your brother's death, then there will be nothing for you to worry about.'

'I can't believe that you are even attempting that justification,' said the solicitor. 'This isn't a police state.'

'Perhaps you could explain this,' said Warren, ignoring her protestations.

He pushed his tablet over, an image on the screen.

'The search team found these at your house. Why do you have keys to your brother's flat?'

*

'His lawyer is right, we can't keep him here indefinitely. He could get up and walk any time,' said Grayson.

Jaidev Patel had refused to comment on whether he had ever actually visited his brother's flat.

'His brother could have given him a key for safekeeping,' Warren admitted.

196

'And we still can't prove that he even drove to his brother's flat the day we told him Anish had died,' said Sutton. 'There are no cameras close enough to the flat to prove he was within a reasonable distance. He could just claim that he was driving around, or near, Middlesbury clearing his head. You'll need witnesses that saw his wife's Audi for that to hold up.'

Warren hissed in frustration. He'd taken a gamble in confronting Patel with the evidence and it had backfired. He knew that even as they spoke, Patel would be busy concocting an explanation. And the moment they released him, he'd likely seek to muddy the waters and dispose of any evidence that he might still have.

'How's his alibi looking for the day of the murder?' asked Grayson.

'Checks out so far,' admitted Warren.

'Then we've got nothing to justify his arrest.'

There was a quiet tap on the door; looking through the window, Warren could see the red of Rachel Pymm's cardigan.

'Come in,' called Grayson.

'Sorry to interrupt, but I thought you'd want to know. We have bad news.'

Warren smothered a groan.

*

Jaidev Patel left the building as soon as he could, with barely a glance back.

'I can't believe it, he actually did stop at a petrol station,' said Warren.

'Yeah, although their records indicate that there wasn't much of a queue,' said Pymm. 'He still had plenty of time to make it to Anish's flat, do whatever he wanted to do, then drive to Cambridge.'

'Well, we can't arrest him for being mistaken about how long it took him to buy petrol,' said Sutton, his mood as dark as Warren's.

Chapter 25

Warren arrived home at an almost decent hour, but Susan wasn't there to make the most of it. It was the final parents' evening of the term and it would be a late one; as Head of Science, in addition to her own pupils she would also be supporting colleagues having awkward conversations with struggling learners.

Too ravenous to cook properly, he popped some frozen potato waffles in the toaster; at least Susan wasn't there to nag him about his diet. As they started to sizzle, he cut thick slices of Red Leicester cheese and splurged a healthy dollop of brown sauce on some slices of bread; at least his waffle sandwich was made with wholemeal.

Waiting for the toaster, he leafed through the junk mail and early Christmas cards on the doormat until his breath caught. He didn't need to open the thick, A4 envelope to know its contents, the discreet logo in the corner told him all he needed to know.

Unbidden, his awkward conversation with Karen Hardwick the previous day came back. If only she knew …

It had been over twelve months since their loss. In the immediate aftermath, Susan had been adamant it was nothing but a setback – tragic to be sure, but just a step on the road to eventual success. Give it a few months and they would try again.

There had been a slight hitch when they were informed that the NHS would no longer fund them for another IVF cycle, meaning they had to pay for it privately. Same clinic, same doctors, but five grand, please.

After the previous year's miscarriage, Granddad Jack had pledged some of his savings to help them. Warren had felt uncomfortable about the offer, but it had soon become a moot point. The heart-breaking realisation that Jack would never be returning to the home he'd lived in since his wedding had been compounded by the fact that the same home would need to be sold to pay for continuing care, and his savings would be similarly ring-fenced.

Jack was frail and in need of assistance, but otherwise fit and healthy. His own parents had both lived far longer than most of their contemporaries and the doctors saw no reason that Jack couldn't enjoy a good few more years himself. Jack currently paid almost eight hundred pounds a week for a room in a residential home. That was only going to get more expensive over time, as his needs increased. The maths had been stark; if Jack lived for another five or more years, then the equity in his house would be all but used up. Warren wouldn't be inheriting anything but memories, and Jack couldn't give them the money to pay for their treatment.

Financially that wasn't a worry for Warren and Susan – between them, their joint salaries were more than enough to pay for several additional cycles of IVF – but it had left Jack even more depressed than before.

And it had become another excuse.

First, they had been too busy to think about the next step; Christmas and New Year had followed an especially gruelling case for Warren. Then there had been the worries with Granddad Jack; finding a suitable care home had taken months, with two false starts, followed by selling his house. It always amazed Warren how some estate agents, despite doing nothing but buy and sell houses all day, still acted as if it was the first time they'd ever done it. Being a hundred miles away hardly helped matters.

Now though, the excuses were running out. Warren could never predict how busy he was going to be, but they'd made it work before – after all, his input in the process was far less than Susan's. Her school was very good about time off for such things, so there was really no excuse for not starting again.

His dinner forgotten, he continued to stare at the envelope. He didn't know how Susan would react to his attempt to reinvigorate the process. Even if she said no, it was something. For months they'd danced around the subject, always too busy or too tired to talk.

Before he could change his mind, he picked the envelope up and slid his finger along the opening. Walking through to the living room he placed the shiny brochure on the coffee table where it couldn't be missed.

He knew exactly what Susan's response would be – that a school night, after a long parents' evening, was hardly the time to discuss something so important. And she was right.

But when was the right time?

Tuesday 6th December

Chapter 26

Warren stifled a yawn with his fist. Two double-strength coffees had barely dented the fatigue from yet another sleepless night. At this stage in a case it was normal for his sleep to suffer; early starts and late finishes propped up by caffeine – not to mention his tendency to eat even more poorly than normal – would leave his mind abuzz. When he did finally drop off to sleep, weird and unsettling dreams were not uncommon.

He had been right about Susan's reaction to the brochure for the fertility clinic. As a couple, they rarely argued about anything of significance and it was unusual for them to raise their voices to one another. Nevertheless, Susan had been far from impressed at Warren 'ambushing her' after a long day at work.

In the end however, his ploy had been successful. Susan had agreed to properly sit down with Warren and discuss their options; Warren hadn't even needed to decamp to the guest bedroom for the night. They had agreed upon Saturday evening; he just hoped that the case didn't throw up any excuses to avoid the issue again.

Warren had decided to start the meeting on a positive note after Jaidev Patel's release. Conscious that the team needed to avoid falling into a rut, and placing all of their investigative eggs in one basket, he turned to Rachel Pymm first for an update on her team's progress tracking down the men that Anish Patel had met through Rainbow Hookups. It wasn't impossible that Anish had been killed by someone he met online, with a motive no more convoluted than simple human jealousy. They still hadn't accounted for Anish's regular stays at the Easy Break Hotel, although the visits didn't seem to correlate with his communications with men he'd contacted through the app.

'The first significant contact he had was with Johnny74 if you recall,' Pymm started.

'The car lover?' said Ruskin.

'Yes, but not to be confused with Car_lover12, who we have also been in contact with,' said Pymm. 'As I suspected, by all accounts it was little more than a casual hook-up with Johnny74,' continued Pymm. 'We did a "bed and breakfast" analysis on the historic location data for his phone and figured out where he usually spends the night. I sent a couple of DCs around to knock on the door and see what he had to say for himself.'

'Anything significant?' asked Sutton. 'It was over a year ago that they first met.'

'Well first of all, he has an alibi for the whole period that we are looking at. He was down in London overseeing a community arts exhibition. He spent the days helping set up and the evenings hosting the event. Naturally, the phone he uses for Rainbow Hookups is a burner, which he left in his flat when he went away. He doesn't like to mix business and pleasure.'

'Convenient,' said Ruskin.

'Perhaps, but he was happy to hand it over to the officers that interviewed him. He admitted that he was still technically in a relationship when he joined Rainbow Hookups, hence the burner. After he became single again, he saw no reason to change phones.'

'How strong is his alibi?' asked Warren.

'We have photos of him in the *Evening Standard* and have confirmed he met with potential sponsors over the course of several days, plus CCTV from his hotel and the train station.

There's just no way that he could have nipped back to the Easy Break Hotel.'

'Did he remember the details of when he met Anish?' asked Warren. 'He wouldn't be the first spurned lover to have someone else kill on his behalf after arranging an alibi.'

'He had to have a bit of a think about it,' said Pymm, 'but when he did remember, he was quite open about what happened that evening. He said that he got the impression that Anish was fairly new to online dating and nervous about being seen in public. They met up for a meal in a restaurant and he thought it was rather sweet that Anish insisted on paying for it.'

'What was he expecting from the date?' asked Warren.

'Well Johnny74, or Mr John Paris to give him his real name,' said that he felt that Anish wasn't clear exactly what he wanted. As for Mr Paris, he said that at the time he was some months out of the aforementioned long-term relationship and was looking for a bit of fun, with something more if he met the right person.'

'And was Anish the right person?' asked Sutton. 'We speculated that Anish may have moved his relationship onto an app-based communication platform, rather than text messages, so we don't know if they continued communicating.'

'Well, he was rather coy about what happened after the meal,' said Pymm, 'but just as we suspected, it seems that it was him that broke off the relationship. If you recall, there was a text message exchange the morning after their date that I surmised was Johnny74 saying "thanks but no thanks". Without being asked he opened his phone and showed the text message exchange between him and Anish; it seemed that they parted on good terms.'

'Sounds like he's unlikely to have been involved,' said Warren. 'Anything on the computer about him?'

'Nothing, not even a speeding ticket. He was quite happy to be fingerprinted,' said Pymm. 'For what it's worth, the lead interviewer has been in this game for years and has a pretty good nose for these things. She reckoned that his reaction when he was told was one of surprise, and though he was sad and shocked, it wasn't over the top for what appears to have been little more than a one-night stand over a year ago.'

'OK,' said Warren. 'Let's move on. Who else have you found? You mentioned Car_lover12?'

'Yes. He was a lot more recent; he contacted Anish on the 16th of June this year,' said Pymm.

'That's barely five months before Anish was killed,' said Ruskin. 'That's not so long for a person to bear a grudge.'

'This one was a little more awkward,' said Pymm. 'The team tracked him down to Stenfield; a couple of uniforms knocked on the door and he almost vomited … his wife and kids were in the living room.'

There was a collective wince. Regardless of their personal views about the rights or wrongs of Car_lover12's clandestine online persona, they were police officers not grubby tabloid journalists seeking to expose the private failings of innocent people.

'There's a possible motive, right there,' said Hardwick. 'Could Anish have threatened to tell his wife? A spot of blackmail could account for his mysterious cash income.'

'He does potentially have a lot to lose,' said Pymm. 'Mr Isaiah Otis is a full-time pastor and youth worker at the Stenfield Community Evangelical Centre. Fundamentalist Christians preaching how you should love your neighbour – but not in the way that Otis loved Anish.'

'What about means and opportunity?' asked Warren. 'How cooperative was he?'

'Once they calmed him down he voluntarily attended the local nick and happily brought his burner phone with him.'

'Did he consent to being printed?' asked Warren.

'Yes, and swabbed, and once he started talking, they struggled to get him to shut up. Poor bloke had a lot to get off his chest, by the sounds of it.'

'I'm assuming I'd have heard about it if he confessed,' said Warren.

'No such luck, I'm afraid,' said Pymm. 'His story is that he contacted Anish and they exchanged a few text messages. He was a little embarrassed, but to be honest they're pretty tame. They agreed to meet for a meal out of the way in Stevenage. He wouldn't say if they spent the night together, but the text the following morning was a simple "thanks for the lovely night" from Anish and a polite, "see you around" from Otis. He claims that they didn't really click and neither wished to continue the relationship.'

'What about WhatsApp or other messaging apps?' asked Sutton.

'His burner phone was too basic to install any,' Pymm scowled in frustration. 'We really need access to Anish's handset to pursue that angle.'

'What about an alibi?' asked Hutchinson.

'The burner phone stays hidden in his car's glove box,' said Pymm, 'and we've tracked his usual mobile phone. Neither have ever been near the Easy Break Hotel, or any place else we know that Anish frequented. Nor has his car, or his wife's car, been photographed anywhere suspicious. He claims to have been home each night and working at the church and youth centre during the days we're interested in. His devices seem to back that up.'

'Any corroboration?' asked Hutchinson.

'Yes, his wife says that he was home each night and he was in meetings each day that the other participants confirm.' Her face took on a sympathetic cast. 'It sounds as though she didn't fully buy the "routine inquiry" line. I wonder if she has been having doubts?'

'Well, not our concern,' said Warren, his words harsher than his tone. 'Keep him on the board until we get the forensics back from the hotel. I suppose he could have hired a hitman if he really hated Anish that much, but I think that may be stretching a bit.'

'Who else have we got left?' asked Sutton.

'Of the five men of interest that we identified from Rainbow Hookups, we still have three outstanding. First off, Blondie92 who contacted Anish on New Year's Day. They texted and called a few times, but we have nothing after January the 8th. That number hasn't been used for months, it seems it was only turned on to make calls and texts to Anish. Bed and breakfast analysis came up a blank also; the phone pings the cell towers too infrequently, from locations all over the place. We have his photo from Rainbow Hookups, I could arrange teams to visit some of the locations and flash it around.'

'Do it,' said Warren. 'I'm very suspicious that he seems to have only used that mobile number to contact Anish. If he did switch SIM cards, could you still track the handset via its IMEI number?'

'We can certainly try,' said Pymm, making a note.

'What about the others?' asked Warren.

'The most recent was HotnReady, back in September. He did a lot of the early groundwork, with some pretty explicit exchanges on the app.'

'He was the one whose profile picture will need to be Photoshopped before we show it to witnesses,' recalled Sutton.

'It looked as though it had already been Photoshopped to me,' said Hutchinson to a round of laughter.

'His and Anish's phones co-located to Middlesbury High Street Saturday evening, before Anish turned his phone off,' said Pymm. 'Mr HotnReady's phone stayed on and went back to his flat just before 11 p.m. Anish's didn't reconnect to the network until just after 1 a.m., back at his own flat.'

'Have we visited?' asked Hutchinson.

'Yes, no sign of him. We have a name from the landlord, Stewart Fallon, but there's nothing on the system. The old lady who lived downstairs says that he was "popular" and had lots of friends visiting him; the interviewing officer described her as the sort of person who lowers their voice and whispers when they say the word "gay". That being said, she claimed he was a nice man, and used to do a bit of shopping for her if the weather was poor. They showed her photos of Anish, and suitably cropped photos of HotnReady from Rainbow Hookups, but she has cataracts and didn't recognise him.'

'Do you think he may be a sex-worker?' asked Sutton.

'Perhaps, or at least very sexually active,' said Pymm.

'So where is he now?' asked Warren.

'She has no idea, she hasn't seen him for days. She said he often disappears for weeks at a time; she's not sure what his job is. His landlord said that his rent is paid by standing order. The phone hasn't been on all week.'

'OK, keep at it. Who does that leave then?'

'Mr Brown Bear.'

'The large Asian bloke with the questionable Rainbow Hookups profile picture,' recalled Ruskin.

'Yes, his former next-door neighbour confirmed that he was definitely closer to fifty than thirty,' said Pymm, 'and the photograph is very flattering, he's a lot heavier than he appears in the picture.'

'Maybe that's why Anish gave him the brush-off, if that's what happened,' said Hutchinson. 'I seem to remember that Anish appeared to break contact after they first met.'

'Hell of a long time to bear a grudge,' said Hardwick. 'It's about a year since they first hooked up.'

'Which brings us back to non-text message communication,' said Sutton gloomily.

'You said former neighbour?' recalled Warren.

'That's where it gets interesting. We have a first name, Deepak, known to everyone as Dippy. It seems that he lived in the house that we tracked the mobile phone to for a number of years with his girlfriend, Joanna Weybridge. She's white and has two kids who clearly aren't his. In February of this year, they started to argue a lot then suddenly, Deepak was no longer around. Then at the end of April, the girlfriend also moved out. He overheard her children talking in the garden; apparently with Deepak gone they couldn't afford the rent.'

'So where is he now?' asked Warren.

'We don't know yet. The burner went dead around the end of February – probably about the time the arguments started. There's also been no activity on his Rainbow Hookups account since then.'

'Sounds like his missus got wind of his extra-curricular interests,' said Sutton.

'Could be blackmail, again,' said Hardwick.

'Do we know if he met anyone else through Rainbow Hookups after he met Anish?' asked Sutton. 'If Anish was the final person he met, that makes him all the more likely to have still been seeing him when it all kicked off with his girlfriend.'

'No way to tell,' said Pymm. 'His profile is no longer visible on searches and when we follow the link from Anish's history, his account is listed as 'archived' since August, due to inactivity. From what I can tell, that happens automatically after six months, which suggests he last used it in February. Unfortunately, only the account owner can see the profile's activity, so we can't access it. The site is hosted overseas and isn't returning our calls.'

'Well, we have a partial name,' said Warren. 'Get onto the landlord and see if he left a forwarding address. If you can't track him directly then pursue the girlfriend, hopefully at least one of them was on the electoral roll.'

*

'Sir, you need to see this!' called Richardson across the office. Warren crossed the room to join her. He'd just left the briefing room, where he had placed a big red cross on the suspects board through the sister and brother-in-law of Latika Luthra, the woman Anish Patel had been planning on marrying. The couple had been in India for the past month visiting his sick father. He'd died a few days previously and three days after the funeral they had flown home. There was no way that either of them could have been involved in the murder.

That still didn't rule out the hitman theory, however, the jaunt had cost the couple the remains of their savings and over-stretched their credit cards, so it was unclear how they could have hired someone, even if they wished to. Again, the experienced nose of the interviewer had come into play and they were satisfied that despite

210

her sharp words, Luthra's sister was genuinely upset that her sister's chance at children and happiness had been so cruelly taken away.

The normally unflappable Richardson sounded excited. Already, there was a crowd around her workstation; even Rachel Pymm had made the journey from her own desk, leaning on her crutches over her fellow DS's shoulder.

Richardson's screen showed a still image of the hotel car park, with Anish's hire car clearly visible.

'This is dashcam footage sent to us by a sales rep staying overnight at the hotel; he checked in on the Thursday night. He didn't recognise the picture of Anish, but he saw the latest appeal on TV and figured he'd send us his dashcam footage anyway.'

The time stamp read 19:02.

She switched images. 'This is from when the rep left Friday morning. He got up early to beat the traffic.'

The picture showed the hire car parked in the same spot as the night before.

Warren blinked. 'Do that again,' he ordered. Richardson complied.

'The car's moved,' he breathed.

The movement was tiny; the car was still parked in the same spot as before, but it had shifted slightly to the left. The front wheels, angled slightly in the first image, were now dead straight.

'When did he move it? Did you miss him coming out of the front door during the night?'

Richardson shook her head. 'Watch this.'

She switched to another window, this time video from a CCTV camera. The timestamp showed just after 1.30 a.m. and the picture was black and white.

'This is from the camera above the service entrance on the corner of the building, next to the access road,' she pointed at the door that the camera was covering. 'We know that nobody came in or out of that entrance during Anish's stay. But look here, at the edge of the screen.'

Light from the streetlamps on the nearby road illuminated the edge of the camera's field of vision. Suddenly a shadow appeared, coming briefly from around the corner of the building from the access road, before disappearing out of shot in the direction of the customer car park.

'Play that again,' ordered Warren. 'Slowly.'

Richardson manipulated her mouse.

'That's the shadow of a person,' said Warren. 'What are they doing wandering across the car park at that time of night?'

'There's more,' said Richardson. She clicked her mouse again, and the video advanced about ninety seconds.

This time the shadow was more boxy; although the object casting the shadow was still out of shot, it was clear to everyone what it was.

'A car, travelling towards the access road,' said Richardson.

'Without its lights on,' observed Pymm.

Warren stood up straight. The footage would be of limited use in court; the person walking was just out of range of the camera – was that deliberate? Then the car, which Warren was certain must be Anish's hire car, was also out of shot. But with the clear evidence from the dashcam footage showing that Anish's car had been moved at some point that night, it was a fair bet that either he, or somebody else, had driven his car around the side of the hotel.

'Does the car continue along the access road to the rear of the hotel?' asked Warren.

'Not all the way. The CCTV above the fire exit is broken, obviously, but the camera over the loading bay doesn't show any movement. But now that we know what to look for, we've found this, twelve minutes later.'

The shadow of the car reappeared; this time there was a faint glow from the leading edge of the shadow. He wouldn't have bet money on it, but Warren got the impression that it was being driven backwards, and they were seeing the flare from the reversing lights.

Warren drummed his fingers on the desk. 'Suggestions?'

'I reckon somebody walked out of the fire exit, up the access road and across the car park, trying to avoid the camera above the service entrance, and then moved Anish's car around to the fire exit, loaded it up and took it back to its parking space,' said Ruskin.

'Loaded up with what?' asked Warren.

'The obvious answer is his body, but we have footage of him leaving the hotel Friday morning.'

'In which case, maybe it was Anish driving the car himself,' said Hutchinson. 'We still don't know why he was checking into this hotel every month. Perhaps he was receiving drugs or stolen goods? He checks in, then in the middle of the night loads up his car before driving away the next day.'

'Seems a bit elaborate,' said Pymm. 'Although it might explain why he prefers to use a hire car, rather than his own vehicle. It puts another layer of protection between him and whatever he's getting up to.'

'Does it though?' asked Ruskin. 'It's easy enough to trace a hire car back to the person that rented it.'

'For the police maybe, but perhaps he's more concerned about the people who he's dealing with, than us?' countered Pymm.

The team fell silent. Thus far, much of their theory was speculation. It still wasn't clear that the shadows on the CCTV footage were even Anish or his hire car. They couldn't be sure that the two things were linked, although the apparent movement of Anish's car that night needed an explanation.

Warren said as much. 'One thing is certain though,' he concluded, 'whatever did happen to Anish had at least some link to that hotel, because I still can't think of any other reason for his body being wrapped in that sheet.'

'Whilst you're here, I think you need to look at this as well,' said Ruskin, moving over to his own workstation.

'I was looking at the list of apps that IT found on Anish's tablet, and I recognised one of them.' He pointed at the webpage. 'He was using a diet and fitness tracker. It's the same one that I've been using for my triathlon training.'

'OK,' said Warren. He recognised the logo from adverts.

'The app is synchronised between his phone, his tablet and the cloud. He used it to keep a log of what food he ate, any exercise he did and body measurements.'

Warren had been thinking about downloading something similar himself in January. With his forty-second birthday fast approaching, he'd reluctantly come to the conclusion that the extra kilos he'd accumulated recently weren't going to magically disappear on their own. As soon as the Christmas and New Year party season were over, he'd have to start doing something about it. He wondered if it could track swimming?

'Anish used it for the past eighteen months,' continued Ruskin. 'I suspect his heart problems were a catalyst.' He clicked on a tab on the webpage. 'And he had some success – he lost twelve kilogrammes and four inches off his waist. His blood pressure, resting pulse and cholesterol were back within the healthy range for a man his age.'

'OK, so what's the problem?'

'Well, he was a creature of habit. According to the timestamps on the log, the last thing he did before going to bed each night was input everything he'd eaten that day. He also listed his exercise, including the steps he'd taken that day – his phone recorded those automatically; he always took a long walk on Tuesdays, Wednesdays and Fridays first thing in the morning. He then manually inputted how far he swam on a Thursday, and how long he spent on the exercise bike and the cross-trainer on a Monday. He weighed and measured himself every Thursday after his swim.'

Warren had a suspicion where this was leading. 'And he definitely did it every day?'

'He had an unbroken chain from the day he started using it. Sometimes he used his tablet, sometimes his phone, but the last thing he did each night was complete his log.'

'Until?'

'Until Thursday the 24th of November. That's the first time since he started that he didn't submit last thing at night. And he doesn't appear to have taken his Friday morning walk either.'

Chapter 27

'DC Hardwick, I have a call for you,' said the support worker on the other end of the line. 'It's a Mr Latham. He says it's urgent.'

It took a moment for Hardwick to place the name.

'Is that DC Hardwick?' asked the owner of Middlesbury Vehicle Rentals when the connection was made.

'Yes, how can I help you?' asked Hardwick, taking a sip of the Diet Coke that was the only thing standing between her and the urge to crawl under her desk and take a nap.

'Sorry to bother you. I didn't think it was important, but my daughter thinks it might be.'

'Well, it's always best to be certain with these things,' said Hardwick, stifling a yawn. 'Why don't you tell me what's on your mind?'

'That car. The one we hired out to the poor man who was murdered?'

'Yes,' said Hardwick, trying to sound encouraging.

'A couple of your officers dropped it back around, thank you. Anyway, it was due its next service, so I took it to the garage that looks after our fleet. There's rarely any surprises with these things, just an oil change, broken bulbs, new tyres, the usual sort of thing.'

Hardwick made an encouraging noise. Her own car was due

its service soon; she could only hope that it needed so little work done.

'The thing is, it didn't need any new tyres.'

'OK,' said Hardwick, slightly nonplussed.

'According to the mechanic, the tyres were almost brand new; just a few hundred miles on them. They're caked in mud, but definitely new. I'm sorry I didn't spot it before, I just gave them a quick once-over when the car was returned.'

'Wait, you're saying the tyres had been changed without your knowledge?' All thoughts of an afternoon snooze vanished.

'Yes. They weren't even the same brand. I've had the odd customer need to replace one if they had a puncture, but I've never had someone change all four. Do you think it's important?'

Chapter 28

Warren called an emergency briefing after he'd relayed the latest findings to DSI Grayson. The German couple that hired the Ford Focus after Anish Patel had driven over 700 miles; it was easy to see how forensics had missed that the tyres had been replaced. The car was now heading back to Welwyn, where it would be processed fully, even dismantled if necessary.

'We are now operating under the assumption that Anish Patel was murdered in the Easy Break Hotel on the night of Thursday November the 24th, and that he was wrapped in a bed sheet, taken to the dumping spot in his hire car in the early hours of the morning, which was then returned to the hotel car park before being dropped back at the vehicle rental place by the killer.'

He turned to Hardwick. 'How confident are you that the person you saw on the reception CCTV on the Friday morning was Anish?'

Hardwick blushed. 'He was wearing the same clothes and carrying his backpack.' Her voice trailed off. 'I just assumed ...'

Warren nodded. There was no point embarrassing her further, these things happened. He made a mental note to get Sutton to check in with her later; he knew she'd be beating herself up over her error.

'Mags, get the Video Analysis Unit to check and see if it really is him. If he was dead by that point, then that must be the killer dressed in his clothes. See if they can find anything we can use to identify them. The killer dropped the hire car back at the rental place; scour the surrounding area for any CCTV. Even a glimpse of the car might tell us when it was returned. The killer needed to get home afterwards, so contact the bus companies.'

'We've gone through the footage from the CCTV outside the hotel with a fine-tooth comb,' said Richardson. 'We assumed initially that the car had been taken from its spot, driven around the corner of the hotel to the fire exit to be loaded up, and then returned to its original space. It then stayed there until after it was picked up the next morning on the sales rep's dashcam. But if that was what happened, that means that whatever was loaded into the boot of that car – and it's almost certainly Anish's body – would have sat in the car's boot in the middle of a car park for several hours, which seems pretty risky.'

She projected a video onto the wall screen. 'Sixty-eight minutes after we believe the car was loaded with Anish's body, this happens.'

This time the shadow was of a person walking briskly back around the corner, again maddeningly out of view of the camera.

'It could be the same person, or it could be a different, unrelated person, but it's now almost twenty to three. It's too early for anyone to be starting or ending their shift, and the kid on the reception desk hasn't moved an inch for three hours.'

'There's a gap in the hedge along the service road that employees use to take a shortcut to the bus stop. Could it just be somebody cutting across the car park?' said Ruskin.

Richardson gave a non-committal shrug. 'It's possible, but I'd wonder why? It's not an especially busy residential area, and the bus doesn't start running again for another couple of hours.

'Anyway, even if the killer spent some time driving around, trying to find a dumping spot, sixty-eight minutes is plenty of time to drive out to the ditch, do what they did and then return, all without triggering ANPR cameras,' she summarised.

'We need to refocus the investigation on the Thursday night, and go back over everything,' said Warren. In front of him he had a hastily scribbled to-do list. 'First of all, alibis: we now need to know exactly what Anish's family were doing on the Thursday night. We also need to double-check the whereabouts of Leon Grime and Nicholas Kimpton.' He turned to Pymm. 'Go back through all of the phone records that we have for that time period. See if they match any of the players.'

He turned to Ruskin. 'It looks as though the killer changed the tyres of the hire car sometime between dumping the body and returning it. Check all the garages in the local area to see if anybody remembers changing all four tyres on a white Ford Focus. Presumably it was a rush job, so hopefully they remember it.'

'What about the forensics in the hotel room?' asked Hutchinson.

'I've asked Andy Harrison to prioritise running all of those fingerprints through the database,' said Warren. 'It'll take some time, but hopefully we'll get lucky.'

'If Anish was killed on the Thursday, then we know that those text messages he sent Friday and Saturday were definitely fake,' said Pymm. 'They must have been sent by the killer, which makes me wonder how he unlocked Anish's phone.'

It was a good question and, depending on how the handset was secured, raised a couple of disturbing possibilities, including torture to get the PIN code.

'How confident are you with the location?' asked Warren. 'Can you tell if they were sent from inside his flat.'

'No, all I've got is the nearest cell tower. It could have been sent from anywhere within a two-street radius.'

'Then let's get door-knocking in the area, see if anyone remembers anyone strange hanging around, or if there's any CCTV or dashcam footage,' said Warren.

He looked around the briefing room. 'We've spent a lot of time assuming that he was killed on the Friday or after. I'll take responsibility for that. However, it wasn't time misspent; we collected a lot of evidence. But let's not jump to any more conclusions. As of now, everyone who was a suspect before is still a suspect now and we don't yet know why he was killed or how. Let's go back over everything again with a fresh eye.

'We will catch whoever killed Anish Patel, and we will get justice for him.'

*

Karen Hardwick wiped her nose on a piece of toilet roll. She'd been in the cubicle for almost fifteen minutes, and the tears had finally subsided. How could she have been so careless? She'd seen the logo on the back of the person departing the Easy Break Hotel, added two and two together and made a million. The Video Analysis Unit had taken her at her word and focused on identifying anyone who may have followed the man they had been told was Anish Patel out the door.

The previous year, Karen had seriously contemplated leaving the police. The offer of a PhD studentship, applied for almost on a whim during her maternity leave, had nearly tempted her to return to the career that she had abandoned when she joined the force. Her role as a single mother had made her re-evaluate her priorities. Life as a research scientist was certainly not an easy option, but the hours would be more regular and she wouldn't be placing herself in harm's way; Ollie had never even met his father – was it right to risk making him an orphan?

And now this mistake. She'd been tired; a restless night with her teething son and the warm, over-heated hotel office had conspired to make her sleepy. Was that the reason for her error? How much time had they wasted? And now it seemed that the car that Anish Patel had hired, and that they had initially dismissed, was a potentially key piece of evidence – that could hardly be considered her fault, but she'd been the one to speak to Richard Latham, could she have questioned him more carefully?

She thought back to the letter that she'd received from the university after declining the offer of a place. It had been personally written by the professor who would have supervised her, expressing his disappointment, but suggesting that she contact him again if she changed her mind.

Should she?

She gave herself a shake. 'Come on Hardwick, get a grip,' she muttered to herself; she knew the real reason for her upset and it wasn't her oversight. Tony Sutton had sought her out and admonished her gently, like any good line manager, but had made it clear that mistakes happen and that DCI Jones wasn't going to hold it against her.

It was because days like this she missed Gary more than ever.

On the first case they'd worked together, he'd made a significant error that had almost derailed the investigation. He'd been embarrassed, but he'd dealt with it. Now she wanted nothing more than to go home, pour a glass of wine and tell him all about it. A hug, a kiss and by early evening, it'd be all right.

But that couldn't happen.

It would never happen again.

Blowing her nose, she stood up. She was nearing the end of her shift, and her parents would be expecting her home to relieve them after an exhausting day with a rambunctious toddler. Gary might not be waiting for her, but the three people she loved most in the world would be back at her flat.

And that almost made up for his absence.

But before then, she had an idea. If her hunch paid off, then perhaps today hadn't been a complete disaster.

*

Back in the office, Sutton picked up a pile of security footage printouts from the morning that Anish Patel supposedly checked out of the hotel.

221

'I've stared at these until I've gone cross-eyed, and I can't work out who is really wearing Anish's clothes. The hoodie is too baggy and there are no face shots, so I've no idea if they have a beard. Whoever they are, they know where the cameras are,' said Sutton, as he leafed through the rest of the pictures. 'Look, they keep their head down all the way across the lobby. They're even wearing gloves, so I can't see what colour their hands are.'

'Deliberate?' asked Warren, as he leaned against Sutton's cubicle wall. 'It would have been a dead giveaway if the person in this picture didn't have brown skin. Not to mention they'd have left fingerprints on the keycard.'

The two men kept on staring, but neither could see anything.

'It could be a sibling, Leon Grime, Shane Moore or even Nicholas Kimpton,' said Warren eventually. He looked at his watch – 7 p.m.; perhaps it was time to call it a night.

He opened his mouth to make the suggestion when his mobile phone started ringing.

Karen Hardwick. She'd left the office without saying anything earlier; her eyes had been puffy and her make-up clearly re-applied. He really hoped she wasn't phoning because she was beating herself up over her slip; it happened to the best of them.

She wasn't.

By the time she'd finished, Sutton had already anticipated their next move, calling out to Moray Ruskin. All thoughts of an early evening had vanished.

'Bring him in,' ordered Warren.

*

Leon Grime looked nauseous as he took his seat in the interview suite. Beside him, the duty solicitor took a sip of coffee, before crossing his legs and resting his pad on his knee. Sutton reminded Grime of his rights, and the reason for his original arrest, making certain he could push his chair back quickly if the man vomited. He hated when that happened.

'I assume that you have re-called my client to unarrest him and release him from his bail,' said the solicitor. 'We have already established that Mr Grime has an alibi for the day that Mr Patel was murdered, and that anyone could have had access to his tool kit.'

It was clear from Grime's countenance that he wasn't assuming any such thing.

'Not yet,' said Sutton. 'We still need Mr Grime to help us clear up some details.'

'And this couldn't have waited?' said the solicitor, looking pointedly at this watch.

Sutton ignored him.

'First of all, let's establish some background,' said Ruskin. 'You've worked at the Easy Break Hotel for sixteen years?'

Grime nodded.

'Where were you before that?'

Grime's Adam's apple bobbed. 'Unemployed.'

'I see. And before then?'

Grime looked down at his hands. 'In prison.'

'For what?' he asked.

Grime continued looking away, his neck flushing pink. His voice was quiet. 'Dealing.'

'Drugs?' asked Sutton. Grime's criminal record was neatly printed in front of them, but it was important to get the man into the habit of answering truthfully – it would make it easier to spot the lies.

Grime cleared his throat. 'And aggravated burglary.'

Sutton made a show of looking over the printout. 'Not much detail on here,' he lied.

'I had a knife in my pocket.'

The two detectives waited.

'The homeowner was in the house. I waved the knife around to make sure she didn't do anything stupid,' he finally looked up.

'But I never used it. It was just for show. I thought the house was empty.'

'But you did punch her, didn't you, leaving her with a broken nose and two black eyes?' said Sutton. 'A seventy-three-year-old widow, in her own house at two in the morning. Her car was on the drive, so the jury didn't believe you thought no one was home. If you hadn't pleaded guilty at the first opportunity you'd have received the maximum sentence.'

The solicitor cleared his throat. 'This offence happened many years ago, when my client was a very different person. He has since lived an exemplary life.'

'Was your employer aware of your previous conviction?' asked Ruskin.

'Never came up,' Grime mumbled.

Sutton said nothing for a few beats, letting the tension build. 'OK, let's go back to the fire door. You said that you were unaware that the door lock was broken, and that the alarm had been bypassed.'

Grime licked his lips but said nothing.

'How is that possible?' continued Sutton. 'You're in charge of maintenance.' He removed a pile of stapled sheets from his folder. 'This is a copy of the logbook that needs to be filled in weekly, as part of the building's safety checks. It's a fire door, so it needs to be inspected regularly.' He pointed to a scrawl at the bottom of one of the pages. 'Is this your signature?'

Grime cleared his throat again, before nodding. 'Yes,' he whispered.

'According to this, you diligently check all of the fire exits each week and sign to say that the locks work and the doors are secure. Either you haven't been doing your job properly, or you've been ignoring the fact that anyone can enter or leave through that door without triggering an alarm. Which is it?'

'No comment.'

His response wasn't a surprise; doubtless his solicitor had

advised him not to engage with the interview and see if they had enough evidence to charge him.

'Your fingerprints are on the junction box that the CCTV camera is wired into, and we know that you have concealed the fact that the camera has been disconnected. Why would you do that?'

'No comment.'

Sutton locked eyes with him.

'Leon, we now have evidence that leads us to believe that Mr Patel was killed on the Thursday night, rather than the Friday morning. The murder most likely took place in room 201. His body was then removed from the hotel via that fire exit. A fire exit that you had ensured wouldn't have CCTV coverage and wouldn't trigger an alarm if it was opened. Anish Patel's body was wrapped in a sheet from the Easy Break Hotel.'

Grime was now a decidedly green colour. Even his solicitor was edging away from him slightly.

'No comment,' he whispered.

'Anish's body was mutilated after he was killed to make identifying him more difficult. Your hammer and Stanley knife were used to do that.'

Grime said nothing.

'The hammer and Stanley knife were found wrapped in towels, again from the Easy Break Hotel. The person who cleaned room 201 didn't report any missing towels or sheets, indicating that either they were replaced or those used in the murder were fresh ones. Either way, the towel and sheets probably came from the locked laundry cupboard next door to room 201. I assume that you have access to the keys for that cupboard?'

'I didn't do it,' said Grime finally, his voice cracking. 'Anyone could have access to my toolbox and the keys to the cleaning stores are hanging in the main office. I was playing pool down the pub on Thursday night, ask anyone.'

'We just have,' said Ruskin. 'Apparently, you went out in the first round. A bit unexpected, you usually make it to the semis

225

at least. In fact, one of the other players said that you practically handed the game to your opponent.'

'Sometimes you just have a bad night.'

Sutton pushed a copy of Grime's mobile phone log across the table. 'According to this, you texted your wife at 7.36 p.m. What did the text say?'

'Just told her that I had a crap game, and I was sticking around for a few more drinks,' said Grime.

'And after the drinks, did you go straight home?' asked Ruskin. 'Your wife says she doesn't know what time you arrived back. She went to bed about ten-thirty and when she woke up Friday morning you were asleep next to her.'

'Yeah, that's right.'

'What time did you get home then?' asked Sutton. 'Kicking out time at the club is about eleven-thirty, and it's what, a ten-minute walk, maybe less?'

'That's probably about right.'

'So, 11.45 maybe? Midnight?' asked Ruskin.

'I guess so.'

'Well that's where things get a bit strange,' said Ruskin. 'You see according to the people you were playing pool with, instead of sticking around and buying your opponent a drink – which is what is expected – you made an excuse about needing to get home to see your wife.'

Grime swallowed. 'They must be mistaken. It was a couple of weeks ago.'

Ruskin made a show of looking at his notebook. 'You left at 7.37 p.m., according to the CCTV from the bar. And despite it being such a short walk, you took your car. We have footage of you getting into it in the car park. Where did you go between texting your wife and finally getting home?'

Grime looked at his solicitor. 'No comment.'

'One more thing,' said Sutton. 'Why did you turn your mobile phone off?'

Wednesday 7th December

Chapter 29

A night in the cells hadn't loosened Leon Grime's tongue. He still refused to explain where he had gone after leaving the pub on the night of Anish Patel's murder. He also refused to make any comment on why he had ignored, or even facilitated, the use of the fire exit at the Easy Break Hotel as a means of entering the building covertly.

The closest they had got to any answer was his insistence that he didn't recognise any of Anish's family, nor had he ever met any of the men that Anish had contacted through Rainbow Hookups. His denials seemed genuine, but given his lack of cooperation so far, nobody was taking them at face value.

'We know that Anish Patel died on the Thursday night, sometime after he checked into the Easy Break Hotel at 6.28 p.m.,' said Warren, addressing the morning briefing. 'The problem is that everything else is supposition. We assume that his body was moved to the dumping site in his hire car, which we believe was caught on CCTV at half past one. We think that the person captured leaving the reception on Friday morning was the killer. But again, we don't know that for sure. We could really do with a much more precise time of death. That may be enough to rule out some of these suspects.'

On a whiteboard, Warren had drawn a grid with a timeline on the left-hand side.

'Let's start by looking for when we know that he was definitely alive,' Warren made a mark at 18:28. 'The Video Analysis Unit are certain that this picture on the reception CCTV is Anish checking in, not somebody dressed in his clothes.'

'He accessed his online banking app at five past eight,' said Pymm. 'It looks as though he was just checking his balance. There were no transactions made.'

'So he was still alive then,' said Warren. 'The question is whether he was alone or somebody – possibly the killer – was with him at that point? How long after then was he killed?'

There was silence around the table; the question was crucial. The footprints surrounding the ditch indicated more than one person was involved in the dumping and mutilation of the body. With the time of death still uncertain, a canny defence solicitor could suggest that their client was either not involved, or only took part in the cover-up. The thought that one of the killers might use the uncertainty to downplay their culpability left a bad taste in Warren's mouth.

When no suggestions about how to narrow down the time of death were forthcoming, Warren decided to leave it with the team to ponder and moved on.

'Where are we with Jaidev Patel on the night of the murder?' he asked.

'A mixed bag,' said Ruskin, who'd coordinated the team probing the man's alibi. 'We tracked down the three friends that he plays badminton with; they played as usual and went for a drink in the bar afterwards. The CCTV clearly shows showing him drinking until just before 8.45 p.m. One of the women was celebrating a birthday, which is why they drank for a little longer than usual.'

'That's a match so far,' said Warren. 'What happened then?'

'That's where it gets interesting. One of the men mentioned in passing that Jaidev said that he could have another drink, because it "wasn't his turn to drive".

'What does that mean?'

'Well, if you remember, Jaidev told us that he caught the bus home that night, which he does so he can have a drink?'

Warren nodded.

'Well, apparently, he always stays for at least one round. Then either he drives home, or he gets picked up. He doesn't catch the bus. In fact, when we looked back over the CCTV for the last few weeks, Jaidev usually picks up his kit bag and leaves the bar about twenty minutes before the bus is due at the stop outside. This week was no different. I followed him on the cameras and he went straight out the door; he didn't even make a detour to the toilet.'

'What are you saying, Moray?'

'I'm saying that I don't think he catches the bus home. One of Mags' team in Welwyn looked at the CCTV footage from the bus that he would have caught that night, and nobody matching Jaidev's description got on. The stop is right outside the sports centre door, so he'd have been waiting in the cold for several minutes before the bus turned up. He's been doing it for years, so you'd think he'd have figured out the timetable by now.'

'So why lie to us?' asked Sutton.

'Could he be worried that he was over the drink-drive limit?' asked Hardwick. 'If he is leaving straight after having a swift one, or maybe more, perhaps he didn't want to admit it?'

'Maybe, but what did he mean when he told his friend that "it wasn't his turn to drive"?' asked Sutton. 'Does he lift-share with one of his playing partners?'

'Apparently not,' said Ruskin. 'The other three all come together, straight from work, and two of the group are a married couple. They all live on the opposite side of town to Jaidev. He makes his own way there and back.'

'Then it sounds as though he's either being picked up, or he's driving another person,' said Hardwick. 'Does he meet someone else in the car park? Perhaps somebody who goes to the centre for a different class?'

'I don't know,' admitted Ruskin. 'The sports centre CCTV doesn't cover the public car park or the road outside.

'There's another thing that I thought was a bit weird. He turns up to the centre in a tracksuit with his kit bag. But he always has a shower afterwards and is smartly dressed when he leaves. I get the shower bit, you don't want to go home all sweaty, but he's supposed to be going home to bed. He's all dressed up like he's going out clubbing.'

Warren tapped his teeth thoughtfully. 'OK, find out who controls those outside cameras, and let's see if we can figure out who he's catching a ride home with. I also want to know how he actually gets to the sports centre. Is he driving himself, or is he being driven there? Maybe he catches a bus, so get back onto the bus company and see if he ever appears on that bus.

'He's lied about how he got home that night. It sounds like he's also lying about going straight there. I want to know why he's not telling the truth, and if it has anything to do with his brother's murder.'

'There's also something else,' said Rachel Pymm. It was her first contribution to the conversation. As the others had spoken, she'd been swiping through her emails on her tablet. She cleared her throat. 'I can't believe I didn't spot it before.'

'Don't keep us in suspense,' said Sutton.

'He plays badminton every Thursday, yes?'

'Yes, he's been doing it for years,' confirmed Ruskin.

'Well, according to the historic location data for his mobile phone, his handset is safely tucked up at home each week whilst he's thrashing a shuttlecock around,' said Pymm. 'Either he's really worried about his phone being stolen whilst he's playing, or he'd rather people don't know where he goes each Thursday.'

'Or he has a second handset that he has neglected to mention,' said Sutton.

Chapter 30

'What have you got to justify the further detention of Leon Grime?' asked Grayson.

The simple answer was 'not a lot'. So far, everything had been circumstantial. The red stains on clothing seized from his flat were not blood. His shoes didn't match the prints where Anish Patel's body was dumped, and neither they nor his coat had revealed any traces of body fluids yet.

The tools that had been used to mutilate Patel's body could have been accessed by other workers in the hotel, and even if they did find his fingerprints in room 201, they would be easily explained away by his role as head of maintenance.

Grime had lied about his whereabouts on the night of the murder and about his involvement with the doctored fire exit. He had also turned his phone off that night, presumably to stop it being tracked. That he had been up to something dodgy was pretty much a given, but was it relevant to their investigation?

'What about a motive?' asked Grayson.

'Nothing substantial,' admitted Warren. 'We can't even show any links between him and Anish's family; there's no overlap in terms of phone records. IT are still looking at his phone but so far as they can tell, unless he's deleted them off his handset, he wasn't a big user of social media or messaging apps.'

'Well he's not even close to the charging threshold,' said Grayson. He looked at his watch. 'What are you waiting on?'

'I'm hoping for the forensics back on his car in a few hours, as well as more detailed analysis of Anish's hire car. We're also going through his financials to see if there is anything interesting.'

Grayson pursed his lips. 'Well, we're pretty confident that Anish's body was driven to the dumping site in his hire car, so any traces of Grime in that car would be difficult to explain away. But I'm worried that we're placing all of our eggs in one basket here, as far as Grime is concerned.'

Warren couldn't disagree. His gut told him that there was something not right about Leon Grime, but they needed more than that. If he wasn't involved, then why were his tools used? Surely that meant the killer had to have at least known where they were? How many of their suspects would have that knowledge? Leon Grime might have been up to no good, but was he involved in the killing of Anish Patel?

One thing was certain though: Leon Grime had been arrested twice now; if he was released a second time, they could pretty much guarantee that whatever evidence existed to explain his behaviour would vanish.

*

The rest of the day passed slowly. By early evening, they needed to make a decision to either release Leon Grime again or apply for an extension to custody. With that in mind, Warren headed towards his office. He hated nagging Forensics. He knew that they worked as hard and as fast as they could, with ever-decreasing resources. He also knew that his was not the only serious crime being investigated at the moment. Nevertheless, he needed to know where he stood.

As he entered his office, his desk phone lit up.

'Andy, your sense of timing is impeccable,' said Warren, recognising the number immediately.

'I live to serve,' said Harrison.

'Go on then, make or break my day,' said Warren, his mouth suddenly dry.

'The vehicle team just reported back on Leon Grime's car. It's early days, and it'll be another twenty-four hours for the fast-track DNA to come through, but we've found traces of blood on the driver's seat, and the windscreen wiper stalk.'

Warren punched the air. Early days it might be, but they'd just got their extension to custody.

Chapter 31

Karen Hardwick's breath curled around her face in the cold, evening air. Standing outside the restaurant, she checked her mobile phone one more time.

No calls, or texts.

She took a deep breath, her heart pounding in her chest. It was go/no-go, as they said in the space program. Either she walked through the glass doors, or she turned around and headed back to the safety of home, and a cuddle with the most important person in her life.

It was the first time that she'd used this babysitter; a lovely, sixteen-year-old girl that lived in the same apartment block as her. Other parents had sung her praises, and finally Karen had relented.

Normally she would call on Gary's parents when she needed childcare. Both retired, they always jumped at the chance to spend time with their late son's only child, and although Karen sometimes found their attentions a bit stifling, she knew that it came from a place of love.

And they didn't charge.

But this time, it hadn't felt right. They'd probably be upset that she hadn't called them, but she knew it was the right decision. She couldn't face them tonight.

Twenty-six months.

Twenty-six months since the senseless death of her fiancé, the father of her beautiful little boy.

Twenty-six months existing, rather than living.

And now, twenty-six months later, perhaps it was time to move on.

She pushed down the feelings of guilt that threatened to overwhelm her and forced her way through the double doors. The blast of warm air and the sudden sound of quiet music and conversation almost made her change her mind.

What the hell was she doing?

Twenty-six months was the blink of an eye. Ollie wasn't even two years old yet, but here she was, galivanting around, trying to replace the father he had never even met.

'Karen?'

Her name came from the direction of the bar. Too late.

She turned and forced a smile. 'Adam,' she managed.

The man slipped off his barstool and headed towards her. Karen started mentally comparing him against the profile on the dating site.

The photo he'd used was clearly a few years old, and he had a bit more of a paunch than the photo he'd chosen, but it looked as though he hadn't told any massive whoppers about his age at least.

And who was she to judge?

Her foray into internet dating had been the result of a very drunken evening with her oldest and closest friend. Jenny had been using online dating sites for years and considered herself an expert – although given that she had yet to find Mr Right, that probably wasn't a ringing endorsement.

Jenny had bullied her into opening an account and then taken charge of writing her profile.

'What are you after? Soul mate, or just a good, hard shag?'

'Jenny! I'm not even looking. I told you, I'm not ready.'

'Bollocks, it's been two years,' she turned to Karen. 'You're beautiful and lovely, and funny and beautiful and lovely and you deserve to be happy.'

'You said beautiful twice,' mumbled Karen, taking another mouthful of the cheap rosé wine that Jenny had brought over. Since the birth of Ollie, she had definitely got out of practice; she'd feel it in the morning.

'Because you are, and it deserves to be said repeatedly. Now let's find a photo.' She opened her camera roll and started scrolling through the images.

'Perfect. Not too demure, not too slutty.'

'You mean desperate,' Karen had slurred.

'Same diff.'

The following morning, the first of the matches selected by the website's algorithm arrived in her inbox. Hungover, guilty, and full of regret, she'd almost deleted her profile there and then, but Jenny had begged her not to. 'At least take advantage of the free trial. If you still feel this way when the month is up, cancel the direct debit before the auto-billing starts.'

So, for the next few days, Karen had looked through her daily suggested matches, her mood swinging from despair, to hope, back to despair.

And then Adam had popped into her inbox.

He wasn't the first match that she'd initiated a conversation with, but he was the first one that she hadn't blocked after two or three exchanges. And the first one that she had agreed to speak to outside of the dating app, giving him the email address that she'd set up specifically for the purpose of contacting strangers on the internet.

After a few exchanges, Adam had finally posted his mobile phone number.

Jenny had been even more excited than Karen, but still texted her list of do's and don'ts.

After twenty-four hours of indecision, she finally called, dialling 141 first to block her own number. You didn't spend years working murder cases and give out your contact details to just anyone.

And here they were.

After an awkward couple of seconds of greeting, the waiter mercifully arrived and took Karen's coat.

'Can I get you a drink?' asked Adam, as he finished the last couple of fingers of the pint of lager in front of his spot at the bar.

'Just a soda and blackcurrant,' said Hardwick. 'I'm driving.'

That was another of Jenny's dos and don'ts; don't drink alcohol, keep an eye on your drink at all times, and make sure that you have your own transport.

Adam ordered her drink and another lager.

He's as nervous as I am, thought Karen. The realisation made her feel better.

On Jenny's advice, Karen had chosen the restaurant. It was a mid-price chain that catered to most tastes, and Karen had been there before. She knew exactly where the rear exit was, and she could be locked inside her car within two minutes.

She was sure dating hadn't been this complicated ten years ago.

By the time the starters had been taken away, the conversation was flowing more freely and soon Karen knew all about Adam's day job as a web designer. It didn't sound like the most exciting of occupations, but she found that oddly reassuring. At least he wouldn't be killed in the line of duty.

'Are you OK, Karen?'

She forced her attention back to Adam, making herself smile. 'Yes, I'm fine.'

Adam nodded, taking a swig of his beer. He'd ordered it after their starters had arrived. Assuming that the beer he was finishing as she arrived was only his first of the evening, that made three by her count. Was three too much on a first date? She'd certainly gone on dates at university that had involved far more alcohol, but was that what she was looking for now?

The main course arrived. Adam had ordered a big, messy burger with all the trimmings, which he bit into with gusto; molten cheese dribbled down his chin. Karen started spooning around her penne pasta with tomato and basil sauce.

Suddenly, there was a commotion from the table behind them. The young couple who had been eating there were heading out the door at high-speed.

A middle-aged waiter raced after them, shouting.

Karen stood up. 'Excuse me,' she said to Adam, as she hurried towards the disturbance. A few seconds later, the waiter reappeared, out of breath and angry.

Before she knew what she was doing, Karen had her warrant card in her hand.

'Is there a problem?' she asked quietly.

'Fuckers did a runner without paying,' the waiter said with a big sigh. 'Second time this month.'

'Did you get their names?' she asked.

'No, they were walk-ins.' He shook his head. 'It's getting harder to tell these days. Years ago, if some scally in a tracksuit and trainers came in, we'd stick them in that corner and keep an eye on them. If they looked like they were going to leg it, they'd at least have to get past half a dozen tables and give us a sporting chance of grabbing them. But those guys were dressed smartly. I should have realised something was dodgy when they didn't take their coats off.'

'What'll happen now?' asked Hardwick.

'We write it off,' he shrugged. 'The boss is pretty good, he doesn't dock our wages or anything, but they had a good meal, with nice wine, I was hoping for a decent tip.' He angled his head upwards. 'At least we'll have got them on the cameras. We'll get headshots circulated around all the local businesses; they won't be welcome anywhere in Middlesbury.'

'Is everything OK?' Adam was standing behind her; his eyes were watery, and a spot of ketchup dotted his collar. Karen was now certain that the beer he'd been finishing as she came in wasn't his first of the evening.

'You know what, I'm not in the mood for dessert,' she said, forcing a smile. An idea was starting to form.

After insisting on splitting the bill two ways, and slipping an extra-large tip on the plate, Karen bid her farewells to Adam.

'That was a lovely evening,' he said, after an awkward kiss on her cheek. 'Can we do it again sometime?'

'Of course, give me a call, yeah?' said Karen, before leaving him to finish his drink. She was already most of the way back to her car, before Adam realised that he didn't actually have her number.

Pulling out her phone, Karen checked the time. It wasn't too late to call, she decided.

Richardson picked up her mobile on the second ring.

'Hey Mags, you still in the office?'

'Yeah, for my sins.'

'I'm going to pop in, I need a word.'

'Sure. Wait, weren't you supposed to be on a date? Andrew, or Aaron or something?'

'Adam, and it's finished.'

'Oh shit, sweetie. Come in and tell me all about it. I'll get the kettle on.'

'No, really, I'm fine. But I've had an idea.'

*

Karen nibbled a biscuit, as she filled Mags in on her date.

'Well, it could have been worse, I suppose,' said Mags philosophically. 'Better that he's a bore, than a weirdo. And he hasn't sent you a dick pic or anything.'

'Mags!'

'Well, you read about these perverts.'

'Don't worry, he hasn't got my number, and I'll block his email address from my dating account. Besides, he knows I'm a copper, he'd be bloody daft to try anything like that.'

'True. Now tell me about this idea you had that caused you to run out on a hot date.'

Karen filled her in on the couple that left the restaurant without paying.

'Rachel said that Anish liked eating out, and that he used his credit card when he paid,' she continued.

'Yeah, it was the only way he could afford that lifestyle.'

'If Anish met his killer through that dating app, or something similar, and paid for the meal with his credit card, then maybe we can use his bank records to track them down.'

Mags gave a cautious nod of the head. 'I suppose we could use the date of the credit card payment, and then track that back to the restaurant and see if they have any CCTV footage from that night,' she frowned. 'The only problem is that most of those meals were months ago. The chances are good that they've recorded over the footage.'

Karen's shoulders sagged.

'Hey, it's a good idea,' said Mags, 'and I'm going to get someone on it first thing tomorrow.'

She stood up and gave Karen a hug.

'Chin up, girl. There's plenty more men out there; somewhere, Mr Perfect is waiting for you to swipe up or down, or whatever it is you do on those apps.'

Karen forced a smile.

The problem was, she'd already met her Mr Perfect, and she wasn't sure if lightning would strike again.

Her phone gave out a strange beep that she was unfamiliar with; her phone was usually set on silent. A text message.

Her heart leapt. Oliver.

Looking at the caller ID, she felt herself relax, it wasn't the babysitter.

It was Jenny, asking how the evening was going.

Suddenly, Karen felt weary. She didn't have the energy to deal with that now.

*

For the first time in days, Warren returned home, if not with a spring in his step, at least feeling a little less worn out. Leon Grime had denied that the blood found in his car was Anish Patel's, nevertheless the magistrate had authorised his continued detention.

At this stage in an investigation, Warren was essentially on call, so sharing a bottle of wine with Susan was out of the question, especially on a school night. Fortunately, after months of careful and diligent experimentation, Tony Sutton had finally identified the best alcohol-free lager on the market. Even better, the M&S Food attached to the local garage stocked it in their chiller cabinet.

For the past year or so, Warren and Susan had been doing their best to cut down on their takeaway habit and eat out a little less; but he was in a celebratory mood, and so had picked up a couple of chilli con carne ready meals and some garlic bread. Hardly a traditional pairing, but Warren didn't care; judging by MasterChef 'fusion' was all the rage these days.

Waiting for the microwave to work its magic, Warren picked up the packet of chilli seeds that Susan had been given by a colleague in work and read the instructions for at least the fourth time. It seemed simple enough; they'd plant them in the New Year, and by the late spring or early summer they'd hopefully be making their own chilli sauce. In theory, you'd think that his biology teacher wife would have naturally green fingers, but they had established early on in their marriage that Susan was an even bigger disaster in the garden than Warren. He wondered if they would be able to arrange for Granddad Jack to come down and stay in the spring. Jack's gardening days were past him now, but he knew the old man would get a kick out of advising Susan and Warren how to finally tackle their back yard. Susan's parents had helped out in the past, but they were busier than ever now they were retired. He'd suggest it next time he phoned.

Warren's mind drifted back to the case. Something about the seeds had triggered a thought. It remained tantalisingly out of reach as he opened a bottle of lemonade; Tony Sutton had found that even the worst of the alcohol-free beers could be improved immeasurably by mixing them with lemonade. Not for the first time, Warren cringed inwardly when he thought about what his younger, student self would have thought if he had known that twenty years later he would be drinking alcohol-free shandy ...

The ding of the microwave brought him back to the present. It also banished whatever idea the seeds had sparked. Warren plated the food and joined Susan in the lounge. He knew that there was no point chasing down the idea. It would come to him eventually; far better to let his subconscious work away at it. Hopefully, it wouldn't wake him in the middle of the night.

Susan moved the pile of tests that she'd been marking onto the floor, clearing a space on the settee.

'Seriously,' she griped, 'my year seven pupils can successfully label the parts of a flower. Yet six years later, a class full of seventeen and eighteen-year-old A level biology students can't tell the difference between the male parts and the female parts of a flowering plant.'

Warren gave her a look of commiseration but said nothing. It would have been hypocritical.

'What?' asked Susan.

Warren had paused, a spoonful of chilli and rice halfway to his mouth.

The flower diagrams and the chilli seeds had merged in his mind. Suddenly, the half-formed thought that had eluded him in the kitchen came rushing back. He placed the spoon back in the bowl, uneaten.

'You haven't even tried it,' said Susan.

'I need to make a call,' said Warren, placing the bowl on the side and heading for the kitchen where he'd left his phone.

Susan sighed, but said nothing. It came with the territory.

'Tony, you got a moment?' asked Warren when Sutton answered.

'Sure thing, Boss.' In the background he could hear Marie, Sutton's wife, asking if he wanted her to put the dinner back in the oven to keep warm. Not for the first time Warren reflected on what police officers' partners had to put up with.

'Leon Grime told us that he'd just taken a load of veg up to his mum's care home and that was why he was late back when we called him in for interview.'

'Yes, but it checked out. ANPR cameras on the motorway show that he was heading back from Newcastle.'

'I know. He also said when we confronted him about the blood in his car, that it was his and he'd cut himself gardening.'

'Yeah, well we won't know if that's true or it was secondary transfer from Anish until tomorrow, even with a rush on the DNA.'

'So twice he's told us that he's a gardener.'

'You'll have to spell it out for me,' said Sutton.

'He lives in a second-floor flat, with no garden. So where the hell is he growing vegetables?'

Sutton paused for a moment. 'Christ, the bugger has an allotment.'

'And what's the betting it has a shed?' said Warren.

Thursday 8th December

Chapter 32

By the time Warren arrived in the office that morning, Karen Hardwick had tracked down the chair of the local allotment association. She gave him a thumbs-up when she saw him enter.

'Yes, we do have a valid search warrant for Mr Grime's allotment and any other outbuildings that he has access to, however we don't know where his plot is. That's why I am calling you,' she rolled her eyes theatrically. Warren could hear a high-pitched squawking from the other end of the line.

'No, it won't be a breach of data protection for you to give us his plot number,' she said politely.

After a few more seconds listening, she finally picked up her pen and scribbled in her notepad.

'Thank you for your help. We'll have an officer waiting for you at the main gates.'

Finally she hung up and let out a puff of air. 'Done. Leon Grime leases a full-size plot just off the A506, roughly half-way between his house and the Easy Break Hotel.'

'That's convenient,' said Warren.

'The chair of the allotment association doesn't know him personally, but according to her records he has rented the plot for the past fifteen years. He keeps it in good order, forks out the forty quid rent each year on time and has never had any complaints,' she looked up and smiled. 'And eight years ago, he applied for – and was granted – permission to erect a wooden shed.'

*

Traipsing around a muddy allotment in December was not Tony Sutton's idea of fun. By contrast, Moray Ruskin was characteristically enthusiastic as they climbed out of the car and made their way through the sturdy double gates. A uniformed constable greeted them as they entered; white-suited technicians could be seen on the third plot from the end, providing entertainment for an older couple who'd given up any pretence of gardening.

'Alex and I have been on the waiting list for a council allotment for the past two years,' Ruskin said. 'We'll never afford a house with a garden, so it's the only way we'll ever be able to grow our own vegetables.'

'You aren't exactly their target demographic,' said Sutton, motioning with his head towards the older couple.

'You'd be surprised,' said Ruskin. 'It's not all old codgers in their eighties. My cousin has had one since his twenties. Mad not to really; for forty quid a year, we'll save a fortune on food.' He lowered his voice slightly. 'Besides, it'll be good exercise for Alex and a lot cheaper than the gym subscription he never uses.'

Sutton laughed. 'You're a bad 'un, Moray.'

The plot had been sealed off, police tape fluttering on metal poles set into the ground. A CSI with a pair of bolt cutters was snipping the padlock off a small shed.

The outhouse was nothing special. It looked a lot like the one that Sutton had in his own garden: a treated wooden frame with a single window and door. The roof was covered in grey, tarred felt and angled to stop water accumulating and Grime had added guttering to channel the rainwater into a large plastic water butt. There was no need on an allotment to store a lawn mower or

250

patio furniture during the winter, so the small building would have ample room for whatever tools and equipment Grime wished to keep in it. And anything else besides.

Deputy Crime Scene Manager Meera Gupta had been assigned this job. Her breath billowed out of her mouth as she spoke.

'As you can see, all of the other plots nearby have similar sheds. I suspect that means that Mr Grime is the only person with access to this one. The association don't insist on having a spare key to the padlock.'

Ruskin made a note to follow up on that; he'd already spotted a couple of Grime's fellow tenants.

'We'll do a quick search of the shed, then get in the dogs. If he's been storing any drugs in here recently they may pick up on residual scent. And the cadaver dogs will find anything with traces of the victim or blood.'

Thanking her, Sutton walked up the pathway to phone Warren and the rest of the team. Ruskin headed toward Grime's nearest neighbour.

The woman was wrapped up well, and Ruskin wouldn't have dared try and narrow her age down to anything more precise than 'over fifty'.

'Oh yes, there's something to do all year around if you plan it right,' she responded to his opening query. 'There are some folks who choose plants that only need working on in the warmer months, but I prefer to be out here all year round.' She gave a sad smile. 'It gets me up and doing something. It's easy to lose track of the days when you're suddenly on your own ...' Her voice trailed off.

'And was Mr Grime here all year round?' asked Ruskin.

'Oh yes, I'd often see Leon, even at this time of year. He was here a couple of weeks ago harvesting some winter cabbage.'

'Was that the last time you saw him?'

'Yes, although I haven't been here as much as I usually am. Just a couple of hours in the morning. Winter's setting in, and

251

even with the best will in the world things quieten down this time of the year.' She pointed towards the other side of Grime's plot. 'You might be better off asking Bert, his other neighbour. He's up here most days as well, but he tends to come a bit later. His arthritis isn't so good first thing in the morning.'

Ruskin made a note of the name. 'Do you know if Leon shared his shed with anyone, or used anyone else's shed?'

'Oh no, nobody does that. What is it they say? An Englishman's shed is his castle? My Ron was always disappearing up here for a bit of peace and quiet. I've no idea how much gardening he actually did during the football season, you can get a good radio signal up here and that sun lounger looked pretty well used. When he … passed … I had a clear-out.' She smiled sadly again. 'Turns out he hadn't given up smoking his pipe after all, the crafty bugger, the shed still smells of tobacco. It reminds me of him …' Her eyes narrowed. 'Whatever it is you find in there, you can pretty much guarantee that it was Leon who put it there.'

'So not his wife then?'

'Goodness, no. I don't think I've ever seen her in the years since Ron passed away and I took over.'

Ruskin thanked her and headed back towards Sutton, who was still on his mobile phone. He looked dejected. Seeing Ruskin, he hung up. 'That was the boss. Bad news: they did an overnight rush-job on the blood found in Leon Grime's car. No match to Anish Patel; it's Grime's. It's just like he said last night when we asked him; he must have cut himself gardening.'

'Bugger,' said Ruskin.

The blood stain in Grime's car was their justification for extending his custody. Now, unless they found something else, it looked like Grime would be walking out of the station later that day.

'Sirs, we've found something.' Meera Gupta was waving an arm in their direction.

The two officers hastened towards her.

252

Beside the CSM, a technician with a litter picker was carefully lifting a grey backpack from behind the water butt.

'Got him,' said Ruskin.

Chapter 33

News of the find from the allotment had travelled fast and the team was in a jubilant mood during briefing. But with no motive established yet, or indication of who else had been involved, they continued to follow other leads. Mags Richardson currently had the floor.

'I've had my team down in Welwyn look at the CCTV from the bus company that serves the sports centre where Jaidev Patel plays badminton. I've also had them going through the CCTV from the public car park adjacent to the sports centre. There is a camera capturing the licence plates of vehicles entering the car park, and another covering a drop-off area outside. Unfortunately, the angle is wrong on that one; we can't see the licence plates. However, they've built up a pattern of his normal movements over the past six weeks. This is a summary; it's an interesting read.'

She projected a colour-coded table onto the screen, divided into two columns.

'As you can see, every other week he catches the bus to the sports centre, and on the alternate weeks drives himself there and parks in the car park.'

She pointed to the second column. 'When he's finished, he

either drives himself home, or on the weeks he goes there by bus, he's picked up by a black Range Rover from the drop-off area.'

'He drives a black Range Rover, doesn't he? Could it be his wife picking him up in his car?' asked Hutchinson.

'That's what I thought at first, but I compared still images of the vehicle that we know he drives, and the one that picks him up.'

She switched to two images side by side. The first showed a black Range Rover exiting the car park, turning left onto the main road. 'This is Jaidev's,' she said.

The second showed what appeared to be the same Range Rover waiting in the drop-off area. The left-hand sides of both vehicles were clearly visible. Richardson manipulated the screen, zooming in on the rear side-window of the car waiting in the drop-off area.

'It looks as though whoever drives this car is a Liverpool Football fan. That's the club decal.' She zoomed into the same area on the car leaving the car park. 'I've no idea what team Jaidev supports, but he doesn't feel the need to place a sticker in the rear window.'

'Nicely spotted,' said Warren approvingly. 'It would seem that Jaidev is being picked up every other week by somebody. What's the betting that on the weeks that he drives himself, he's the one picking up that person?'

'I wouldn't bet against it,' said Richardson.

'So, who else do we know that drives a near-identical black Range Rover to Jaidev Patel?' asked Warren.

'Manoj,' said Richardson, 'and on the night of Anish Patel's murder, Manoj's wife, Lavanya, claimed that he was home with her. However, the neighbour across the road has CCTV.'

'Don't tell me,' said Warren. 'He wasn't in when he said he was?'

'No. We have footage of his Range Rover pulling into his drive at 17:49. It's dark, and the camera is using infra-red, but the plate is readable. Three hours later, the car leaves. It doesn't return until five past two the next morning.'

'Are we sure he's driving?' asked Sutton.

She shook her head. 'No. The windscreen is tinted, and the night vision on the camera isn't good enough; his wife claimed that he was home with her all night. Their kids are too young to drive, so at least one of them left the house. Which means that they are both lying.'

'Great work, Mags,' said Warren. 'So, where are these two going every Thursday night, when they claim to be at home with their wives, bathing their kids? And why do they feel the need to leave their mobile phones at home? And most importantly, where did they go on the night that their brother was murdered?'

'Bring them all in,' he ordered.

*

Leon Grime looked decidedly impatient when he was led into the interview room. After the formalities had been completed, Tony Sutton and Moray Ruskin got down to business.

'We've had the results back from the DNA test on the blood that we found in your car,' started Sutton. 'It seems that you are correct and that it is your blood.'

Grime smiled and leaned back his arms folded. 'Good, can I go now?'

'Not just yet,' said Sutton. 'We have a few more questions that we wish to ask you.'

Grime gave a big sigh. 'Fine, whatever. Can we just get on with it?'

'What were you doing on the evening of Thursday the 24th of November?' asked Ruskin.

'I've told you before, I ain't got nothing to say about that night,' said Grime.

'You were first arrested on Saturday the 3rd of December,' said Ruskin. 'Where did you go when you left here the following morning?'

'Straight back to bed for a kip.' Grime's voice was aggressive.

'Any witnesses?'

'Just my wife. Ask her.'

'And how long were you there for?' asked Sutton.

Grime gave a shrug. 'Until I went to work the next morning.'

Ruskin looked over at Sutton. 'He's right, Sir. According to his mobile phone records, he never left home.'

Grime smirked. 'There you are.'

Sutton looked at his notes and frowned. 'And you definitely didn't leave the house until the following morning?'

'Nope. Stayed in with the missus, watched a bit of telly, had something decent to eat and got an early night.'

'Do you have a brother, Mr Grime?' asked Ruskin.

Grime blinked. 'No, I had a sister but she died years ago. Car accident.'

'I'm sorry to hear that,' said Sutton. 'Do you have kids?'

'No. Look, what is this all about?' asked Grime.

'I'm beginning to wonder that myself,' interrupted the solicitor.

Sutton ignored him. 'So, if you were at home and you don't have any siblings or kids, who was it that was down your allotment on Sunday morning, about an hour after you left the station?'

Grime opened his mouth, before closing it again. After a few seconds he tried again. 'That's nonsense. I never went anywhere near my allotment that day.'

'Are you sure? We have a witness that saw you.'

Grime's right eye twitched. An interesting tell that Sutton noted for future reference.

'They must be confused.' He licked his lips. 'You've seen them up there, coffin dodgers the lot of them. Reckon they haven't got a clue what day of the week it is half the time.'

'The witness was pretty confident about the day,' said Ruskin. 'He asked if you'd watched the match the night before.' He looked at Grime. 'Your old man was a Chelsea fan, wasn't he? That's why you've always supported them, even when you lived in Newcastle. Three-one against Man City; he was surprised you'd missed it, but you couldn't really tell him that we don't have Sky TV in the custody suite.'

Grime's eye twitched again.

'So, what was so urgent about your allotment that you needed to race down there, barely an hour after a night in the cells, leaving your phone at home?' asked Sutton.

Grime was silent for a few seconds. 'No comment,' he said eventually.

'Well whatever it was, it didn't seem to involve much gardening,' said Ruskin. 'According to our witness, you were there for less than ten minutes. What was it you were doing?'

'No comment.'

'What did you take away in that blue sports bag he saw you with?' asked Sutton.

'No comment,' repeated Grime.

'Well, I'm sure we'll figure out what it is sooner or later,' said Sutton. 'You'd be amazed how sensitive the noses are of those sniffer dogs.'

Grime swallowed but said nothing.

'More importantly,' said Sutton, 'what did you bring in that bag?'

'No comment,' said Grime.

Sutton opened the folder on the desk next to him and took out a series of colour images. He pushed them across the table, one by one, as he drove his point across.

'Do you recognise these, Leon?'

Grime looked at the picture in front of him and shook his head. 'No, I've never seen them before.'

'Really? They were hidden between the water butt and the wall of your shed.'

'I told you, I've never seen them before.'

'Are you sure? This was the hoodie that Anish Patel was wearing the night he was murdered. The same hoodie that somebody other than Anish was wearing the morning after he was killed.'

258

'No, I've never seen it,' said Grime, shaking his head violently.

Sutton passed over another picture. 'These were also found at the scene. We've taken imprints of the keys and they match Anish's flat.' He pushed another picture across the table. 'And this wallet belonged to Anish. There's no money in it, but as you can see it contains his driving licence and his credit cards.'

'No, no, no,' Grime was shaking violently. 'I've never seen them before. They've nothing to do with me.'

'These jeans and shoes match those that he was wearing that night,' said Ruskin. Grime continued shaking his head.

Sutton placed a final photograph on the table, this one a composite of two images.

'What about this grey backpack? Everything else was inside it.'

He pointed to a black logo on the rear of the bag, then pointed to a similar looking logo on the one slung across Patel's shoulder as he entered the hotel lobby. 'It looks very much like the bag that Anish Patel used for overnight hotel stays.'

Grime turned to his solicitor. 'Can't you do something? They planted that evidence.'

'Now why would we do that, Leon?' asked Sutton.

'I don't fucking know, do I?' shouted Grime.

'OK, calm down, Leon,' said Sutton.

'No, I won't fucking calm down. This is a stitch-up. You've just decided to pin it on the ex-con. You've looked at my record and thought, I know, he's got form. He's spent time inside. No need to bother looking any further.'

Grime had turned an alarming shade of red and was breathing heavily.

'Perhaps a break would be a good idea,' suggested Sutton, beating the solicitor to it by seconds.

'Why, so you have time to plant more evidence?' Grime started to stand up and Sutton braced himself.

'Sit back down, Leon,' ordered Ruskin getting to his feet. At six feet five inches, he towered over the handyman.

Grime dropped back into his chair, but Sutton could see that it wasn't because he was intimidated by Ruskin's size.

'Shit,' he muttered, jumping to his own feet. 'Somebody get a first-aider in here,' he shouted towards the video link.

This was not how they wanted the interview to end.

*

'Looks like it was a panic attack, rather than anything more serious,' said Warren as he passed Sutton a glass of water. Sutton nodded his thanks.

'But what about you?'

'I'm good,' said Sutton, the colour having finally returned to his face.

'Are you sure you don't want to go home?' asked Warren.

'I said I'm fine,' snapped Sutton. He took a sip of his water. 'Sorry, didn't mean to be rude.'

Warren perched on the end of his desk. He'd been friends with Sutton too long to let it go at that.

'Your hands were shaking, and you were grey by the time we got down to the interview suite. Poor Moray didn't know who to go to first,' said Warren.

'It's nothing. Seriously, I just got a bit excited is all,' he stuck out his arm. 'Feel my pulse, steady as a rock.'

'I know, I spoke to Sergeant Subramanian after she checked you over,' Warren waited until Sutton met his eyes. 'No bullshit, Tony, it's just us in here. How are you really?'

Sutton leaned back in his chair. 'I'm OK, really I am. The pills keep my blood pressure and pulse rate down, and sometimes that makes me a little light-headed,' his voice strengthened. 'It's nothing I can't handle. I had a check-up less than a month ago, and my consultant told me to just take it easy. No running around, light exercise only, try not to get too stressed.' He raised a hand to stall Warren. 'She's not worried, so I'm not worried. And neither should you be.'

Warren looked at him for a long moment, before finally nodding. 'OK, we'll play it your way. But for Christ's sake, if you are feeling ill, stop and take some time out.'

Unbidden, the memory of Sutton collapsing, his tongue flopping around and his eyes rolling sprang to mind. Felled by a mini-stroke as they chased after a serial killer, Warren still felt that he'd let his friend down, even though there was nothing he could have done. He pushed the image away, although he suspected it would make an unwelcome return in his dreams that night.

'Well I'll say one thing, that panic attack put the kybosh on our questioning,' said Sutton.

'Yeah, hell of a reaction,' mused Warren.

'We had him by the bollocks. He's looking at a long stretch inside,' said Sutton.

'Yeah. Maybe,' said Warren.

Sutton eyed him carefully. 'You don't sound convinced.'

Warren gave a sigh. 'We're a long way from closing this. If nothing else, he can't have been acting alone; it would probably have taken at least two people to manoeuvre Anish's body in and out of the boot of his car, and who went to his flat to send those text messages from Anish's phone? A phone that is still unaccounted for? We've got CCTV and witness statements that place Grime at work when the texts were sent.'

'Well, we thought that anyway,' said Sutton. 'There were two sets of shoeprints at the dumping site.'

'So, who has he teamed up with?'

Sutton thought for a moment. 'I suspect we won't know that until we figure out a motive.'

'Exactly. And why kill him at the Easy Break Hotel, wrap him in a sheet and use his own tools to mutilate him? That just leads us back to where he works.'

'True, it's shitting in your own nest,' said Sutton. 'But you'd think if he was innocent, he'd be falling over himself to tell us what he was doing that night.'

'Which brings us back to Anish's brothers,' said Warren. 'What the hell were they doing that means they left their phones at home so they couldn't be tracked? Is it too much of a coincidence that both they and Grime are lying about their whereabouts that night? How are they linked?'

'Maybe his family aren't involved,' said Sutton. 'They're arseholes, and clearly up to something, but maybe it is just a coincidence?'

'In which case, what's Grime's motive?' asked Warren. 'We know that he removed something from that shed of his, but whatever it was, it only half-filled a gym bag.'

'In which case, the obvious conclusion is drugs,' said Sutton. 'A few tightly wrapped bricks of cocaine or heroin would not only be worth a few grand, he'd be in a whole heap of trouble if we'd found them, and not just from us. I doubt he's at the top of the totem pole.'

'Which makes more sense,' said Warren. 'If Anish and his brothers were shifting drugs through the hotel and got greedy, then there's no way those above Grime are going to let that go.'

'But there's more bothering you, isn't there?' said Sutton.

'Yeah. And when Leon Grime's ready to be interviewed again, it should be the first question his solicitor asks.'

Sutton though for a second. 'He'll want to know why, if Grime had the presence of mind to go and remove whatever dodgy gear was stashed in that shed, he left a bag containing Anish's belongings where it could be easily found?'

Chapter 34

Manoj Patel, and his wife, Lavanya, were brought to Middlesbury station separately, having both been picked up from their places of work. The officers that fetched them were careful not to allow the couple to contact each other, although they allowed Lavanya to call her sister-in-law, Reva Vasava, to arrange childcare for later.

To minimise any chance of the two brothers getting their stories straight, DSI Grayson had persuaded Cambridgeshire police to make a couple of their interview suites available for Jaidev Patel and his wife, Kamala. Warren had despatched Richardson and a small team to see if either of them were willing to shed light on the brothers' Thursday night outing.

Not wanting a repeat of his previous encounter with Manoj, Warren delegated David Hutchinson and Moray Ruskin to interview him, and assigned Rachel Pymm and Karen Hardwick to speak to his wife. Both interview suites were fitted with video feeds and Warren settled down with the team to watch the interviews in the briefing room.

The first to be interviewed was Lavanya Patel.

'Thank you for attending today, Lavanya,' started Pymm.

Patel looked nervous.

'Why am I here? The kids will be wondering where I am.'

'We won't keep you any longer than necessary,' said Pymm, in a tone that managed to sound both reassuring and firm.

Pymm opened her notebook. 'You spoke previously to my colleague, DC Hardwick.'

Patel nodded. Hardwick smiled politely.

'We're just trying to clear up a few details from that interview,' continued Pymm, 'now that you've had a chance to think about things.'

She let the statement hang in the air. Patel swallowed.

'You told me that Thursday the 24th of November, your husband, Manoj, was at work during the day and then home for the evening,' said Hardwick, consulting her own notes.

'Yes, that's right.'

'What time does Manoj finish work typically?'

Patel paused for a moment. 'Usually he works from about nine until half past five.'

'He works at the Everyday Essentials on Perry Road?'

'Yes, he's the manager.'

'I see. So he closes the shop and comes home at about five-thirty?'

'No, the shop is open until ten. We have a sales assistant who works there in the evening. Manoj gets home between five-thirty and six.'

'And that's it for the evening?'

'Yes. Manoj keeps his phone on in case there are any problems. It's only a ten-minute drive.'

'What about the Thursday night? Was that a normal evening?' asked Pymm.

'Yes, I'd say so.'

'I know it's some time ago, but can you remember what you did when Manoj got home that evening?'

'I don't know. I guess we had dinner, then bathed the boys and put them to bed.'

Patel took a sip of water.

264

'And what then? What time do you go to bed?'

'Look, what is this about?'

'We're just trying to get a feel for what happened that night, Lavanya. It helps us build a timeline.'

Pymm's tone was reassuring, but it was clear that Patel was uncomfortable.

'We go to bed between ten and eleven, I guess. Sometimes we watch a movie.' She smiled, but it didn't quite reach her eyes. 'We have two small children, our days of late-night partying are behind us.'

Pymm returned the smile. 'I remember it well.' She leaned forward. 'Trust me, in a few years you'll be glad that you know where they are and what they're doing.'

'So, neither of you went out again that evening?' asked Hardwick.

Patel paused and took another sip of water. 'No, hang on. Manoj popped back out to the shop. We got a call; the till was playing up. He nipped over to reset it.'

Upstairs, Warren clapped Sutton on the back. 'Excellent, she's starting to panic. She's making lies up on the spot, she won't be able to keep her story straight.'

Back in the interview suite, Pymm and Hardwick sensed the shift. Pymm decided to give her a little more rope to play with.

'How annoying, does that happen very often?' she asked.

'Now and again.'

'I'll bet it happened right in the best part of the film, that's usually the way,' commiserated Hardwick.

'Yeah, I had to pause it whilst he was gone,' said Patel, her shoulders relaxing slightly.

'How long did you have to wait?' asked Hardwick.

'Umm, not long. Twenty or thirty minutes, I suppose. I loaded the washing machine and the dishwasher and made the boys' lunches. Saves a bit of time in the morning.'

'And he took his own car?'

'Yes, his is parked in front of mine on the drive.'

'What film were you watching?' asked Hardwick.

'Err. Something on Netflix,' said Patel. 'Some Bollywood musical, you probably wouldn't know it,' she added hastily.

'You're probably right,' said Pymm, turning over a page in her notepad. 'The sales assistant at the shop – her name's Kelly, I believe?'

'Uhm, yes, I think so.'

'It's strange, because we had a chat with her, and she didn't mention Manoj coming back to work Thursday night.'

Patel swallowed again. 'She must have forgotten. It happens all the time.'

'I thought you said it only happened "now and again",' said Hardwick.

Patel glanced down at the table. 'I guess she must have been confused. Not a lot happens in the shop in the evening, it's pretty boring. She probably got her days muddled up.'

Pymm carefully placed her notepad on the desk. She looked squarely at the woman in front of her, the woman now picking at a loose thread on her sleeve and tapping her foot on the floor.

'OK, Lavanya, time to stop playing games. We know that your husband's car returned to the house at 17:49. It then left three hours later and didn't return until five past two. One or both of you were out of the house the night that Anish was killed. I want to know which of you left that night, where you went and what you were doing.'

Patel's eyes were starting to shine.

'Did Manoj go out that night?' asked Hardwick, her tone softer than Pymm's.

Patel's lower lip trembled and she shook her head slightly. Whether it was a denial, or she didn't want to speak, was unclear.

'Did you leave the house that night?' asked Pymm.

Patel looked up at the ceiling, the tears starting to run down her cheek.

Finally, she spoke.

'I want a lawyer.'

*

'Good work, you two,' said Warren. They were a long way from the truth of what happened that night, but cracks were starting to appear in the couple's alibi.

'Manoj Patel has decided to meet us head-on and request a lawyer straight off the bat,' said Hutchinson 'They just arrived and they're having a conference now.'

'Hopefully, Manoj will be expecting us to question him further about Jaidev's movements on the day we told the family about Anish's death,' said Warren.

'Sounds like a good opener, Sir,' said Hutchinson, a note of relish in his voice. He clapped Ruskin on the shoulder. 'Ready to go and meet Mr Charming?'

'Lead on,' said Ruskin.

*

Manoj Patel glared at the two officers throughout the interview preliminaries, speaking only to confirm his name. Beside him his solicitor – a portly, middle-aged man that neither officer had met before – sat similarly mute, his pen poised over his notepad.

'Thank you for coming to see us again, Manoj, I appreciate that this is a difficult time for you and your family,' started Hutchinson. It never hurt to try and get the interview off to a cordial start.

Patel curled his lip. 'Didn't give me much choice, did you?'

'Well, as the officers explained, you are not under arrest. You have attended the station, voluntarily, to give a statement to help us with our enquiries.' He inclined his head towards the solicitor. 'As I am sure your legal representative has explained to you.'

Patel gave a sneer and leaned back in his chair, arms folded.

'I imagine you have spoken to Jaidev about what happened the day that we visited your father to break the news of your brother's death. I wonder if you could tell me what you recall about that day?'

Patel said nothing and just glared. Hutchinson and Ruskin waited patiently. Eventually, after a few tense seconds, he straightened in his chair.

'Fine, whatever. My sister, Reva, called me to say that police were at the house. Something about Anish being dead. She was pretty cut up and wasn't making a lot of sense. I jumped in the car and drove over. I met the officers that were there, and then stayed the rest of the evening with my family.'

'Did you go straight there?'

'Pretty much. I called Kelly, the girl who does the evening shift and asked her to come in early. It took about fifteen minutes for her to arrive, then I left and drove over,' he sneered. 'You can check the speed cameras, if you like; see if I stopped off to get petrol first.'

'You and your late brother didn't see eye-to-eye?' said Hutchinson.

Patel sighed. 'We've been through this before. No, my brother and I had our differences.'

'So, you weren't in contact?' continued Ruskin.

'No. We hadn't spoken since he moved out of Mum and Dad's house.'

'What about by phone?'

'No, I didn't even have his number.'

'What about his flat, did you ever visit there?'

'Are you deaf or something? No, I was not in contact with my brother. I did not call him. I did not visit his flat.'

Up in the main briefing room, the team were gathered around the main screen.

'Good, he's getting annoyed,' muttered Warren. 'Keep on pushing his buttons boys, don't give him time to think it through.'

'But Jaidev was in contact with him, wasn't he? In fact, he visited his flat,' Hutchinson was saying.

'Yeah, well Jaidev always had a bit of a soft spot for Anish. He's as bad as Reva.'

'And you didn't approve? You followed your dad's orders and left him well alone,' said Ruskin. 'Like a good boy?'

'Hey, fuck you. You know nothing about my family.'

'Officers, I remind you that Mr Patel is here voluntarily. I insist that you treat him with respect, or I shall be advising him to end this interview and leave.'

Ruskin raised his hands. 'Sorry, you're right. That was out of line.'

Hutchinson repeated the apology.

'Tell me, Manoj. What happens to your father's business when he dies?' Ruskin asked after a moment.

'What has that got to do with anything?'

'Just answer the question, Mr Patel,' said Hutchinson.

'We inherit it, obviously.'

'And who is we?'

'Me and my brothers and sister.'

'And what happens now that Anish is dead?'

'I dunno, ask my father.'

Hutchinson opened the folder again and removed the photocopy of the will that Reva Vasava had brought into the station.

'This is a copy of your father's will. Are you familiar with it?'

Patel shrugged and said nothing.

'It has been amended recently, are you aware of the nature of those changes?' Hutchinson continued.

'No comment.'

'According to those changes, the will is to be split between all four children, providing they are married with children.'

'No comment.'

'As it stands, if your father were to have died before Anish passed away, Anish would not have been eligible for a share of the business?'

'Well, obviously,' said Patel.

'Why obviously?' asked Ruskin.

'Because he's fucking gay, and he would have to marry a woman and have kids of his own.'

'Well, UK law recognises the marriage of same-sex partners, and adopted children are regarded, for inheritance purposes, in the same way as biological children,' said Hutchinson. 'It sounds to me as though you are familiar with your father's will, namely the clause he inserted defining marriage as between a man and a woman, and children as being biologically related.'

'No comment.'

'Tell me, Manoj, were you aware that your brother had recently been seeing a woman, with a view to getting married?' asked Hutchinson.

'This is fucking ridiculous. Anish was a poof; everybody knows that.'

Hutchinson continued, regardless, 'And that they were looking at having children of their own?'

Patel threw his arms up and looked at his solicitor. 'Seriously, do I have to listen to this shit?'

'You are free to leave at any time,' said his solicitor, his own voice carrying an edge of annoyance.

'OK, let's change the subject,' said Hutchinson, not wanting Patel to end the interview. 'Tell me about that shop you manage. Who's this Kelly for a start?'

Patel shrugged. 'What's to tell? It's a corner shop and newsagent. Fags, booze, newspapers, a couple of shelves of food.'

'Open late?' asked Ruskin.

'Yeah, till ten o'clock. You'd be amazed how many people fancy a Ginsters and twenty Bensons on the way home from the pub.'

'Must be hard, working all those hours,' Ruskin commented.

'Kelly does the evening shift after she's finished college. She has keys and locks up.'

'On her own? That's quite trusting. What if there's a problem?' asked Hutchinson.

'She has my number, she can call me if she needs to, I'm only ten minutes away. And there's CCTV and a panic button. I empty the till before I leave and she can't open the safe, so there's no point trying to rob her.'

'Do you get a lot of problems?' asked Ruskin.

'No, the area's OK and she's got her head screwed on. I can't remember the last time I had to go out there.'

'So, you haven't been called back after work recently?' asked Hutchinson.

Patel's eyes narrowed. 'No, why do you ask?'

'Do you drive a black Range Rover, Mr Patel?'

'Yeah.'

'And you park on your drive at home when you're not at work?'

'Yeah, 'course. I don't understand, where is this going?'

'Does your wife drive?'

'Yes, she has a Vauxhall hatchback.'

'Does she ever drive your car?'

'No, she doesn't like it; she says it's too big. We didn't bother adding her to the insurance.'

Hutchinson opened his notepad. 'When you were interviewed previously, you stated that you spent the evening of November the 24th at home.'

Patel licked his lips. 'I might have, I can't remember. I was still a bit dazed after everything, you know?'

'You did. I have the transcript of your interview here,' said Ruskin.

The solicitor looked at the proffered print-out. Patel ignored it.

'Is this your mobile phone number?' asked Hutchinson, passing over a sheet of paper.

'Yeah.'

'According to historic location data for that evening, your phone didn't leave the house.' Hutchinson looked at Patel, who was now looking slightly shifty. 'Presumably, that's the number Kelly would phone if she had a problem?'

'Yeah.'

Hutchinson opened his laptop. He spun it around so that Patel and his solicitor could see the screen.

'This is CCTV footage of your driveway, the night that Anish was killed. The night that you said that you stayed in with your wife. Where were you going at eight forty-five, Manoj?'

'I don't know, I can't remember.'

'Your car doesn't return for over five hours. Where were you?'

Patel went quiet. He looked over at his lawyer. 'No comment.'

'You've been lying to us, Mr Patel. I'll ask again, where did you go the night that your brother was murdered, and why did you leave your phone at home?'

'No comment.'

Hutchinson looked over at Ruskin, who gave a tiny nod.

'Manoj Patel, I am arresting you on suspicion of the murder of your brother, Anish Patel, on or around November the 24th. You do not have to say anything. But it may harm your defence if you do not mention when questioned something which you later rely on in court. Anything you do say may be given in evidence.'

'What! Are you fucking kidding me?'

'No, Mr Patel, this is not a joke,' said Hutchinson sternly. 'You have lied to us about your whereabouts on the night of your brother's murder. You have repeatedly expressed your dislike of your brother, and we believe that you stand to gain financially from your brother's death, particularly now that we know Anish was actively looking to circumvent the restrictions placed in your father's will.

'I suggest that this would be a good time to tell us where you were on the night of your brother's murder and what you were doing.'

Patel folded his arms. 'No. Fucking. Comment.'

'Then this interview is suspended. You will be remanded in custody, whilst we execute a search warrant on your house, your vehicles and your place of work.'

Patel remained silent, as he stared over Hutchinson's shoulder, seething.

*

'Manoj Patel's fingerprints don't match the partial print found on the door handles in Anish's apartment,' said Rachel Pymm. 'We're still waiting for them to process Jaidev's.' Jaidev Patel and his wife had refused to tell Mags Richardson his whereabouts the night of the murder. Nevertheless, given that they had caught Jaidev in a lie about his movements that night, the desk sergeant at Cambridge nick had authorised his detention. His wife had been bailed.

'No surprise, I think his insistence that he had no contact with his brother is probably the only thing I believe from his interviews,' said Warren.

'That's backed up by the phone records we have, for his personal handset at least,' said Pymm. 'The only calls we have between Anish and his family are those calls to Jaidev and his weekly calls to his sister. Pretty much everything else was one-sided from Anish, and it looks as though they were ignored.'

'Unless they were using a messaging app,' Ruskin reminded them.

'Forensic IT have both his and his wife's phones, and are looking at what apps they have installed,' said Pymm, 'but don't hold your breath.' She frowned. 'What we really need is Anish's mobile phone, there are no messaging apps installed on the tablet that we recovered from his flat.'

'And Manoj could have an unregistered phone,' said Sutton. 'We know that both he and Jaidev left their usual phones at home that night, so unless they're completely incommunicado, they must have at least another handset between them. There are loads of calls and texts from unregistered phones on Anish's call list that we haven't managed to link to the people he met on Rainbow Hookups. He could be the owner of one of those numbers.'

'Well, if he was using a burner phone, perhaps it'll turn up during the search,' said Warren.

Lavanya Patel had been informed of her husband's arrest, but on the advice of her solicitor had said nothing further. Eventually, Grayson had authorised her release on conditional bail, after her arrest on suspicion of conspiracy to pervert the course of justice.

Pymm's desk phone rang; she looked at the caller ID as she picked up.

'Meera Gupta,' she mouthed; Gupta was leading the search teams at Manoj Patel's house.

Warren raised an eyebrow; he wasn't expecting to hear anything for at least a few hours.

He tried to listen in on the call, but Pymm's side of the conversation was maddeningly vague.

'Well?' he asked when she hung up. She started to manipulate her computer mouse.

'Well, so far they haven't recovered any burner phones. They've bagged some clothes to look for traces of Anish's blood, but aren't hopeful.'

'OK, but I'm sure she wasn't calling to tell us that.'

Pymm smiled sweetly and pointed to her computer. 'Take a look at what she just emailed me. They've been into the garden shed and look what they've discovered underneath an old carpet.'

Chapter 35

'My client has explained why he sometimes stores excess stock at home, rather than at the newsagent,' said Manoj Patel's solicitor.

Patel's second interview of the day was going about as well as the first. After furnishing Hutchinson and Ruskin with an obviously prepared explanation for why there were six hundred cartons of cigarettes hidden in his shed, he'd folded his arms again and refused to say anything else. His solicitor was getting as exasperated as his client; he probably had better things to do with his evening than sit in an over-heated interview suite, going around in circles.

'You say it's for security,' said Hutchinson, 'but I fail to see how a rickety wooden shed with a cheap padlock is more secure than your shop, which has metal shutters, five-lever mortice locks, CCTV and an alarm monitored 24/7 by a private security firm. It's also damp, which can't be good for keeping tobacco dry.'

'It is secure if no one knows they are there,' said Patel, finally breaking his silence, 'and the cartons are wrapped in plastic, aren't they?'

The explanation was certainly logical, if nothing else.

'Look, I fail to see how the way that the Patels choose to run their business has anything to do with your investigation,' said the solicitor. 'You are supposedly looking into the circumstances of Mr

Patel's brother's death – an affair that he categorically denies any involvement in. I don't see the relevance of this find.' He pushed his glasses back onto his nose. 'In the interests of disclosure, I would be interested in knowing about anything relevant that you have found during your intrusive search into Mr Patel's house, business and vehicles.'

'All in good time,' said Hutchinson with more confidence than he felt.

The solicitor wasn't fooled.

Manoj Patel's scowl remained fixed as the two officers suspended the interview again.

*

'We'll get an extension to custody granted, no question, but we need more to justify holding him beyond tomorrow,' said Grayson. 'What have we got in the pipeline?'

Warren sighed and took a sip of his coffee. Grayson had taken pity on him and brewed him a cup of his private stash.

'Manoj claims to have had no contact with Anish recently. We now know that both Manoj and Jaidev left their phones at home that night, perhaps to avoid being tracked. That raises the possibility that they may have access to another phone, which may account for one of the unregistered numbers on Anish's phone records. We're addressing that as a matter of priority.'

'Supposition,' said Grayson.

'We know that Anish's body was carried to the ditch in the hire car, but there may be secondary transfer in Manoj's Range Rover if he got in it after killing Anish.'

'Anything so far?'

Warren didn't say anything.

'I thought so,' said Grayson. 'And there are no tyre tracks matching a Range Rover at the site. What else have you got?'

'Jaidev's fingerprints match the partial on Anish's door handle.'

'Which he has explained away as a visit last year to check how he was,' Grayson reminded him.

'Forensic IT are looking at both brothers' devices for evidence of contact, plus their wives' phones.'

'And how long will that take?'

'Longer than we have,' admitted Warren.

'I take it we have no ANPR records that show any of the Patel family's vehicles near the hotel on the night of the murder?'

'No, although it is possible to get from Cambridge to the hotel, and from the hotel to the dumping site, without passing fixed cameras. If they drove below the limit, they wouldn't have triggered the speed cameras either.'

'Speculation,' said Grayson.

Warren bit his tongue. Grayson wasn't being obtuse, he was doing his job, and he wasn't saying anything that Warren didn't know himself. The case against the two brothers was flimsy at best. Releasing them on bail again whilst they investigated further was almost inevitable. Warren didn't even ask about mounting surveillance on them to stop them destroying any evidence; the cost alone would be prohibitive and they'd need a lot more than they had to persuade a magistrate to sign a warrant.

'What about Jaidev?'

'Jaidev's wife claimed that he came straight home and stayed in for the rest of the evening. In theory, Manoj could have dropped him off before he went and did whatever he did that night, but she's now no commenting, so we don't know if that's what happened.

'A rather big fly in the ointment is that Jaidev and Manoj appear to leave their phones at home every Thursday night. So, whatever they're up to, it wasn't just that night.'

Grayson grunted. 'There could be an entirely innocent explanation for the brothers leaving their phones at home – maybe they're going for a pint and don't want their wives phoning them to nag them that the kids need bathing?'

'So why not say that?' asked Warren.

Grayson drummed his fingers on the table as he thought about it. 'I don't know,' he admitted eventually.

'I think their wives might be the key to this,' said Warren. 'Manoj's wife is clearly protecting him; I think she knows exactly what her husband was up to that night. I also think Jaidev Patel's wife knows more than she is letting on. And she's certainly pissed off with him after he racked up two speeding tickets in her car.'

'Well, you know the law as well as I do, Warren. Neither wife can be compelled to give evidence against their husband. You'll have to figure out how to get them to do so voluntarily.'

He sighed and picked up their mugs, crossing his office to his coffee machine. He didn't need to ask.

'So, if means and opportunity are still up in the air, that leaves motive.' He slopped milk into both mugs. 'Give me your best theories.'

'Leading contender is the business with the will, but here is another idea that I've been kicking around, ever since we found those cigarettes in Manoj Patel's shed,' said Warren.

'Go on.'

'It turns out that the Patel family business has form for selling dodgy fags under the counter. Assuming that those cigarettes aren't legit, then that raises a whole load of other issues.'

Grayson blew the steam off his coffee. 'So, we're back to the organised crime angle?'

'Possibly, although I haven't worked out the connections yet. It could just be a falling out between the brothers; no need to involve outside parties.'

Grayson's eyes narrowed in concentration. 'You think that Anish Patel got wind of their scam and threatened them?'

Warren shrugged. 'Maybe, I'm just throwing it out there.'

'That still doesn't explain why he was in that hotel, or why he had been visiting it so regularly. And why would Anish have been meeting his brother – or brothers – there? There are plenty of other places they could have met up.'

'Which leads us back to Leon Grime,' said Warren. 'His tools were used to mutilate Anish and his belongings turned up at Grime's allotment. He has no alibi for that night, and it's looking increasingly like he was dealing – the sniffer dogs have indicated that there were probably drugs stored in the shed recently. Forensics have ripped up the floor for more detailed analysis.'

'These gangs aren't too fussy about what they deal in,' allowed Grayson. 'Profit is profit, so he could also have been supplying the Patels with dodgy cigarettes, but it's still looking pretty flimsy.'

'I know,' said Warren quietly.

'Until Trading Standards get back to you and tell you whether those cigarettes are dodgy or legitimate, it's all speculation,' said Grayson decisively. 'And even if they are suspect, it's quite possible they have nothing to do with this case. You'll get a pat on the back I'm sure for finding them, but our aim is to solve Anish Patel's murder, not work out if his family have been diddling Her Majesty's Revenue and Customs.'

*

On the other side of town, Moray Ruskin stepped out of his car and pulled his coat tighter. An icy-cold drizzle had started an hour or so previously, and the constant stopping and starting as he'd traipsed around town hadn't given the engine time to fully warm up. Nevertheless, after spending most of the day in a stuffy office, he'd relished the chance to head outside and visit some of the garages that may have changed the tyres on Anish Patel's hire car.

JJ Car Repairs looked more like a wrecker's yard than a garage. A badly mangled people carrier with no wheels rested on top of a rusted set of jacks, next to the shell of a small hatchback of indeterminate make and model. Loud rap music blared out from inside the workshop.

It was the fourth garage that Ruskin had visited in the past couple of hours; it would be his last stop before heading back to the station he decided.

With no obvious doorbell, he banged his fist on the steel double-doors.

Nothing.

He tried again, harder. Still nothing.

'Hello, anyone in there?' he called out.

He was about to give up and walk in, when one of the doors squeaked open. A shaved head atop a pale face, bisected by what could only be a knife scar.

'Yeah? Oh fuck, what do you want?'

Ruskin was dressed in a suit, with a smart black coat. He wasn't wearing a uniform, but yet again he had been identified as a police officer before he'd said anything. Alex said it was something about the way he held himself. Ruskin figured it was just a skill possessed by those with a guilty conscience.

'Mr Johnson?' The advert on the local business directory listed the proprietor of the business as a Joe Johnson.

'Yeah. Who's asking?'

'DC Moray Ruskin, I want to ask you some questions about a customer that you may have served.'

Johnson gave a sigh, but pulled the door fully open, and walked back inside. Ruskin took that as an invitation.

'The sign outside says that you replace tyres?'

'Yeah, so?'

It wasn't the warmest welcome that Ruskin had ever received, but at least Johnson turned off the radio.

'Were you open for business on Friday the 25th of November?'

'Yeah, I work Monday to Friday and Saturday mornings.' Johnson still had his back to Ruskin, as he opened a pack of cigarettes, ignoring the 'No Smoking' sign on the wall.

'Do you remember if you replaced all four tyres on a white Ford Focus?'

'Dunno, I do a lot of Fords.'

'I have the licence number here, if that helps?'

'Doubt it; I don't usually make a note of registrations unless it's an insurance job.'

'The vehicle was a hire car. It had a green sticker from Middlesbury Vehicle Hire.'

Johnson paused in the lighting of his cigarette, a frown creasing his forehead. 'Now that you mention it, yeah I did. Weird, I don't usually see hire cars.'

Ruskin felt his pulse rise. 'Can you remember anything about it?'

Johnson flicked his lighter and took a deep drag. He let out a steady stream of smoke.

'Like I said, weird. Bloke phoned me at stupid o'clock, like just after six. Good job I'm an early riser. I told him to come round in an hour as I don't open that early and I'd do it whilst he stayed. But he wouldn't wait. In the end, he offered me another hundred to open up and do it then. All four tyres as well. I figured, what the hell? Got a bit of grief off the missus 'cause she had to get the kids ready on her own, but I wasn't going to turn that down.'

'Did he say why he wanted it done so quickly?'

'Nope, none of my business.'

'Did he give a name?'

'Not that I recall.'

'Can you describe him?'

Johnson shrugged. 'To be honest, I just took his money and did the job as quick as I could.'

Ruskin wasn't sure if he believed him but decided not to press him yet.

'I don't suppose you have CCTV?'

Johnson just looked at him.

'How did he pay?'

'Cash.'

'Did he sign an invoice?'

'No, I just logged it in the book.'

Ruskin suspected that whatever note Johnson had made for his accountant probably wouldn't include the hundred-pound sweetener.

'Can you tell me what tyres he bought?'

Johnson sighed again, before walking over to a cluttered folding table with a portable credit card reader and a locked cashbox. He opened a hard-backed ledger.

'Full set of Runways. They're not standard issue for that model, but they're cheap and they do the job. Besides, that's all we had in stock. If he wanted Goodyears like the ones he already had, he'd have needed to wait for the delivery on Monday.'

'One last thing,' said Ruskin, 'I don't suppose you kept the old ones?'

Johnson smirked. 'You're in luck, I'm not due to get them taken away until next week. Follow me.' He set off towards the rear of the workshop, Ruskin scurrying to keep up with the much skinnier man. His coat was stained with rust by the time he reached the back door.

'Knock yourself out, officer.'

Ruskin smiled tightly, as he thanked the man. Forensics were not going to be happy; JJ Car Repairs changed a lot of tyres.

Friday 9th December

Chapter 36

With Leon Grime in custody, along with both of Anish Patel's brothers, the investigation had moved into high gear and morning briefing was a busy affair. Ruskin had just finished telling the team about his success the day before.

'Trading Standards have got back to us about that stash of cigarettes we found in Manoj Patel's garden shed,' said Hardwick. 'They're dodgy, just as expected.'

She opened her notepad. 'There were eight different brands – all of the usual ones that you'd expect to see in a newsagent. All have a duty-paid sticker on them, but the stickers are fake.'

'What about the fags?' asked Sutton.

'They're probably legit, contraband rather than counterfeit, but they're testing them to see if they've bulked them out with anything nasty. Trading Standards reckon they're brought in illegally from overseas, where you can buy them for a fraction of the price they sell for here. People nip abroad and fill their suitcases with them. Rebranding them so they look like they are UK-bought isn't that difficult; most punters would never notice the difference. The gangs are even getting kids into it now; the profit on a couple of full suitcases easily covers the cost of a cheap weekend in Europe and a bit of spending money for the smuggler.'

'How much money are we looking at here?' asked Warren.

'Well, we don't know how much they are being sold for. Six hundred cartons is six thousand packs, and if we take an average of about £9.50 per pack if they were sold at full UK prices, then we're looking at over fifty grand in resale value. And with roughly eighty per cent of a pack's price being duty and tax, that's forty grand that the taxpayer never sees.'

'How much profit would he have made?' asked Pymm.

'If the smugglers sold them for three quid or less per pack, and he sold them on at full-price through the newsagent, then that's six or seven quid profit per pack; that haul in his shed could return up to forty thousand.'

Sutton let out a low whistle. 'That's forty thousand reasons to kill someone.'

'How does this link to Anish?' asked Warren. 'Assuming it does, and isn't just a coincidence, where was he in the supply chain? Was he sourcing the cigarettes or just passing them on?'

'If Anish was Manoj and/or Jaidev's middleman, it would explain his trips to the hotel,' said Hutchinson.

'I'd place good money on the transaction being facilitated by Leon Grime through that dodgy fire exit,' said Sutton. 'And given what we've found down his allotment, it looks as though he was in deep enough to take part in Anish's killing.'

'I can see now why Anish used a false name and a hire car,' said Pymm. 'You wouldn't want these sorts of people knowing your real name or where you live, especially if drugs were involved.'

Warren frowned. 'The problem is it still seems an awful lot of trouble to go to. I understand the hire car, but why go to the expense of arranging a hotel room? Surely a pub car park or an unlit layby would do the job just as well? How long does it take to fill a car boot with cartons of cigarettes?'

'Maybe it appealed to his sense of adventure,' said Sutton. 'That flat of his is like a shrine to spy movies.'

Pymm wrinkled her nose. 'I don't know, I agree with the chief. It still doesn't smell right.'

*

Another night in custody, and a lengthy consultation with his solicitor, had finally convinced Leon Grime to tell the truth. Or at least a heavily redacted, limited version of the truth, all written out carefully in a statement that gave away very little.

'Mr Grime admits that he has turned a blind eye to comings and goings through the fire exit at the Easy Break Hotel.'

It was hardly news, but at least he had started to open up.

'A little over a year ago, Mr Grime became aware of a problem with the alarm on the fire exit during one of his regular inspections. He mentioned it in passing to colleagues at the hotel, who urged him not to fix it, saying it could be useful when taking additional cigarette breaks. The hotel had recently undergone a change in management and some staff felt that the new regime was somewhat draconian.'

'Which colleagues?' asked Sutton immediately.

'Mr Grime would rather not say; he does not wish to get them into trouble.'

Sutton bit his tongue. Everybody in the room knew that was a lie, but so far Grime was being cooperative – after a fashion – and he didn't want to jeopardise that. The questions that Grime chose not to answer, and the partial truths he was giving, revealed more to Sutton and those watching than the handyman probably realised.

'What about the CCTV camera?' asked Ruskin.

'There have been issues with the CCTV system in the hotel for some years. It's well known that the system is old and needs replacing. The time that the fire exit alarm stopped working coincided with one of the periodic outages of the system. When the system was fixed, management immediately noticed staff standing outside the fire exit taking unauthorised smoke breaks and sanctioned them accordingly.'

The solicitor cleared his throat; Sutton doubted he believed the statement that he was reading any more than anyone else did.

'It was suggested to Mr Grime that the next time the CCTV system went down, it might be better if it wasn't repaired.'

Sutton pretended to give consideration to what Grime's solicitor had just read.

'Thank you, Mr Grime. Just a couple of things we need to clear up. First, you suggest that both the CCTV camera over the fire exit and the alarm stopped working spontaneously, and you agreed to leave them unfixed to help colleagues go for a smoke break?'

'Yeah, that's right,' said Grime. It was the first time he had spoken since the interview had started. Beside him, his solicitor maintained a poker face. Doubtless he would have counselled Grime to keep his mouth shut and let his written statement – such as it was – do the talking. However, Grime knew that the statement was a half-truth at best; answering Sutton's follow-up questions was the only way he could strengthen it. And as the wording of the police caution warned 'it may harm your defence if you do not mention when questioned something which you later rely on in court'.

'But you did more than that, didn't you, Leon? Your finger-prints were all over the inside of the junction box for the CCTV camera and the wiring for the contacts on the fire exit.'

Grime had clearly been prepared for the question.

'Well obviously. I had a look inside to see if I could fix it.'

'Which you couldn't – or rather wouldn't. So why didn't you call in the CCTV company?'

Again, Grime was prepared. He'd clearly spent a significant amount of time thinking through the possible questions that he might be asked and decided that having already admitted to facilitating the use of the fire exit, there was little to be lost by confessing that he had stopped the service contract to the company.

'They were taking the piss. They charged a bloody fortune for maintaining a so-called "legacy system". Everyone knew that it was going to be scrapped as part of the refurb, so I figured I'd save the hotel some money.'

'Very noble of you,' said Sutton, not even trying to conceal the sarcasm. He leaned backwards in his chair. 'You see, this all leaves us with a problem, Leon. It's looking very much as though the killer of Anish Patel entered the Easy Break Hotel through that doctored entrance, and likely disposed of his body through there also. On the night of his killing, you cannot account for your whereabouts. In fact, you've actually lied about that night. Anish Patel's body was mutilated after death using your tools and wrapped in hotel bedding that you had access to. The motive for killing Mr Patel is, as yet, unclear. But I would be willing to bet that it has something to do with whatever you were storing in your allotment shed. The shed where we found Anish's clothes, wallet and keys.'

Sweat had started to bead on Grime's forehead and he was breathing heavily; his solicitor looked over at him with concern. Noting the man's discomfort, and unwilling to risk another panic attack, Sutton glanced at Ruskin.

The younger officer locked eyes with Grime. 'Look, Leon. You need to start helping yourself here.' He softened his tone. 'Work with us. We know that it took more than one person to kill Anish and dump his body. Who else was involved? It'll go a lot better for you if you give them up and cooperate.' He opened his hands in a gesture of trust. 'Honestly? We don't think you were the person that instigated this. We think you got in over your head. Perhaps you were brought in to help clean things up? But unless you start assisting us, we can't help you.'

Grime shook his head, his tone one of abject misery. 'I didn't kill him, I wasn't involved. I don't know how those clothes got there. Anyone can get access to my toolbox.'

'Then if you weren't involved,' said Ruskin, 'what were you

doing that night? Tell us where you were so we can rule you out. Whatever it was you were doing that night, it can't be as bad as what you are being accused of here. Give yourself a chance, Leon.'

Grime continued to stare at the table. Eventually he spoke, his voice low and scratchy.

'I can't.'

Sutton and Ruskin waited for a few moments longer.

Eventually Sutton gave a big sigh. 'Well, don't say we didn't give you the opportunity, Leon. Interview suspended.'

290

Chapter 37

Donnie Campbell picked at his collar and swallowed; a slim, dark-haired man, he looked young to be running a hotel, but given the place's recent problems he might have been the only applicant for the job. He'd been interviewed as soon as the Easy Break Hotel became the focus of the investigation; now he was back at the station.

'Leon Grime,' said Sutton, before sitting back and waiting for Campbell to fill the silence. He'd come fresh from the interview with Grime and had teamed up with Karen Hardwick, who had met Campbell previously.

'Yes, our head of maintenance. I am aware that he has been arrested.'

'Tell us about him,' said Hardwick.

Campbell puffed his lips out. 'What's to tell? Leon's worked at the Easy Break Hotel for sixteen years or thereabouts. He started long before my time, obviously.'

'And how is he?' asked Sutton.

'No complaints; in fact, he's very reliable. The previous manager was impressed with him.' He paused, clearly choosing his words carefully. 'That wasn't necessarily a glowing endorsement. My predecessor wasn't as hands-on with the details as he should have been. Things … slipped a bit towards the end.'

'The food poisoning incident,' said Hardwick flatly.

Campbell winced. 'Yeah. That happened less than a month after I arrived as deputy manager,' he gave a short humourless laugh. 'Fortunately, he did the decent thing and fell on his sword. We sacked the chef, bloody piss-artist, closed for three weeks whilst we deep-cleaned everything, retrained all of our kitchen staff and got the lawyers in. I hadn't been in the post long enough to blame, so they offered me the job as overall manager.

'It turns out that Leon was one of the few people who had raised concerns about the chef. But my predecessor just dismissed him – what does the handyman know about food hygiene? Turns out, more than they gave him credit for.'

'So you're happy with Mr Grime?'

'Well, yeah. He can be a grumpy git at times, but I like him.'

'Were you aware of his history before he worked at the Easy Break?' asked Sutton.

'Look, I heard about it on the grapevine, nothing official you understand. I'll be honest, had I been the one hiring him back then, then bollocks to the Rehabilitation of Offenders Act, I'd have taken somebody different. But he's worked at the Easy Break for years and nobody has a bad word to say about him. I guess everyone deserves a second chance.'

'Tell me about the fire exit next to the kitchen,' said Sutton.

Campbell blinked. 'I don't see why … ah, that bloody CCTV camera. It's been playing up for months.'

'Have you tried to contact the security company to get it fixed?' asked Hardwick.

'Yeah, Leon's been on at them for ages to sort it … oh. I see.'

Sutton contemplated him for a moment. Unless he was a very good actor, he was only just starting to join the dots.

'What if I told you that the alarm on that door had also been tampered with, so that it could be opened without alerting the front desk?' said Hutchinson.

'But why would …?' Campbell paused for a second. 'Well that

292

explains why there are always so many cigarette ends on the floor outside that door.' He frowned. 'Are you suggesting that Leon deliberately sabotaged that door so staff could go outside and have a crafty smoke?'

'That's what he claims,' said Sutton.

Campbell scowled. 'Bloody snake in the grass. I know that some of the staff thought I was being a bit harsh when I banned them from smoking out the front and started timing their breaks, but he was always very supportive of me. I'll bet he was laughing behind my back all that time.'

'Can you think of any other reason that Leon may have disabled the alarm and CCTV on the door?' asked Hardwick.

'No? Why? Wait, you don't think that's how the killer got in and murdered that poor man in 201, do you?' asked Campbell, his voice rising in alarm.

'Perhaps. But the door was tampered with long before Mr Patel was killed,' said Sutton. 'Were you aware of that door being used in the evenings. Perhaps for deliveries?'

'What, like pizza?' asked Campbell, before he suddenly placed his hand over his mouth. 'Oh, shit. You mean drugs?'

Sutton gave a shrug. 'Perhaps.'

The manager shook his head vigorously. 'No. Not at all. I can't believe anyone …' He gave a quiet moan. 'This job was supposed to be a stepping-stone to better things; turning around a failing hotel would look great on my CV.' He groaned again. 'Now all people are going to see is that the kitchen was closed down a month after I arrived, then a customer was murdered in one of the rooms, and to cap it all, an ex-con has been selling drugs under my bloody nose.'

Sutton and Hardwick glanced at each other. It would seem that Campbell really had been absolutely clueless about what was happening in the establishment he had been running.

The young man slumped in his chair. 'I can't believe it,' he muttered. 'Leon was one of my best employees. Hell, when I first took over, he got me out of a hole. Without his help, we'd never have reopened as quickly as we did.'

'How do you mean?' asked Sutton.

'He pointed me towards Nick Kimpton.'

'The chef?'

'Yeah. Obviously, when we let the previous chef go, we had to hire someone new. Unfortunately, we weren't exactly top of anyone's list.'

'And so you appointed Nick Kimpton?' said Hardwick.

'Yeah, turns out he and Leon had known each other for years. Leon said he knew what he was doing, and he needed the work. So, I had him in and interviewed him.'

'How much did you know about him before you employed him?' asked Sutton, trying to sound casual.

'I know he'd been struggling to find work since he'd moved to the area. Mostly cash-in-hand, farm jobs, that sort of thing. But he was desperate to get back into the kitchen. Apparently, he'd been pretty good back when he was a lad, but life had got in the way. I think he has a kid and a dodgy ex. Anyway, he checked out and frankly, beggars can't be choosers.'

'How has he been?'

'No complaints,' said Campbell. 'In fact, I've been pretty impressed. We aren't exactly the Ritz, but he runs a tight ship and he works bloody hard. I've popped in unannounced a few times and he keeps the place spotless; our TripAdvisor ratings have climbed again. Non-guests come over especially for his curry night; he found a local supplier that makes samosas and bhajis and all that. They're really good. We freeze them, but they cook up lovely.'

Hardwick frowned. 'What's the name of the supplier?' she asked.

Campbell shrugged. 'Dunno. Sunny's Sundries or something?'

Chapter 38

Warren opened the team briefing with a summary of the interview he'd just conducted with Kelly Drake, the young woman that Manoj Patel employed to run his shop in the evenings and on the weekends. He'd invited her in on a hunch, and it had paid dividends.

'Rather than closing the shop as soon as he heard about his brother's death, Manoj called in Ms Drake and asked her to start her evening shift early. And it seems that the wheels of commerce continued as normal the following day, with Manoj claiming that he was "too busy to waste time wallowing in grief".'

From the looks on his team's faces, they were as disgusted by the man's callous attitude as he was.

'However, Ms Drake noticed that the cigarette kiosk was unusually empty, despite having been fully stocked the previous day. When she questioned Manoj, he claimed that he'd had a call from the supplier to say that there was a quality control issue. She thought it strange, as it seemed to affect multiple brands from different manufacturers.'

Grayson snorted his disbelief. 'Now why would he be so keen to remove those cigarettes the day after we told him his brother died?'

'It's almost as though he expected us to stumble across them,' said Sutton.

Grayson tapped his teeth with a pen. 'What have Trading Standards said about this?'

'I spoke to the local enforcement officer,' said Hardwick. 'He reckons that there was a problem with dodgy fags being sold at one of Gotam Patel's other businesses, specifically the one run by Jaidev Patel. They investigated and were – in his words – satisfied that the scam was orchestrated by a rogue, junior employee, who had been fired as soon as Jaidev Patel realised what he was doing. The packets of cigarettes still on the shelves were ones that they missed when they removed the illegal stock.'

'That's pretty much what Kelly Drake told me,' said Warren. 'Apparently one of their cousins was trying to make a bit of money on the side.'

'And Trading Standards took that at face value?' said Sutton.

Hardwick gave a humourless laugh. 'Their budget has been slashed by a half since 2010; apparently they "don't have the resources or the time to chase every case of dodgy fags".' She gave a tight smile. 'That being said, they are very grateful for our find in Manoj Patel's garden shed and will be pursuing it vigorously.'

'Couldn't happen to a nicer man,' said Hutchinson.

'Well we've certainly put a smile on Trading Standards' face,' said Grayson. 'But I want to know why, if Jaidev or Manoj were involved in Anish's death, they waited until the day that we told them about it to hide the cigarettes? He'd been dead for almost a week by that point.'

'Well, the killer clearly intended for the body to remain hidden for longer, and when it was found, for us to struggle to identify it,' said Sutton. 'Maybe Manoj was looking for somebody else to take the cigarettes off his hands until things settled down again?'

'So how does the Easy Break Hotel fit into all of this?' asked Grayson.

'Leon Grime recommended Nicholas Kimpton for the role of

chef and Kimpton sourced Indian side dishes made locally by Suniti's Sundries, the catering company run out of Reva Vasava's kitchen that she took over after her mum died,' said Hardwick.

'And an analysis of the ANPR data from traffic cameras out towards Cambridge, shows that Jaidev Patel's Range Rover travelled down the A506 in the direction of Middlesbury, regular as clockwork, once a month,' said Richardson. 'He isn't picked up on the cameras at the traffic lights just past the hotel, which suggests he could have been turning into there.'

'So now we just need to figure out what role Anish played,' said Sutton.

'If Jaidev was delivering trays of frozen samosas in his Range Rover, perhaps he was picking up cartons of dodgy cigarettes at the same time?' suggested Ruskin. 'If they used the broken fire exit to hide what they were doing, then Jaidev would have known all about it.'

'So what was Anish doing?' asked Richardson. 'His visits were similarly frequent, but never on the same day as his brother.'

'Delivering money?' suggested Hardwick. 'Presumably they had to pay for the cigarettes. And if Anish was skimming some of the cash off, and his brother and/or Grime and Kimpton found out, that could explain why they killed him.'

'But why involve Anish at all?' asked Warren. 'Surely it would be easier for Jaidev to just hand over an envelope of cash when he picked up the cigarettes? And even if they were letting them have them on credit, with Anish paying for them once they'd sold enough, why would he need to go to all the trouble of booking a room for the night?'

'Perhaps it was a separate deal entirely?' suggested Ruskin. 'Jaidev is sourcing cigarettes for the family newsagents, whilst Anish is picking up drugs; we're fairly certain Leon Grime was storing drugs in his garden shed before he got cold feet and removed them. Either brother could have introduced the other to Grime or Kimpton and then they did their own thing.'

'But that takes us back to why was Anish going to the trouble of booking a room for the night? Why not just turn up, take the drugs and go?' said Grayson.

The room fell silent. What were they missing?

'Well, we all know who we need to speak to next,' said Warren eventually.

'Oh, happy days,' muttered Richardson.

*

Gotam Patel was alone when David Hutchinson and a team of detectives and CSIs arrived unannounced at his house to execute a search warrant and interview him. At the same time as they were persuading a shocked Patel to accompany them, a second team were knocking on the door of the converted barn that his daughter, Reva Vasava occupied with her husband, search warrant in hand.

'Am I under arrest?' asked Patel. The older man was haggard. Hutchinson detected a faint whiff of alcohol; however, his voice was clear and he looked fit to be interviewed.

'Not at this time, Mr Patel, but we do need you to help us with our enquiries.'

Hutchinson waited, whilst Patel glared at him. After a few moments' stand-off, the older man eventually gave a sigh, his shoulders slumping. 'Let's get this over with then.'

Just like his sons, Patel insisted on having a solicitor, and there was a delay whilst Patel was booked in. That suited Warren and the team fine; it gave them time to plan an interview strategy.

Warren had decided to take a lead on the interview – he was keen to speak to the patriarch of the Patel family himself, after watching interviews with the rest of his family. He paired himself with Moray Ruskin; it would have been cruel to inflict the man on Richardson again.

Patel was already present in the interview room with his

solicitor, a sharply suited young man Warren hadn't met before. The Patel family used a Cambridge-based firm; he hoped that there wasn't too much discussion between the firm's lawyers, although there wasn't much he could do about that. After Ruskin had finished the formalities, Patel nodded curtly.

Warren started. 'On the day that we informed you of Anish's death, you alluded to his "lifestyle" and expressed your disapproval. You claimed not to have had contact with your son. However, when giving us your formal statement, you declined to give us any more details. Since then, we have spoken to your family and neighbours, who have given us their version of events. I realise that this is a sensitive subject, but I am inviting you to describe, in your own words, your relationship with Anish and help us determine any motive for his murder.'

Patel stared over Warren's shoulder; his jaw moving as he ground his teeth. Finally he spoke, his voice quiet.

'You must think me a very bad father, DCI Jones.'

Warren said nothing.

'I loved my son – I love all of my children – very much. But sometimes, the choices that they make can be … disappointing.'

Patel's back was rigid, his voice betraying no emotion, but Warren could see the pain in his eyes.

'Anish was a homosexual. I know that it is not a fashionable view these days, and perhaps I am out of touch, but I was brought up to believe that is against the natural order of things. I still believe that.'

Beside Warren, Ruskin's face was a mask. For a moment, Warren regretted bringing the young officer with him, before pushing the feeling aside. Ruskin was an experienced and professional police officer who regularly dealt with individuals who viewed his life and marriage as illegitimate. In the months after Gary Hasting's death, Tony Sutton had accused Warren of being over-protective towards Ruskin, seeing in him the man he felt he had failed to protect. Sutton had been right, of course, and

Ruskin had proven himself to be more than capable of handling himself. Warren wouldn't patronise the man by excluding him from an interview just because the person they were speaking to might say unpleasant and hurtful things.

'When did you last have any contact with Anish?' asked Warren.

'The day he moved out. Friday October the 16th 2015. I still remember that day.'

'Do you know where he moved to?' asked Warren.

Patel gave a tiny shake of the head. 'I didn't ask, and he didn't tell me.'

'What about your other children? Did they have contact with Anish?'

There was a long pause. 'Yes. I told them not to. I forbade them to contact him, until he changed his ways.' Patel sighed. 'But I know that Reva still spoke to him. Maybe Jaidev also.'

'But not Manoj?'

'No. I don't think so.'

'And how did you feel about that, Gotam? About them going against your wishes?'

This time the pause was even longer, and Warren wondered if he had pushed the man too far.

'I will not lie. I was angry at first, but then I thought about what Suniti would have said.' The man's voice caught slightly. 'She would not have approved of me seeking to divide our children. So, I decided not to speak of it. If they wished to talk to their brother … well, they are adults.' Patel's face turned hard. 'Is that all you want to ask me, DCI Jones? Have you dug deep enough into our family's pain, or do you want more?'

'I'm very sorry for any distress that this might be causing you, but we need to find your son's killer. Anything you can tell us might help. Why do you think Anish's sexuality might have contributed to his death?'

Patel said nothing, his teeth grinding. Warren prepared himself for a sudden termination of the interview.

Finally, Patel relented. 'I know that you will probably dismiss my views as foolish. As out of touch, even, but that lifestyle … the people he would come into contact with when he fulfilled his … needs. I worried about who he might meet; you read about these things. And our family is wealthy. Anish was so naïve.' He paused, and for the first time Warren caught a glimpse of a frightened father. 'If the wrong person found out about how much money our family has, I worried what they might do. It seems I might have been right.'

The man's eyes were now shining, and he rubbed them with the back of his sleeve. When he spoke again, his voice was rough. 'Anish was a spendthrift. I'm sure you have seen the car he drove, and the way he dressed. He was an attractive target. An easy target.' His voice became angry and he started jabbing the table. 'That is who you should be looking for, DCI Jones. Who took advantage of my son? Not chasing his brothers and sister. Look at his Facebook. Check his emails. That's where you'll find his killer.'

Patel collapsed back into his chair, the fire leaving him as suddenly as it had appeared.

'I promise you, Mr Patel, we are following every lead,' said Warren quietly.

Patel had a mercurial temperament to say the least. Warren had no idea how his next line of questioning would be received.

'Can I ask you what will happen to your business when you are gone?'

A look of confusion crossed Patel's face. 'I don't understand what you mean.'

'Will your children inherit your business when you die?'

'What sort of a question is that?' His voice was angry once more.

'I'm sorry, but I need to ask,' said Warren firmly.

'Well yes, of course. They have worked very hard to help build it up, for many years.'

'And would Anish have inherited a share of the business?'

Patel said nothing for several long seconds, before pouring himself a beaker of water from the jug on the table.

'All my children are included in my will, as long as certain conditions are met.' He took a large sip of the water, then stared at the cup, avoiding eye contact.

'And what are those conditions, Mr Patel?' asked Warren.

The solicitor stirred. 'I don't see that is any of your concern, DCI Jones.'

Warren took out the copy of the will that Vasava had given him. The letterhead of the solicitor's firm could be clearly seen.

'Where did you get that?' demanded Patel.

Warren ignored the question. 'It says here that your children will only inherit if they are married at the time of your death. And the document specifically states that a marriage is defined as between one man and one woman. Presumably that would have excluded Anish?'

'That is none of your business, DCI Jones.' Patel turned to his solicitor who interjected again, although with little conviction. It was a reasonable line of questioning.

'Tell me, Mr Patel,' said Warren, 'were you aware that Anish was in the process of arranging a marriage with a young woman that he had met recently?'

'You have said that I am not under arrest, I would like to end the interview,' said Patel. He was gripping the plastic beaker so tightly, Warren worried it would split.

'Did you know, Gotam?' repeated Warren.

'My client has expressed a clearly stated wish to terminate the interview,' warned the solicitor. Patel had placed his water down and was plainly about to walk out.

Warren ignored him, hoping to goad Patel into staying. 'You see, to some that could be seen as a motive for murder.'

'What! How dare you say such a thing?' Patel stared at Warren in disbelief.

'I advise you not to say anything else, Mr Patel,' said the solicitor forcefully.

Warren shrugged, hoping he'd read the situation correctly.

He had.

'To say such a thing …' Patel ignored his solicitor's pleas to say nothing. 'I loved my son, how could you say that I murdered him?'

'Did you know about his plans to get married? To ensure that he qualified for a share of the inheritance that you had attempted to deny him?'

'This is ridiculous,' stated Patel, but Warren could see the truth in his eyes; the man had known, or at least suspected.

Warren decided to push a little harder.

'Were you also aware that Anish was investigating the possibility of fertility treatment to help him start a family? Thus circumventing the stipulation that your heirs also have to have children – biological, not adopted – in order to qualify for a share of the inheritance?'

Patel blinked. Now he looked more confused than angry. 'You must be mistaken, DCI Jones.'

'It's here, in black and white,' said Warren, pushing the document across the table. He pointed to the highlighted clause.

'This is not an up-to-date copy of my will,' said Patel, after fishing a pair of reading glasses from his shirt pocket and taking a closer look. He passed the document to his solicitor.

Now it was Warren's turn to be confused.

Patel pointed to the signature and date at the bottom. 'I have amended my will since then.'

'You've altered it? When?'

Patel sighed. When he finally spoke, his voice was tinged with weariness.

'You are right; I did change my will to try and stop Anish from inheriting a share of my business. But that's because it would not be fair for him to share in the fruits of our hard work.'

Patel removed his glasses and rubbed them on his jumper.

'Manoj, Jaidev and Reva helped their mother and me run our business from the day they left school. Anish didn't.' Patel's voice hardened. 'He did not deserve to share in the rewards that our sacrifices brought.'

'So you are saying that after you altered your will, you had another change of heart? You got rid of the clauses insisting that your heirs had to be married with children of their own?'

'They still need to be married,' said Patel.

'But they don't need to have their own children? Why did you change your mind?' asked Warren.

'I would like to speak to my solicitor in private,' said Patel.

*

Moray Ruskin slid into his chair and gave a big sigh.

'Are you OK?' asked Hardwick. Warren had told everyone to take a break before they reconvened to go through the interview feedback.

'Yeah, I'll be fine,' he muttered.

Hardwick looked at him with concern. The young Scotsman was usually a source of good humour, it worried her to see him so down. She suspected she knew why.

'Come on, you need coffee,' she said, standing up. 'I'll even treat you to a chocolate muffin.'

Ruskin gave her a tired smile and clambered to his feet. 'Well if you put it like that …'

*

The coffee shop franchise that now ran the staff canteen was quiet when Hardwick and Ruskin entered, and they easily found a private table.

'What's bothering you, Moray?' asked Hardwick. In the months since returning to work, she'd struck up a friendship with her fellow DC, acting as an unofficial mentor to the less-experienced officer. She'd found spending time with newer members of the team, such as him and Rachel Pymm, to be less emotionally draining. Ruskin had only known Gary briefly, and Rachel had never met him. Most of her other colleagues had served alongside Gary for years before his violent and unexpected death, and she knew that working with her brought up memories for all of them.

'It's the way that Anish Patel has been treated by his family – especially his father – because he's gay.' He gave another sigh, fiddling with the wooden stirrer that had come with his coffee. 'It kind of reminds me of Alex's situation.' A mixture of sadness and anger flashed across his face. 'You heard about our wedding, right?'

Hardwick nodded. She hadn't been invited to Moray's wedding, as she barely knew him at that time, but she had spoken to those members of the team that had attended.

'None of Alex's family came. It wasn't a surprise of course; his parents disowned him the day he came out. I've never even met them. He puts a brave face on it, but I know how much it hurts him.'

'Why did they react that way, if you don't mind me asking?' asked Hardwick.

Ruskin snorted. 'Why do you think? Religion. I'm not even sure what flavour of Christianity they supposedly follow, but it's clearly one that ignores all the bits in the Bible about love. Look, I get that some churches feel unable to marry same-sex couples, but these days few cast out members who are gay. Love the sinner, hate the sin and all that. It's just cruel. I would never say it to his face, but you've got to question how much a parent actually loves their kid if they would rather follow the edicts of some two-thousand-year-old book than accept who their child falls in love with.'

'I'm not going to disagree with you about that,' said Hardwick, 'but I'm not sure if that's the reason the Patels shunned Anish. Jaidev suggested it was more to do with the conservative-minded circles that Gotam Patel moves in rather than religion. They aren't even that religious, and from what I've read, it shouldn't really be an excuse.'

'I can't decide if that makes it worse or not?' said Ruskin. 'If he can't even use religious commandments to justify his views, what does that leave? Bigotry? Hatred? Just plain, old-fashioned, being a tosser?'

'I don't know,' said Hardwick eventually, reaching across the table to squeeze his hand.

Ruskin gave a weak smile. 'Thanks, Karen. Thanks for letting me blow off some steam.' He gave a small chuckle. 'Did I ever tell you about when I came out to my parents?'

'No, I've not heard that story.'

'I was at university. My sister had known for years, but she respected my decision not to tell Mum and Dad – they can be a little old-fashioned.

'Anyway, I used play football for the university's LGBTQ team. One year we won the league, and the local paper took photos. It wasn't until after I'd told Mum and Dad that I was going to be on the paper's website I remembered our shirts were covered in loads of LGBTQ logos.'

'Oh, God,' said Hardwick, covering her mouth.

'Anyway, I spent all night practising how I was going to tell them. By the time I rang them I had a little speech worked out with bullet points.'

By now, Hardwick was unable to stop her giggles. 'I'm sorry, I shouldn't laugh. Please, carry on.'

'So I called first thing Sunday morning, all fired up. Mum answered, but I never rang at that time, so she thought I'd been kicked off my course or I was ill; I couldn't get a word in edge-ways. Eventually, I just blurted out "I'm gay!"'

'What did she say?'

'"Of course you are, your father and I have known since you were a teenager. Have you met somebody?" I was actually

306

disappointed that I didn't get to use my speech. I think I still have it somewhere. Mind you, I got it in the neck from my sister. She said that Mum phoned her afterwards and said that now I probably wouldn't be giving them grandkids, it was all up to her. She was not impressed.'

Hardwick laughed. 'That's brilliant.'

'Yeah, when I met Alex and brought him home, Mum and Dad were great,' Ruskin smiled. 'They loved him to bits. Mum was so angry when his parents refused to come to the wedding that in the end she offered to walk him down the aisle at the same time Dad walked me.'

'God, that's beautiful,' said Hardwick. Suddenly her eyes filled with tears. She had never got her opportunity to walk down the aisle; before she knew it, it was Ruskin comforting her.

'We're a right pair, aren't we?' she managed eventually. She cleared her throat. 'Anyway, back to your problem. Perhaps you should speak to DCI Jones, if it really bothers you this much. He's pretty understanding. Perhaps he can reassign you so you don't have to deal directly with the Patels? There's plenty of other ways to contribute to the investigation.'

Ruskin shook his head. 'No, I'm a professional; if I can sit across from somebody who has just committed murder or abused a kid, I can sit opposite somebody who hasn't received the memo that it's the twenty-first century.' He waved his hand around the canteen. 'And besides, I'm not going to give up this opportunity. DCI Jones and DI Sutton are probably the highest-ranking officers in the force – perhaps any force – that still interview suspects. And the clean-up rate for serious crime in Middlesbury is second-to-none.'

Hardwick agreed. Middlesbury – and Warren Jones – were all but unique. Middlesbury's position as a 'first response' CID unit covering Middlesbury and the surrounding villages at the north-ernmost tip of the county was an anomaly within Hertfordshire Constabulary, which had years ago consolidated all of its major crime into one unit, along with Bedfordshire and Cambridgeshire.

For years, there had been those who wished to close Middlesbury down and absorb it into the Major Crime Unit. But for all the money that would save, it was hard to argue that their approach didn't work. The same went for DCI Jones, whose hands-on style, tolerated and even encouraged by DSI Grayson, delivered results that were the envy of his peers.

After her brief thoughts of leaving the police the previous year, she had come to realise that despite all the ghosts that sometimes haunted Middlesbury CID, she didn't want to be anywhere else.

*

'Reva Vasava knew that her father had amended his will again, but she gave us the old copy. Why?' said Warren. The team had watched the interview with Gotam Patel on the video feed.

'And she came to us,' said Sutton, 'pointing her finger at her father as a possible suspect in the killing. Why?'

'I figure there are two possibilities,' said Ruskin. His chat with Hardwick had helped him clear his mind, and he was back to his usual self. 'Either she genuinely thinks that her father was responsible, or she's framing him.'

'Framing him why?' asked Warren immediately.

'She could be protecting herself, or her brothers,' said Pymm. 'After all, they stand to gain the most now that Anish is dead.'

'Gotam claims not to know anything about Suniti's Sundries supplying the Easy Break Hotel,' said Hutchinson. 'He says that he leaves Reva to run that part of the business all by herself. Which makes you wonder if she could be laying another trail back to her father, if we don't believe his denials.'

'What does Jaidev say? Does he admit to delivering to the hotel or knowing Leon Grime and Nicholas Kimpton?' asked Pymm.

'No comment,' said Sutton, who'd spent a fruitless twenty minutes with the man.

'Well, let's keep our knowledge of that connection to ourselves for the time being,' said Warren. 'I don't want word getting back to anyone at the hotel that we're looking at them. If Kimpton is involved, he probably thinks he's in the clear at the moment.'

'What would happen to the inheritance if Gotam Patel went down for murder?' asked Ruskin. 'Could they inherit sooner?'

'I doubt it,' said Richardson. 'I looked at that will and aside from those specific clauses aimed at blocking Anish, it looks like a fairly straightforward division of his estate. If anything, mounting a defence against murder would eat into that estate. The solicitors that have represented them so far don't come cheap.'

'Could it be a power grab?' asked Sutton. 'That business is worth millions. With old man Patel out of the way, they could take over the running of the firm. Perhaps they want to wind it up and divvy up the assets now, rather than waiting until he dies?'

The team fell silent, as they pondered the suggestion.

'It seems quite a convoluted way to do it,' said Warren finally, 'and it still doesn't explain why Reva brought us that out-of-date copy of his will. It also doesn't address the question of whether they were involved in the murder, or whether Reva just saw an opportunity when Anish was killed.'

'I also wonder why he didn't just strike Anish from the will and leave his share to the local donkey sanctuary,' said Richardson.

'Shame?' suggested Pymm. 'A will is a public document; there would have been questions asked about why Anish was deliberately missed out of it.' Her mouth twisted. 'For all his claims that he loved Anish, he still seems more bothered about Anish's sexuality tainting his legacy. By slipping in some clause that Anish couldn't meet, the family could just brush it under the carpet.'

'Possible,' conceded Warren. At the moment however, it didn't really matter what the man's motive was; the fact was, he had done it, and it was perfectly legal to do so under English law. There were far more pressing questions that needed answering.

'Anything back from the search teams yet?' asked Sutton.

'Hutch called in a few minutes ago,' said Pymm. 'They've

seized the footage from Gotam's CCTV system. There's a camera outside the front of his house that covers the driveway and the entrance of the converted barn that Reva and her husband live in. That should help confirm if they left the house the night of the killing. In addition, both the house and the barn have a number of connected smart home devices. A technical team are going to do an audit of them to see if they can pull any useful information off them.'

Sutton grunted. 'Even your home spies on you these days.'

'It gets better,' said Pymm. 'Those nice fancy Range Rovers that the brothers and their father drive have advanced telematic systems. All of their journeys are logged with Jaguar Land Rover. And Reva's Merc is similarly connected. The vehicle unit down in Welwyn are raising warrants to see if they can get a copy of that data from JLR and Mercedes.'

Sutton whistled. 'That's a potential gamechanger; the brothers have an irritating habit of leaving their mobiles at home. Still bloody creepy though.'

'I'm not going to disagree, but let's not look a gift horse in the mouth,' said Warren. It wasn't an exaggeration to claim that some crimes that might not have been resolved in previous decades had been cracked wide open by the fact that most people now carried an electronic spy in their pocket in the shape of their smartphone. Nevertheless, part of Warren missed the anonymity of years gone by. Maybe he was just getting old.

'Whilst we're waiting on that, what else have they found at the properties?' he prompted.

'It's early days,' said Pymm. 'They're going through their wardrobes and laundry bins looking for any bloodstained clothes. Whoever sliced his fingertips off and smashed his teeth in must have carried some evidence with them.'

'They've had plenty of time to dispose of anything,' pointed out Hardwick.

'True, but as the saying goes, every contact leaves a trace,' said

Pymm. 'They're going to dismantle their plumbing and washing machines to look for Anish's blood. A dog team are on their way in case there are any blood spots too small to see.'

'Well, let's hope they get lucky,' said Warren, looking at his watch. 'In the meantime, Gotam Patel's day is going to get even worse. A team from Trading Standards are due any moment to have a little word about those dodgy cigarettes that his sons have been selling under the counter.'

Chapter 39

'The hoodie found at Leon Grime's allotment is from the same batch as the one Anish bought from Middlesbury Sports and Leisure,' Sutton told the afternoon briefing. 'If what we believe is true, and Anish was murdered on the Thursday night, then that's his killer wearing his clothes on the hotel reception CCTV. Forensics are looking for any trace DNA or other evidence they may have left behind, but it'll likely be a mixed profile; it'll take time to separate the wearer from Anish.'

'What about the rest of the clothes that were found?' asked Warren.

'The jeans look similar to the ones on the CCTV,' said Sutton, 'but we can't be certain they're his without matching the DNA. But any foreign DNA will be hard to explain away.'

'And his shoes?'

'That's more interesting,' said Sutton. 'Andy is pretty confident that his shoes match one of the sets of footprints on the grass verge next to where his body was dumped.'

'Well, we know that Anish was dead before he was laid in that ditch, so he can't have been walked down there,' said Warren. 'Which means that there were definitely two people, because one of them was wearing Anish's shoes. Anything from his wallet and keys?'

'Nothing useful,' said Sutton. 'There's no cash but his bank cards were there. No surprise; his bank records show that nobody was foolish enough to use a dead man's credit card. His driver's licence was also present, so the killer knew his address and could send those text messages from nearby.

'Unfortunately, Forensics haven't found any useful trace evidence yet. The backpack is the wrong type of material to easily retain fingerprints and the wallet doesn't even have Anish's on it, so the killer clearly made the effort to clean it.'

'Which does beg the question why Leon Grime still had it?' said Warren. 'You'd think if he was that forensically aware he'd have ditched it – cut all the cards into small bits, scattered them in waste bins around town then stuck the wallet in a plastic bag with a brick and chucked it in the river.'

'You should have been a criminal, Boss, you're a natural,' said Sutton.

'What about the keys?' asked Warren, after the laughter had died down.

'Again, no fingerprints. Two of the keys matched Anish's flat's front door. There was no car key, which makes sense given that he left his car at Middlesbury Rental Vehicles.'

'So, what are we missing? We have his outer clothing, wallet and keys stuffed in the backpack he was using that night,' asked Warren.

'Just his phone,' said Pymm. 'That's been off the network for two weeks, handset and SIM.'

'It was a nice one as well,' said Sutton. 'This year's latest model. Maybe the killer will try to sell it?'

'We can only hope,' said Warren. 'Unfortunately, there is little of any use from any of the cars being investigated. No trace linked to Anish in Leon Grime's car. Similarly, nothing of any interest in Anish's Mercedes, which is hardly surprising. The GPS shows that it never went anywhere near the Easy Break Hotel that night, or any other night. Nicholas Kimpton doesn't own a vehicle.

'They're still finishing up the hire car, but it had been given a really good clean, inside and out, with the couple that hired it next saying it smelled strongly of cleaning products. Theirs are the only fingerprints. Mr Latham, the owner of the hire car firm, confirms that he hasn't valeted it for weeks, so it's suspicious that there's no trace of Anish or previous customers. Even the keyfob is spotless. There are some fibres that are being checked against the other customers to see if they can isolate anything from the killer.

'We know that whoever drove the car on the Friday morning was wearing Anish's clothes, and we're fairly certain that there were two people at the dumping site. Any fibres that don't match Anish or other customers could be from the second person.'

'I've had no luck tracking down where the car was cleaned,' said Hardwick. 'Nothing on the CCTV from local garage fore-courts, and if the killer used a hand carwash, they either can't or won't remember him,' she said. 'Interestingly though, the carpet covering the spare tyre is missing. Latham is confident it was there when Anish hired the car.'

'Which suggests that they may have placed Anish in the boot to transport him,' said Sutton. 'Can we rule out that he died in there? He had a dicky ticker; if they were kidnapping him for money, they could have driven him somewhere, opened the boot and had a nasty surprise.'

'I'll check with Prof. Jordan,' said Warren. 'But aside from the bump on the back of his head, he reported no other fresh bruising; you'd have thought he'd have been bouncing around in there. Either way, we need to find that carpet; they got rid of it for a reason.

'Where are we with the tyres, Moray?'

'Forensics believe they have identified the tyres that were replaced on the hire car,' said Ruskin. 'Mr Latham confirms that it should still have had the original Goodyears that it came with; he was not impressed that they were replaced with cheaper Runways. The good news is that the original tyres are caked with mud. The soil specialists are doing a comparison with the dumping site, but the tread patterns match. I think we can be pretty certain that the car was used to dump Anish's body, and then had the tyres switched to hide that it had been there.'

'Speaking of the killer, what can the garage owner tell us?' asked Warren.

Ruskin scowled. 'Two-thirds of bugger-all. He reckons it was still dark that time of morning, and the guy was wearing a black hoodie and gloves; he claims not to even remember if he was white, black or Asian. The customer handed over the keys and the cash outside, then disappeared off for twenty minutes or so. When the job was finished, Johnson left the keys in the ignition. Easy money.'

'And that's all he saw?' Sutton's tone was sceptical.

'So he says, although he's agreed to look at some headshots after I hinted that our forensic accountants might need to look closely at his paper ledger,' Ruskin smiled. 'Just as a point of interest, I walked to Anish's flat and back to the garage within twenty minutes.'

'So the same person could easily have sent that text,' said Sutton.

Warren looked back over his notes. 'This customer rang Mr Johnson's mobile to open up early. Do we have his number?'

'Johnson claims that the number was withheld,' said Ruskin.

'I'll bet he does,' muttered Warren. 'OK, raise a warrant for his phone records. In the meantime, I need to have a conversation with the CPS about Leon Grime. We've got until tomorrow to decide if we have enough to charge, or if we have to release him again.'

Saturday 10th December

Chapter 40

Warren wasn't sure exactly what he was expecting when the man known as HotnReady on the Rainbow Hookups dating site dropped by the station, after being told that the police were looking for him. His profile on the website and the account of his neighbour had certainly painted a different picture to the smartly dressed research scientist that had been signed in at the front desk.

'It sounds as though Dr Stewart Fallon leads a bit of a double-life,' relayed Hutchinson to the team briefing. 'He's openly gay and certainly not ashamed of it, but he'd rather his co-workers and friends and family don't see his online dating profile.'

'I'll bet,' said Sutton.

'Anyway, he says that's why he uses a burner phone; he likes to keep that side of his life separate.'

'Do you think he might be a sex-worker?' asked Hardwick.

'I don't think so; he was somewhat affronted when I dropped a hint that he might be. He admits to enjoying "the single life" as he puts it, but he thinks the old lady downstairs, who he says is "as blind as a bat", probably mistakes his brothers staying over, or work colleagues crashing on the sofa after the pub, for sexual conquests.'

'What did he say about Anish?' asked Warren.

'Straight up admitted to meeting him, no pause,' said Hutchinson. 'He said that the two of them had a few drinks, then Anish came back to his. They had sex and he stayed a few hours and then they went their separate ways. Both of them were after nothing more than a bit of fun, and that's all they had. No more contact since then.'

'Well, that fits the mobile phone activity and location data,' said Pymm. 'They contacted each other mid-week at the end of September with a couple of texts, then Anish's handset co-localised with Fallon's handset on the high-street just before 7 p.m. on Saturday October 1st. Anish turned his phone off, but Fallon's phone does a circuit of the bars, before going back to his flat where it stayed. Anish's phone turned back on just after 1 a.m., outside his own flat. There was no more contact.'

'I'm getting tired of asking,' said Sutton, 'but did they communicate via WhatsApp or other apps?'

'He claims not,' said Hutchinson with a shrug.

'So, what about an alibi?' asked Warren. 'And where has he been the last couple of weeks? His neighbour claims he disappears a lot.'

'The regular disappearances are to do with work apparently,' replied Hutchinson. 'He's a physicist and he often travels abroad to conferences. As to the last couple of weeks, he and a dozen of his university friends were having a final blow-out in the Canaries before two of the group have a baby and they have to start acting like grown-ups.'

'Yeah, kids will do that,' interjected Pymm. 'We haven't had a week of hedonism and drunken debauchery since I got pregnant with Tilly. She's thirteen now; God, I'm sick of Center Parcs.'

As the laughter died down, Warren put a line through the man's name. He'd turn it into a cross when they'd finished checking out his story.

'What about Mr Brown Bear and Blondie92?' asked Sutton.

'No luck with either yet,' said Pymm. 'The mobile phone companies report that neither men's SIM cards or handsets have been used recently, so we can't locate them.'

'Any luck tracing Mr Brown Bear's partner?' asked Warren.

'Her house hasn't been let since she left, as it's being renovated. The neighbour says that Ms Weybridge had lived there long before Brown Bear — or rather Deepak — came on the scene. He thinks he was some sort of casual labourer. It was rented in her name, and he wasn't on the electoral roll or council tax records, presumably so they could claim the twenty-five per cent single adult discount. She paid that in cash at the Post Office, and the landlord's name was on the utilities bills.'

'What about a forwarding address?' asked Sutton.

'None for Deepak, which is not surprising,' said Pymm. 'If he was dodging council tax, he was probably flying under the radar. The landlord also claims not to have anything for Ms Weybridge. He reckons she agreed to give up her deposit in lieu of her final month's rent and then cleared off. He said that she had a Liverpool accent, and mentioned "going back to live with her mam". Either way, nobody with that surname has appeared on the electoral register this year at a new address.'

Warren chewed his pen thoughtfully. 'She must have been paying her rent somehow. Does her landlord have her bank details?'

'Nope, she paid by cash, and before you ask, she paid her TV licence at the Post Office the same way.'

'DVLA?' suggested Richardson.

'Neither of them owned a car,' said Pymm.

'It's the twenty-first century, how can someone be untraceable when we have their full name and their last known address?' asked Ruskin.

It was a rhetorical question, but Pymm answered anyway. 'Not everyone has a bank account that lets them pay by direct debit, so companies still have to accept cash or cheque. I'll bet there's a substantial difference between the amount of rent she paid and the rent her landlord declares for tax purposes.'

'Not unheard of that end of town,' said Sutton.

Ruskin snorted. 'Alex used to rent a room in a four-bedroom house at uni. There were actually five rooms, with the bloke in the box room paying his rent in cash.'

'She had kids,' said Hardwick. 'They must have been at a local school. Could we find her that way? Even if the kids had their father's surname, she would be registered as a contact. What about the doctor and dentist or even benefits?'

'If their home life was that unsettled, they may have been known to social services,' suggested Richardson.

'Well, that's given you plenty to keep busy with,' said Warren. 'We still don't have a clear motive yet and there's no guarantee that the Patel brothers were involved in Anish's death, so keep on looking. In the meantime, Leon Grime is due in court this morning after we charged him last night. I need to go and plead our case to the magistrate, otherwise our number one suspect will get bail.'

*

'Remember that helpful neighbour of Manoj Patel's with the CCTV camera?' said Richardson, as soon as Warren returned from court. The magistrate had been sympathetic to the CPS's decision to charge Leon Grime and had remanded him in custody for conspiracy to commit murder. They couldn't prove that he was the one who had killed Anish Patel – and the cause of death was still outstanding – but the court had agreed that there was sufficient evidence linking Grime to the events that night for a case to be answered. Grime had been led away still protesting his innocence.

'The neighbour that showed Manoj Patel was lying about his whereabouts the night that Anish was killed?' Warren answered her.

Richardson passed over her tablet computer. 'This is a log of every car entering or leaving the house. It's pretty much what you'd expect: Manoj coming and going around the time he says he leaves for work, his wife's car doing the school run and after-school clubs. Then the usual to-and-fro you'd see from a family with young kids at the weekend.'

'Go on.' He'd heard Richardson's stomach rumbling as she entered his office; she wouldn't postpone her lunch break without good reason.

'This is from the day that the family were told about Anish's death.'

Richardson switched to a video clip. Warren watched as a car pulled into Manoj Patel's empty driveway, the rear of the vehicle just visible. A few seconds after stopping, someone – presumably the driver – appeared in shot. Only the person's lower torso was visible, making identification impossible. But it wasn't necessary; they had the car's licence plate.

Opening the boot, the person reached inside and pulled out a cardboard box. Warren squinted at the logo on the side of the box.

'Now we know where he got those dodgy fags from.'

Chapter 41

'Sir, you have a visitor downstairs. They're quite distraught and insist that they need to speak to you now,' Janice was standing at the office door. 'Do you want to talk to them, or shall I tell them you're busy?'

After Richardson's revelation, Warren was busy, preparing for another interview with the Patel brothers. Nevertheless, in his experience, people tended not to walk into the station without good reason.

'Who is it?'

Janice told him.

'On my way.'

The two brothers weren't going anywhere and he really wanted to hear what his visitor had to say.

*

The face of Reva Vasava, Anish Patel's sister, was puffy from crying. Unlike the last time she had arrived at the station unannounced, she wasn't wearing her expensive cashmere coat and jewellery. She also had her solicitor in tow. The lawyer held a thick manila envelope in one hand and a laptop case in the other.

'I wish to make a statement,' she said, the moment Warren greeted her at the front desk.

'Follow me then,' said Warren, heading towards interview suite one. 'Have DI Sutton meet me,' he instructed the desk sergeant. The timing couldn't have been better. The team had planned on bringing her in after they had interviewed her brothers again, to address the issues raised in her father's interview the previous day.

'You've arrested my brothers over Anish's murder,' she started, after Sutton had joined them. It wasn't a question.

'That's correct,' said Warren, eyeing her carefully.

'May I ask why?' Her voice betrayed her lack of confidence.

'I'm afraid that I can't give details of an ongoing investigation.'

Vasava bit her lip, before taking a deep breath. 'My brothers cannot account for their whereabouts on the night of Anish's murder.'

Warren said nothing.

'You have also found a significant number of illegal cigarettes in Manoj's garden shed.'

Again, Warren said nothing. Apparently, Vasava had more to say, and he was interested to know how much of what she told him she knew for a fact, and how much she had worked out. It was clear that the family's solicitors were pooling information, making Warren doubly wary about how much information to disclose in each interview.

The question on his mind was, why was Vasava here? Did she have information that she wished to share? She had, after all, been the one to first draw their attention to the clause in Gotam Patel's will that effectively cut Anish out of his inheritance – a revelation that now raised more questions than it answered.

On the other hand, was she simply on a fishing expedition? Or was it something more devious? Was she trying to muddy the waters to protect or even implicate her brothers and father?

'I imagine that you believe that my brothers killed Anish because of some business arrangement that went wrong?' she continued.

Warren kept quiet, knowing that the best strategy was to let her fill the silence. Now he was really intrigued. The motive that Vasava suggested was certainly one that the team had been actively considering. Had she deduced this herself or was she floating the hypothesis to see his reaction, because she knew it was true?

'Or perhaps you believe that my brother was killed to protect our inheritance and hide the shame that Anish was bringing on our family through his lifestyle? Perhaps you think that we decided he didn't deserve to inherit a share of the wealth that the rest of us worked so hard to create?'

For the first time since the interview began, she looked at Warren square in the eyes.

'You probably think that when we found out that Anish had found a way around those clauses in our father's will that we decided that the only way to stop him taking what was ours was to kill him?'

The air in the room was electric. Even the solicitor, who had already heard everything that Vasava was planning on telling them, seemed transfixed. Beside him, Sutton remained immobile.

'Well, you are right about some of it. But my brothers didn't kill Anish. They are just too stupid and stubborn to save themselves.' Tears formed in her eyes. 'They're trying to protect me. And because of that, they're going to go to prison. I can't let that happen.'

*

Vasava's solicitor opened her laptop.

'I have here a prepared statement that Mrs Vasava would like to be entered into the record. I'll provide you with a written transcript once I have read it out.'

Warren agreed. Beside him, Sutton moved to a more comfortable position.

'I would like to start by stating that my brothers, Manoj and Jaidev Patel, did not kill our younger brother, Anish Patel.'

Seated beside her solicitor, Vasava closed her eyes, her face a mask.

'On the night of Thursday November 24th, my brothers, Manoj and Jaidev, attended an unofficial social gathering in a warehouse on the Fowler Industrial Estate. Entry is by invitation only. My brothers have been going there at least once a week for the past few years. Because of the unofficial nature of the club – and the entertainments provided within – Manoj and Jaidev thought it wise to leave their personal mobile phones at home, taking only an unregistered pay-as-you-go phone with them.'

'What type of entertainments?' asked Sutton.

Ordinarily, the investigators would be reluctant to break the flow of what was clearly building up to a confession of some sort, however the statement was pre-written and they would receive transcripts afterwards. Furthermore, Vasava's willingness to answer awkward questions would give an insight into how much the statement was her own words and how much it had been 'massaged' by her solicitor to paint her in a more flattering light.

The solicitor said nothing, studiously not looking at her client. Would Vasava heed her advice not to incriminate herself further, or give Warren and Sutton a show of good faith?

Vasava swallowed. 'Gambling. Drugs. Girls.'

Beside him, Warren felt Sutton shift slightly. The type of establishment that she was describing was more the purview of the Serious Organised Crime unit, who typically played their cards close to their chest. Nevertheless, DSI Grayson was usually made aware of such activities within Middlesbury, if only to stop CID inadvertently interfering with ongoing operations. He hadn't mentioned the club to either of his senior officers. Had Vasava revealed the existence of somewhere as yet unknown to SOC?

'How do you know about this?' asked Warren. It didn't seem like the sort of place one would boast about to loved ones.

Vasava closed her eyes briefly. 'Manoj's wife told me. After he was arrested.'

'She knew about it?' Warren's suspicion that the family had been talking to one another and swapping stories after the brothers' arrest appeared to be well-founded.

'Yes,' Vasava swallowed. 'Manoj can be very ... controlling. He believes that what he does in his own time is his own business and nobody else's. Lavanya has very little influence over my brother. He's very like our father in that way.'

The description certainly chimed with the impression that Lavanya Patel had given in interview, with her hasty and clumsy attempts at lying to cover for her husband. Not for the first time, Warren wondered what life was like behind the closed doors of Manoj and Lavanya Patel's home.

'And what about Jaidev?' asked Sutton. 'Was his wife Kamala also aware of what he and his brother were up to?'

Vasava gave a tiny shrug. 'I don't know. She's never spoken to me about it ... but she must suspect something. I think she's in denial.'

'So why didn't either of them tell us this themselves?' asked Warren. 'If they could have supplied an alibi for that night, we might not even have arrested them.'

Vasava snorted. 'Why do you think? They're never going to willingly admit what goes on in there.' She shook her head slightly. 'Not to mention the curse of all the men in my family: arrogance and sheer bloody stubbornness. They know they didn't murder Anish, so to their mind, there's no way they could be convicted of it. Far better to listen to their solicitor and keep their mouths shut, and it'll all go away in the end.' Her voice dropped. 'Bloody fools, do they think that innocent men never go to prison?'

She folded her arms and looked over at her solicitor again, who cleared her throat slightly. Warren motioned for her to continue reading from the statement.

'The cigarettes that were found in Manoj's garden shed were illegally imported from Eastern Europe. They were sold through the newsagents our family manage at full price. The profit was taken as cash.'

The revelation told them nothing new; it merely confirmed what the team had already deduced. But why was Vasava admitting to it? Was it a show of good faith, or was she playing a game with them?

'And what was Anish's part in this?' asked Warren.

Vasava looked over at her solicitor, who continued reading from her laptop.

'Anish agreed to store the cigarettes in his apartment, for a fee. He gave a key to Jaidev, who would periodically drive over and pick up a few cartons to replenish those that had been sold. When you came to the house to tell us that Anish had been murdered, we knew that as soon as I gave you his address, you would search his flat and the cigarettes would be discovered. Jaidev drove over, removed the remaining boxes and hid them in Manoj's shed.'

'Why was Anish involved?' asked Sutton. 'I thought he had nothing to do with the family business?'

Vasava sighed. 'He didn't, but he needed the money. Anish was … profligate. He liked to live the high life. Fancy clothes, expensive meals, a flash car. He was drowning in debt.'

She paused. 'And we needed somewhere to store the cigarettes. We couldn't risk storing them in the shops, in case we got raided by Trading Standards again. Jaidev had no space to store them. Manoj … well, he knew Lavanya wouldn't approve. The one place we knew Dad would never find them was Anish's flat. Everyone was a winner.'

That at least explained why Anish had kept his expensive suits on a wheeled rail, rather than in his wardrobe – he'd needed that space to store the cigarettes.

'I thought you said that Manoj believed that what he got up to in his own time wasn't any of his wife's business?' Sutton said.

'I think Manoj is starting to realise that the way he has treated

Lavanya over the years might just come back and bite him on the arse.'

'He was worried that she might report him to the police or Trading Standards?' said Warren.

'Worse, she might tell our father.'

'So, your father was unaware of this business arrangement?' asked Warren.

'No, he wasn't aware, and he would have been furious if he found out.' A faint smile returned. 'For all their bluster, my two brothers are very scared of what my father would do to them if he caught them selling illegal cigarettes out of his shops. He has spent a lifetime building up a reputable, honest business.'

Vasava leaned forward, her voice becoming more earnest. 'What you have to understand is that for my father, appearances are everything. He craves the respect that his parents never had. His name is above each of our shops and it is his reputation that would be destroyed if one of them were raided. He was beside himself when Jaidev was almost prosecuted by Trading Standards a couple of years ago. He made it very clear to my brothers what the consequences would be if such a thing happened again.'

'And what would those consequences be?' asked Sutton.

Vasava's eyes flashed and her mouth tightened. 'He would disown them. To his mind, that would be the only way that he could save face. Our father owns our houses and pays our mortgages. His name is on the ownership documents for our cars. He employs us and he employs our partners. All that would be gone—' she clicked her fingers '—just like that.'

'OK, I get that,' said Sutton. 'But if he's willing to disown Manoj and Jaidev for being in trouble with the police, then why didn't he disown Anish for being gay?'

'Because to do so would be to admit it,' said Vasava. 'I'm not sure exactly what he tells his friends about why he so rarely sees Anish, but I'm certain that it has nothing to do with Anish's sexuality. They probably don't even know that he has been cut off.'

'So why do it?' asked Warren. 'Why rock the boat? It looks to me as if you've all got it pretty good.'

Vasava's eyes flashed again. 'Because we don't have any control. He pays us the bare minimum; we own nothing. Our wages cover our bills and our food; anything else and we have to ask him for a handout.

'I'm thirty-two years old. My brothers are in their forties. We have lovely houses and expensive cars, but we have to ask our dad to open his wallet if we want to buy something nice for Christmas. My TV packed up last year; I had to take Dad to the showroom to choose a new one, because he was paying for it. Do you know how that feels? At thirty-two?

'My husband wanted to take me away as a surprise for our anniversary. Dad knew where we were going before I did, because he put down the deposit.

'We can't get a credit card with a decent limit because according to our bank statements, we don't earn enough to pay off the balance. When I first got married, Dad applied for one on my behalf,' she snorted. 'I was delighted; it never occurred to me that the statements would go to him, because it was all in his name. He came into the house one morning – oh yes, he has keys to all of our houses, another reason we paid Anish to look after those damned cigarettes – brandishing the statement, demanding to know what I'd been buying from Victoria's Secret that cost almost two hundred pounds.' Her voice cracked. 'It was my husband's birthday, and I'd bought something sexy to wear and, well something to help us as a couple. The humiliation …'

She stopped and took a deep breath. 'The money made from selling those cigarettes was our money. Money he knew nothing about. Money we could spend how we wished. Is it any wonder Anish was so bad with his finances? When he moved away and started having to look after his own affairs, he couldn't cope. On his salary, he had no business driving that car or wearing those clothes. Without the money from looking after those cigarettes, he'd have been out on the street.'

Her piece said, Vasava sagged back in her chair.

Warren looked over at the solicitor, who was scrolling down the statement.

'That's pretty much everything that Mrs Vasava wished to say,' she said. 'I'll still send you the formal version.'

'Then I think that now would be a good time for a break,' said Warren, rising to his feet.

'There's one more thing,' said Vasava.

She licked her lips. Her solicitor looked over in surprise.

Reaching into her purse, she withdrew a piece of paper. 'These are the numbers for Manoj and Jaidev's second mobile phones.'

*

Warren called a quick team briefing. Vasava's revelations had answered a number of questions and confirmed several of the team's suspicions. But the list of questions that she hadn't answered was even longer.

'Pretty convenient that her brothers' alibis are essentially that they were visiting some sort of illegal gentleman's club,' said Hutchinson. 'What are we supposed to do? Knock on the door next Thursday and ask if any of the dealers or prostitutes can remember if the brothers Patel were there that night? We don't even know what time Anish was killed; they could have bumped him off on the way home.'

'The club could be another link to Leon Grime,' said Sutton. 'We suspect that he was dealing drugs, and that he was also out and about somewhere he shouldn't have been that night. Perhaps that's how they all met each other? Maybe he introduced them to Nicholas Kimpton so they could use their catering business as a cover? This story about Anish looking after dodgy fags for them to sell through their shops might just be the tip of the iceberg.

They could have been selling drugs also. A pint of semi-skimmed, twenty dodgy Bensons and a gram of your finest coke, please.'

'She's also given everyone a bloody big motive to kill Anish,' said Ruskin. 'What if he was the one that threatened to tell their father what was going on?'

Warren turned to Pymm and Richardson. 'Reva gave us what she claims are the numbers to her brothers' burner phones. Work your magic. If we can prove or disprove the brothers' alibis, we're halfway there.'

He turned back to the team. 'OK folks, Reva Vasava has drip-fed us just enough to potentially clear her brothers. Now let's turn the screws and get her to tell us what's really been going on. But before we do that, I have a phone call to make.'

'Me too,' said Sutton, to no one in particular. Ever since Vasava had mentioned her brother's heart condition again, an idea had been forming. He couldn't believe they hadn't thought of it before.

Chapter 42

Reva Vasava was more composed when they restarted the interview a little over two hours later. She probably thought that whilst she may have got her brothers into trouble over their illicit Thursday evening excursions, and landed them in hot water with Trading Standards, she had at least removed the threat of murder charges.

'Tell me about the deal with the cigarettes,' started Warren, once the recording had resumed. 'How did Anish get involved?'

The details of the operation would be of far more interest to Trading Standards and SOC than Warren, but he needed to know how relevant the arrangements were to the investigation into Anish Patel's murder. They'd decided not to broach the subject of illegal drugs yet; he didn't want her to stop talking.

'Anish became involved in November of last year, after he moved out of Dad's and started having to pay his own rent,' said Vasava. 'I could see from his Facebook posts that his outgoings must be far more than his salary. Jaidev texted him and asked him if he wanted to take part in a business deal. Anish was reluctant, but he couldn't afford to turn down the money.'

Sutton looked down at the phone records Rachel Pymm had furnished him with before they resumed the interview. He gave a tiny nod. Anish had swapped text messages with Jaidev's personal phone that November. A few days later, a further exchange had been via Jaidev's burner phone.

'Go on,' said Warren.

'Jaidev would meet Anish in a layby after dark on the A506 and transfer the cartons from the boot of his Range Rover to the boot of Anish's Merc.' She gave a sad smile. 'That was Anish's idea. He loved a bit of cloak and dagger; all those years watching spy films and heist movies ...' Her voice trailed off. She cleared her throat and continued. 'He didn't want the neighbours to see Jaidev coming in and out of his flat. When Jaidev pointed out that meant he wouldn't be able to pick up the cigarettes when he needed them, Anish insisted that Jaidev only come by in the afternoon when his neighbours were at work, and fill a bag-for-life so they couldn't see what he was carrying. Silly sod. We all knew his neighbours wouldn't even notice, but if it kept him happy ...'

'Did Anish ever meet the supplier?' asked Warren.

'No, he didn't want any part of that.' She looked down at the table, guilt passing across her face. 'He didn't really want to be involved at all, but like I said, he needed the money.'

'Did the exchange ever take place anywhere else?' asked Sutton.

'You mean like the hotel where he was found?' she asked. 'No, the layby was out of the way. He wouldn't have wanted to be so exposed. God, listen to me, I'm even speaking like him.'

'So neither you nor your brothers had any link to the Easy Break Hotel?' asked Warren.

'No, I've no idea why Anish was there,' she replied.

'Thank you, Reva. That's been very helpful,' said Warren.

Some of the tension drained from her shoulders.

'Why did you tell us you thought your father killed Anish?' asked Sutton.

Vasava licked her lips. When she spoke, her voice was measured, the words practised. 'The day that you told us Anish was killed was very difficult, and my father was upset. He had a lot to drink, and things were said.'

'What things?' said Sutton.

'He said that it was all Anish's fault. That he brought it on himself, parading around town and shaming us all.' She closed her eyes. 'He said that if Anish had so little respect for himself and our family, then perhaps we were better off now that he was dead. That we could move on.' She covered her mouth, stifling a sob.

'Did he ever threaten Anish in that way?' asked Warren. 'Did he speak to Anish at all after he moved out? Try to persuade him not to be so – I don't know – open about his homosexuality?'

'As far as I know, they didn't say another word to one another from the day Anish moved out. He wouldn't even speak to him when he changed his will the week after Anish left.' Again, her voice cracked. 'He wrote a letter outlining what he had done and made me post it; he didn't even want to know his address.'

Vasava sniffed and wiped her nose with a tissue handed to her by her solicitor. 'The thing is, Anish was respectful. He didn't "parade around town". He just quietly got on with his life. It wasn't that he was ashamed or anything, he just didn't want the hassle from Dad and his brothers.'

'Do you think he hoped to reconcile with your father one day?' asked Warren.

'I think so. Despite everything, family was important to him.'

'You showed me a copy of the will,' said Warren, moving the topic back to the matter in hand. 'Why did you do that?'

'I guess it sort of made sense that Dad would be angry that Anish was trying to get around those hateful clauses … and I thought that maybe he was angry enough to kill him.'

'And now? Do you still think that he was angry enough to kill him?' asked Warren.

Vasava was quiet for so long, Warren considered repeating the question, before she finally replied, her voice like that of a small child.

'I don't know.'

Her answer hung in the air.

'How did your father know about Anish's plans to get married?' asked Sutton.

'Sorry?'

'Well, if he knew that Anish was trying to circumvent those clauses, he must have known that Anish was planning on getting married and having a baby,' said Sutton. 'How did he know?'

'I'm not sure.'

'You said that Anish and your father hadn't spoken to each other since he moved out, and Anish hadn't formally announced his engagement yet, so how did your father know of his plans? Did you tell him?' asked Sutton, staring hard at her.

Warren opened the file in front of him and removed a collection of stapled sheets.

'This is the copy of the will that you brought to me. You helpfully highlighted the clauses that your father added the week after Anish moved out.'

Vasava nodded.

'Remind me what these new clauses stipulate?'

Vasava cleared her throat again. 'That in order to inherit his share of the business, Anish needed to be married to a woman and to have had a child with her.'

'Which presumably meant that at the time that your father changed the will, Anish believed that he had, to all intents and purposes, been disinherited?'

'Yes.'

'When did Anish tell you that he had met a woman willing to marry him?' asked Sutton.

'Early summer, I suppose. June maybe? I can't remember exactly.'

'And you've never met this woman?' asked Sutton. 'Do you know her name?'

'Latika, that's all I know,' said Vasava. 'Why? Do you think she's involved in his death?'

'Do you know when they actually first made contact?' asked Warren, ignoring the question.

'No, it was sometime earlier in the year.'

'What did you and Anish speak about when he phoned you on May 2nd?' asked Sutton.

'I don't know,' said Vasava. 'It could have been anything.'

'That wasn't when he told you about this Latika?'

'I don't think so, no.'

Sutton opened the folder and removed a folded print-out. 'Well it's strange, because on that day, about an hour or so after you finished your call with Anish, you friended Latika on Facebook; it must have taken you a while to figure out who she was on Anish's friends list, but I suppose the date they became friends helped. Of course she didn't know that you were Anish's sister. He never told her your married name and Reva is a common enough first name, but you came up as mutual acquaintances, so she accepted. We didn't make the connection immediately, because like a lot of teachers she doesn't use her real name on social media. Neither for that matter do you.'

Vasava looked away.

'The two of you got on pretty well,' continued Sutton. 'Well enough that you started following her on Twitter and Instagram. Why would you do that, Reva? Keeping an eye on the future sister-in-law? Perhaps you were hoping to pick up a bit of dirt that you could use against her? Maybe keep her in line later?'

'No comment,' said Vasava eventually.

'Let's go back to the changes in the will,' said Warren. 'Even if Anish was going to get married to Latika, they still thought they needed to have a child.' He pulled another collection of stapled sheets out of the folder. 'Is that why you decided not to tell Anish that your father changed his will again on February 15th this year? To remove the stipulation that you had to have children to inherit?'

'I didn't …' Tears pooled in her eyes.

338

'Don't try and claim you didn't know,' snapped Sutton. 'Your father says he changed it because you begged him to.' His voice softened. 'You and your husband can't have children, can you?'

'That's none of your business,' she said, with a sob.

Warren hardened his heart, pushing away the empathy he felt for someone in a situation so similar to his own. 'He agreed to remove the need for you to have children, but you still have to be married.'

'Which means that you can't divorce your husband, even though you want to. It would bring shame on the family, and we all know how your father feels about that. I bet you must really hate him sometimes,' said Sutton.

'You see, this is what I think happened here,' said Warren, taking over again. He could see Vasava wilting under the dual onslaught. 'I think that you used your knowledge of Anish's plans with Latika to keep up the pressure on him to continue his little business with Jaidev. Obviously, when you finally persuaded your father to alter his will so that you and your husband didn't need to have children, you kept that to yourself. Clearly if Anish were to have children, he would need medical assistance, especially if they didn't want to risk passing on the faulty gene that he inherited from his mother. Genetic testing and IVF is expensive if it's not offered on the NHS, and you wanted Anish to continue feeling under financial pressure.'

Vasava's lip started to tremble, but she said nothing.

'Now, here's where it gets interesting,' said Warren. 'There was no need for you to show that outdated copy of the will to us. You could just as easily have brought in the latest version; it still says that Anish has to get married. But I think you realised that if we tracked down Latika, we would soon realise that she and Anish were only aware of the earlier version of the will and we might start asking awkward questions about why you hadn't told him that things had changed.'

Vasava remained silent, the tears starting to return.

'I think there is also another reason,' said Warren. 'You hate your father. Whether you truly believed that he killed Anish or not probably doesn't matter, you wanted to cause him pain. But you also loved your brother and felt guilty about the way that you had used him and the way he had been treated by the rest of your family, but especially your father. By pointing a finger at him, even if he wasn't convicted, you knew his reputation would be ruined. His friends and business colleagues, whose respect he so craved, would see all his dirty laundry – at least as he sees it – hung out in public. Anish is dead, so it can't hurt him anymore, so why not punish your father?'

'No comment,' whispered Vasava.

Undeterred, Warren continued. 'And I think there's yet another reason. You hoped that directing our attention towards your father might steer us away from your brothers. Do you think your brothers killed Anish or arranged to have him killed?' he asked.

'No! They wouldn't,' said Vasava. 'I've told you where they were that night.'

'Yes, you have. You've also given us a compelling reason why they might have wanted to have him killed on their behalf,' said Sutton.

'What do you mean?' she demanded.

Warren ignored her and reopened the folder. 'Forgive the crudeness of a spreadsheet, but you only gave us your brothers' mobile phone numbers a couple of hours ago.' He spun the sheet of paper around so she could see it clearly.

'This is location data for Jaidev's burner phone and Anish's phone. As you can see, they converge at this spot on the A506 for seven minutes at 19:55 on Saturday November the 7th of last year. I'd say that's plenty of time to transfer two large boxes of cigarettes from the back of Jaidev's Range Rover to Anish's Mercedes, and hand over five hundred pounds in cash, wouldn't you?'

Vasava looked over at her solicitor. She'd already confirmed that was how the arrangement had worked, but Warren could see the frantic calculations going on behind her eyes. She had to wonder what else Warren was planning on hitting her with, and how Warren knew how much money had switched hands.

Eventually she nodded.

'The same thing happens again, on January 30th this year,' said Warren. 'Was it the same arrangement as before? Two boxes, in exchange for five hundred quid?'

Vasava agreed.

'April 24th. Same again?'

'About then.'

'So roughly every two or three months, five hundred pounds each time?'

'Yeah.' Vasava's tone was resigned.

'So, when did it change?'

'I don't know what you mean,' she said. Warren could see that she did.

'You should know that a few minutes ago, I called Latika. She was well aware of the money that Jaidev was handing over to Anish every few months and wanted no part of it. She's something of a high-flyer and ambitious. She wants to be a head teacher by forty. The last thing she needed is a husband with a conviction for handling illegally imported cigarettes, no matter how peripheral his role was.

'Was that why Anish phoned Jaidev on July 10th, an hour after he had promised Latika that he would stop? To tell him that the deal was off? Slight mistake that, calling Jaidev's personal mobile phone, not his burner. Latika says he agreed to keep on looking after the cigarettes that he already had, but he didn't want any more.'

'No comment,' said Vasava.

'You see,' said Sutton, 'that could be seen by some as justification for killing someone. How much profit did Jaidev make from each of those cartons Anish was storing? He was happy to hand over five hundred quid for your brother to just stick them in the bottom of his wardrobe, so I imagine he was doing OK out of the deal.'

'No comment,' said Vasava finally.

'But of course, that wasn't the end of it, was it?' said Warren. 'By my sums, you must have pretty much used up the cigarettes that you had by the end of July. Which left Jaidev with a dilemma. Did he stop the scam or find somewhere else to store them?'

He leaned back in his chair. 'Stopping the scam wasn't really an option, was it? Quite aside from the money, he'd have to think about the logistics of hiding the sudden change in the books. Your father might have left the day-to-day running of the shops to your brothers, and he put Manoj in charge of the accounts, but he still kept an eye on things. When Jaidev first came up with this plan, I imagine he ran down the orders from the wholesalers over time, claiming that people were smoking less, and substituting his own packs for the ones that you were no longer buying legitimately. It's probably easy enough to hide those off-the-book sales on your old manual tills.

'Eventually it must have reached the point where you had too many contraband cigarettes to safely store in the shop. Was that when Jaidev decided to enlist Anish?'

Vasava ignored him.

'Anyway, the problem is if you stop selling the illegal cigarettes, how do you suddenly ramp the legitimate sales back up again without it being noticed? Customers will start to complain pretty quickly if their favourite brands keep on selling out, but your dad would be suspicious if orders to the wholesaler suddenly doubled.'

'So that means that if Anish stopped storing them, you'd need to find somewhere else to keep all those cigarettes,' said Sutton. 'Jaidev hasn't got enough room to swing a cat, and Manoj is too scared of the missus; hell of a problem. So, what happened? Did Jaidev offer Anish more money?'

'No comment.'

It was clear that Vasava had decided to stop digging her hole any deeper.

'Did you know that Anish and Latika were planning on announcing their engagement at Christmas? After all, he proposed in September. You and he had a special relationship,' said Warren. 'He felt he could tell you things that he couldn't tell anyone else.'

The flash of pain and guilt in her eyes told Warren he'd hit a nerve.

'Did Anish want more money?' asked Sutton. 'I hate to stereotype, but Indian weddings have a reputation for being no expenses spared. I know that's traditionally paid for by the parents, but with the image that Anish cultivated there would be an expectation that the engagement ring would be something special; it's not like he could ask his dad for the money. Did you offer him more cash to continue storing those cigarettes behind his fiancée's back?'

'No comment,' whispered Vasava.

'Which leads us back to a motive for Anish's killing,' said Warren.

'If Jaidev refused to give Anish more money, then that doesn't leave Anish with too many options,' said Sutton. 'Except one.'

'Did Anish threaten to tell your father about the illegal cigarettes unless he got a better cut?' asked Warren.

Vasava looked away. Her lip trembled.

'Yes,' she said finally. 'But they didn't kill him. I know they didn't kill him.'

'Why are you so sure?' asked Sutton. 'You can't know what your brothers were up to twenty-four hours a day.'

'I just do,' she said.

'A little earlier, you said that neither you nor your brothers had any link to the Easy Break Hotel,' Warren pushed a photograph across the table. 'This is an image from a traffic camera showing your brother Jaidev's Range Rover in the vicinity of the hotel; a journey he makes once a month. Why would he be in that area?'

Vasava's eyes narrowed. 'No comment.'

'Well, here's the thing Reva. We know that the catering company that you run – Suniti's Sundries – supplies the Easy Break Hotel. We also know that when Jaidev does his deliveries, he doesn't use their loading bay, or come through reception. Which suggests that he knows all about the CCTV blind-spot on the fire exit. The same fire exit that Anish's body was removed the night that he was murdered. So you can see how that looks to us.'

'No comment,' she whispered once more.

Both officers could see in her eyes how close she was to breaking. Sutton looked over at Warren, who nodded. It was time to ask the question that both men had been pondering ever since her opening statement, hours earlier.

'Why did you say "They're trying to protect me. And because of that, they're going to go to prison. I can't let that happen"?' asked Sutton.

Vasava's hands tightened.

'Does it have anything to do with the night of Sunday the 14th of August,' asked Warren. 'The night that Jaidev turned up at Anish's flat to try and persuade him to continue storing cigarettes?' He pushed over another sheet of mobile phone location data, a third number highlighted. 'The night that you accompanied Jaidev?'

Seconds ticked by. Eventually Vasava let out a breath. 'Yes, I did say that, didn't I? They are protecting me because I'm their little sister.'

'And?'

'And they do not want me to go to prison.'

'And why would they think you are going to go to prison?' asked Warren, although he already knew the reason why.

Beside her, her solicitor stirred, but Vasava ignored her.

'Because the whole bloody idea to make money from selling those damned cigarettes was mine,' she snorted. 'My brothers are many things, but businessmen they are not. I found the suppliers and I worked out how to adjust the sales figures to keep Dad

344

from noticing what was going on. Jaidev nearly brought the whole thing crashing down when he screwed up and got raided by Trading Standards but whose idea do you think it was for us to blame it on our dopey cousin?

'And you're right, Jaidev does deliver our food to the Easy Break Hotel. He uses the side door, because we have a deal with the chef. He forges an invoice for thirty per cent more than I report, and we split the difference,' she said. 'It's hardly worth it.'

'And what about the cigarettes? Is Leon Grime your supplier?'

She frowned. 'No, I don't know that name.'

'He works at the Easy Break Hotel. Were you picking up your cigarettes from him?'

'No, it's completely separate. Jaidev met a man at the nightclub.' Now there was bitterness in her voice. 'Those brothers of mine are bloody idiots. They're so arrogant. They're convinced that they can't possibly go to prison for Anish's killing, so they're saying nothing. All my life, they've protected me, their little sister. And I love them for it, I really do. But they should have told the truth. I'm a big girl; I knew what I was getting into.' She looked Warren and Sutton squarely in the eyes, one at a time, before turning to her solicitor, her tone almost apologetic. 'I know that I'm in trouble,' her voice trembled. 'And even though you'll do your best for me, I'm probably going to end up in court – or worse. But I can't let Manoj and Jaidev risk prison for Anish's murder to protect me.

'I persuaded Anish to continue storing the cigarettes for us, and yes I offered him more money – from my cut of the profits, before you ask, seeing as it was my idea to get him involved anyway.' She looked away briefly, shame creeping into her voice. 'And yes, I did threaten to tell Latika's family about the true reasons for their relationship.'

She took a shuddering breath. 'So as far as Manoj and Jaidev were concerned, I'd sorted the problem. They had no reason to kill him. You've said it yourself that losing Anish has caused us more headaches. Why would they have murdered him?'

'And your father?' prompted Sutton.

'Dad was angry at Anish after he moved out, but again he'd had his revenge, effectively cutting Anish out of his will. And if Anish decided to get married and have a kid to make himself eligible for his inheritance, then so much the better; nobody need know that he was gay and we could all go back to ignoring the elephant in the room.'

'So, who did kill Anish, and what was he doing at the Easy Break Hotel?' asked Warren.

'I don't know; really I don't.'

Warren believed her.

Chapter 43

Warren and Sutton returned to the office after the interview with Reva Vasava had been concluded. They'd formally arrested her after her admissions regarding the illegal cigarette operations, so she wasn't going anywhere; Serious Organised Crime and Trading Standards wanted a chat. In the meantime, it gave the team time to plan their next move. Despite what Vasava had told them, they hadn't ruled out a link between the family and Leon Grime, and had yet to address the subject of drug dealing. The motive for Anish Patel's death was still unclear.

Sutton plucked a yellow Post-it note off his screen. He smiled and phoned the number on it.

Five minutes later, he rapped on Warren's office door.

'We've got a time of death.'

*

'I tracked down the technician that identified Anish Patel from the serial number on the pacemaker that he was fitted with.'

The main briefing room was filled with everyone currently on shift, even Grayson; all eyes were on Sutton.

'Anish was fitted with a fairly standard model. I won't bore you with the technical details, suffice to say that Anish had an arrhythmia – an irregular heartbeat – caused by a genetic mutation that he inherited from his parents. It was undiagnosed in his mother and caused the heart attack that killed her. Anish was on anti-arrhythmia medication that worked well, but his cardiologist decided to fit him with a pacemaker as a precaution.

'Pacemakers send a regular pulse of electricity to the heart to keep it in check. Anish's wasn't an ICD – an implantable defibrillator – so it wouldn't have shocked him if he went into full-blown cardiac arrest.'

Sutton projected a graph onto the wall screen.

'Besides helping keep a heart in rhythm, they are also a diagnostic tool. It basically acts like a simple ECG machine and records the heart's activity, which the cardiologist can then look at during a check-up.' He pointed to the graph. 'This is a recording of Anish's heart earlier on the Thursday. As you can see, the trace is fairly regular. I'm told that his cardiologist was pleased with his response to his medication and had no concerns.'

'This is from a few minutes before Anish died.'

Sutton switched slides. The difference was immediate. The gaps between the peaks were still regular but noticeably farther apart.

'His pulse rate was abnormally slow at this point.' He changed slides again.

'As you can see, the gaps between the peaks have now become very irregular. The pacemaker did its best, but it was fighting a losing battle.' Sutton pointed to the end of the graph; the flat line unmistakable to anyone who watched TV. 'He entered full cardiac arrest at 20:28.'

Sutton gave a moment for the importance of the timing to sink in.

'His brothers can't have been with him,' said Pymm. 'Manoj was at home in Cambridge, and Jaidev was still drinking in the sports centre bar.'

'We also have a cause of death,' said Warren. 'Cardiac arrest after he entered arrhythmia. And that might change everything.'

This time it was Hutchinson who spotted the problem. 'It might not be murder. It could have been natural causes.'

'Unfortunately,' said Sutton, 'the pacemaker data tells us what his heart was doing, and when it was doing it, but it doesn't tell us why.'

'So why dispose of the body that way?' asked Ruskin. 'I get that it must have been pretty scary to suddenly find yourself with a dead body, but what they did to him …'

'I see two possibilities,' said Warren. 'First of all, perhaps the person – or persons – believed that they were responsible for his death. We know that he had sustained a significant blow to the back of his head at some point that evening. Perhaps they thought that was what killed him?'

'Could it have been the cause?' asked Hardwick.

'Inconclusive,' said Sutton. 'There was significant trauma, but the neurologist that Prof. Jordan consulted couldn't say if it was enough to kill him.'

'Which leaves the next possibility,' said Warren. 'The person who was with him did something that led to the arrhythmia – perhaps unintentionally. They then panicked and decided to dispose of the evidence.'

'Could he have died during sex?' asked Pymm. 'We still don't know why he was at the hotel. We know that at least some of the men he met on Rainbow Hookups were closeted. The person he was with could have been scared that whatever they were up to might become public knowledge.'

Sutton shook his head. 'I asked that exact question. The technician thought it unlikely. His pulse, even before it started to slow down, and he entered arrhythmia, was fairly normal. Sexual arousal usually results in an increased heart rate. Plus, he was fairly fit, he exercised vigorously twice a week with no apparent ill effects.'

'You said that his cardiologist was pleased with the way he responded to his medication,' said Richardson. 'Do we know if he had taken it that day? My dad's getting a bit forgetful, and Mum always knows if he hasn't taken his pills first thing because he gets tired and out of puff later in the day. If Anish had forgotten that day, then maybe he was at a greater risk of problems by the evening?'

'Could be,' said Sutton. 'His pills were one-a-day, slow release. Assuming he usually took them first thing in the morning, it could have easily been thirty-six hours or more since he last had one if he forgot that morning. Unfortunately, we can't tell if there are too many pills left in the packet.'

'What about toxicology?' asked Hardwick. 'Would the medication levels in his bloodstream answer that question?'

'The blood tox results are due back soon,' said Warren. 'I could ask Professor Jordan if they are able to add that to the screen, although I imagine that will take longer.'

'Well, either way,' said Grayson, 'I still want to know why his body was disposed of and attempts made to conceal his identity. He was found by chance, and somebody sent text messages from his phone to make it appear he was still alive. Were they just buying time to clean up after themselves?'

He looked around the room. 'It may transpire that Anish Patel died of natural causes. But in the meantime, nothing changes. We continue to treat this as murder. We'll let the defence and the CPS fight over the charges.'

*

It was late in the evening and most of the day shift had finally left. Warren, Sutton, Ruskin and Richardson remained, seated around Richardson's workstation.

Warren looked over at Sutton; the bags under his friend's eyes were pronounced. There was someone that needed to go home. Grayson beat him to the punch.

'Great work today, people,' he said, shrugging on an expensive-looking, full-length raincoat as he exited his office. 'I just got confirmation that SOC are going to raid that "gentlemen's club" that the brothers Patel frequented.'

He looked out of the darkened window; icy rain battered the glass, with some of the fatter drops lingering and joining together. 'Get yourselves home,' he ordered. 'The forecast is for snow flurries later, you don't want to get caught out.'

'Nothing you can't cope with, eh, Moray?' asked Richardson as Grayson headed towards the lift.

'Yeah, I still can't get used to the way England grinds to a halt as soon as more than a millimetre of snow falls,' replied the bearded Scotsman as he retrieved his cycling helmet from beneath his desk.

'So, you'll be cycling home in nothing but skimpy lycra then?' teased Sutton.

'I might put some gloves on,' Ruskin allowed.

Warren smiled, enjoying the banter but too weary to contribute.

'Grayson's in a bloody good mood, considering we've just lost one of our most promising lines of inquiry,' said Richardson, once the lift had whisked the Superintendent out of earshot.

'Of course he is,' said Sutton. 'We've just uncovered a major drugs and gambling ring and got full confessions from Reva Vasava and Jaidev and Manoj Patel regarding a cigarette smuggling operation. That's red faces all around for SOC, you know how much he'll enjoy that. I'll bet you he'll be down in Welwyn tomorrow first thing, rubbing it in before he makes it in here for the day. He might even give us some of the credit.'

Sutton was probably right, but Warren struggled to match Grayson's mood. Whittling down the suspect list was an essential part of any investigation, but it was only helpful when the actual culprits remained on the list, and Warren wasn't entirely convinced that was the case. They still had no idea who was with Leon Grime that night, and he still refused to admit to being involved. And they still had no clear motive; there was too much of Anish Patel's day-to-day existence that remained a mystery – his killer could well have come from a part of his life that they knew nothing about.

A few minutes earlier, he'd released both of the Patel brothers on bail after re-arresting them on suspicion of a raft of charges relating to their illegal cigarette operation. Exactly who amongst the three siblings had played what part was for SOC and Trading Standards to determine. It also sounded as if they and a number of local businesses would be getting a visit from HMRC to determine how much tax they had defrauded through under-reporting the sales of Suniti's Sundries.

They were welcome to them; Warren had no desire to clap eyes on any of them again. No family was perfect and Warren tried not to judge those in situations that he'd never experienced personally, but in this case, the way Anish Patel had been treated by those who should have loved him the most left a sour taste in his mouth.

Rachel Pymm had continued to work her magic throughout Reva Vasava's interview and during the follow-up with her brothers. By the time Warren had elicited admissions from both men about their true whereabouts on the night of Anish's murder, Pymm had confirmed the location of their mobile phones at the warehouse on the Fowler Estate. She'd also chased up the manufacturers of the family's various prestige vehicles, who used the GPS trackers embedded within them to verify that they had driven there in Manoj's Range Rover and remained for several hours; certainly long after Anish was confirmed dead.

They'd also confirmed that Gotam Patel's Range Rover was parked in his driveway, alongside Reva Vasava's Mercedes, all of that night. The smart CCTV camera and security system that protected both residences showed that Anish's father, his sister and her husband had all been home that night, as had their mobile phones, which had remained connected to the houses' wireless routers. Snippets of a voice recording of Gotam Patel using the smart speaker in his home to turn up the heating that evening, and Reva Vasava using hers to play music, were merely icing on the cake.

'Fancy a quick pint, Warren?' asked Sutton. 'The Prince and Pauper has finally started stocking passable alcohol-free beers.'

'Not tonight, mate.'

Sutton nodded his understanding. Despite the day's successes, neither man would feel like celebrating until they'd got justice for Anish Patel. Besides which, Warren and Susan were due an important conversation that they'd been putting off for far too long.

Sunday 11th December

Chapter 44

Mornings off, even at the weekend, were rarer than hen's teeth at this stage of a major investigation. Nevertheless, Warren had made a promise to himself that he would at least have a leisurely breakfast with his wife. It was now well into December, and Christmas was fast approaching. The festive season had been overshadowed the previous year by the couple's recent loss, and Warren was determined to make up for that.

He'd also sent a text the previous evening, ordering the rest of his team to have a lie-in – nobody was to set foot in the office before 10 a.m. At least the threatened snow hadn't materialised.

The previous night's discussion had gone better than Warren had hoped. He'd arrived home late and was worried that despite his best intentions he would need to postpone their talk until the following morning. But Susan was waiting for him, and to his surprise not only was the brochure from the fertility clinic open, the clinic website was displayed on her laptop.

'We have the money, we should do it,' she greeted him.

Warren had been expecting, if not an argument, then at least a lengthy conversation. But if there was one thing he had learned about his wife, it was that when she made a decision the last thing she wanted to do was dither.

That night as they lay in bed, Susan started talking. It was pitch-black, but he could tell from her voice that if he turned the light on, he'd see the shine of tears in her eyes.

'I'm scared.'

The statement was as profound as it was simple.

'When the first couple of attempts failed, when the pregnancy tests came back negative, I was able to kid myself that it wasn't a big deal. It was disappointing but life goes on, you know? I was lying to myself, but I could cope. After all, we'd been trying the old-fashioned way for so long, I was used to it. I didn't let myself truly feel hope.'

She gave a big sigh. Warren said nothing, just squeezed her hand.

'When I got pregnant last autumn, I finally started to let a bit of that hope in. I knew that there was a long way to go – for any pregnancy, let alone twins – but I couldn't help myself.'

Her voice caught and Warren kissed her head. There was nothing he could say. There was nothing he needed to say; he just needed to let his wife speak without interruption. All she wanted was for him to listen.

'When we lost them, it just hurt so much. I wasn't ready for it; I never realised how much worse it would be than the other times.'

She turned her head. 'And I'm scared how much it'll hurt again.'

Warren recognised all the feelings she was describing. The constant disappointments, month after month, as they tried to get pregnant. Then the cautious optimism that he too had tried to repress, which nevertheless was soul-crushing when thwarted by another failed implantation.

And then the excitement that he just couldn't dampen when the pregnancy test finally came back positive. He remembered the fear in the pit of his stomach as they went for the ultrasound and then the elation as the ultrasound detected not one, but two tiny heartbeats.

Then the elation turned to dread; he was going to be a father!

How the hell was he qualified to be a dad? To two of them. What if he messed up? What if he was a disappointment? What if he couldn't be there? If he was snatched away like Gary Hastings?

Yet despite knowing it intellectually, the only fear he never really considered was Susan losing the babies. Miscarriage happened to other couples. They'd fought so hard for these babies, surely the universe – surely God – had decided it was time to reward them? And to reward them with not one but two?

But it wasn't to be. The 11th of November 2015 was the day the universe showed it wasn't ready to let them off the hook just yet.

The pain had nearly broken him; Susan too, although she had tried not to show it.

But her steadfast avoidance of the topic in the months gone by had made the damage clear to him. He'd felt himself sinking into despair. How could he fix something when he couldn't even address the problem?

Would they try again, or not? He didn't know, but he knew that it was a decision that they had to make together, and to do that they had to talk. And so he'd taken the gamble. Asking for the brochure, if only to act as a catalyst for a conversation that he didn't know how to start otherwise.

Finally Warren had whispered back in Susan's ear. 'I'm scared too.'

Chapter 45

'Gamma Hydroxybutyrate,' said Professor Jordan. The toxicology report had finally returned, and he'd phoned immediately.

'GHB,' said Warren. 'Isn't that used as a date rape drug?'

'That's one of its uses. Slipped into someone's drink, it makes them drowsy, and also affects short-term memory, so when the victim wakes up, they have no recollection of what happened to them. At higher doses it can cause cardiopulmonary arrest – basically a heart attack.'

'And there were traces of it in Anish's blood tests?' said Warren.

'Yes, but unfortunately, even if Mr Patel did consume the drug, and it did lead to his death – entirely possible, given his pre-existing heart condition – it might not have been administered non-consensually. The drug is used recreationally, particularly in the gay and rave communities. It causes a feeling of euphoria and sometimes increased sexual arousal.'

Warren considered what Jordan had said. Anish had been using the hotel covertly, perhaps for sexual relations. Could he have been using GHB recreationally?

Was his death an accident?

*

'We've traced Mr Brown Bear, one of Anish Patel's contacts from Rainbow Hookups,' said Pymm. Warren and Sutton were standing next to her workstation. 'Karen's idea about tracing his ex-girlfriend through her kids' school paid off; the girls had their father's surname, but she was listed on the system as sole contact. They moved back to her mum's in Warrington, but the previous school got a request for records from the new school. We have his full name, Deepak Basu, and his address.'

'What has he got to say for himself?' asked Warren. Anish had made contact over a year ago, and as far as they could tell it was him that had ended the relationship a week later. But if the man's former neighbour was correct then maybe he held Anish responsible for what appeared to be the subsequent breakdown in his relationship with his family? If Anish had been the one to tell his girlfriend of their affair – perhaps as some sort of extortion attempt – that could well have left the man angry enough to kill him, although why it had taken so long was something Warren was keen to know.

'I'm afraid he hasn't got anything to say for himself,' said Pymm. 'Ms Weybridge confirmed that part of the reason they broke up was because she found his burner phone and read the text messages that he was exchanging with men, but she said the relationship was failing already. He was struggling with a cocaine and drink habit that couldn't be funded entirely from his wages as a builder, especially since he had a tendency not to turn up to work.'

Warren had a feeling he knew where this was going.

'He died of heart failure, probably from the coke and booze, back in October. He was dead long before Anish was killed.'

'Damn.'

Pymm lowered her voice, 'We also got a trace on Anish Patel's missing mobile phone, it just connected to the network. It's using a different SIM card but the handset's IMEI number matches. It's on the Chequers Estate.'

'What a surprise,' said Sutton. 'Where else would a murder victim's stolen mobile end up?'

Warren glanced over his shoulder. Karen Hardwick had her back to them, typing at her computer. He lowered his voice also.

'Tony, arrange for a team to go and pick up whoever is using it. Keep it quiet, there's no need for Karen to get wind of this just yet.'

Sutton's face turned grim. 'Yeah, I get it. Nothing but bad memories on that estate.' He looked at his friend. 'You OK?'

Warren nodded, not trusting himself to speak. He was just glad that he didn't have to go himself; the memory of Gary Hastings' blood-soaked body in the passenger seat of Warren's car brought a lump to his throat.

Like Sutton said, there was nothing but bad memories there.

*

'The person with Anish's phone is downstairs in interview suite one,' said Sutton an hour later. 'She'd just put a brand-new SIM card in it.'

'Where did she get it?' asked Warren.

'She claims to have bought it second-hand on eBay,' said Sutton.

'Do you believe her?'

'Not for a second. She's on the system; dealing, shoplifting, a couple of busts for soliciting.'

'Could she have been involved in Anish's murder?' asked Ruskin.

Sutton shrugged. 'Impossible to tell, but at the moment, she seems more fussed about being caught with stolen property. My guess is she bought it down the pub, no questions asked.'

'Well, let me know when she's spoken to her solicitor and you can go and put the frighteners on her,' said Warren.

'Sir, you're going to want to see this,' Mags Richardson called Warren over to her workstation.

'The team in Welwyn have been looking through CCTV footage from the cameras along the A506. There is a camera overlooking the bus stop just along from the Easy Break Hotel.'

Warren looked over her shoulder.

'The video isn't great, because it's dark, but I have footage from the same camera over the previous two weeks. Here are the best screenshots. Look at the timestamp.'

Each of the images over the previous two weeks were taken at the same time, plus or minus about two minutes. In each, the same figure was clearly recognisable.

'OK, that makes sense,' said Warren. 'We'd expect him to pass by at that time.'

'This is the night of the murder. We've played it for an hour either side, and guess what?'

'He doesn't pass the camera,' said Warren. 'So where was he?'

'Exactly. Now let's fast-forward a few hours.' She manipulated the mouse.

The image changed. Now the figure was clearly visible again. Warren looked at the time stamp. 02:56.

'Got you,' said Warren.

Chapter 46

Amber Mackie was on edge. Despite her forced appearance of calm – folded arms, chewing gum and humming to herself – the tension in her face was obvious, as was the jiggling leg under the table.

'Do you know why you are here, Amber?' started Ruskin, after identifying himself and Mags Richardson.

Mackie gave a shrug and looked over the two officers' shoulders.

Richardson pushed an A4 colour photograph across the table. 'Can you tell me who this mobile phone belongs to?' she asked. The actual handset had been couriered to headquarters in Welwyn Garden City for forensic analysis.

'Me. I bought it on eBay.'

'When?' Ruskin asked.

'Dunno, last week sometime.'

'Do you have a receipt, or proof of purchase?'

'No. Chucked it in the recycling bin, di'n't I?'

'We saw no sign of it when we looked,' said Richardson.

'Bin men must have been.'

'No, recycling's tomorrow,' said Ruskin. 'What about an email receipt? Perhaps you could log into your account and show us who the seller is.'

'Look, what is this really about?' interjected the duty solicitor, a middle-aged black woman in a trouser suit. 'A detective constable and a detective sergeant seems like overkill to establish the provenance of a mobile phone.'

Richardson glanced over at Ruskin. The interview strategy called for a phased release of information to the suspect. She decided to increase the pace slightly.

'The mobile phone was stolen from the victim of a serious crime.'

'Woah!' shouted Mackie. 'I ain't been involved in nothing. I just bought a second-hand phone.'

'Then perhaps you could tell us your whereabouts on the evening of Thursday, November the 24th?'

Mackie paused. 'I ain't done nothing. I just bought a phone, that's all.'

'A phone that we know was stolen on the night of November 24th.'

'Nothing to do with me.'

'So where were you then?' pressed Ruskin.

Mackie licked her lips. 'No comment.'

'Look, Amber, we know that you didn't buy that phone on eBay,' said Richardson. 'Either you stole it from our victim, or you received it from somebody else linked to that person. Now I need to know what you were doing that night, and if you have an alibi, who you got the phone from.'

Mackie looked at her solicitor, who sat stony-faced.

'I ain't a grass,' she muttered eventually.

Richardson opened her folder again. 'Do you recognise this man?' she asked.

Mackie shook her head.

'How about you actually look at the photo, first?' suggested Ruskin.

'I ain't a grass,' repeated Mackie, but she glanced down at the picture, despite herself. Her eyes narrowed, and she stopped chewing. A second later, her eyes widened again.

'Fuck off. No way. No way am I involved in that.'

'Do you recognise this man?' asked Richardson again.

'Shit. Of course I do. That's the bloke on the news. They found him murdered in a ditch.'

'That's correct. This phone,' Richardson gestured towards the picture, 'belonged to the victim, Anish Patel. It hasn't been seen since the night he was killed. Now, as I said before, either you were there and took the phone, or you got the phone from somebody else.'

'I wasn't there, I swear,' Mackie's voice had taken on a pleading tone. 'You've got to believe me.'

'Then where were you?' asked Ruskin. 'You have to help us to help you here. That phone links you to a murder victim. We need to know where you were that night.'

'I was at home,' Mackie sobbed. 'I scored some really good gear, and I took it all. I didn't wake up until the next morning.'

'Was anyone with you?' asked Ruskin.

'No. I live on my own now.' She turned to her solicitor, who cleared her throat.

'Ms Mackie has been struggling to stay clean and sober for the past year. Her eight-year-old daughter is currently with foster carers. In order for Amber to get her daughter back, she has to prove to the court's satisfaction that she is a fit and capable mother.'

'They won't let her live with me if I'm still using,' said Mackie, the tears now running freely down her cheeks. 'You can't tell them what I said,' she cried. 'You can't tell the court I'm still using. It's just now and again, hardly ever.'

'I'm afraid that's not up to me,' said Richardson softly. 'But what I do know, is that you being involved in a murder investigation is not going to help get your daughter back.'

'Tell us who you got the phone from, Amber,' said Ruskin. 'Help us solve this murder and I'm sure the judge will take that into account.'

'What about the handling stolen goods?' asked Mackie. 'I'm on probation.'

'Again, that's not up to me, but I can have a word,' said Richardson, ignoring the scowl from Mackie's solicitor.

'OK, OK. I bought it down the pub. Fifty quid.'

'Which pub?' asked Richardson.

'The Rising Sun.'

'Who from?' asked Ruskin.

'Just some bloke.'

'We'll need more than that,' said Richardson. 'What's his name?'

Mackie looked helpless. 'I don't know.'

'Describe him.'

'I dunno. White, blonde hair.'

'That's not very helpful, Amber,' said Ruskin.

'What can I say? I never spoke to him before. I needed a new phone, 'cause my last one was nicked by my ex. A mate said that he knew someone who could get one. The next night he turned up, I gave him some money and he handed it over.'

'And there's nothing else you can tell us about him?' said Richardson. 'Young or old? Tall or short? Slim or fat?'

'I don't know,' sniffed Mackie. 'I wasn't in a good state, you know?'

The two detectives looked at each other in exasperation; the phone was potentially a direct link to the killer but the woman in front of them was pretty much useless.

'He was wearing a Chelsea top,' she said suddenly.

'Well that narrows it down,' said Ruskin. He had a feeling that there was more that Mackie wasn't telling them. What was she holding back?

Mackie looked down. For the first time since she'd arrived, she looked slightly ashamed.

'I couldn't really afford fifty quid. So, I asked my mate if he reckoned I could get a discount from him if, you know.' She made a gesture with her hand and wrist, her fingers circled.

'He just laughed and said I was barking up the wrong tree; I wouldn't be his cup of tea.'

*

Warren had called a team meeting; the pieces were flying in thick and fast and he needed everyone fully briefed.

Mags Richardson had the floor. 'Credit again goes to Karen for this particular idea,' she said. 'We used the purchase history on Anish's credit card to see if we could secure any CCTV footage of who he had been associating with recently. As you all know, he very much enjoyed eating out. He also liked a weekend away.'

She opened up a presentation on the wall screen.

'Most of the CCTV has gone of course, but we did get lucky with a few bits. For example, we have footage of Anish with Isaiah Otis, AKA Car_lover12, having a meal in Stevenage back in June. That footage was retained because of a pending court case concerning a member of staff accused of dipping their hand in the till.'

'That confirms what he told us,' interjected Sutton.

'More interesting is what we found on these dates,' said Mags. 'Again, we used his credit card records and retrieved CCTV from these premises.'

She projected a compilation of images onto the screen, each of them date-stamped.

Immediately, the room exploded into a babble of excited observations; Warren couldn't keep track of who was saying what.

'They're all the same bloke.'

'It looks like they went away for the bank holiday.'

'A long weekend in July.'

'They were seeing each other for months.'

Grayson, who had been sitting quietly at the back anticipated Warren's next request. 'I'll get a warrant for a real-time intercept on his phone. No problem at all now.'

Before Warren could acknowledge him, Janice poked her head around the door. 'Sorry DCI Jones, but I have Andy Harrison on the phone. He says it's important.'

'I'll hold the fort,' offered Sutton. If what Harrison had was urgent enough that he'd phoned, rather than just emailed, it was worth answering the call.

'The fingerprints from Anish Patel's hotel room have come back,' said Harrison as soon as Warren picked up. 'Sorry it took so long, but it isn't the cleanest of establishments, so there were a lot of them.'

'I understand. What have you got for us?'

'Most of the prints were unusable, but of those that were, most had no hits on the database, or were identified as members of staff. I've sent a list to you in an email. There are also some that are too blurry to run through the system, but we could probably match by eye if you can get us a suspect.'

'What about the ones that came up on the system?' said Warren.

'Two of them are current members of staff, but I think the most interesting is likely to be the set we found on the back of the bed's headboard. Alongside Anish Patel's.'

'You're right, that is interesting,' said Warren, his pulse starting to increase. 'Tell me about them.'

'Unfortunately, these were the blurred ones, but we have prints from digits on both hands, just like Patel's, on the rear edge of the headboard. Pointing downwards.'

Warren tried to picture the scene. 'As if Anish and this person were holding the headboard?'

'Exactly. Not inconsistent with what you believe he was meeting these people for. There were plenty of other fingerprints in a similar position – try not to think about that next time you check into a hotel with the missus.'

'I wasn't, until you put the idea in my head,' said Warren, already clicking on his email as he hung up.

He scanned the list of names. Harrison was correct, most of

the staff prints were workers that probably had a legitimate reason to have been in the room. Except for one.

'What the hell were you doing in there?' asked Warren out loud.

Warren stood up and strode briskly back to the briefing room.

'Perfect timing, Sir,' said Mags Richardson as he entered. 'I was just sharing this with the team. It came in moments before you called the meeting.'

On the screen, black and white CCTV footage was coming to an end. She restarted it from the beginning.

A smile crept across his face.

With the fingerprints from the hotel room, the CCTV showing Anish's previously unknown relationship, and the testimony from the woman who had bought Anish's mobile phone, combined with this newly uncovered footage, Warren could feel all the pieces of the puzzle finally coming together.

'Bring them all in and let's see if we can finally put this to bed,' he ordered.

Chapter 47

After the briefing, things moved quickly: warrants were applied for and granted, arrest teams sent out and witnesses located, authorization from the bean counters to fast-track forensics reluctantly given and real-time intercepts on phone locations approved.

This time, Shane Moore, the trainee chef from the Easy Break Hotel, was accompanied by his father. As Ruskin set up the recording, Hardwick studied the teenager. His neck was slightly pink, and he seemed to have difficulty making himself comfortable. Unless Hardwick was very much mistaken, Shane Moore was a man – a boy, she corrected herself – with something he'd like to get off his chest.

'Do you know why we've invited you back, Shane?' asked Hardwick, her tone kind, but firm.

Moore's neck reddened still further. 'It's about the night that bloke was killed, isn't it?' He swallowed, and his father placed a comforting hand on his forearm. 'I didn't tell you everything.'

'Go on,' said Hardwick. Beside her, Ruskin remained silent. It was clear that with gentle persuasion, Moore would tell them everything he knew. Ruskin was aware that at times he could be perceived as … intimidating.

'Look, I haven't seen anything with my own eyes, OK, so, I

don't know what's really going on.' He fingered the array of studs in his left earlobe.

'Why don't you tell us what you think,' she encouraged.

'I think that sometimes there are deliveries.'

'At the loading bay?'

'No, at the fire exit. I can hear when the door is opening and closing, it makes a loud squeak. Sometimes I hear people walk down the corridor, open the fire door, and speak to somebody outside. Then the door closes again. It isn't long enough for a smoke break.'

'And does this happen often?'

Moore looked at his hands. 'Most evenings.'

'And did it happen the night of Thursday November 24th?'

He nodded, still staring at the table.

'Is there anything else you are not telling me, Shane?' asked Hardwick softly.

Moore continued looking at the table.

'Go on, son,' said Moore Sr. 'Tell them what you told me.' It was the first time that Moore's father had spoken since the initial introductions.

Eventually Moore spoke. 'It's about Nick …'

*

Nicholas Kimpton was arrested at the same time his trainee, Shane Moore, attended the station for further questioning. The chef had vehemently denied murdering Anish Patel as his rights were read to him, but Hutchinson had detected a note of resignation beneath his protestations.

'Do you recognise this mobile phone number?' asked Warren, pushing a slip of paper across the table. To maintain consistency, Warren had chosen to interview Kimpton again, with a constable to observe and take additional notes.

The man was a ghostly white under the room's lighting. His

eyes were bloodshot and slightly puffy, as if he had been crying. Warren wasn't surprised. If they were right, and he had been involved in the death of Anish, he was going to prison for a very long time. Right now, he was probably wondering how on Earth it had all come to this.

Kimpton looked at it and shrugged. 'No idea. Who does it belong to?'

Warren ignored the question and produced a sealed plastic evidence bag containing a black Samsung phone. 'Is this your only phone? It was in your pocket when you were arrested.'

'Yes.'

Warren produced a Force-issue mobile phone. 'Can you tell me its number?'

A look of puzzlement on his face, Kimpton reeled it off. Warren typed the number into the police handset and composed a text. A few seconds later, the phone in the evidence bag lit up, and made a loud 'ding' noise.

'That's the noise that your phone makes when it receives a text. Now I'm going to ask you again, Mr Kimpton, is this your only handset, and do you recognise the number I showed you a moment ago?'

Kimpton paused, looking to his solicitor for guidance. His solicitor said nothing.

'No comment.'

Warren produced another evidence bag, this one containing an older black Nokia handset. He slid it across the table. 'This phone was found in your house, hidden behind some DVDs on a bookcase in the living room. Do you recognise it?'

Kimpton licked his lips. 'No comment,' he repeated.

Warren picked up his police-issue mobile phone again. 'I am entering the number that I just showed you. We've checked the SIM card and this phone regularly receives text messages from another, unregistered number. We don't know what those messages are about – yet. Forensics are currently recovering

373

everything that you've got rid of – but those texts do coincide with evenings that our victim, Anish Patel, used the Easy Break Hotel. They are typically sent about an hour after he checks in.'

The number entered, Warren stopped typing. His finger hovered over the send button.

'On the night of his murder, this Nokia received one of those text messages. It then received a further six messages and a call, which this handset replied to, between 19:32 and 20:28. We'll know pretty soon what those messages were about, but why don't you save us all some time and tell us now?'

'No comment,' Kimpton whispered.

Warren pressed send. A moment later the phone in the evidence bag made a loud quacking noise.

'According to a witness, the phone that they heard on the night of the murder – a phone that we have tracked to the Easy Break Hotel that night – makes a noise like a duck quacking when it receives a message. Our forensic IT department have been through your personal handset and they can find no ring tone matching that description.'

Warren gestured toward the black Nokia in the evidence bag. 'I believe that you were carrying this phone that night. And all the other nights that Anish checked into the Easy Break Hotel. Can you explain this?'

'This is rather circumstantial, DCI Jones,' interjected Kimpton's solicitor. 'I'm sure that particular ringtone has been downloaded by thousands of people. Besides which, many people have more than one mobile phone.'

'The phone isn't mine,' said Kimpton.

'Really, then who does it belong to?'

Kimpton licked his lips. 'I found it a few days ago in the car park of the hotel. I was thinking about selling it, you know making a bit of cash.'

'I see. A bit of a coincidence, don't you think?'

'Just thought I was lucky.'

'So why was it hidden in your flat?'

Kimpton blinked. 'Look, I thought it might have been stolen. Then when that bloke was murdered, I thought maybe it was linked to his killing. I panicked and hid it.'

'Why didn't you hand it into the police? It could have been a crucial piece of evidence.'

Kimpton looked down at the table. 'Yeah, I know I should have. But like I said, I panicked. And then you started questioning me and all and I thought maybe if you found it, you would think I was involved.'

Kimpton's solicitor's eyes narrowed. He could see the inconsistency, even if his client couldn't.

'So why didn't you dispose of it?' asked Warren.

Kimpton licked his lips. 'I figured that when it all blew over, I still might be able to flog it. It's a bit old, but I might have got some beer money.' He looked up. 'I'm really sorry; I know it was stupid.' He sat back in his chair, a look of relief finally passing across his face.

'OK, Nick, I can see how that would happen, but you're going to have to help me out with a few of the details here,' said Warren. 'How long would you say you've had the phone? You found it after the murder? What day?'

Kimpton paused. 'I'm not sure.'

'Ballpark figure; a week ago, longer?'

'Yeah that's probably about right. A week or so.' Kimpton was looking visibly flustered. Beside him his solicitor opened his mouth as if to object. Warren jumped in quickly before he got a chance.

'Where did you find it again?'

'The car park. Behind a wheelie bin.'

'How did you see it, if it was behind a bin?'

'Dunno, I just spotted it out of the corner of my eye.'

'So, it was easy to see?'

'Yeah, I guess so.'

'But not so easy that a trained crime investigation team, doing a fingertip search of that entire car park, would find it?'

Kimpton paused. 'I must have found it before you guys turned up.'

Out of the corner of his eye, Warren could see the man's solicitor trying to formulate some sort of objection, so he spoke quickly.

'Well Mr Patel was killed on the night of Thursday 24th November, his body wasn't found until the Sunday and it took us until Friday 2nd December to identify the Easy Break Hotel. That means you must have found the phone between the 24th and the 2nd?'

'Yeah, sounds about right,' said Kimpton before his solicitor had a chance to interrupt.

'Well here's the problem, Nick, you said that you found the phone a few days ago,' started Warren.

'Mr Kimpton was rather imprecise on the timing,' interrupted the solicitor.

'But you reckoned a week was about right?' persisted Warren. 'That's what you said.'

'I suppose that I might have been a little confused,' said Kimpton. 'I think I found it more recently.'

Warren suppressed a smile, Kimpton had finally noticed he'd walked into a trap of his own making and was now trying to leap back out. Unfortunately, he'd chosen the wrong direction to jump. His solicitor rolled his eyes.

'Well we first brought you in to make a statement on Saturday the 3rd; that's just over a week ago, and you say that you found the phone a few days ago. But you also say that you panicked and hid the phone after we interviewed you. Which is it, Nick? Did you find this phone before or after you became aware of the murder?'

'No comment,' said Kimpton eventually. Beside him, his solicitor relaxed slightly. At the moment, Kimpton was his own worst enemy; he really needed to keep his mouth closed. Warren hoped that he could persuade Kimpton not to.

'Well, I don't suppose it really matters,' said Warren. 'You found a mobile phone, you decided not to hand it in, and here we are. There are other, more important things I need to clear up, and I could really use your help. Can you do that?'

'I would advise my client that he is under no obligation to make further comment in this interview,' interjected the solicitor.

'Of course, but we'll let Mr Kimpton decide for himself,' said Warren, addressing his remarks directly at the solicitor. The two men locked eyes briefly.

'First of all, the ringtone on this phone matches the one that witnesses say they heard in the kitchen that night, which is one of the few places inside the building that a mobile phone signal can penetrate. They've also heard it on previous occasions, for that matter.'

'Which you said was probably just a coincidence,' said Kimpton, clearly unable to obey the sound legal advice that he was being given. 'Loads of people have that ringtone. Maybe it was one of the waitresses' phones?'

'I don't believe I said it was "probably a coincidence" that it had that ringtone, I said that it "seemed a bit of coincidence" that you should find a mobile phone with the same ring tone as one heard in your kitchen by witnesses on the night of the murder,' said Warren mildly. 'But for what it's worth, none of the serving staff working that night have that ringtone.'

Kimpton blinked again.

'But anyway, I have a more pressing concern. Regardless of when you claim you actually found this phone, it was sometime after the night that Anish was murdered. However, according to the historic location data for the handset, it has regularly been in the vicinity of the Easy Break Hotel since the SIM was activated back in January of this year. Obviously, the signal in the building is a bit patchy, but we're confident that the owner of this phone works at the hotel.'

'Then there's your killer,' said Kimpton. 'It must have been another member of staff.' He leaned forward. 'Have you checked out other people who work there?'

'Like who?' said Warren. 'Perhaps you could help us there. Is there anyone that you think might have been responsible?'

Kimpton leaned back in his chair, a thoughtful look crossing his face. 'I don't know. Let me have a think about it.' He turned to his solicitor. 'I'd like to take a break now, I need a pee.'

'Of course,' said Warren. 'Interview suspended.'

*

'Get ready for the bullshit,' said Sutton, as he handed Warren a cup of coffee.

'It doesn't matter,' said Warren. 'We both know who he'll try to pin it on. I just hope he keeps on ignoring his solicitor's advice to keep his mouth shut.'

'Well so far, you're playing him like a cheap violin,' said Sutton.

'How is everything else going?' asked Warren.

'No luck yet; nobody was home, but we've got teams out searching. The warrant has come through for the real-time intercepts, Rachel is speaking to the phone company right now.'

'Good, keep me posted. Interrupt the interview if you need to.'

The desk sergeant popped his head around the door. 'He's done, Sir. Mr Kimpton's ready when you are.'

Sutton clapped Warren on the back. 'Go get him.'

*

'The evidence disclosed is flimsy at best,' said Kimpton's solicitor. 'You seem to be basing Mr Kimpton's entire arrest on a ringtone installed on a phone that you have yet to establish Mr Kimpton was even in possession of the night that Mr Patel was killed. My advice to my client remains that he should not cooperate with what is clearly a desperate fishing expedition aimed at reinvigorating a stalled investigation.' His mouth tightened. 'Nevertheless, Mr Kimpton is a civic-minded individual, and he has insisted that he wants to offer whatever assistance he can.' He looked sideways at Kimpton. 'Whether I believe it to be wise for him to do so or not.'

Warren nodded gravely, his tone dripping with false sincerity. 'Then I thank Mr Kimpton for his help and look forward to hearing what he has to say.'

He turned to Kimpton expectantly.

'Obviously, I don't know for sure that he is guilty, and I'd be as shocked as you are if he was involved, 'cause he's a mate, but have you considered Leon Grime?'

'Leon Grime? The handyman?' Warren injected a note of surprise into his voice. 'Why do you say that?'

'Leon has a record. You know, dealing and all that. I think he also has a violent past. He spent some time in prison.'

'I see.' Warren thought it best not to remind Kimpton of his own chequered history.

'The thing is, Leon was told about the broken lock on the fire door ages ago. And he was supposed to get the CCTV fixed. I figured he was probably up to something when he didn't get it sorted, but it was really handy for nipping out for a fag without anyone knowing. Leon's office is close to the kitchen and you can get a signal in there also. I reckon if the volume on his phone was turned up really high, you could hear it in the kitchen, if it was in his office.'

Warren pinched his bottom lip thoughtfully. 'That's really interesting.'

Beside Kimpton, his solicitor stared into space, his face carefully neutral.

'So, what do you think he was up to?' Warren asked.

'If I had to guess, I'd say that he was probably receiving deliveries, you know drugs or stolen gear. He wouldn't want that on

379

CCTV, and the alarm system would log every time the fire door was open.'

'Hmm. Pretty smart,' said Warren. 'Where does the mobile phone come in?'

'I guess whoever was delivering the drugs sent him a text when they were outside. He must have lost it at some point, and I found it.'

With Kimpton cooperating – after a fashion – Warren decided not to interrupt him and press for further clarification of when Kimpton had supposedly found the phone. It was clear that under the right circumstances, the chef was incapable of staying silent. Warren decided to let him keep on talking; hastily constructed lies were always the most damning.

'Well, what you've said makes sense. The only thing is Mr Grime's shift typically ends before the text messages were received, on the nights that Anish checked into the hotel.'

'Leon was always hanging around the building at odd hours. I just figured he was on call.'

'So, where does Anish come into it?'

'I can't help you there. Maybe he was a customer, or Leon was taking the drugs up to his room?'

'And you think something went wrong, and Anish was killed?'

'Sounds logical.' Kimpton relaxed into his chair again.

'I guess that would explain why Mr Grime's fingerprints were found in room 201,' said Warren.

'There you go then,' said Kimpton, a look of relief crossing his face.

'Mind you, he was the hotel's handyman; we might have a problem proving that his fingerprints shouldn't have been there.'

'I suppose so.'

'Well, it confirms what we already know. Mr Grime has admitted that he was receiving drugs and stolen property through that door. We currently have him in custody.'

'Well then,' said Kimpton, a note of triumph in his voice. 'You've got your man.'

'However, I have been wondering why your fingerprints were in the room. I mean you're the chef, why would you be up in a guest's room?'

Kimpton tensed. 'I don't know what you mean.'

'Your fingerprints were in room 201. On the edge of the sink in the bathroom. Both sides, as if you were gripping the sink bowl. Fortunately for us, the cleaning staff at the Easy Break Hotel aren't the most assiduous. The inside of the sink was nice and glistening, but they'd clearly not bothered to wipe the outside.'

Kimpton started to speak, then thought better of it.

'Why are the fingerprints of the hotel chef in a guest's room on the second floor? You've never taken advantage of the twenty per cent staff discount, why would you? You only live a short cycle ride away?'

'No comment,' managed Kimpton.

'Going back to the phone location data. We've tracked the Nokia with the quacking ringtone to the hotel – unfortunately, we can't be any more precise than that. We can't tell if it was in Mr Grime's office, or the kitchen. But what we can do is show that it has spent time in your flat, for several months before you claim you found it. Why is that?'

Kimpton had gone pale. He swallowed hard before answering. 'Leon comes around mine occasionally, you know just to chill, watch the footie if Chelsea's on. Maybe he was carrying it then?' he managed.

Warren took his time writing on his notepad. 'I'll be sure to check that out. In the meantime, why don't we move on? Remind me, what time did you finish work the night of the murder?'

Kimpton swallowed again; he eyed the jug of water on the other side of the room but obviously decided that to ask for water might be seen as evasive.

'About 10 p.m.,' he said.

'Your usual time?'

'Yes.'

Warren opened the folder in front of him, taking out a series of glossy photographs.

'You're a man of habit, I'll give you that.' He fanned several of the pictures across the tabletop.

'There's a CCTV camera on a pole next to the bus stop nearest the hotel. These photographs show you passing it on the way home from work, every evening. They're in black and white as they're using night vision, but we have some shots of you cycling home after the morning shift, which are in the daylight and full-colour.' He pushed one of them across the table. 'Is that you in the photograph?' Warren asked.

Kimpton stared at the picture. His throat bobbed. 'Yes,' he managed finally.

Warren pointed to the picture, turning slightly towards Kimpton's solicitor. 'As you can see, Mr Kimpton rides quite a distinctive bicycle. White and red stripes, with reflective safety tape wrapped around the frame. His lights are also quite old-fashioned; filament bulbs rather than the newer LED ones, and look, he even has a bell. Mr Kimpton's fingerprints are on the handlebar grips, so we know that it's his. Or at least it is now; it was stolen from some poor student last year.'

Kimpton closed his eyes briefly.

'You also wear a fluorescent green jerkin with reflective strips, and a helmet with reflective tape. That makes it really easy to identify you on the night-vision cameras, even if we can't see your face clearly.'

Kimpton said nothing. Warren continued. 'Now on the night that Anish Patel was killed, you didn't pass that camera at your usual time. We have you on the other side of the road travelling to work, but nothing when your shift ended. Obviously, we've allowed for the vagaries of human memory, and checked the footage for a couple of hours either side. We figured you might have left at a different time to normal – after all, you sent Shane Moore home early that night, shortly after the quacking phone received a text message.

'Which was very generous of you, by the way, offering to load the dishwasher yourself. Shane wasn't going to argue, obviously, although he did say it was a bit strange that when he came in the next morning the dishwasher was still running, as if you hadn't actually set it off the night before. Why was that?'

'Just forgot,' mumbled Kimpton.

'Well anyway, guess what? We did eventually find you on that CCTV footage. A hell of a lot later than you originally said; 2.56 a.m. in fact.' Warren thrust the last CCTV image across the table.

'What were you doing at the Easy Break Hotel between the end of your shift and five-to-three the night that Anish Patel was killed?'

Nicholas Kimpton looked as though he had been kicked. He covered his face, and his shoulders started to shake. Eventually, he composed himself enough to speak. When he did, his voice was thick.

'OK, OK. I'll tell you everything. But I didn't kill him.'

'Then who did?' asked Warren, his voice now gentle.

Kimpton looked up and for the first time, Warren thought he glimpsed the truth in his eyes. And real fear.

'I'll give you his name. I'll give you everything, but you have to promise me you'll make sure my daughter is safe. He said he'd kill her if I said anything.'

Chapter 48

Warren entered the main CID office at a jog; already the office was on high alert.

'I'm trying to get Abbey Fields Primary School, where his daughter's dance class is held, on the phone, but it's a Sunday,' said Pymm. 'We've got officers banging on his front door, but no reply. Neighbours haven't seen him. We haven't managed to get a real-time intercept on his mobile yet.'

'Shit,' said Warren. Kimpton had given them the name of the man they'd been trying to identify for the past several hours. The search had just become significantly more urgent. Kimpton's neighbours had witnessed his arrest; if the news found its way to their suspect he might assume that Kimpton was talking and come good on his threat to harm the little girl.

'What about the mum?' he asked.

'Also engaged, and she's ignoring the call-waiting signal. I've contacted her mobile provider to see if they can break into the conversation and warn her, but it'll be a couple of minutes until they can set that up.'

'There are three units on their way,' confirmed Hutchinson. 'ETA two minutes.'

Warren looked at the clock. It was just after three; a dozen small children would be finishing their class, Kimpton's five-year-old daughter amongst them.

Sutton sat down heavily, his face pale.

'You OK, Tony?' asked Warren.

'Yeah, just a bit breathless. The adrenaline does that sometimes.'

'I've got some camomile tea,' said Pymm. 'It'll help relax you.'

Sutton shook his head. 'Don't worry, things aren't that bad.'

Warren started to pace. The two minutes stretched endlessly. The primary school was on the other side of town, several miles away. Even with blues and twos, there was no way Warren or anyone from his team could be there in less than ten minutes; like it or not, they'd be sitting this one out, waiting for news to be relayed to them second-hand.

'How would he even know about Kimpton's daughter's dance lessons?' asked Ruskin.

'Bloody Facebook,' said Pymm. 'Her mum posted a picture of her in her tutu and Kimpton shared it,' she scowled. 'It doesn't take a great detective to track down the dance teacher's website. Those pictures are a child-molester's dream, especially when you don't have any restrictions on who can view your feed.'

Unable to bear it any longer, Warren picked up a radio, selecting the correct frequency.

'Arriving on scene,' came a voice from the handset.

'I see him,' said a second voice a beat later.

Warren bit his tongue; they didn't need him clogging up the airways and distracting them. He turned the volume on the radio up to maximum and set it on a desk near the centre of the room. By now nobody remained at their workstation; everyone was huddled around the piece of black plastic and electronics. Even Grayson had emerged from his office, his face pinched with worry.

For the next few seconds, the team listened intently, trying to decipher the overlapping voices from the open channel.

Suddenly the airwaves were full of screams – a mixture of adults and what could only be small children.

'Put the knife down, and move away from her,' came a raised voice, cutting through the babble. Warren's breath caught in his throat. Beside him, Sutton leaned forward, breathing deeply as if he was about to faint.

'Put the knife down, now!' ordered another voice.

'Oh, Christ,' muttered Pymm.

A moment later there came the sound of rapid clicking, followed by loud breathing and the sound of pounding feet from whoever had the channel open.

'One down, we need an ambulance,' came the voice a few moments later, struggling to be heard over the sounds of panic.

Unable to help himself, Warren reached for the radio. 'Do you have her? Is she safe?'

The shouting in the background continued for a few more agonising seconds before a voice finally broke through the noise. 'All good, she's fine. Suspect is detained. Ambulance is for suspect.'

A collective sigh of relief went around the office and Warren felt the tension drain out of him. He felt a thump on his shoulder: Grayson, the release of stress making him uncharacteristically effusive. 'Got the bastard,' he said, a huge smile across his face.

Warren grinned back, agreeing with the sentiment, if not its accuracy. As it stood, they were a long way from even charging the man currently recovering from a 50,000 volt Taser shock, but for the moment he'd take the victory.

After sharing a few more congratulatory handshakes, Warren made his way back to Sutton; already colour was returning to the man's face. 'Tony, why don't you sit this one out?' he asked quietly.

'You must be kidding,' said Sutton clambering to his feet. 'Let's nail this fucker to the wall.'

*

The response from Nicholas Kimpton was a mixture of relief that his daughter was unharmed, and weary recognition that it was time to come clean. He spoke for almost two hours before being led back to his cell.

Warren was tired, but he knew that the end was in sight.

'He's in a meeting with his solicitor,' said the custody sergeant when asked about their recently apprehended suspect. 'The doctor's been and pronounced him fit enough to be interviewed; just a few cuts and bruises from when he face-planted after the Taser. He's currently under arrest for attempted kidnap and possession of a bladed article in a public place.'

'Good,' said Warren. 'That'll keep him off-guard for the time being, I don't want to give our game away too soon.'

He looked over at Sutton. 'Fancy a bite to eat whilst we plot our interview strategy?'

'Sounds like a plan. It's been a while since we did the old good cop, bad cop routine.'

Warren smiled. He'd missed his old friend.

*

'My client would like to stress that this has all been a big misunderstanding,' started the solicitor.

'I see,' said Warren. 'Then perhaps you can explain why you were standing near a primary school, waving a knife around when the kids were being let out?'

The man opposite them stared down at the table. His slumped shoulders suggested compliance, but there was a hardness behind his eyes. He wasn't going to make their job easy.

'I wouldn't characterise it as "waving a knife around",' interjected the solicitor.

'How would you characterise it, Mr Beechey?' asked Sutton, looking directly at the blonde-haired man. The suspect was dressed in a paper forensic suit; the tracksuit and Chelsea football shirt that he'd been wearing at the time of his arrest had been taken for processing. The man who called himself Blondie92 on the Rainbow Hookups dating site shrugged but said nothing.

'OK, Jake,' said Warren. 'Let's start at the beginning. Why were you hanging around Abbey Fields Primary School?'

'I wasn't hanging around, I just happened to be there.' It was the first time that Beechey had spoken other than to confirm his name and address.

'Really?' said Sutton.

'Yeah, there's a newsagent round the corner. I was going to buy some fags.'

'Why there?' asked Sutton. 'You live miles away.'

Beechey shrugged again. 'Was up that way, and I decided to stop off.'

'Why were you up that way?' asked Sutton.

'Just was. Decided to get some fresh air.'

'You drove there though, didn't you?' said Warren.

'Yeah, so?'

'Well, it's just that you parked in the drop-off area where the parents wait,' continued Warren. 'Seems a bit weird, given that there is ample parking around the corner at the newsagent, and the road outside was full of parents waiting for the dance class to end.'

'I saw a spot and took it,' said Beechey.

'You also arrived just before 3 p.m. Which again seems odd. Why did you sit in your car for ten minutes, and only get out when the kids were released?' asked Warren.

'I was listening to the radio.'

'Why did you hide your face with a baseball cap and a hoodie?' said Sutton. 'You also kept yourself turned away from the school's CCTV cameras.'

'So you say,' sneered Beechey. 'It's December, innit? I was trying to keep warm.' He gave an open-handed shrug. 'And I don't know where the school's security cameras are, do I?'

'The woman you approached. Who is she?' asked Warren.

'Don't know what you mean.'

'In addition to the school's security cameras that you happened to be looking away from, there is a traffic camera mounted on a pole across the road, and we have a very good shot of your face as you turn away from the school's CCTV. You very clearly step out of your car and walk towards a woman waiting by the gate. She didn't seem thrilled to see you.'

Beechey paused for a moment. 'I recognised her. She's my mate's ex.'

'Which mate? What's his name?' said Sutton.

'Can't remember. Just some bloke I used to know.'

Warren gave a dramatic sigh. 'Look, Jake, it's been a long day. None of us want to be here. We've got a statement from the woman you spoke to, Jasmine Whitey, and the other parents waiting to pick up their kids. You approached this woman and said, "Nick says hello". Now we can clear all of this up, here and now, and then we can move on. But if you won't even admit to basic details that we can easily verify, nobody is going home any time soon.'

Beechey reached for his cup of water and took a slow sip, before he spoke. His eyes were cold and calculating.

'I used to know her ex years ago. I just thought I'd say hello. I was curious. He said he had a daughter; I thought it'd be interesting to meet her.'

'Her ex being Nicholas Kimpton? The chef at the Easy Break Hotel?' asked Warren.

'I suppose. Like I said, I haven't seen him for ages.'

'If you haven't seen him for ages, why did you say, "Nick says hello"?'

'Couldn't think what else to say.'

'So, then her daughter came out the school gate. What happened then?'

'I said something like, "Oh, this must be Kayla."'

'And then?'

'A police car pulled up and some bastard started shouting at me to get away from her.'

389

'And was that when you pulled the knife out?'

'No, it wasn't like that.'

'So, what was it like? Because I've seen the CCTV and read the witness statements, and that's what it looks like to me, her mother, the other parents present and the police officers on the scene.'

'I had my hands in my pockets. I started to take them out and I accidentally took out the knife I had in there.'

'Why did you have a knife in your pocket?' asked Sutton

Beechey swallowed. 'I dunno, I just did. I must have put it in there by accident when I was pottering about the house.'

Warren had to give the man some credit; his story was just plausible enough that it might cast enough doubt on his intentions to result in an acquittal. The video footage clearly showed that he had kept his hands in his pockets when speaking to Whitey and he had only removed them when he was first instructed to get away from her and her daughter. The weather was certainly cold enough to justify keeping hands in pockets whilst standing around chatting.

'So, it was all a big misunderstanding?' said Warren.

'Yeah.'

'So why did you try to grab Kayla and run?' asked Sutton.

'I panicked, didn't I? I thought that copper was going to shoot me, like I was a terrorist or something.'

'So, you were going to use Kayla as a shield?' Sutton stated.

'No, of course not.' Sweat was starting to bead along Beechey's forehead. The air of confidence that he'd projected since he'd entered the interview suite was starting to crack. 'Like I said, I panicked. I wasn't thinking straight. Anyway, I let go of her immediately.'

That was a generous interpretation of events; Kayla had snatched her arm away.

'There was no need for that fucker to tase me,' continued Beechey. 'I should sue.'

Beechey's solicitor winced and leaned forward. 'I think Mr Beechey is understandably distraught by what occurred. And I believe he wishes to apologise for all the confusion and upset that he has caused.'

Beechey scowled, before finally nodding. 'Yeah. I shouldn't have said anything to her. I'm sorry if I upset anyone.'

'I'm sure that Ms Whitey will be delighted to hear your apology,' said Sutton, 'and little Kayla will sleep a lot easier tonight.' He didn't even try to hide the sarcasm.

'Is that it? Can I go now?' asked Beechey.

'Not just yet,' said Warren. 'Let's just go back to your relationship with Mr Kimpton. How long have you known him?'

'I don't really see that this is relevant,' said Beechey's solicitor. 'I think we've established that Mr Beechey made a mistake. It's getting late, and while I appreciate that this incident needs proper investigation, no harm was done, and I don't think it is in anyone's interest to prolong matters unnecessarily.'

Warren gave a tight smile. He could tell from the solicitor's demeanour that whilst he clearly didn't know why Warren and Sutton were so interested in his client, he'd realised it would probably be in Beechey's best interests to conclude matters as quickly as possible.

'Indulge me. How long have you known Mr Kimpton?'

'A few years.'

'And how did you meet?'

'Can't remember.'

Warren opened the folder in front of him and removed a printout. 'Let's see if I can jog your memory. Did you know Mr Kimpton before the two of you shared a cell at The Mount Prison between April 2009 and January 2010?'

Beechey opened his mouth, before closing it.

'And what about since? Have the two of you kept in touch? You know, reminisced about the good old days?'

'No comment.'

It was Beechey's first flat-out refusal to answer a question. It looked as if they were finally getting somewhere.

'Mr Kimpton hadn't met Ms Whitey at the time you were in prison and so obviously hadn't fathered Kayla. So how did you know about her, if the two of you didn't stay in touch?' asked Sutton.

'No comment.'

'Where were you on the night of Thursday November 24th?' asked Warren. It was time to get down to what they really wanted to talk about.

'I was home in my flat all night.'

'Was anyone with you?' asked Warren.

'Nah, I was on my own. Just playing on my phone, you know.' There was a crafty look in Beechey's eyes. Whether by accident, or design, he knew that the iPhone on which he conducted most of his daily business was sitting in his flat all night, and the phone's location data would show that.

Warren opened the folder again, removing a photograph of Anish Patel. 'Do you recognise this man?'

Beechey looked at the photograph carefully. 'He looks familiar.'

'According to your phone logs, you texted this man on Monday the 4th of January this year. The two of you exchanged eight texts that day, then two more texts and a phone call the following day and a final series of texts on the Wednesday.'

'Oh, yeah,' said Beechey, 'I remember now. We met up for a drink.'

'And you haven't seen him since?'

'Nah, he wasn't my type.'

'What do you mean by "not your type"?' asked Sutton.

Beechey shrugged. 'A bit old for me.'

'But he was honest about his age on Rainbow Hookups,' said Sutton. 'You knew what to expect.'

'Some people look older than their years in real life,' said Beechey. 'You know how it is; appearances can be deceiving.'

'They certainly can be,' said Warren, pausing for a moment to let Beechey ponder the significance of his comment.

'Have you spoken to him since the 6th of January? In person or by text or phone?'

Beechey shook his head. 'Like I said, not my type. We had a drink, then that was it. I guess he felt the same way, he didn't call me either. I didn't see him again, until I saw his face in the paper.'

'Do you recognise this number?' asked Warren, pushing a piece of paper across the table.

'No, never seen it before.'

'Are you sure about that?'

He nodded.

'Have you ever been to the Easy Break Hotel on the A506?' asked Sutton.

'No, I don't think so.'

'Not even to visit your old mate, Nick? He works as a chef in the kitchen.'

Beechey's eyes narrowed. 'Like I said, I don't think so.'

'Well, the phone that this number is attached to certainly has. It's been to the Easy Break Hotel nine times over the past year. Funnily enough, it only ever seems to go there when Anish Patel – that's the name of the person you met on Rainbow Hookups by the way – checks in.'

'Like I said, I don't recognise the number.'

'Interestingly, the SIM card was activated just under a year ago, the day after you last texted Mr Patel using the phone number you gave him on Rainbow Hookups. Since then it has only ever contacted Mr Patel, and two other numbers, and spends much of its time switched off. You've not communicated with Mr Patel again using the number you gave him when you first made contact on Rainbow Hookups.'

'You need to listen more carefully,' snapped Beechey. 'I told you, I don't recognise that number and I only ever met Anish once; that's why I never contacted him again.'

'Strange. Because it seems that wherever this phone goes, your

393

phone also goes. Except when it goes to the Easy Break Hotel. When your phone stays in your flat. With you, apparently,' said Warren.

'Well, I can't help you there,' said Beechey.

Warren opened his folder again, removing another picture, this time of a black Motorola handset.

'Do you recognise this phone?'

Beechey swallowed again.

'It was in the glovebox of your car. We found it when we impounded it, after today's ... incident.'

'Not mine. Somebody must have left it in there.'

Warren pulled out a picture of a white Samsung. 'What about this phone?'

'No.'

'We recovered this one from somebody who claims that you sold it to them.'

'She's lying, I've never seen it before.'

'How do you know it was a she?' asked Sutton. 'DCI Jones made no mention of the person's gender.'

'I dunno.'

'Jake, let's cut the crap,' said Warren. 'Your fingerprints are on the back of this phone that you sold for fifty pounds down the Rising Sun pub. There's a nice clear thumbprint from when you removed the SIM card, and the buyer recognised your picture.'

Warren could almost see Beechey's mental pivot.

'OK, I admit. I found it.'

'Where?'

'In some bushes.'

'Where?'

'I can't remember.'

'When?'

'A week or so ago.'

'And why did you try and sell it?'

'Why do you think? It's a nice phone. I figured that whoever

394

lost it had probably already claimed on his insurance, so no harm done. Finders keepers, right?'

'No, not right,' said Sutton. 'But again, why do you say "he"? We haven't said anything about who owned the phone.'

'Just assumed,' said Beechey.

'Who does own the phone?' asked Warren.

'Like I said, I don't know.'

'Well you texted it,' said Warren. 'In fact, you texted it several times – as you set up your date with Anish.'

'Wait? You mean that's Anish's phone?' said Beechey. He covered his mouth with his hands, his voice muffled. 'Fuck ...' Suddenly he leaned back in his chair, shaking his head violently. 'No, this is bollocks; you're trying to set me up.'

Warren ignored him. 'This phone also received a single text from the black Motorola that you claim you don't own, that somebody apparently left in your glovebox. Now what are the odds of that?'

'No, this is bullshit.' He turned to his solicitor. 'Tell them; they can't do this. I know my rights; they can't just lie to me.'

Warren continued to press, holding up the photograph of the Motorola found in the glovebox. 'The only other number this phone contacts regularly belongs to your mate Nicholas Kimpton, a phone with a distinctive ringtone, that he initially claimed to know nothing about either – I tell you Jake, with all these phones that people claim to know nothing about, my head's beginning to spin.'

'I think it's about time you came clean and told us what happened the night of November 24th,' said Sutton. 'The night that Anish Patel was killed at the Easy Break Hotel, before being hidden in a ditch and mutilated to conceal his identity.'

'I don't know nothing about that,' said Beechey. 'You can't prove nothing. I wasn't anywhere near that hotel.' He slumped back in his chair, arms folded and glared at both men.

Warren glanced at Sutton. 'I think that now would be a good

time for us to tell you that we have Mr Kimpton next door. And he's been telling us a very interesting tale.'

'He's a liar, he's full of bullshit,' snapped Beechey.

'Really? Then perhaps you'd like to tell us what took place that night. Let us know your side of the story.'

Beechey started to 'no comment', before changing his mind. 'Nothing to tell,' he said eventually. 'Whatever he's said is bollocks. He's trying to frame me.'

'How is he trying to frame you? What do you think he's told us?' asked Warren.

'Don't answer that,' Beechey's solicitor instructed him firmly, before turning to Warren. 'DCI Jones, you cannot expect my client to answer questions about a conversation that he has not personally witnessed.'

'Of course, that would be unreasonable. Let's go back a bit then. Tell me about your relationship with Anish,' said Warren.

'No comment.'

'You said that you hadn't had any contact with Anish since your first date?'

'No comment,' mumbled Beechey.

'Well, let's just assume that you have had recent contact, shall we,' continued Warren, 'given that a phone that we found in your car, and which location data shows can normally be found within a few metres of your own iPhone, was also located to the Easy Break Hotel on the same nights that Mr Patel checked in. I assume it was your idea to meet up with Anish there?'

'No comment.'

'Well, Mr Kimpton claims that you contacted him last year and asked him to do you a favour. To let you in through the fire exit whenever you texted him. Why did you want him to do that?'

'No comment.'

'Is it because you didn't want anyone to know about your meetings with Anish?' Sutton pressed.

'No comment.'

'It all seems a bit strange to me,' said Warren, his tone thoughtful. 'I get that Anish was in a delicate personal situation, which was why he checked in under the name of Mr Smith and paid cash, but he still came in through the main reception where the CCTV cameras could see him. Yet you made sure that there was no video evidence of you coming and going. Why is that? We know that you aren't ashamed of being gay, you're quite open about it down at the Rising Sun, and your friends and family all know.'

Beechey gave a slight smile. 'Like you said, there's no CCTV footage of me entering the hotel. Nick's full of shit. In fact, I wouldn't be the least bit surprised if that phone in the glovebox of my car belongs to him. I give him a lift occasionally.'

'I thought you hadn't seen him since you left prison?' said Sutton.

Beechey shrugged. 'OK, so I lied about that. I figured if I said that I spoke to him recently, you'd keep me here even longer, and I couldn't be done with the hassle.'

'So, you're saying that Nick is blaming you for the murder of Anish and trying to frame you by leaving that phone in your car?' said Warren.

Beechey frowned; it was clear that the constant switching between Warren and Sutton was having the desired effect. 'I ain't saying anything, figure it out yourself, you're the detectives.'

'OK, Jake. Yes or no: have you been meeting Anish Patel at the Easy Break Hotel?' asked Warren.

Beechey paused for a long moment, before glancing at his solicitor.

'I want to speak to my lawyer.'

*

'They're going to throw each other under the bus,' opined Hutchinson.

'I suspect that you're right,' said Warren. 'Do we have anything back from the search teams or forensics?'

'They're doing a rush job on everything that they find,' said Pymm. 'No idea when they'll have news.'

'What's the plan, Chief?' asked Sutton, biting into an apple. 'Do we plough on tonight or pick up again tomorrow when we have more evidence from forensics?'

'We have Beechey on the back foot. I reckon he's going to hit back with a new story to explain any forensics that he thinks we're going to find. What I don't want is for him to spend all night polishing his story and plugging any holes in it. Let's continue, hear what he has to say and then pick it apart. Kimpton isn't going anywhere; he won't have any idea what Beechey is claiming, so we'll let him sweat overnight.'

There were general nods of agreement around the table.

'I want to know anything that comes in from forensics or the search teams immediately,' ordered Warren as he and Sutton headed back down to the interview room.

He looked at his watch; they had a long night ahead of them.

*

'I didn't kill Anish Patel,' Jake Beechey was white under the harsh, fluorescent lighting. 'Nick Kimpton did. I just helped introduce them.'

'Go on,' said Warren.

'I met Anish on Rainbow Hookups. We got on OK, he was a nice enough bloke, but we didn't really gel. But I thought that he might get on all right with Nick Kimpton.'

Warren and Sutton were careful to keep their expressions neutral; neither man had foreseen this turn of events.

'What do you mean by "get on all right"', asked Warren.

Beechey spread his hands. 'You're right, me and Nick spent some time together in prison. We got to know each other pretty well. Actually, very well, if you know what I mean.'

'Go on,' said Warren.

'Well, you know how it is. Nick just said it was a prison thing, and when he got out, he kind of denied it ever happened, which is cool. Plenty more fish in the sea and all that. And then he met Jasmine and had his little girl, Kayla,' Beechey snorted. 'But I knew. That wasn't really him, not deep down – why do you think they broke up?'

'Jasmine found out he was gay?' asked Sutton.

Beechey shrugged. 'Dunno if she ever figured it out, but he finally did. Anyway, he messaged me the back-end of last year and we hooked up again.'

'So, the two of you are in a relationship?' asked Warren.

Beechey shook his head. 'No, nothing like that, he's just a mate. But he's lonely, you know? And I was worried about him. He was too shy to go to gay bars and didn't want to join a dating site. But after I met Anish, I figured he might like him.'

'And so they started a relationship?' asked Warren.

'Yeah, I guess you could call it that. Anish's family were right bastards from what he told me and they wouldn't speak to him because he was gay, so he was lonely as well. He used to keep his sexuality private because he couldn't be done with the grief. Nick was still finding his feet, and didn't want everyone knowing, so they were a good fit. I guess that's why he used a new phone; to keep it discreet, like.'

'What else can you tell us about their relationship?' asked Sutton.

'Well, I can only tell you what Nick told me,' Beechey warned. 'But basically, Anish was into spy movies and all that shit, and he wanted to keep things quiet because of the problems with his family. Nick also wanted to keep things private, so every few weeks, Anish would book into the hotel under a false name and pay cash.

'Nick would finish his shift, wave goodbye to everyone, and then sneak back into the hotel through a dodgy fire exit to spend the night with Anish.'

Warren looked over at Sutton. Beechey's account certainly fit many of the facts that they had so far, even if it was unexpected.

'So, what happened the night he died?' asked Warren, deciding they'd circle back and pick apart the rest of Beechey's story later.

'I don't know. I just got a call from Nick, in the early hours of Friday morning. He said he was in the middle of some sodding field, and he needed me to come and pick him up.'

'So, you just dropped everything, jumped in the car and drove to a field in the middle of nowhere?' said Sutton.

Beechey looked down at the tabletop. 'Yeah. I wish I'd never answered that fucking phone.'

'So then what happened?' asked Warren.

'I picked Nick up. He was carrying a grey backpack and wearing gloves. I asked him what had happened and what the hell he was doing in a field in the middle of the night, but he didn't want to talk about it. I was like, cool, OK, whatever. I just wanted to get back to bed, and really didn't want to know what shit he was involved in. I dropped him back at the Easy Break Hotel and forgot about it.'

'Really? You completely forgot about it?' asked Sutton.

'Yeah, until I saw the news. I recognised Anish obviously, and I started to wonder what the fuck Nick'd got himself into. So, I rang him and demanded he tell me what happened.'

Given the probable date, that matched a call between the two men's personal phones.

'He claimed that they had had their usual meet-up,' continued Beechey, 'but Anish was acting really weird and collapsed, hitting his head on the desk. He wasn't breathing, and Nick shit himself. He knew that if he called the police, they would want to know what he was doing in the room. With his record, he reckoned they'd assume that he killed Anish, so he panicked. He waited until it was late at night, then he put Anish's clothes on, moved his car around to the fire exit, wrapped his body in a bed sheet and then drove him out to some ditch. He dumped the body under a bridge and said that he tried to make him as hard to identify as possible.'

'How?' asked Warren.

'I dunno. I think he cut his fingertips off and smashed his jaw in with a hammer. Real gangster movie shit.'

'Then what happened?'

'He dumped the car and called me. After I dropped him back at the hotel, he went back into the room to try and clean it up. The next morning, he walked back into work, just like normal, to avoid suspicion. Then he dressed like Anish and checked out through reception, circled back and went back in the fire exit, got changed again and went back to the kitchen and finished his shift, cool as you fucking like.'

'What happened to Anish's car?' asked Sutton.

Beechey shrugged. 'Dunno, he just said he dumped it.'

'Did you know he was due to meet Anish that evening?' asked Sutton.

'No, he didn't mention it the last time we spoke.'

'When was that?' asked Warren.

Beechey shrugged. 'A couple of days before? I didn't know anything about it until he called me to come and pick him up.'

'And what did he say when he called for you to pick him up?' asked Warren.

'Just that he was stuck in the middle of a field and really needed a lift. He gave me the directions and I drove out there.'

'And you expect us to believe that you got out of bed, without any explanation, and just drove out there?' Sutton didn't even bother to try and hide his disbelief.

'Well, he's a mate, ain't he? I figured I'd ask him about what happened when I saw him. Besides, his teeth were already chattering, I reckoned he'd freeze to death if I didn't go out there and fetch him quick.'

'And what did he say happened, once you'd rescued him?'

'Nothing, he was stressing loads and wouldn't speak to me, so

I stopped at a garage to get him some fags to calm him down. I reckon that must have been when he put that bloody mobile phone in the glovebox of my car.'

*

This time it was Warren who asked for a break, deciding to call it a night, and resume the interview the following morning. As Beechey was led to his cell for his legally mandated rest, Warren almost envied him. He knew that eight hours' shut-eye was not in his immediate future.

'They're both full of it,' said Hutchinson.

'Makes it easier for us,' said Warren. 'We'll let them go to bed thinking they've got one over on us, rather than lying awake all night making up better lies.'

'In the meantime, we need to work out who did what,' said Grayson.

'Forensics may be able to help us there,' said Sutton, reading a printout that had been left on his desk. He handed it over.

Warren smiled. 'That'll do nicely.'

Monday 12th December

Chapter 49

Warren's eyes felt as though they were full of grit. He'd made it home sometime after 2 a.m. and collapsed on the bed in the spare room to avoid disturbing Susan. He must have slept, but the 6 a.m. alarm on his phone seemed to go off only moments after his head hit the pillow.

Tony Sutton didn't look much better, but Warren knew there was no point trying to persuade him to take it easier. Warren slurped at his coffee; Sutton claimed that going cold-turkey from caffeine after his stroke meant that he now no longer needed a morning boost to get going first thing. Warren wasn't sure if he envied or pitied him.

The briefing room was filled to capacity, with incoming and outgoing shifts jostling for space. By now, Warren could name most of the seconded detectives and support workers from Welwyn. He made a note to thank each of them over the next couple of days for their hard work.

'Right people, today is crunch day,' said Warren, his voice slightly hoarse. 'In custody, we have Nicholas Kimpton, chef at the Easy Break Hotel. We also have his old friend, Jake Beechey – known to us before yesterday as "Blondie92". They are currently blaming each other for the death of Anish Patel, with the other merely helping to cover things up. Still in the mix is Leon Grime, the Easy Break Hotel's handyman, who Nicholas Kimpton is also pointing a finger towards. He has already been charged, but denies everything. A team will be heading to the Mount Prison to confront him with everything we were told yesterday, to see if he changes his mind about cooperating.'

Warren took another sip of coffee, hoping it would lubricate his throat.

'So far, we have two competing narratives, both of which largely fit the evidence that we have to date. I'll run through them both before we start picking holes.

'Nicholas Kimpton's story is that he was sucked into this whole thing unwittingly when Jake Beechey called him, saying that Anish Patel had died unexpectedly in room 201. Up to this point, Kimpton believed he had simply been helping an old buddy meet up for illicit sex sessions by letting him in through a fire exit that Leon Grime had conveniently allowed to remain non-functional, we believe to facilitate drug dealing.

'In his version of events, he now believes that there was more to Beechey and Anish's meetings than sex, and that in fact Leon Grime was involved in a drug deal with both men that went wrong. He initially claimed that a mobile phone with a distinctive quacking ringtone was found behind a bin in the hotel car park and that it might have belonged to Leon Grime, but has now admitted that he owns the phone and that it was this second phone that Jake Beechey contacted when he wanted to be let into the hotel. He still insists however, that Leon Grime was a central part of the drugs conspiracy.

'Kimpton claims that Beechey contacted him via text on the quacking phone and insisted that he help them dispose of Anish's body. He is adamant that Beechey and Grime were responsible for dumping the body and the attempts to conceal its identity, and that Kimpton remained at the hotel during this time to try and clean up.

406

'It was Beechey who wore Anish's clothing and was captured on the reception CCTV leaving the hotel, whilst Kimpton started his shift in the kitchen, thus providing himself with an alibi. Leon Grime was subsequently given the job of disposing of Anish's backpack, clothing and personal effects. Beechey was supposed to have disposed of Anish's mobile phone, but decided to sell it on.

'It is Kimpton's assertion that he only went along with the plan because Beechey threatened the safety of his daughter. Yesterday's events suggest that was at least partly true.'

Around the room pens were frantically scribbling on notepads and fingers blurring across device keyboards. David Hutchinson was going to have some stiff competition if he wanted to get his question in first like he usually did.

'Second story of the day is that of Jake Beechey. He too claims to have been sucked unawares into this whole sorry tale. His version of events is that he and Kimpton became sexually intimate whilst sharing a cell at the Mount Prison. Upon release, they initially lost contact, which was when Kimpton met Jasmine Whitey and fathered young Kayla. However, after the breakdown of that relationship, he contacted Beechey again, who helped him to explore the other side of his sexuality by introducing him to our victim, who Beechey had met through the Rainbow Hookups dating app. Kimpton bought himself a new phone solely to conduct this affair; a very simple model that he downloaded a quacking duck ringtone to.

'Both Anish and Kimpton wished for their relationship to be discreet, which is why Anish booked into the Easy Break Hotel under a false name and paid cash. Kimpton would finish his shift and ostensibly leave for the day but would use the fire exit to re-enter the hotel and spend the night with Anish.

'Beechey claims he knew nothing about Anish's death, but received a phone call in the early hours of the Friday morning from a distraught Kimpton, who was standing in the middle of a field needing a lift. Our knight in shining armour raced out

407

there and picked him up, returning him to the Easy Break Hotel. During that journey, Kimpton apparently planted the phone that had been used to conduct his affair with Anish in the glovebox of Beechey's car to frame him. Beechey then returned to bed and forgot all about it until seeing Anish on the news.'

There was a chorus of disbelieving snorts.

Warren pressed on. 'Beechey claims that he found Anish's phone abandoned in some bushes and decided to sell it. Again, Leon Grime was involved in the whole affair in some capacity, but Mr Beechey is unclear on the details. He is also yet to fully explain how yesterday's misunderstanding with the knife after Kimpton's daughter's dance lesson came about.

'So, in summary, both men are blaming each other and Leon Grime, whilst seeking to minimise their own involvement in the affair. Nicholas Kimpton admits to helping cover up an unfortunate death because of a threat to his daughter. Jake Beechey denies any offence beyond naivety and not reporting his suspicions to the police. Leon Grime claims to have no knowledge or involvement in the whole affair.

'Any questions?'

Hutchinson's hand shot up so fast he nearly knocked Rachel Pymm's glasses off.

*

By the time the briefing finally drew to a close, Warren had added a considerable number of new questions to the list that needed to be asked of the three men they had in custody.

In addition, new forensic leads had come in overnight, with more promised. Grayson had opened the proverbial cheque book and authorised fast-track analysis where possible and Rachel Pymm had corralled extra analysts to ensure that the new information was curated promptly.

Soon the room was almost empty, with only Warren's core

team and DSI Grayson left. For the next hour or so, they would all work together to draft the interview strategies that would finally bring all the pieces together and deliver Anish Patel the justice he deserved.

But first, coffee.

Chapter 50

Warren decided to maintain the status quo for his first interview of the day, opting to lead the interview with Nicholas Kimpton as he had previously, with a specialist uniformed constable as an additional note-taker.

Kimpton was no stranger to the hospitality of a custody cell overnight, but that familiarity didn't make it any easier; his eyes were red-rimmed, his ever-darkening stubble a stark contrast against his pasty complexion. He looked exhausted.

'We've been looking into the information you gave us on Leon Grime yesterday and it's been very helpful. Why don't you begin by telling us a bit about him?'

Kimpton puffed out his lips. 'Where to start?'

'How did you meet? You weren't in prison together.'

'Nah, Leon served his time ages before I did. We didn't speak about it that much – better to look forward than backwards and all that – but I don't think we had any mates in common. We met down The Clock House, playing pool.'

'So you knew each other quite well?'

'Yeah, I suppose. I had to quit the pool league in the end because it clashed with my evening shift at the Easy Break, but we'd still go for a beer sometimes and shoot a few, just to keep my eye in. He'd come around mine now and again and watch the footie.'

'Were you employed when you met?'

'Not really,' said Kimpton.

'I'll be honest,' said Warren, 'Leon's not been very forthcoming with us. Does he have any hobbies that we should know about?'

Kimpton frowned as he thought. Warren waited patiently.

'Well aside from the pool, he was a keen gardener.'

'Really, I thought he lived in a flat?'

'He had an allotment; he used to go down there most weekends.'

'Did you ever go with him?'

'Nah, I'll cook it but I ain't bothered about growing it,' Kimpton paused. 'To be honest, I think it was an excuse to get away from his missus. He had a shed down there and I reckon he used to hide from her. You'll understand if you've ever met her; she's a bit full-on.'

'Yes, I hear she's quite the character,' said Warren. 'Have you spoken to her since Leon was arrested?'

'No, I ain't seen her for ages.'

'Well thank you Nick, that's been really helpful,' said Warren carefully writing 'Allotment' and 'check shed' on his notepad in big, easy-to-read handwriting. Out of the corner of his eye he saw Kimpton relax slightly.

'Back to Leon,' said Warren. 'He recommended you for the job at the Easy Break Hotel, I understand?'

'Yeah, they were short-handed after they fired the dickhead that gave everyone food poisoning, so he put in a word for me.'

'And did you know about his – shall we say, activities on the side? – before you started working there?'

'No, we never spoke about it. He knew that I wasn't interested in getting involved in any of that sort of shit again; it's already cost me too much. It was a big enough fight as it was to get shared custody of Kayla. That last stint … she was old enough

411

to know something was wrong. I can't risk jail time again for something so stupid.' He shook his head and his eyes started to shine. 'I can't believe that bastard Jake has got me into this … and Leon … I thought we were mates …' His voice was thick with emotion.

'Speaking of Jake, tell me about your relationship with him,' said Warren, allowing some sympathy to creep into his voice.

'Well you know the basics. We shared a cell in the Mount for a few months; we became pretty tight. I'd been in for a while already when he arrived, and I'm a bit older, so I sort of looked after him until he found his feet.'

'And you stayed friends afterwards?'

'Yeah, we kept in touch. We both ended up living around Middlesbury, so we'd meet up and go for a drink.'

'And when you were sharing a cell, were you sharing anything else?' asked Warren.

Kimpton's brow creased. 'What do you mean?'

'Were you and Jake Beechey intimate in prison?'

Kimpton reacted as if he'd been slapped. 'What? No! Why the fuck would you think—'

His solicitor cleared his throat loudly and with a visible effort, Kimpton calmed himself.

'Look, Jake's gay. So what? You've been watching too much TV. Sure, there are blokes that hook up and I suppose some of them would even deny they were really gay, just desperate, but that wasn't what we were like. I'm not saying Jake didn't have sex with people whilst he was in there, but it wasn't any of my business. Besides, I have a daughter; it's obvious I'm straight.'

'OK, Nick, I apologise. It was a lazy stereotype,' said Warren. Was Kimpton's outburst genuine, or to mangle the famous saying, did he protest too much?

'So, my next question is, how did Leon and Jake know each other?'

'I'll be honest, I didn't know they did. I'm guessing it was a

412

drugs thing. Like I said, I'm not into that stuff anymore. I'm pretty sure Leon isn't gay, if that's what you're thinking.'

'It seems like a bit of a coincidence, all of you coming together at the Easy Break Hotel; Jake and Anish hooking up and using the place where you and Leon Grime both work. I'm struggling to join the dots here. What do you reckon?'

Beside Kimpton, his solicitor cleared his throat loudly again. Kimpton ignored him, licking his lips. His hairline looked damp, but when he spoke, his voice was steady.

'I've been thinking about it and I'm sure it was drugs. Apparently, that Anish bloke's family had a load of newsagents. I reckon Leon was using him to sell his gear through them.' He gave a small shrug. 'You know what those dodgy Asian places are like.'

Warren ignored the casual racism. 'So where did Jake come in?'

'I think he was stringing Anish along; making him think that they were in a relationship and then getting him to shift drugs through his shops.'

'So you reckon Leon Grime and Jake Beechey were in partnership, persuading Anish to sell their drugs?'

'Dunno for sure, but it makes sense to me.'

'And obviously Leon Grime would know about the doctored fire exit,' said Warren.

'Exactly,' said Kimpton.

'That makes sense, I'll look into it,' said Warren. 'Now tell me about the night Anish died. What happened after Jake Beechey texted you? What did the text say?'

Kimpton closed his eyes, pain crossing his face.

'He said "get up here now. Room 201. Shit's hit the fan."'

'Did he say what the "shit" was?' asked Warren.

'No, but I figured I'd better get up there and see what was happening, so I ducked out and went up the emergency stairs. He was waiting for me in the corridor.'

'What was he like?'

'Scared. He was pacing up and down. I asked him what was

happening, but he just grabbed me and pulled me into the room,' he shuddered. 'Anish was lying on the bed and his eyes were closed. I thought at first he was sleeping, but then I saw that he wasn't breathing, and his lips were a sort of bluish colour.'

'What did you do?'

'I asked them what happened.'

'Who's them?' asked Warren.

'Jake and Leon.'

'Leon was in the room when you entered with Jake?'

'Yeah, he was just standing at the end of the bed, breathing really hard.'

'What did they say happened?'

Kimpton took a deep breath. 'Jake said that he and Leon were talking to Anish. Anish was standing at the end of the bed. He suddenly said he felt dizzy and went all wobbly then fell down and hit his head on the edge of the desk. He wasn't breathing, so they dragged him onto the bed. One of them took his pulse and saw he was dead.'

'Who took his pulse?' asked Warren.

'I don't know, they didn't say.'

'And nobody thought to call an ambulance?'

Kimpton looked down at the table. 'That's what I said. I should have pushed, or done it myself, I know, but they said he was dead and there was nothing we could do,' he looked back up. 'I could see that it was an accident or a heart attack or something, because he hadn't been stabbed or shot or anything. He looked kind of … peaceful.'

Warren felt an urge to ask how long Kimpton had been a Fellow of the Royal College of Pathologists or held a Home Office licence, thus qualifying him to make such a judgement, but he didn't want to antagonise Kimpton and risk him shutting down.

What it did mean was that if Kimpton's account was true – and Shane Moore's statement seemed to corroborate the timings – then there were approximately ten minutes between Anish Patel's pacemaker recording his cardiac arrest and Jake Beechey texting Kimpton. Could an emergency call have got paramedics to the hotel in time to save Anish? What about the defibrillator next to the reception desk? Leon Grime would surely have known about that. Warren suspected that such a lengthy period of inactivity would come back to bite everyone involved in the affair when the case was finally presented to a jury.

'Then what happened?'

'I went back down to the kitchen and told Shane to go home early. I spent a few minutes tidying up so nobody would get suspicious, and then went back up the emergency stairs.'

'And then what?'

'Leon and Jake were back in the room and Leon had some cleaning stuff. I asked them what they were going to do with it and Jake said that they had to get rid of the body and clean up so nobody knew they were there.'

'Did they say why? If Anish just collapsed and it wasn't their fault, then why would they be worried about reporting his death?'

Kimpton paused. 'Look, it was really obvious that whatever they had been up to with Anish was dodgy and probably illegal. For months, I just thought I was helping a mate get his leg over, you know? I was letting a non-guest into a guest's room through the fire exit and I'd definitely have lost my job if I got caught, but it wasn't a big deal. The duty manager is never in at that time, and everyone uses that door for fag breaks, so who was going to tell on me?'

'But you said that you thought there were drugs involved. Did you just come to that conclusion there and then, or did you suspect it before that night?' said Warren, staring hard at Kimpton. The chef visibly wilted.

'Look, Jake never said anything to me. Nor did Leon, but I started to suspect that Leon had his own reasons for keeping that fire door broken. You could hear the door opening and closing from the kitchen. It didn't stay open long enough for a fag break, and it always seemed to be Leon opening it, even though he should have gone home ages ago. I didn't ask, because I didn't want to know.'

'And what about Jake?'

Kimpton looked down at the tabletop. 'Something wasn't quite right. I knew that Jake used dating apps, but he did it just to get a shag; he wasn't interested in a relationship. But he happened to mention this Anish guy more than once. Anyway, one night we were both really drunk, and he showed me a picture of Anish from Facebook.

'He was smartly dressed and standing in front of a sports car. Jake zoomed in on his wrist and started saying how the watch was a legit Rolex and that he'd never seen him wear the same one twice.

'The thing is …' Kimpton paused and started again. 'Look, I don't want to sound racist, because I'm not and neither's Jake, but Anish … Well, he's Asian. And about forty. And bald.'

'And that surprised you?'

'Yeah, he didn't seem Jake's type. I asked him once about how he met men and he showed me that app he uses and all of the blokes he'd bookmarked were white guys in their mid-twenties, buff with blond hair. None of them looked like Anish.

'Anyway, I thought that maybe he was just stringing him along; nice meals out, no need to pay for his drinks. Anish was really into spy movies and stuff, so he got a kick out of acting like he was a secret agent. I figured Anish could afford it because his family had loads of businesses, so where was the harm?' He frowned. 'What do they call a rich bloke who has a young, pretty girlfriend who he buys stuff for?'

'A sugar daddy?' suggested Warren.

'Yeah, basically that's what I thought Anish was.' His face darkened. 'But then I heard rumours. That Jake had been seen hanging around with dealers. And not just the blokes who sell you a bag of weed or a couple pills in the pub toilet.'

'Do you know the names of these dealers?' asked Warren.

416

Kimpton shook his head vehemently. 'No idea.'

Warren couldn't tell if his denials were genuine or he just didn't want to say.

'And then, when I saw that Leon was involved,' continued Kimpton, 'it just all kind of made sense.'

'When you were in the room, did you see any evidence of a drug deal?'

'Not really, but there was a black kit bag in the corner of the room. Leon took it with him when he left.'

Warren thought back to the CCTV of Anish entering the hotel reception. He'd been carrying a grey backpack – almost certainly the one that they'd found at Grime's allotment – but no black bag, which suggested any such bag had been brought to the room after Anish had checked in.

'Can you describe the bag?' he asked.

Kimpton shrugged. 'Just a sports bag; cheap-looking. With handles that you carry, rather than straps for your back. I didn't see any logos or anything.'

It was hardly conclusive proof, but the report back from the dog handlers had indicated that once-upon-a-time, drugs had probably been stored in Leon Grime's allotment shed.

'So, let's continue. You're in a room with a dead body. Jake and Leon don't want to call the police or an ambulance, so they decide to dispose of the body and clean up the room. What happened next?'

'Well, I said that I didn't want to get involved, but Jake said I was already involved because I had been letting him into the hotel and that if I said anything, he'd tell the police that I was there when it happened and that he'd take me down with him.' Kimpton gave a shuddering breath. 'And then he says he knows all about Kayla and her mum. He had this really scary look in his eyes. I'd seen it before, in prison, when he got mad at someone … and I figured if he was involved in drugs, then he might even ask one of the other dealers to solve the problem …'

'OK, so walk me through what happened over the rest of the night,' said Warren, trying to keep him focused.

'Well, we knew that we couldn't do anything with the body until everyone else in the hotel had gone to sleep.' A look of shame crossed his face. 'Jake said that Anish was creeping him out, so he put a bed sheet over him. And then we just waited.'

Warren had a sudden, surreal image of the three men sitting quietly around as if participating in an Irish wake or performing shemira. And then he felt his mood darken as he remembered his own experiences of sitting with a dead person – some peaceful, some less so.

He pushed the thoughts away and focused on his next question. 'That's it? Did anyone leave the room in that time?' he asked.

'No, Jake said he wanted everyone together. There was a bathroom so we could go for a piss and there were those see-though cups sealed in a plastic bag so we could drink some water. He wouldn't even let me go for a fag.

'About 1 a.m. Jake reckoned it was quiet enough that nobody would see us. Leon told him where the CCTV cameras were outside and Jake went to fetch Anish's car around to the side of the building,' he swallowed. 'He put Anish's hoodie on in case anyone spotted him.'

'What did you and Leon do?' asked Warren.

'We waited until he got back and then Leon and Jake took the rest of his clothes off him. Jake put his jeans and shoes on and put everything else in his backpack.' Kimpton's voice quietened. 'Poor bastard hadn't even had time to unpack his wash kit. Then they wrapped him in a bed sheets. He wasn't stiff yet, so Jake sort of lifted him over his shoulder and took him down the stairs with Leon to the car.'

'Then what?'

'I stayed, stripped the bed and remade it using fresh bedding from the laundry cupboard in the corridor, then rearranged the covers so it looked like it had been slept in. I wiped down the desk and the bathroom and replaced the towels and glasses. There wasn't really any blood from where he hit his head, but I gave that a clean as well. Then when they got back, I cycled home, as I figured people would be suspicious if it looked like I'd stayed in the hotel all night. Leon went home to his missus and Jake stayed in the room until the next morning. After I started work again, he left the room dressed in Anish's clothes and walked out the front of reception, using the drop box for the keycard. Then he drove Anish's car back to the hire place.'

'And what about when they disposed of Anish's body. What happened then?'

'I don't know, I really don't, I wasn't there. I just thought they were going to dump him by the side of the road or in a ditch or something. I didn't know they were going to … you know …' He made a vague gesture towards his hands and face.

'Going to what, Nick?' pressed Warren.

'You know, cut his fingers off and smash his teeth in.'

'They said nothing about that as you all sat around his cooling body for what four, five hours?'

'No, they must have decided it in the car when they were taking the body away.'

'So when did they fetch the tools?'

Kimpton blinked. 'Then maybe they decided to do it before then.'

'When? You said that nobody was allowed to leave the room.'

Kimpton's eyes jumped from side to side. 'They must have come up with the idea when I went back down to the kitchen after Jake showed me the body. I guess Jake could have grabbed the tools from Leon's office when he went to fetch the car.'

'OK,' said Warren. 'That all makes sense.'

Kimpton leaned his elbows on the table, exhaustion etched on his face.

'I think we can see that Mr Kimpton made some very serious errors of judgement on the night that Mr Patel tragically died,' said his solicitor, who up until this point had mostly been making notes. 'He was in the wrong place at the wrong time, and clearly acting under duress. If it transpires Mr Patel did die of a heart attack or natural causes, then my client, who was not present at the time, cannot possibly be charged with murder. And if the facts were to suggest that Mr Patel's demise was precipitated by the events that took place in that room, then again, all my client is guilty of is allowing Mr Beechey access to the hotel. Naïve yes, but he could not reasonably have foreseen how the evening would unfold.'

'I shall take that under advisement,' said Warren. The solicitor hadn't wasted his breath asking for Kimpton to be released on bail. Warren had been granted an extension to custody and he fully intended to use it. And even if Kimpton's version of events were true, he would need that time to determine if there were additional charges to be brought, such as preventing a lawful burial.

'Interview suspended,' said Warren standing up.

Kimpton wasn't going anywhere for the foreseeable future.

*

'Nicely done, Warren,' said Grayson as Warren re-entered the CID office, where the interview had been streamed on the briefing room screen. 'It looks like you got everything out of him that you wanted.' He handed Warren a steaming cup of coffee without asking; from its rich odour it was clearly freshly brewed from his personal stash – he was obviously pleased with how the day was progressing so far.

'Where are we with the searches, Tony?' asked Warren.

'They've pretty much finished with Jake Beechey's flat and very interesting it was too.'

Warren listened carefully as he ran down the list of what they'd found. He caught himself almost smiling. He and the team had developed a theory about what they thought had really transpired that night, and it looked as though they were largely correct.

'What about forensics?'

'Coming in thick and fast,' said Pymm as Warren moved over to perch on the edge of her desk. 'Andy Harrison reckons most of the fast-track we've sent in over the past couple of days will be completed in the next few hours.'

'It gets quicker all the time,' marvelled Warren. 'Pretty soon we'll be getting results back almost as quickly as they do on TV.'

'Only if they give us the same budget,' grumbled Grayson as he joined Warren. 'The money they spend on filming just a couple of episodes of those glossy American shows dwarfs our entire annual forensic allowance.'

Turning back to her screen, Pymm started to run through what she'd been sent so far. Warren felt a stirring of excitement, and he could see that Sutton and Grayson felt the same. The proverbial light at the end of the tunnel was getting ever brighter.

'One last thing,' said Pymm as she finished. 'Mags left you a little present before she and Moray headed over to the Mount to speak to Leon Grime.'

'She found some CCTV?' asked Warren.

'Yep, and it's everything you wanted.'

Warren looked at the clock next to the wall-map of Middlesbury.

'Care to join me for elevenses whilst we plan our interview strategy, DI Sutton?' asked Warren.

'I'll grab my wallet,' said Sutton.

'My treat,' said Grayson, fishing his own wallet out. He was *very* pleased with the way the day was going.

Chapter 51

Jake Beechey projected an air of arrogant confidence when Warren and Sutton started the morning's interview, but behind his sneering visage, there was a note of worry.

'Before we start, Mr Beechey would like me to read out a prepared statement for the record,' stated the solicitor.

'Please, go ahead,' said Warren, trying not to sound too enthusiastic. Beside him, Sutton kept his face neutral, giving no sign that he'd just lost ten pounds in a bet that the two men had agreed before the interview started. Sutton had been certain that Beechey would go for a 'no comment' interview. Warren had disagreed. Beechey already knew that Kimpton was trying to blame everything on him. Whether through fear or arrogance, Warren was confident that Beechey wouldn't be able to let things stand without trying to fight his corner. It remained to be seen if he had more to say on the matter beyond his statement.

'First of all, Mr Beechey would like to repeat his apologies for yesterday's incident after the dance class. He had visited the school in the hope that he could persuade Ms Whitey to speak to her former partner, Nicholas Kimpton, and ask him not to embroil him in the unfortunate death of Anish Patel. As we saw from yesterday's interview, he was right to be worried that Mr

Kimpton would attempt to shift the blame onto him, when he was only guilty of being naïve.'

Warren and Sutton said nothing; Beechey kept his eyes averted.

'Mr Beechey would also like to retract his claim that he found Mr Patel's mobile phone in the bushes. In reality, Mr Kimpton had given him the phone a few days after my client had been called out to pick him up on the night that Mr Patel died. Mr Kimpton was, in fact, the one who found it. He asked Mr Beechey to sell it on his behalf, splitting the cash between them. Mr Beechey fully accepts that he should not have agreed to this but had no idea that this phone belonged to Mr Patel until you informed him yesterday. Mr Beechey's criminal record is such that he was afraid to admit to handling what – in hindsight he realises – were stolen goods. When it became clear to him that the phone belonged to the unfortunate Mr Patel he panicked, worried that he would become even further implicated in a situation he had nothing to do with.'

His piece said, the lawyer closed the laptop.

'Thank you,' said Warren. He turned to Beechey. 'Let's return to the other mobile phone. The one that we found in the glovebox of your car.'

'The one that Nick left in the glovebox of my car,' said Beechey.

'Which you never saw before?' said Warren.

'Yeah, that's right.'

'Why would Nick Kimpton text himself?' asked Sutton.

'What do you mean?' asked Beechey, blinking at the apparent change in direction.

'You reckon that the phone found in your glovebox belongs to Nick Kimpton. Every night that Anish went to the Easy Break Hotel, that phone texted Nick Kimpton's other phone; the one with the quacking ringtone. Why would he text himself? It doesn't make sense.'

Beechey frowned. 'I don't know, you'll have to ask him.'

'We will,' Sutton assured him.

'Do you ever use WhatsApp, Jake?' asked Warren.

Beechey shrugged, his tone nonchalant. 'Sure, who doesn't?'

'And whom do you contact through the app?'

'Family. Mates. The usual.'

'We've looked at your personal phone and we can't find any messages exchanged with Anish, even when we looked as far back as January when you and Anish were getting to know each other,' said Sutton.

'I never spoke to him on WhatsApp,' said Beechey. 'We just used old-school texting.'

'What about when you contacted him using the phone found in your glovebox?'

'Nope, hasn't even got WhatsApp installed.'

Beechey's solicitor winced.

'How do you know what apps are installed on that phone?' asked Sutton immediately. 'You said you'd never seen it before.'

Beechey looked over at his solicitor.

'You know, we can't find any trace of Mr Kimpton's fingerprints on that phone,' said Warren, not giving Beechey time to think up a suitable response to his faux pas.

'He must have wiped it down, he ain't daft,' said Beechey.

'Wiped it down and then placed it in the glovebox of your car? Why would he do that?' asked Warren.

'To stitch me up, obviously.'

'Why? You were mates. Why would he kill a man, then think, "you know what, I'll pin this one on Jake Beechey"?' asked Warren.

'Don't know, you'll have to ask him,' mumbled Beechey.

'OK, cut the crap, Jake,' snapped Sutton. 'Your fingerprints are on the phone, even if Nick Kimpton's aren't.'

Beechey opened his mouth again, before thinking better of it and reached for his glass of water. He took a slow sip, his eyes narrowed and calculating.

Would he 'no comment'? It was probably the wisest thing to do at that moment, but it wouldn't look good when they showed the interview to a jury. Or would he try and talk his way out of trouble?

'I found the phone in the glovebox a few days ago,' he said eventually. 'I played with it to see if I could work out who it belonged to, but the messages were wiped. I figured it probably belonged to Nick.'

'So why didn't you give it back to him?' asked Warren. 'I thought you two were mates?'

'I couldn't see why he'd have left it in the glovebox. Then I remembered how flustered he was when I picked him up that night. I got a really bad feeling, and then when I saw Anish on the news …'

'Then why did you hang onto it?' asked Warren.

'I thought it might be evidence. I was trying to decide if I should hand it in to the police and tell them about my suspicions or if I should chuck it and forget all about it. I didn't want to get Nick into trouble.' His voice quietened. 'He's a good man, I can't believe he'd kill someone, I figured it was all just a coincidence. But now I know the truth …'

Sutton snorted. 'Pull the other one, Jake, it's got bells on it.'

Beechey glared at him, but remained silent.

'Jake, do you know what end-to-end encryption is?' asked Warren.

Beechey paused for a moment before eventually nodding. 'Yeah, I read something about it on the internet.'

'So, you know that Facebook, the owners of WhatsApp, are unable to tell us the content of any messages passing through their servers?' said Warren. Beechey nodded. 'And that the messages are actually encrypted and decrypted on the users' handsets, so that if the app is deleted, or the phone is wiped, they can't be retrieved?'

'Yeah, I suppose.'

'Well here's the thing. That handset did have WhatsApp installed, but it was deleted.'

'So, the messages are gone?' asked Beechey.

'Yes, all gone,' said Warren.

'So, we'll never know what Nick said to Anish?'

'Not using that handset, no,' said Warren. 'But there are two sides to a conversation.'

'But Anish's handset was also wiped,' said Beechey.

'Yes, it was,' said Warren. 'I imagine you did that before you tried to sell it on in The Rising Sun.'

Beechey said nothing. He'd already admitted to trying to dispose of the phone.

'Did you look at the messages before you wiped them?'

Beechey reached for his glass of water again. This time his sip was even slower, the calculations going on behind his eyes even more frantic. Would he incriminate Kimpton further? Or would he decide that admitting he had browsed the phone's contents would make it more difficult for him to claim that he couldn't be certain who the handset originally belonged to?

'No, I never read them,' he shrugged. 'None of my business.' A faint hint of a smirk played around his lips.

'Anish Patel's handset was a top-of-the-range Samsung – this year's model. Pretty expensive, which is why you were so keen to sell it on, I guess,' said Sutton.

'Yeah, so?'

'Anish wasn't perhaps as flush with cash as he liked to portray sometimes,' said Warren.

Beechey shrugged as Warren continued. 'So, he saved a bit of money and got the nice, snazzy handset, but bought the model with the smallest storage.'

Again, Beechey shrugged, but a crease had appeared in his forehead.

'I made that mistake once,' said Sutton. 'Within six months I had to delete something every time I wanted to take more than a couple of photographs. It drove me nuts when we were on holiday in Canada. I was going to back up everything to one of

426

those cloud storage websites, but the data-roaming charges would have bankrupted me if I couldn't find free WiFi.'

'So?'

'Did you know that Anish's handset had a MicroSD card?' asked Warren.

'What do you mean?' asked Beechey.

'You know, one of those tiny memory cards that you can buy if your phone memory keeps on filling up? They only cost a few quid, it's much cheaper than backing everything up to the cloud if you're outside the EU.'

Beechey's swallowed.

'Anish set the phone to save everything onto the card,' said Warren. 'Photos, music, WhatsApp conversations …'

'How was Antonelli's?' asked Sutton. 'I'm thinking of taking the missus there for our anniversary. Is the food any good?'

Beechey's eyes told them he knew exactly where this was going.

Sutton opened the folder sitting between him and Warren and pushed a glossy photograph across the table.

'This is a still from CCTV footage in Antonelli's restaurant where you and Anish enjoyed a nice meal on Saturday the 19th of June. That's what? Five months after you supposedly decided not to meet up with Anish again, and instead introduced him to your mate Nick?' He leaned forward and squinted at the picture. 'Looks like lasagne. If it's as good as my wife's, I may be tempted to book a table.'

'She does make a very nice lasagne,' confirmed Warren. 'How was Brighton? Perfect timing for a long weekend. Nice weather, the schools hadn't started summer holidays, so not too busy.' He pushed another photograph over. This time it was one of a hotel reception desk. 'Mr and Mr Smith: very romantic. The owners always like to get a picture of their guests as they come in, you know, just in case. Anish's credit card took a bit of a pounding that weekend.'

'I'll bet Bacton was busy,' said Sutton. 'August bank holiday weekend, lovely weather, Norfolk's finest beaches according to the Tourist Information Centre.' He slid several photographs over. 'We don't have pictures of everywhere you went that weekend, since not all the bars keep their CCTV that long, but we do have some lovely ones of the two of you drinking in the Fisherman's Rest, because they have a new system with a massive hard drive.' He pointed at the two of them standing at the bar. 'Looks like Anish is buying the drinks again.'

Sutton sat back, his arms folded.

Beechey licked his lips. Finally he placed his elbows on the table, his head in his hands. His voice was muffled, but clear enough to understand. 'OK, I admit it. The phone was mine and I was still seeing Anish behind Nick's back.'

'So you were at the Easy Break Hotel the night that Anish died?' said Warren.

'No,' Beechey shook his head. 'I used to meet up with Anish now and again, but never at the Easy Break,' he snorted. 'I like a bit of excitement as much as the next bloke, but I ain't silly enough to cheat on my mate at the place where he works.'

'So why did you lie about the phone, Jake?' asked Sutton.

Beechey gave a sigh. 'I knew how it would look, so I figured I'd point the blame back at Nick, he was the one who did it after all.' His tone turned pleading. 'But everything else I've told you was the truth, I swear. I didn't kill him.' His voice caught. 'And I did love Anish.'

'Do you think Nick might have known about the affair?' asked Warren.

Beechey fell silent, before his eyes widened. 'Son of a bitch … he did know! He knew all about it. That's what happened.' His words were now coming out so quickly Warren could barely keep up with them. 'He found out about us and killed Anish, then tried to pin the blame on me! He even gave me Anish's phone to get rid of. That absolute bastard!'

*

Warren had been happy to suspend the interview for a break. He needed to stretch his legs and wanted to catch up with the rest of his team.

'Well done both of you,' said Grayson as he met Warren and Sutton by the entrance to the CID office. 'You're playing those two jokers perfectly. Every time they have enough rope to hang themselves, you feed them some more.' He turned to Warren. 'Brilliant move with WhatsApp, I had no idea that you could back it up to a memory card and then read the messages on another device.'

'You probably can't,' admitted Warren. 'I imagine they're still encrypted. You can thank Rachel Pymm for that particular piece of techno-bullshit.' He smiled. 'Besides, if you listen carefully to the recording, you'll hear that I never actually said that we'd read the messages. Beechey just assumed we had and decided it was time to come clean about who the phone really belonged to.'

Grayson chuckled. 'Nice one.'

Warren headed to the water fountain, before making a beeline for Pymm's desk.

'I hear you've been putting a good word in about me with the boss,' she greeted him.

'Yes, I told him not to trust a word you say about mobile phone apps. Seriously though, that was a brilliant idea. Now stop resting on your past successes and tell me something new.'

'Mags and Moray have finished interviewing Leon Grime. You'll get the full report when they get back from the Mount, but Moray thought you'd want a quick summary before then. I saved it as a voicemail for you.'

She pressed play on her phone handset.

Warren winced; beside him, Sutton jumped. 'Christ, somebody has to let that lad know that phones were invented so that you could communicate over long distances without needing to shout.'

Pymm reached for the volume control on the handset as the two men listened intently. Ruskin's report was short and succinct.

'Just what we suspected,' said Sutton, smiling broadly.

'What else have you got, Rachel?' asked Warren, recognising from long experience when Pymm was probably holding back the best bit to create a little more drama.

'The fast-track DNA and the other evidence has come through,' she reached over to the laser printer by her desk and handed over a sheaf of paper. 'Exactly what you were hoping for, plus a little bonus on the fingerprint page.'

Warren flicked through the sheets to the section on fingerprint analysis.

'Got you, you bastard,' he said.

Chapter 52

The long, electronic beep from the interview suite's recording equipment signalled the start of the day's second round of interviews.

'Thank you for your help earlier, Mr Beechey, you've given us a lot to consider. I just wondered if you would be prepared to go through everything you've told us, so we've got it all clear?' Warren started.

'Yeah, sure.' Jake Beechey was slouched in his chair, giving the impression of a man whose cares had been lifted. Now that the finger was pointed firmly at his former cellmate, Beechey probably saw his current situation as an improvement.

'You met Anish Patel through the Rainbow Hookups website in January of this year. You didn't hit it off immediately, and instead introduced him to your friend Nicholas Kimpton, who started a relationship with Mr Patel, meeting him every few weeks in a room at the Easy Break Hotel?'

'Yeah, that's right.'

'However, you continued to conduct an affair with Mr Patel behind Nick's back, including weekends away?'

'Yeah.' Beechey looked down at the table.

'Why Anish?' asked Warren.

'What do you mean?'

'Let's be blunt here, Jake. You're a good-looking lad in your twenties. You aren't short of a bit of company if you want it, and you've had plenty of success on the Rainbow Hookups app. Anish Patel, by all accounts, was a lovely man, but he was close to forty, was embarrassed about being bald, and was of Asian heritage. Very different to your usual type. So why Anish? What was it about him that attracted you to him?'

'Dunno,' mumbled Beechey.

'I think we all know why, Jake,' said Sutton. 'Money. Tell me, did you ever pay for anything when you went out with Anish?'

Beechey said nothing.

'You're a bit of a parasite, aren't you, Jake?' said Sutton, ignoring the frown from the man's solicitor. 'You not only saw a wealthy man with cash to splash around, you also saw a lonely man. A man who had been rejected by his family, who was still finding his feet but finally embracing who he was. A man who would be flattered that a young, handsome guy like yourself, was interested in more than a one-night stand.' Sutton stabbed a finger in Beechey's direction. 'You saw an opportunity.'

'So fucking what?' snapped Beechey. 'So what if he paid for everything? That's not a crime. Anish was an adult, we both had fun. He enjoyed being seen with me and I enjoyed being taken to fancy restaurants where the starter costs more than I usually pay for a whole meal. It was a nice change to visit a pub without worrying that my debit card would be rejected when it was my turn to get the drinks in.' He gave a defiant shrug. 'Everyone was a winner.'

'Let's return to the matter in hand,' continued Warren. 'You never met Anish at the Easy Break Hotel, to avoid bumping into Mr Kimpton?'

'No, I steered well clear,' said Beechey, his voice still sulky.

'However, you believe that Nick may have become aware of the affair, and decided to kill Anish and then blame it on you? As some sort of revenge.'

'Yeah.'

'OK, thank you for your cooperation … eventually,' said Warren.

Beechey waited patiently, whilst Warren made notes on his pad. Beside him his solicitor didn't look nearly as relaxed as his client.

'I asked you earlier why Nick would be texting himself,' said Sutton. 'Obviously, we now know that the phone in your glovebox belongs to you.' He leaned forward slightly. 'So now there's a different question. Why were you texting Nick's quacking burner phone every time Anish checked into the Easy Break Hotel?'

Beechey's eyes widened and he reached for his glass of water again; a sure-fire tell that he needed time to think about his answer.

'I set them up,' said Beechey. 'So, I just wanted to give him a bit of encouragement, you know?'

'Really?' said Warren, his tone neutral.

Beechey managed a nod.

Sutton opened the evidence folder. 'You told us that you'd never visited the Easy Break Hotel.' Beechey's eyes flicked toward the folder and he swallowed.

'If that's the case, can you tell me why your fingerprints were found on the headboard of the bed in room 201, alongside Anish's?'

The colour slowly left Beechey's face. He continued to hold his glass of water to his lips, even after he'd drained it. Warren held his breath. Beside him, Sutton sat sphinx-like; even Beechey's solicitor seemed at a loss.

'Jake, would you like me to repeat the question?'

'No comment,' whispered Beechey finally.

Warren opened the evidence folder again.

'Can you tell me what this device is? We found it hidden behind the toilet cistern in your flat.'

'No comment,' said Beechey.

'For the benefit of the recording, I am showing Mr Beechey a picture of a miniature covert video camera and charger,' said Warren.

Warren pointed to the photograph. 'Our forensics team have measured the diameter of the camera and it fits perfectly into a recently filled-in hole in the wall of room 201, above the TV, directly overlooking the bed. Now why would you have such a device, Mr Beechey, and why would you install it in a hotel room that you claim you never visited?'

'No comment.'

'They aren't cheap, but then I suppose it's all about the return you get on your investment. You were using this to blackmail Anish, weren't you?'

'No comment.'

'You've been using this every time you and Anish visited the Easy Break Hotel; gathering evidence that he was a homosexual. What did you threaten to do with the footage, Jake? Send it to his family? Or were you going to distribute it on a website?'

'No comment.'

'It didn't work though, did it?' said Sutton. 'Despite appearances, Anish didn't have any money, did he? In fact, he was pretty much skint. On the night that Anish Patel died, you confronted him with the footage. How much did you ask for?'

'No comment.'

'What did you do when he told you he couldn't pay? Was that why he died?'

'No, it wasn't like that,' said Beechey.

'Really, then what was it like, Jake?'

'This is bullshit,' snapped Beechey. 'It's just a coincidence. There's nothing on there to show that I was doing any of that.'

Warren smiled at him, but there was no humour in his eyes. 'Are you sure about that, Jake?'

He opened his laptop. 'It looks as though you had the common sense to dispose of the memory card. But you really should have got rid of the camera as well,' he tutted. 'You forgot about the camera's internal memory. It's only a tiny amount; it'll only store a few minutes footage, which is why you needed to buy a

434

memory card. But the first time you used it, you didn't think of that, did you?'

The laptop had already been set up and Warren pressed play. The screen came to life with a surprisingly clear video recording of a hotel room bed. A date stamp in the top right corner showed Thursday the 21st of January, the date that Anish Patel had first checked into the Easy Break Hotel. The sound was muffled, but voices could be heard in the background. With a twinge of sadness, Warren realised it was the only time he had ever heard Patel's voice.

Beechey closed his eyes as the video continued. His solicitor watched transfixed as the two men came into view. Beechey was easily recognisable, his blond hair spikey; Patel wore a checked shirt and pale trousers. Patel said something, the sound too indistinct to make out the words fully. Beechey responded and both men laughed. Beechey pulled off the red sweater he was wearing, followed by his football top, exposing his distinctive Chelsea tattoo. Patel sat down on the bed, facing the camera directly, before Beechey moved to stand in front of him. It was unclear what the two men were doing, but after a few seconds, Patel's shirt came undone. Moments after that, Beechey's belt came off.

Abruptly the recording stopped.

'Out of memory,' said Warren. 'I guess that's why you bought the memory card that we found cut into little bits at the bottom of your kitchen bin; you wanted footage of the good stuff. We've sent it off to a specialist forensic unit who are pretty good at piecing these things back together.'

'It was Anish's idea,' said Beechey.

'What was?' asked Sutton.

Beechey waved at the laptop. 'This whole thing. He was really into movies, the thought of pretending to be secretly videoed, like some sort of Cold War spy, really turned him on,' Beechey shrugged. 'I didn't mind, it sounded like a bit of a laugh. That's why he always wanted the same room each time.'

'Seriously?' said Sutton. 'I can accept that you and he fancied spicing things up a bit, but you expect us to believe that he drilled a hole into the wall? Why not just stick the camera on top of the TV with a bit of Blu Tac?'

'He was a perfectionist.' He sat back with his arms folded. Yet again, Beechey had come up with an explanation that, whilst bizarre, was just about feasible. However, the tabletop on which he'd been resting his hands moments before, retained a faint outline from his perspiration.

'So, let's start all over again, shall we, Jake?' said Warren, allowing a note of irritation to creep into his voice. 'Despite what you told us earlier, you did in fact visit the Easy Break Hotel to meet up with Anish Patel. Why didn't you tell us that in the beginning?'

'Well, it would have looked bad,' said Beechey, after a long moment.

'And how is Nick involved?' asked Warren.

Now the pause was longer. Warren glanced at Sutton. It was time to stop letting Beechey play his games; he'd wasted enough of their time already. They had everything they needed and he was sick of hearing the man's lies.

'We know that Nick didn't call you up in the middle of the night asking for a lift because he'd killed Anish and wanted to pin it all on you,' he said.

Warren opened the folder again, and started spreading sheets of paper across the table, pointing to them in turn.

'Anish's hoodie. We know it's his, because it has his DNA on it. It also has your DNA on the hem of the sleeves and the neck. You were the person on the hotel CCTV walking out the entrance dressed in Anish's clothing.'

He pointed to the next sheet. 'JJ Car Repairs. You phoned him the morning after Anish's death and paid him to switch all of the tyres on Anish's hire car to disguise the fact that it had been used to dump his body. Very clever, but we have call logs and location data linking the phone that we found in your glovebox to the garage. He also recognised a photo of you. As did the person who saw a man matching your description standing outside Anish Patel's flat on both the Friday and the Saturday mornings, as you powered up his phone and used it to send text messages to his workplace and his sister. It's only a ten-minute walk to Anish's flat from the garage, which is convenient.'

'You were in that room when Anish died, weren't you?' said Sutton. 'You then tried to cover up his death by dumping his body in a ditch and tried to buy yourself some time by mutilating his body so it wouldn't be easily identified, and impersonating him so that we'd think he was still alive after he left the hotel. For the past twenty-odd hours you've been spinning us a pack of lies. Now stop wasting our time and tell us what really happened.'

Beechey placed his head in his hands, his shoulders shaking. 'Yeah, you're right. I was there, but I didn't kill him.'

'Then what happened?' asked Warren.

Beechey gave a long, shuddering sigh.

'Anish checked into the hotel and asked for room 201. He did all his usual shit with the hire car and the false name because that's what excited him. Then he WhatsApped me to let me know he had checked in. I walked down to the Easy Break, and when I got there, I texted Nick to let me in. I went up to the room and Anish was there.'

Beechey swallowed and turned to his solicitor, who obligingly poured him some more water. Warren and Sutton waited patiently. It had taken hours for the story to trickle out and neither man was naïve enough to believe that Beechey had completely given up trying to fool them, but by now Warren was confident that they could identify and counter any more of Beechey's lies.

'Anish was looking a bit hot, so I went to the bathroom and poured him a glass of water, then we sat down on the bed. We talked for a bit but then Anish stood up and said he wasn't feeling very well,' Beechey swallowed. 'I asked him what the matter was, and his knees suddenly gave way. He went down backwards and smacked his head on the edge of the table.' Beechey's voice turned pleading. 'You've got to believe me; I didn't kill him. He just collapsed.'

'So what did you do?' asked Warren.

'Well, he was still mumbling, so I just lifted him up onto the bed. I wasn't sure what to do. Then I noticed that he'd stopped breathing, I checked his pulse and saw that there wasn't one. He was dead.'

'Why didn't you call for an ambulance?' asked Sutton. 'Or phone down to reception for the duty first aider?'

Tears had started to form at the corners of Beechey's eyes. 'I panicked. I knew that if I phoned an ambulance they'd call the police. I wasn't supposed to be in there and there's no sign of me on the CCTV. Anish had checked in under a fake name so the first thing they'd want to know is what the hell was going on? Why had I sneaked into his room like I had something to hide? He had a bump on the back of his head – did that kill him? They'd never believe I wasn't responsible ... And he was dead. He wasn't breathing and I couldn't find a pulse. It was too late for him and Anish wouldn't have wanted me to go to prison.'

Warren looked at Sutton. Finally, they were nearly there.

'Tell us what happened next and how Nick Kimpton and Leon Grime fit in.'

Beechey nodded. 'I will, but I need a toilet break first.'

Warren repressed a sigh. 'Fifteen minutes,' he said firmly.

*

'I can practically smell the bullshit wafting down the corridor,' said Sutton. 'He'll be in there making up lies as quickly as he can.'

Warren and Sutton had taken the opportunity to return to the CID main office and review the next stage of their interview strategy. Mags Richardson and Moray Ruskin had returned from the Mount Prison and filled in more details of their visit with Leon Grime.

'Well, it can't be helped,' said Warren. 'He was entitled to a break. Besides, every time he's tried to twist the truth so far, he's just made things look worse when we've shown he's lying. If he has any sense at all, he'll finally shut his mouth and no comment.'

'You reckon he'll be able to do that?' asked Ruskin.

Warren smiled. 'Not a chance.'

*

Warren had been right; Beechey was unable to keep quiet. For the next half an hour, he described what had transpired in the hours and days after Anish Patel's death. Eventually, he finished.

'Thank you, Jake,' said Warren. He leaned back and placed the cap back on his biro. He shook his head, sadly. 'Any idea why Anish collapsed?' he asked casually.

Beechey shrugged. 'No idea. One minute he was standing up, the next he was down on the floor,' he frowned. 'Didn't the autopsy say why he died?'

'Cardiac arrest. Heart attack. Any idea what triggered it?'

Beechey shrugged again. 'No idea.'

'What were you in prison for, Jake?' asked Sutton. 'The last time,' he clarified.

Beechey blinked. 'Umm, robbery.'

Sutton started to read from one of the sheets piled on the desk in front of him. 'You were convicted of robbery and theft. The victim met you on another dating app and after going for a few drinks invited you home. He claims that he fell asleep, and that when he came around you were having sex with him.'

'That was never proven,' interjected the solicitor.

'That was bollocks,' agreed Beechey. 'We were both drunk. He made it up to try and stitch me up after I said I didn't want to see him again.'

'Fair enough, those charges were dropped through insufficient evidence,' said Sutton. 'However, you were convicted of stealing his bank card and then withdrawing money from his account.'

'No comment,' said Beechey.

'This is old ground,' said the solicitor. 'Mr Beechey has served his time for that crime.'

Sutton ignored him. 'To use someone's bank card, you have to know their PIN code. You and your victim only met in person for the first time that evening. I don't believe that he willingly gave you his PIN, and neither did the jury, which is why they convicted you of theft.'

'What were the charges that the CPS eventually dropped against you, Jake?' asked Warren.

'No comment.'

Sutton handed over the sheet and Warren read aloud. 'You were originally charged with robbery and theft, plus sexual assault and administering a substance with intent. What substance are they referring to?'

'No comment.'

'According to the original investigation,' said Warren. 'The victim reported symptoms prior to passing out consistent with ingestion of gamma hydroxybutyrate, better known as GHB, or GBH on the street. The tabloids call it a "date rape drug".'

'No comment.'

'The drug produces euphoria and disinhibition, and after it's been used, amnesia – in other words at lower doses, the victim will relax and let their guard down, perhaps do and say things that they wouldn't normally, like give their PIN code to a virtual stranger.'

'No comment,' said Beechey again, despite no direct question being asked.

Warren ignored him and continued. 'At higher doses, the victim becomes insensate and can easily be sexually assaulted. After the attack has been concluded and the drug wears off, the victim has little or no memory of the events that have just occurred. That's

440

why your previous victim didn't remember you stealing his bank card or giving over the PIN, and which is why you managed two trips to the cashpoint – one just before and one just after midnight, each time drawing out his daily limit. He does have some memories of the sexual assault.'

'Not proven,' said Beechey, affecting a bored tone.

'Mr Beechey is correct,' agreed his solicitor. 'Those charges were dropped due to a lack of evidence. I would ask you to remember that, DCI Jones.'

'Why was there a lack of evidence?' asked Sutton.

'Probably because they did tests and didn't find any GHB in his blood,' sneered Beechey.

'Even though they found a glass vial in your apartment with traces of the drug in it?' said Warren.

'Circumstantial,' interjected the solicitor again. 'There is no evidence that Mr Beechey used the drug on the complainant and therefore no inference should be made from Mr Beechey being in possession of it.'

'GHB is known to break down in the body extremely quickly,' said Warren. 'Most studies agree that within eight hours, the amount of drug detectable in the blood even from somebody who took a very large dose, is indistinguishable from the levels found in the body naturally. Eight hours had easily passed before your victim was in a fit state to report what had happened to the police.'

Beechey shrugged.

'Of course, you knew all this, because you'd researched it on the internet. How many victims did you successfully rob and assault before you were convicted, Jake?' asked Warren.

'No comment,' said Beechey.

'Well, there were six different complaints lodged against your profile on the dating app before you were blocked. All of them said they had been robbed of money and valuables, but few if any of them reported it to the police and there was not enough evidence to charge even when you were arrested.'

'You got greedy, didn't you Jake?' said Sutton. 'That last victim, the one that reported you: you never denied that you went back to his flat, so finding your fingerprints there wasn't incriminating, but your mistake was stealing his bank card. The machine photographed you when you withdrew the cash.'

'I still fail to see the relevance of this,' interrupted the solicitor. 'This is all supposition based on allegations that have never been proven.'

Warren turned back to Beechey. 'We found two vials of GHB hidden under that loose floorboard in your kitchen. GHB is a class C substance, prohibited under the Misuse of Drugs Act.'

Beechey snorted. 'Big fucking deal. I'm a gay man, everyone uses it. Ain't no proof I gave it to Anish.'

'Well, it's interesting you should say that,' said Warren. 'You see I think that one of the reasons that you didn't want Anish's body to be found so soon was that you wanted time for the drug to be broken down in his system. We didn't find his body for three days. Much longer than the eight hours or so that it takes for the drug to disappear from someone's body.'

'Well, there you are then,' said Beechey, hints of the maddening smirk returning. 'No evidence.'

'Of course, that's in living people,' said Warren. 'When you die, the heart stops pumping and the major organs such as the liver stop working.' He felt a surge of satisfaction as the blood started to drain from Beechey's face. 'The levels of GHB in the body will rise slightly after death, and everyone has some in them because it's a naturally occurring chemical in the nervous system. But there are well-established threshold concentrations for blood and urine, above which a forensic pathologist can confidently state that the victim was administered GHB before death. Anish's levels were significantly above that threshold.'

Warren's smile was humourless. 'You screwed up, Jake. You got the dose wrong. The last victim you tried this on had been out drinking and then the two of you stopped off at the chippy on the way home. Anish came straight from work. He was on a diet and sometimes skipped meals, so he had an empty stomach.'

Beechey said nothing. After a moment he reached for his glass of water. Warren and Sutton kept their faces immobile. Would he take the bait?

'It was Anish's idea,' said Beechey.

'What was?' asked Warren, although he knew exactly what Beechey was going to claim.

'The GHB. He'd read that it could enhance sexual pleasure and he wanted to try it.'

'And the supply in your flat?' prompted Sutton.

Beechey swallowed. 'I said I'd get some.'

'Here's the problem with that scenario,' said Warren. 'Anish had a serious heart condition, for which he was receiving treatment. I spoke to his specialist and she said Anish had made significant lifestyle changes over the past eighteen months. It is very, very unlikely that he would have risked taking a drug such as GHB, which at high doses can have significant effects on the heart rate.'

Beechey said nothing.

'Did you know that Anish had a pacemaker?' asked Sutton. 'Very sophisticated things these days, they can record hours of the heart's electrical activity. We even know the exact moment he went into cardiac arrest, twenty-eight minutes past eight. But his heart rate had been gradually slowing down for twenty minutes beforehand. In fact he had almost certainly passed out some time before he suffered his heart attack. Was that when he fell and hit his head?'

'No comment,' whispered Beechey.

'You know what's even more interesting,' said Warren. 'In order to use his phone to send those misleading text messages, you needed to know his PIN code to unlock his phone. You drugged him and then asked for his PIN code, didn't you?'

'No comment,' said Beechey, his voice even quieter.

'Now why didn't you ask him for the PIN to his bank card?'

'No comment.'

'It's because the last time you did that you were photographed at the cashpoint,' said Sutton.

Beechey said nothing.

'You figured it'd be far better to transfer the cash directly from his account. If Anish threatened to call the bank, you had those nasty little videos to make him change his mind.

'I'll bet you couldn't wait, could you? All that money. You must have been gutted when you saw his balance. All that effort, all those months grooming your rich sugar daddy and finally, when you decide you've had enough fun and it's time for the payout, it turns out he had less than twenty-five quid left on his overdraft and his credit cards were maxed out. Appearances can be deceiving, can't they? I'll bet that's why you decided to try and sell his phone, instead of destroying it. In fact, you actually lost money that night, after paying for new tyres on the hire car.'

Beechey placed his hand over his mouth, the 'no comment' barely audible.

'But you know what the sickest thing is?' said Warren. 'The PIN code that unlocked his phone wasn't the same as the one that unlocked his banking app. You needed his fingerprint for that. We have the exact time the app was accessed. Five past eight.'

Warren stabbed a finger at Beechey. 'That's why you didn't call an ambulance as soon as he collapsed. Whilst Anish Patel was dying from an overdose of a drug that you administered to him, you were busy using his fingerprint to try and steal his money.'

Chapter 53

Warren and Sutton re-entered the main CID office to a round of applause. Supervising the charging of Jake Beechey with the murder of Anish Patel and a raft of other offences had been one of the most satisfying things Warren had ever done.

Beechey's biggest mistake had been arrogance; he should have followed his solicitor's advice and given a no comment interview. But he had been convinced that he had been clever enough to outsmart the detectives and that he could spin the events of that night to portray himself as nothing more than an unwitting dupe. Beechey had lied again and again throughout the interview, repeatedly changing his story as Warren and Sutton had countered his falsehoods. And that, Warren suspected, would be the most damning thing of all. No jury liked to see someone lying and taking them for fools. And judges liked it even less.

After a few more handshakes and backslaps, Warren made his way back over to Sutton.

'I think it's time to put Nick Kimpton out of his misery,' he said. 'Care to join me?'

'Love to,' said Sutton.

*

Nicholas Kimpton's face was pinched with worry. He'd spent the hours since the morning's interview back in his cell, but it didn't look as though he'd used that time to catch up on his sleep.

'Good news, Nick, we've charged Jake Beechey with the murder of Anish Patel,' started Warren after introducing Sutton to him and his solicitor.

'Thank God,' whispered Kimpton.

'You realise that there will be charges relating to your involvement in the disposal of Mr Patel's body, don't you?' said Sutton.

'Yeah.'

Given what he'd originally been arrested for, he probably felt grateful that he had got off so lightly.

'Now we're going to need your assistance tidying up a few details,' said Warren.

Kimpton nodded, eager to help.

'In your earlier interview, you said that you suspected that Jake Beechey had been stringing Anish Patel along for money, letting him pay for everything?'

'Yeah, that's right.'

'Were you aware that Mr Beechey was intending to extort money from Anish by covertly filming their meetings and threatening to release the recordings?'

Kimpton's eyes widened. 'No, of course not. I had no idea the bastard was planning that. If I'd had any idea that was what he was doing, I'd never have let him into the hotel. Shit …'

'Well the camera was well hidden,' said Sutton. 'Anish always insisted on the same room, 201. We thought that it was just because it was the closest room to the emergency stairs, which makes sense because it means Jake could come in and out of the fire exit without being seen. Now we realise that Jake encouraged him to book that room because there was a hole drilled in the wall where the camera was fitted.'

'We still don't know how Jake got into that room to fit the camera,' said Warren.

'Well it's obvious, innit?' said Kimpton. 'Leon Grime. He had access to the room whenever he wanted, and the tools to fit it.'

'That makes sense,' said Warren. 'By the way, thanks for telling us about Leon's allotment, it was really helpful.'

Kimpton nodded in acknowledgement.

Sutton opened his notepad. 'So now that we've charged Mr Beechey, we need your assistance to nail down the final details. The problem is that Mr Beechey destroyed the memory card from the camera and so we have no footage of what actually happened in the room that night. Can you check that I have everything correct here?'

Sutton read through a summary of the statement that Kimpton had given that morning.

'This is what I'm still not clear on,' said Warren. 'We know that Jake was planning to use those recordings to extort money from Anish, and you reckon that Leon Grime helped by installing the camera in the room. But we also know that Leon was involved in selling drugs. You aren't the only person who was suspicious about the late-night comings and goings through the fire exit, and thanks to your tip-off, the drug dogs indicated that his allotment shed was probably used to store his supply at some point in the past. I'm not quite joining the dots here. Any thoughts?'

Kimpton pinched his bottom lip in thought. 'I wonder if Anish was getting cold feet about the drug deal? Maybe they were using the video recordings to keep him in line?'

'Do you think they could have confronted Anish the night that he died?' said Sutton. 'And during that altercation he fell and hit his head?'

'Yeah, that makes sense. Maybe that's why Leon and Jake were both in there, they were putting the frighteners on him?' Kimpton scowled. 'I never really believed Jake when he said that Anish had just collapsed, it didn't seem to make any sense.'

'Well that's certainly a good story,' said Warren. 'The problem is it doesn't quite work.'

'What do you mean?' asked Kimpton, a note of suspicion creeping into his voice. Beside him his solicitor looked up.

'When was the last time you spoke to Leon Grime's wife?' asked Sutton.

'Ages ago,' said Kimpton confidently.

'According to your phone logs, you last called her back in September.'

'Yeah, that's probably about right. Leon used my phone when he forgot to charge his.'

'How would you describe your relationship with her?' asked Warren.

Kimpton shrugged. 'I knew her to speak to through Leon; she was my mate's wife,' he grimaced. 'Not really my type, if that's what you're suggesting. Twenty years too old for a start.'

'No, we're not suggesting that at all,' said Warren. 'She's just a friend's wife. And you just knew her in passing …' He paused. 'But you knew her well enough that the first thing she did when Leon was arrested was knock on your door and ask you if you knew anything about it. Leon first met her after his own spell in prison and he hasn't been in trouble since, so she didn't really know what to do. She thought you might be able to help. Why did you lie about meeting her?'

'I thought it would look bad,' admitted Kimpton. 'And I didn't want to be linked to him.'

'So you knew that Leon had been arrested on the 3rd of December?'

'Yeah,' said Kimpton.

'We went to see Leon Grime in prison this morning,' said Warren. 'Up until now, he's denied any involvement in this whole affair. But he also couldn't account for his whereabouts that night. You're right about the drugs; he's been dealing them out of the fire exit of the hotel for the past year or so. He stored them in his allotment shed. Quite a good little racket; good enough that he even bunged you a few quid to look the other way.'

'Bullshit!' snapped Kimpton. 'He's just being spiteful because I've told you what he and Jake did that night.'

'Either way, he claims that he wasn't at the hotel that night, that he was playing pool. But we know that wasn't entirely true, he ducked out early.'

'Well there you go,' said Kimpton.

'He ducked out early to meet his supplier,' continued Warren. 'A charming individual already known to our colleagues in the drugs division for his alleged enthusiasm in going after the relatives of those he perceives as a threat: kids, wives, elderly mothers in care homes, you get the picture. Leon was seriously contemplating standing trial for Anish Patel's murder rather than using this rather dangerous and violent man as an alibi.'

Kimpton snorted. 'And you believe this crap?'

'Have you ever visited Leon Grime's allotment?' asked Sutton. Kimpton hesitated. 'No, he's told me about it, but I've never been there. I'm not the green-fingered type. Like I said before, I'll cook it, but I ain't going to grow it.'

'Well, that's not completely true, is it?' said Warren. 'According to Leon's wife, you went down there earlier this year to help Leon bring his harvest back. You then cooked a lovely roast dinner for the three of you.'

'No comment,' muttered Kimpton.

'The point I'm making,' said Warren, 'is that you knew all about Leon's first arrest. You also knew that he was unlikely to have an alibi for the night Anish died – at least one that he would want to share with the police. And you knew exactly which allotment plot was his.'

'No comment,' repeated Kimpton.

'There was always something that bothered us,' Warren continued, almost conversationally. 'Anish's backpack was hidden behind the water butt attached to the shed. Leon has admitted that he hid drugs inside the shed. So why would he conceal the backpack containing Anish's clothes – covered in blood because

449

the person who mutilated him was wearing them at the time – outside the shed? It was hidden from view but it was never going to fool a search team for long. It's almost as if the person concealing them there wanted them to be found.'

He turned his laptop around, so the screen was visible.

'This is CCTV footage taken from the outside the main gates to Leon's allotment, at 1.26 a.m., the night that Leon was in custody for the first time.'

The footage was black and white, but clear enough that Kimpton's distinctive striped bicycle was recognisable, as was the grey backpack over his shoulder. Kimpton pulled up to the gates and dismounted. Using the bicycle as a ladder, he boosted himself up and over the gate. He was inside the allotment within fifteen seconds of arriving.

'Very smoothly done,' commented Sutton. 'I guess you could say that breaking and entering is like riding a bicycle, you never forget how to do it.'

The video continued playing in real-time and barely two minutes later, Kimpton reappeared. This time he used a low wall to give him the extra height he needed and was back over the gate and cycling away within seconds.

He no longer had the backpack over his shoulder.

The room fell silent as Kimpton and his solicitor absorbed the damning evidence.

'Leon Grime had absolutely nothing to do with the events of that night, did he?' said Warren.

Kimpton looked to be on the verge of tears, and he gave his head a tiny shake.

'So why drag him into it?' asked Sutton. 'If nothing else, I thought he was your mate?'

Kimpton took a shaky breath and let it out.

'Most of it was just like I said. Anish collapsed when he was with Jake, I knew nothing about what was going on until he texted me to tell me to get up to room 201. Jake threatened me

450

if I didn't help him out. He planned it all. He drove Anish's body out to the ditch, wearing Anish's hoodie, leaving me to clean up the room. The next morning he left dressed in Anish's clothes and got rid of his car.

'I spent the rest of the day in a daze, you know? Like it was all some shitty nightmare that I couldn't wake up from. When I finished my shift that night, I got home and who was there? Jake. Sitting outside my flat door, with a black bin bag. Fuck knows who let him into the building. He followed me into the flat, then tipped up the bag and the backpack fell out, and he was like "it's your problem now, deal with it."' Kimpton looked down. 'I knew exactly what he was doing; he was getting me more involved. He'd told me what he'd done to the body, so I knew the clothes and everything would be covered in blood and DNA and stuff. Unless I wanted to go down for it, I had to work out how to get rid of them, and I had to keep my mouth shut. As if threatening my daughter wasn't enough to keep me quiet.'

'So where does Leon Grime come into it?' asked Warren.

'Jake told me that he'd cut off Anish's fingertips and smashed his teeth in with a hammer. I asked him what he'd done with the hammer and knife and he said he'd wrapped them in a towel and dumped them near the body. He'd worn gloves, so he figured it didn't really matter if the police found them. I kind of forgot about that until Leon was arrested and I realised that you must have linked the tools back to him.' Kimpton wiped his nose with the back of his hand and gave a loud sniff. 'It seemed so obvious, you know? You guys already suspected Leon was guilty. His missus said that he couldn't give you an alibi for that night, so I thought if I shifted the blame onto him, me and Jake would be in the clear. I knew you were already searching his flat, so I went and planted the backpack down his allotment. I didn't have a key to the shed, so I just hid it behind the water butt. I figured you'd be down there that morning, find the bag, and case solved.' He snapped his fingers. 'Leon would deny everything of course, but unless he was willing to risk his wife and his mother's life, he couldn't give you an alibi, so he'd go down.' Kimpton smiled humourlessly. 'But that didn't happen. You didn't know anything about his allotment, so you kept on investigating and that's when it all fell apart.'

Kimpton leaned forward, his tone pleading. 'I was an absolute shit, I agree. But everything I did was to protect my daughter and happened after Anish died; I just helped clean up the room and get rid of the backpack. I didn't mutilate his body or anything. Jake came up with this whole plan, I just thought I was helping a mate have a bit of fun. I had no idea he drugged him and was taping it all to blackmail him.' He cleared his throat. 'I want to put it on the record that Leon Grime was not involved in any way with what happened that night. He should be released immediately.' He looked down at the table. 'And please tell him I'm really sorry.'

'I'm sure he'll be delighted with your apology,' said Sutton.

'Where did you work before you started at the Easy Break Hotel?' asked Warren.

'Here and there,' muttered Kimpton.

'Can you be more specific?' asked Warren. 'What sort of work did you do?'

'A bit of kitchen work, general maintenance, anything to pay the bills really,' said Kimpton; he kept his gaze away from them.

'Any farmwork?' asked Sutton. 'We're a semi-rural area.'

'Yeah, a bit,' he admitted.

'How did Jake know where the tools were?' asked Warren.

'What do you mean?'

'Well, you said that you knew nothing about Jake's plan to mutilate Anish's body until after he did it. But he used Leon Grime's tools. We know that Leon wasn't present that night and whilst anyone working in the hotel would know the keycode to his office where he kept them, how would Jake Beechey know it unless you told him?'

452

'I don't know,' said Kimpton.

'That ditch is in the middle of nowhere,' said Sutton, 'and it's a perfect spot to dump a body; underneath a bridge, concealed from the road, you can only really see it from the field. A field that wasn't due to be ploughed until after the New Year. That gives you months of breathing space to figure out what you're going to do when his body is finally found. But who would know about that spot?'

'We found two sets of footprints at the scene where Anish's body was found,' said Warren. 'The first matched Anish's own shoes. We know that he didn't walk there himself, so that must have been whoever was wearing his shoes. Leon Grime wasn't there – and none of his shoes match anyway – so who owned the pair of size ten men's Nike trainers, Nick?'

Kimpton said nothing.

Warren produced a still image from the bus stop CCTV of Kimpton cycling to work. The image had been blown up, and was grainy, but the Nike swoosh logo was easily visible on the white trainer. 'We've measured the width of the pedal and used it as comparison, and it would appear that these white trainers are size ten. What have you done with them, Nick? They aren't in your flat.'

'No comment.'

'It doesn't matter,' said Warren. 'We've been looking through your bank statements and you bought something from the discount shoe store in town back in October. They're going through their sales records to identify what you purchased.'

'You helped mutilate Anish's body, didn't you,' said Sutton. 'You and Jake stripped him, wrapped him in a bed sheet, placed him in the back of his hire car and then drove him to a secluded spot that you were familiar with from when you did a bit of cash-in-hand work at Carrington Farm. You then removed his fingertips with a craft knife and smashed his teeth in with a hammer; how did that work Nick, did you take a job each – or did you both have a go?'

By now, tears were flowing freely down Kimpton's cheeks. 'He made me do it,' he sobbed. 'He knew all about my daughter and he said he'd hurt her if I told anyone what happened. But it was all his idea and I didn't know anything about what he was planning, I thought he was just stringing Anish along, getting him to pay for stuff, I had no idea he was filming him and blackmailing him. I never even met the guy. And the night he died, I just thought it was like Jake said; he just collapsed. I didn't know anything about the GHB.'

'Stop lying,' countered Sutton. 'You were in on this from the start. You planned it all with Jake from day one. He's told us all about it.'

'He's the one lying,' wailed Kimpton. 'He's still trying to set me up. Can't you see that he's telling you stuff so you think he's cooperating and he'll get a lesser sentence?'

'We never told you Anish was drugged,' said Warren quietly.

'What? You did,' insisted Kimpton.

'No, we didn't; we never mentioned it,' said Warren firmly. Beside Kimpton, he could see that his solicitor had noted his client's slip-up.

'How did Jake know about the fire exit?' asked Sutton, getting his next question in before Kimpton could think up a lie. 'This whole plan only works if that fire exit has no working alarm and the CCTV is broken, so that Jake could enter and leave the hotel at will. That's something that only an employee of the hotel would know. Jake had no other connection to the hotel aside from you.'

'No comment,' said Kimpton.

'And what about the spy camera?' asked Warren. 'It could hardly be left in the room in case another guest or the cleaners found it. You went in and fitted it before Anish arrived each time and took it away after he left.'

'No, I didn't,' said Kimpton.

'That's why they only ever met up on a Thursday; it's the quietest night of the week and nobody likes being so far from the lifts, so it's almost guaranteed that room 201 is available. You knew that because you worked there.'

'No, that was all Jake's idea,' said Kimpton. 'Jake sold that idea to Anish as part of the whole spy-movie thing.'

'You used the master keycard to gain access to the room,' continued Sutton. 'Not too difficult, it's behind the reception desk. You probably thought you were clever, wiping it down after you used it that night, but you screwed up. There are three different cards. I don't know what particular night you used the one with your fingerprints on, but it's a lovely impression. We've spoken to the manager and he can think of no legitimate reason for the hotel chef to be using the master keycard for the guest bedrooms.'

Kimpton was shaking his head; whether he was denying what Sutton was saying or denying the situation he was in, was unclear.

'And then there was the camera itself,' said Warren. He pushed a large, coloured photo of the tiny device across the table. 'You were very careful to wipe it down after you removed it the night of Anish's death, before you gave it back to Jake. You even filled the hole in and painted over the top.' He pushed over a second photograph. 'But you forgot the memory card, or rather the inside of the protective cover on the back where the card slots into. There are clear thumbprints from when you removed the card after each recording session and gave it to Jake to save the video.'

'You were in this from the start,' said Sutton. 'You planned this alongside Jake and you helped him as he groomed Anish and took advantage of him. And you knew that Jake was planning on drugging Anish that night to finally get your pay-off. In fact, it was you who pushed Jake to end it all that night. After all, Jake was having a great time: expensive meals, free drinks, weekends away ... but so far, you'd not seen a penny. Christmas was coming and you needed cash.

'It was your idea to finally pull the plug: to drug Anish on the night of the 24th and drain his account the month before Christmas. It doesn't matter that you weren't the one to slip the

GHB into Anish's glass of water or use a dying man's finger to unlock his banking app; you planned it along with Jake Beechey and so you are equally culpable.'

Warren locked eyes with the distraught chef. It took all his self-control to clear the disgust from his tone.

'Nicholas Kimpton, I am charging you with the murder of Anish Patel.'

Epilogue

Warren entered the office of Assistant Chief Constable Mohammed Naseem. These informal debriefings had become something of a ritual over the years. As always, the expensive-looking notepad that Naseem would record the details of the case in sat on the desk. Rumour had it that at least one major publisher was courting him, interested in his memoirs; several of Warren's cases were likely to feature heavily in the book. Unfortunately, Naseem would never be allowed to publish whilst still serving; Warren hoped that Naseem wasn't planning on retiring any time soon. He'd come to respect, and even like the man.

Naseem pushed a cup of coffee over without asking. It seemed that he'd given up trying to compete with John Grayson and bought himself the same machine. Warren's nose told him that he had also sourced the same blend.

'How is the case proceeding?' he asked.

'It's getting there. We have supposedly full confessions from both Beechey and Kimpton, but their defence teams are still quibbling over who was the more responsible. I don't think we'll ever really know if Anish collapsed and banged his head, or was pushed, but the GHB almost certainly triggered his heart attack.

The CPS are still keen to go with murder, not manslaughter, but it may come down to the jury on the day.

'We found the carpet from the boot of the hire car, complete with traces of Anish's blood, in a black bag at the local tip, alongside white trainers that we've matched to Kimpton and the shoeprints on the grass verge. He won't be able to wriggle out of being present when Anish was mutilated.'

'Good,' said Naseem. He took a sip of his coffee. 'Mind you, I do wonder sometimes if you and your team have enough to keep you busy.'

'Sir?'

Naseem smiled. 'You were supposed to be solving a murder, but you decided to help out Trading Standards and Serious Organised Crime along the way.'

Warren laughed. He'd received a call just that morning from DCI Carl Mallucci at SOC, who'd had the grace to congratulate him on a job well done. Apparently, Leon Grime had panicked after his initial arrest and returned his drugs to his supplier; this hadn't been received well. In the end, aided by a potential sweetener in the form of a reduced sentence, Grime had been convinced that the safest course of action for him and his family was full-cooperation with the Drug Division.

'And from what I hear, that poor man's family have also got what they deserved,' said Naseem.

Warren agreed. Bringing Anish Patel's killers to justice was intensely satisfying; but seeing his family also answering for their crimes was nearly as pleasing. Anish Patel's treatment had been heart-breaking. The Patel siblings were cooperating fully with Trading Standards and SOC in an effort to reduce their sentences, but it was inevitable that they'd all spend at least some time behind bars. It was just a shame that Gotam Patel would not be charged with any offences, although the apparent closure of several Everyday Essential corner shops and the destruction of his precious reputation brought some small measure of redress.

Niceties observed, Naseem removed the lid of his fountain pen. They'd been through this before, and so for the next hour Warren ran through the case, including all the little details that he knew the ACC liked.

Finally he finished. Naseem slipped the lid back on the pen.

'It's ironic really. Had Anish not been so obsessed with spy movies, this whole plan might never have happened.'

Warren agreed; the whole affair had left him especially feeling sad. A lonely man, bullied even by his family, he had been looking for nothing more than somebody to show him some kindness and affection. And his trust had been betrayed on all levels.

'I expect you'll be taking a few of those rest days you've accumulated,' said Naseem eventually.

'Yes, Susan got us some last-minute tickets for a West End musical – no idea which one, it's a surprise – and booked us a room near Tower Bridge as a pre-Christmas treat. We'll catch the train as soon as she finishes school.'

'Sounds like a well-deserved break. And will you be going back up to Coventry to see your grandfather?'

Warren hid his surprise; he had no idea that Naseem had such a detailed knowledge of his family life.

'Yes, he's in a nursing home now, but he'll be joining us at Susan's parents for Christmas.'

'Splendid,' Naseem paused. 'The West Midlands Police is a fine force,' he said finally. 'You spent the first part of your career there, I understand.'

'Yes, about fifteen years,' said Warren. Where was this going?

'Plenty of prospects for an ambitious officer up there,' said Naseem.

'I suppose, I've not really looked,' said Warren, a small, but prudent white lie.

Naseem nodded slowly. 'Well, don't be too hasty, should you spot anything interesting. Hertfordshire has plenty of scope for career advancement at the superintendent level; there are always resignations, retirements, that sort of thing,' he paused. 'Including some upcoming opportunities close to home.'

Acknowledgements

Wow, it's hard to believe that it's that time again – writing the acknowledgements for another DCI Warren Jones! It's incredible to believe that ten years have passed since I first sat down at my keyboard and started writing what would eventually become *The Last Straw*. Eleven books on and it still seems unreal. I want to thank everyone who has taken the time to read one. Sometimes publishing can be a bit of a numbers game, but when I look at how many copies have been sold or borrowed from libraries it's humbling to realise that behind each one is a real person who has read something that I wrote.

With every book the team behind me gets bigger, and every time I worry that I will forget somebody. So, in anticipation of my inevitable goof, I apologise sincerely and hope that you know how much I appreciate your help.

First of all, a big thank you to the team at HQ Stories and HarperCollins, in particular my two editors for this book, Abi Fenton and Dushi Horti. It has been a delight working with everyone again and as always, the book is immeasurably improved every time you give feedback. Before it reaches HQ though, there are three more sets of eyes that have combed through the manuscript: Cheryl, Mum and Dad. Thank you so much for your input;

Mum and Dad's 'editorial meetings' via our Sunday afternoon family video-conferences were a blast!

As always, I have sought the expertise of those more learned than myself. My favourite lawyers, Caroline and Dan, have kept me on the straight and narrow for years when it comes to police procedure. Thanks guys. I would also like to thank Naomi at Slee Blackwell Solicitors for taking the time to answer a random question out of the blue, from a stranger claiming to be a writer, concerning the rules governing the drafting of wills. Bob Gitsham was an invaluable source of information concerning how a kitchen in a hotel would be organised. As is always the way, much of our conversation didn't make it into the final book, but that which did was crucial to the plot.

Richard Latham very generously donated the use of his name for a character through the annual CLIC Sargent Good Books auction (www.clicsargent.org.uk), which supports children affected by cancer. I hope you enjoy your appearance, and thank you so much for supporting such a wonderful charity.

Most of this book was written and edited during lockdown, so I want to thank our wonderful NHS and the key workers (including the police) that have kept the country running, and the scientists that have worked tirelessly to give us hope that next year will be better.

Finally, it has been a difficult, and at times disappointing year for everyone, but I know that it would have been far harder without my beloved Cheryl. I love you, and fingers crossed *it* will have happened by the time I write next year's acknowledgements!

Best wishes,
Paul Gitsham

Keep reading for an excerpt from *A Price to Pay*...

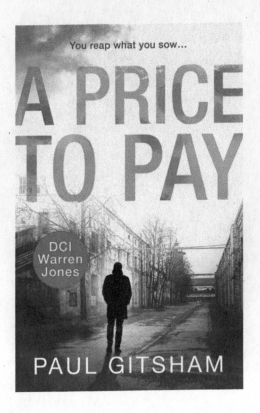

Keep reading for an excerpt from A Price to Pay

Prologue

The branches whipped at her face as she crashed through the trees.
Her breath caught in her throat, her lungs labouring to keep up.
Behind her, dogs barked and snarled, and she heard the shouts of
her pursuers. The further into the woods she plunged, the darker
it turned, the thickening canopy of leaves blocking ever more light.

A sudden burst of pain sent her sprawling to her knees, a fist in
her mouth muffling her cries.

She couldn't go on anymore.

She couldn't.

Maybe if she turned around and went back they'd forgive her.

Maybe if she begged ...

A shot rang out.

Going back wasn't an option.

She'd just seen what they did to deserters.

She'd seen what they did to women like her.

She gritted her teeth, forcing herself back to her feet. She needed
to continue her flight, putting as much distance as she could between
her and the following men, before running was no longer possible.

She pushed on. The dogs were louder, and she shuddered at the
memory of them. Huge, slavering things – she'd seen the way they
attacked the dead rabbits thrown to them; chained up all day, they

would be beside themselves at the prospect of a real, live prey to chase down.

The road was only a few hundred metres away; a busy, two-lane highway, the hiss of traffic was audible even at this time of night. There's no way her pursuers would risk chasing her onto it.

She stumbled again, her foot sinking into a depression in the soft earth. She tried to get up, she really did, but she was exhausted.

What had she been thinking? Nobody ever escaped. Those who tried were dragged back and used as an example to everyone else.

Another shot cracked the night sky open.

It was closer than the last, and the dogs were even louder.

The extra surge of adrenalin was enough to spur her on.

But her pace was now little more than a brisk walk.

It was the best she could do.

The sound of the road, the sound of freedom was getting louder, but the sound of the dogs was getting louder more quickly.

Another unseen obstacle, and she ended up flat on her face.

What was the point? Everything that she loved in the world was now gone. She rolled onto her back, too exhausted to care about the blood trickling down her face from her broken nose. She felt her eyes close. Just a few seconds' rest ...

This time the shot was so close, she heard the leaves above her rustle.

No! She wouldn't give in. Too much had already been sacrificed. If she gave up, if she died here, those sacrifices would have been in vain, and the memory of his selfless love would die with her.

Clambering back to her knees, she half crawled, half walked, towards the road.

This time when the pain came, there was no ignoring it.

'No, no, no,' she whimpered. Not now. Just a few minutes more.

Behind her, she heard the baying and snapping of the dogs and the shout of their handlers.

It was over. The dogs would be on her in seconds. There was no way she could keep ahead of them now. Sinking into the soil, she *prayed to a god who seemed to have been deaf to her pleas for as long as she could remember.*

Please make it quick.

She fell to her side, welcoming the encroaching darkness, looking forward to the release from suffering.

Suddenly, bright, dazzling beams of lights cut through the trees, turning night into day wherever their dancing cones landed. Overhead the night was shattered by a loud clattering. Now she could hear the handlers shouting, calling back their snarling charges.

But she was too far gone to care, wave after wave of pain passing through her, until eventually the darkened forest turned pitch black and she remembered nothing more.

Monday 2nd November

Chapter 1

It had been a fairly quiet few weeks. Some might even say boring. DCI Warren Jones felt his head start to dip and he dug his nails into the palms of his hands. Nodding off in the middle of a budget meeting before they even got to the coloured printouts of this year's projections would be rude, especially in a room full of his peers, some of whom seemed to regard it as the most exciting event in their calendar.

There weren't even any decent biscuits.

What he wouldn't give for some real policing right now. A good, meaty case he could get his teeth into, with leads to chase down and suspects to grill.

The current speaker switched slides. A quick look at the graph with its downward trends told Warren everything he needed to know. Fewer front-line officers, less money to pay for outsourced forensics services, and another cull of support staff. It didn't seem as though the cuts extended to turning the heating down in the briefing rooms, although it was a mystery to him why this even required a meeting; an email would have sufficed.

Warren resisted the urge to look at his phone sitting face down on the desk in front of him. He hated when people did that; it was the height of bad manners.

On the opposite side of the room, the door opened, and a middle-aged man with a name badge on a Hertfordshire Police lanyard came in. Apologizing to the speaker, he scuttled around the table. Warren saw glimmers of disappointment on the faces of his colleagues as the support worker passed them by. He felt a surge of much-needed adrenalin as it soon became apparent that the man was heading for him.

'Lucky bugger,' muttered the DSI sitting next to him.

The man leaned down and spoke quietly into Warren's ear.

Hiding a smile of relief, Warren apologized to the rest of the attendees and made his way to the door. Clearly, somebody upstairs had been listening to his silent pleas.

Be careful what you wish for.

*

The crime scene was already surrounded by a cordon when Warren arrived. An ambulance, lights off, sat silently. Two paramedics sat on the back step of the parked vehicle, keeping the chill, November air at bay with a Thermos of coffee. Their patient was well beyond anything they could do.

Parking up, Warren signed the scene log and fetched his murder bag from the boot. He would wait until the last minute before putting on his paper Teletubby suit, gloves, booties, hairnet and facemask. Even at this time of the year it would get uncomfortably sweaty very quickly.

Already there were swarms of white-suited crime scene investigators going about their business. He wondered if they ever got used to the protective gear, or if they just learned to put up with it.

The smell of tobacco smoke was accompanied by the sound of rustling. Warren turned to see Detective Sergeant Shaun Grimshaw heading his way. The man's paper suit was folded down, so that only his legs were covered. He carefully stubbed out his cigarette on the edge of his packet, before placing it inside the box.

At least he wasn't contaminating the crime scene, thought Warren, though to be fair, they were still well outside the police tape.

'I take it you've been in already?'

Grimshaw nodded. 'Yeah, it's a bloodbath.' He motioned toward the paramedics. 'Nowt for them to do, that's for sure.'

'Talk me through it before I go in and see for myself.'

Grimshaw turned and pointed down the street. 'The victim's in the rear ground-floor room of the massage parlour. According to the girls who were working, it's one of the clients. A white male, mid-twenties I'd say. He was on his back, relaxing after a full-body massage. The girl servicing him said she'd popped out of the room to let him chill out for a bit and was fetching fresh towels for the next client, when she heard a scream.'

'What do you mean, "servicing him"? Are we talking sex work?'

Grimshaw shrugged. 'Supposedly it's not that type of place, but who knows? I've seen the two girls working here, and they're above the local average, if you get my drift.'

Warren let the insinuation slide; he'd speak to the Sexual Exploitation Unit later, and see if they had any intelligence on the establishment.

'Then what?'

'The girl ...' he looked at his notebook 'Biljana Dragić, raced back in and she reckons there was somebody in a black hoodie removing a knife from the middle of the victim's chest. She said the window was open, and he climbed out, ran across the yard and through their back gate. She didn't see his face.

'She called for help and tried to stop the bleeding with towels. Another girl, Malina Dragić, heard her, came in and tried to help her, but they reckon he was already dead.'

'The same surname and it sounds Eastern European. Are they related?'

'Sisters, and they are Serbian nationals. With work visas. They were very keen for me to know that.'

'Where does the back gate lead to?'

'There's an alleyway. He could have gone either direction, towards the high street or into the estate behind. Jorge's already down there with a team of uniforms looking for witnesses.'

'It's the middle of the afternoon on a Monday. There should have been someone around,' said Warren. 'Presumably the killer was covered in blood, and you say he took the knife with him?'

'Yeah, the girls reckon he pulled it out. There are bloody smears on the window where he escaped.'

'Then either he's run away covered in blood, he's stopped to take his clothes off and ditched them, or he got changed. Get a team out looking for the knife and any discarded clothes.'

'Will do.'

'Whilst you're at it, get Mags Richardson to start collecting CCTV and licence plate numbers. If he didn't escape on foot, he might have used a vehicle.'

'It's a slightly dodgy area; Jorge reckons some of the houses might have security cameras out the front, so he's got his team looking for that as well. There's CCTV in the reception area and out the back, but none in the actual massage rooms. I guess you don't want that sort of thing on camera.'

Again, Warren ignored the implication.

'How many staff and clients were on the premises at the time?'

'There were no other clients at the time of the murder – it's pretty quiet this time of the week. There were just the two masseuses.'

'What about the owner?'

'She's on her way.' He looked at his watch. 'She'll be here any minute now, I reckon, in this traffic.'

'I want to speak to the masseuses when Forensics have finished with them.'

'You might need a translator. Their English is pretty basic.'

'Get one organized. Do we know who the victim is?'

'Just a first name, "Stevie", and a mobile number. They're pretty old school; they use a paper diary to book in clients.'

'Bag the diary as evidence. Send the mobile number back to Rachel Pymm and see if she can do anything with it. Who's the crime scene manager?'

'Andy Harrison.'

Warren nodded his approval. So far, everything had been done by the book.

'Good work, Shaun. I'll go and take a look.'

*

The rather grandiosely titled *Middlesbury Massage and Relaxation Centre* was a converted detached house, similar to dozens of small business across the town. The small garden at the front had been tarmacked over to create enough space for two medium-sized cars, whilst the large bay windows had been covered in signage advertising the services offered within, and products customers could buy to supposedly re-create the experience at home.

Warren stepped carefully onto the metal boards laid down by the CSIs to preserve any trace evidence such as footprints in the entranceway.

Inside, the wall between the entrance hall and what would originally have been a spacious front sitting room, had been knocked through to make a large reception-cum-waiting area with a desk, computer, till point and several comfy chairs. Towards the back were two small tables, each with a comfort-able-looking recliner and a more practical work chair. Judging by the bottles of nail varnish and acetone on the tables, this was where the manicures and pedicures took place. Even through his mask, Warren's nose was assaulted by a heady mix of different scented oils.

Standing in the hallway beyond, Warren recognised the portly form of CSM Andy Harrison talking to another white-suited technician. The veteran CSI broke off when he saw Warren enter.

'Come in, DCI Jones. We'll have to forgo the kiss on both cheeks and the handshake; we don't want to contaminate the scene.'

The longer Warren knew the man, the stranger his sense of humour became; he supposed it was a natural response to the things the man dealt with every day.

'The victim is in the back room. We've finished the preliminaries and we're waiting for the pathologist to come and take a look.'

'What's the layout of the rest of the property?'

Harrison pointed towards the rear.

'These old houses had galley kitchens leading through to an outside toilet and coal shed. When they converted this one from residential to commercial, they made use of the existing plumbing and kept a small sink and kitchenette for staff use. The old out-buildings now house a washing machine and a tumble dryer; it looks as though they wash their towels and uniforms on site.' He rotated on the spot. 'Upstairs, the front bedroom is also kitted out as a massage suite, the original bathroom has been split in two and turned into male and female toilets, and the small bedroom has been turned into a store cupboard. It appears that the staff also keep their personal belongings in there and use it to get changed.'

Warren followed him through; Grimshaw hadn't been exaggerating, it really was a bloodbath. Here, even the scented candles, still guttering in the wind from the open window, were unable to mask the cloying smell of fresh blood.

The victim was a young man, probably in his twenties. White, with dark hair, he lay on his back, his body nude from the waist up, revealing a bulky torso that suggested hard work rather than hours spent in the gym. A gash to the left of his chest had leaked enough blood to obscure the tattoos that crossed his pectoral muscles and shoulder.

The attack had clearly been very quick. The victim's blood-covered hands indicated that he had made some attempt to cover the wound.

'The pathologist will confirm, obviously, but I'd say the knife was quite large and it penetrated at least one of the chambers of his heart. I wouldn't be surprised if it was given a twist on the way out.'

Warren tore his eyes away from the wound to focus on the victim's face. The man's eyes were open, staring sightlessly at the ceiling, his mouth open in surprise. The blood loss had left his skin waxy in appearance, making the two or three days' stubble on his cheeks and chin stand out even more.

'The witnesses said that the killer escaped through the window,' said Warren. Even from his vantage point on the opposite side of the room, he could see bloody marks on the window frame.

'That's what it looks like at the moment, although we've not lifted any prints. I'd say the killer was wearing gloves. We'll look in more detail when the body's been removed, and we can move around more easily.'

Warren pointed to a number of evidence bags sitting on a chair in the corner.

'Are those his personal belongings?'

'Looks that way. The larger bags contain clothing. Blue jeans with leather belt, a black T-shirt with some rock band I've never heard of, and a brown leather jacket. He kept his socks, shoes and underwear on. The smaller bags contain his wallet, keys and mobile phone, which were in the inside-left pocket of his jacket.'

'We need to identify him, so I'll sign for those and leave the clothes with you.'

Warren collected the bags, before taking another look around the room.

His first impressions were that the murder had happened exactly as Grimshaw had stated. The killer came in through the window, stabbed the victim as he lay helpless on the massage bed, before taking the knife with him, leaving through the window.

He looked again at the victim's wide-staring eyes and his surprised expression.

Something wasn't right about the scene, but he couldn't quite put his finger on it.

*

Back outside in the fresh air, Warren wasted no time taking off his paper scene suit. Early evening and it was already dark. He handed the evidence bags over to Shaun Grimshaw whilst he undressed.

'We need to identify the victim. Take a look in his wallet and see if you can find a name. The bus service around here is crap, so he may have parked up nearby. Use the key fob to check the cars nearby; we might be able to identify him that way. Bag his phone and ask IT if they can unlock it. This doesn't look like a random killing, so I want to know who he's been in contact with.'

Grimshaw opened the evidence bag containing the wallet and started leafing through it.

He let out a heartfelt groan. 'You are never going to believe who it is.'

A Letter From Paul.

Wow, time for another thank you to my readers. Whether you have been with Warren and the team since his first appearance, or this is your first experience of the series, I hope it has lived up to your expectations.

It's been a funny old year! If you haven't read the book yet, let me reassure you that the novels in my series are typically set three or so years before their publication date, so there will be NO MENTION of the big C!

Please, dive in and if this book helps distract you for a few hours, then I've done my job.

Keep safe and thank you.

Paul.

Dear Reader,

We hope you enjoyed reading this book. If you did, we'd be so appreciative if you left a review. It really helps us and the author to bring more books like this to you.

Here at HQ Digital we are dedicated to publishing fiction that will keep you turning the pages into the early hours. Don't want to miss a thing? To find out more about our books, promotions, discover exclusive content and enter competitions you can keep in touch in the following ways:

JOIN OUR COMMUNITY:
Sign up to our new email newsletter:
http://smarturl.it/SignUpHQ
Read our new blog www.hqstories.co.uk
🐦 : https://twitter.com/HQStories
f : www.facebook.com/HQStories

BUDDING WRITER?
We're also looking for authors to join the HQ Digital family!
Find out more here:
https://www.hqstories.co.uk/want-to-write-for-us/
Thanks for reading, from the HQ Digital team

If you enjoyed *Out of Sight*, **then why not try another gripping mystery from HQ Digital?**

If you enjoyed *Out of Sight*, then why not try another gripping mystery from HQ Digital!